BR_____
by initiation

THE
Underworld

MAGGIE COLE

PULSE PRESS INC

To all my romance addicts who've
crushed on their childhood friend,
had endless dirty thoughts,
and resisted the never-ending
ache you wish you could escape...
Feel free to use this one for
motivation.

xoxo—
Maggie

Mafia Wars
universe

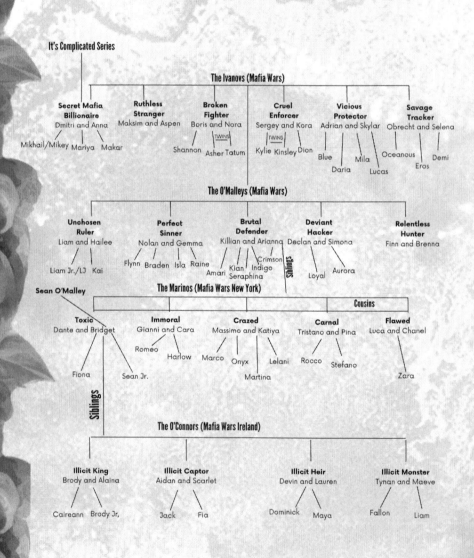

It's Complicated Series

The Ivanovs (Mafia Wars)

Secret Mafia Billionaire	Ruthless Stranger	Broken Fighter	Cruel Enforcer	Vicious Protector	Savage Tracker
Dmitri and Anna	Maksim and Aspen	Boris and Nora	Sergey and Kora	Adrian and Skylar	Obrecht and Selena

Mikhail/Mikey Mariya Makar

TWINS
Shannon Asher Tatum

TWINS
Kylie Kinsley Dion

Blue
Daria

Mila
Lucas

Oceanous
Eros

Demi

The O'Malleys (Mafia Wars)

Unchosen Ruler	Perfect Sinner	Brutal Defender	Deviant Hacker	Relentless Hunter
Liam and Hailee	Nolan and Gemma	Killian and Arianna	Declan and Simona	Finn and Brenna

Liam Jr./LJ Kai

Flynn Braden Isla Raine

Amari Kian Indigo Crimson
Seraphina Siblings

Loyal Aurora

Sean O'Malley

The Marinos (Mafia Wars New York)

Cousins

Toxic	Immoral	Crazed	Carnal	Flawed
Dante and Bridget	Gianni and Cara	Massimo and Katiya	Tristano and Pina	Luca and Chanel

Romeo
Harlow

Marco Onyx Lelani
Martina

Rocco Stefano

Zara

Fiona Sean Jr.

Siblings

The O'Connors (Mafia Wars Ireland)

Illicit King	Illicit Captor	Illicit Heir	Illicit Monster
Brody and Alaina	Aidan and Scarlet	Devin and Lauren	Tynan and Maeve

Caireann Brody Jr,

Jack Fia

Dominick Maya

Fallon Liam

THE
Underworld

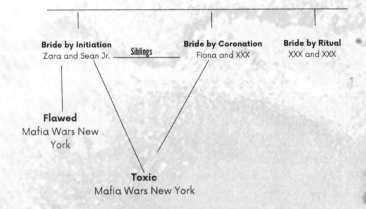

Bride by Initiation
Zara and Sean Jr. ——— **Siblings** ———

Bride by Coronation
Fiona and XXX

Bride by Ritual
XXX and XXX

Flawed
Mafia Wars New York

Toxic
Mafia Wars New York

Sean
O'Malley Jr.

Preface

In my father's day, Mafia wars existed all over the world. Crime families formed alliances for protection against their enemies. Bridges were built or burned with secret meetings.

On the turn of a dime, wars could erupt. Organizations could thrive or turn extinct, and everyone around would know about it.

The details might not be public, but the destruction and proof regarding who won or lost, glared in the light until it blinded anyone who wanted to see it.

Today, things are different.

Alliances exist, but you always question if you can trust them. It doesn't matter if it's your blood relative, best friend, or lover. Those closest to you can turn at any time.

And Darknet deals are made in the deepest crevices of Hell. The carnage stays hidden, only for those who suffer or bask in their demented glory to see.

Unless you personally step through the satanic door, you'll never know your true enemy. So the days of Mafia wars are over. There's only one place that now determines who survives and who dies.

All the power lies in a more sophisticated, faster moving, scarier universe.

Discipline, vengeance, and loyalty lie within a secret society where only the chosen can enter. But beware. You'll always want to climb to the next level, knowing there's more power in reach but that it's almost impossible to take. So choose your wife carefully. There's no advancing to the next level without her. She better have the same ambitions as you because once you get initiated and say your vows, there's no going back, even in death.

Only those branded with the sacred skeleton know who the trusted members are, and they call their world one thing.

The Underworld.

Sean
O'Malley Jr.

Chapter ONE

"Happy birthday, dear Shannon, happy birthday to you!" everyone in the pub sings and then cheers erupt so loud, I cringe.

My cousin, Shannon, beams, her face glowing from all twenty-eight flickering candles decorating the luxurious chocolate cake.

"Make a wish," Aunt Nora chirps, her excited smile growing as tears well in her eyes.

Uncle Boris tugs Nora closer to him, looking just as proud as his wife.

Shannon blows a long breath of air over the cake, extinguishing the candles.

A deafening round of applause and hollers sound throughout the pub again, and Zara raises onto her tiptoes to lean into my ear and state, "Time for another drink."

The hairs on my neck rise, and a feeling I keep getting in my gut reappears. It happened the moment she walked into the pub wearing a short minidress and stilettos. Her dark hair hangs in long curls, those blue eyes, fringed with long lashes, sparkle, and her plump, red-stained lips keep making my mind buzz with indecent thoughts.

I try to ignore it. Zara is my sister's best friend, and we've known her since childhood. Fiona would never shut up if I made a move on her. It doesn't matter if I'm 36 and Zara's 30. The fact we're adults doesn't stop my sister from constantly warning us to not cross the line. Plus, Luca, Zara's father, would kill me if I tried anything with her.

Yet I don't argue or stop myself from following her to the bar. "Another pint and..." I glance at Zara's empty martini glass and tease, "What fancy drink is it tonight?"

She bats her lashes, her gaze swirling with mischief and something else...something inviting and taboo.

I'm imagining things, I remind myself.

She smirks, eliminating the room in my pants to the point it hurts.

Jesus. I need to get a grip.

It's Zara.

She chirps, "It's a chartreuse martini, Sean."

I groan, pretending to be annoyed, stating, "I'm not even going to ask what that is, how to spell it, or where you discovered it."

"Good. I can't tell you anyway."

I arch my eyebrows and lean closer to her. "Why is that?"

She studies my face for a moment, pursing her pink, pouty lips, then licks them, tilting her head to the side.

My blood heats further, and an ache hits me below the belt.

She replies, "It was at a secret place."

"Well, now you have to tell me," I claim.

"So a pint and chartreuse martini?" Molly interjects in an irritated voice.

I snap my attention toward her. "Sorry. Yes."

She keeps her frown in place, grabs a pint, and holds it under the tap, pulling the lever toward her.

"What's up her booty?" Zara murmurs in my ear.

I clench my jaw, wishing my dick would settle down.

Don't go there.

I glance at Molly, the bartender who's worked at the O'Malley pub for as long as I can remember. She's always either happy or moody. You never know which Molly you're getting, but I'm used to it. So I shrug, answering, "Who knows."

Molly slaps down my pint and then grabs the metal shaker.

Fiona steps between us. "Make that two, Molly. Please and thank you."

Molly barely looks at her and mutters, "Sure."

"What's wrong?" Fiona asks.

Leave it to my sister to stir up that hornet's nest and dive right into Molly's drama.

"That's my cue to go outside," I announce, grabbing my pint and quickly making my way toward the exit. Relief fills me the farther I get away from Zara. I tell myself it's just the alcohol making me react to her.

It takes a while to get to the back of the pub. It's full of O'Malleys, O'Connors, Ivanovs, and Marinos. There's no one here I don't know, and I get pulled into several conversations. By the time I finally step outside, my cock feels normal, but my problem has followed me.

Even though it's cold outside, Zara's sitting in a chair, her long legs crossed and covered in goose bumps. She taps her pale-pink nails on the table, lost in whatever she's reading on her phone. And she doesn't look happy. She pins her eyebrows together, seeming anxious or maybe even upset.

MAGGIE COLE

Against my will, I weave through the handful of people, take off my sports coat, and put it over her shoulders.

She glances up in surprise.

I pull out the chair next to her and plop down. I grin, putting my face beside hers, and ask, "Is your world falling apart?"

She tears her gaze from mine, taking another glance at her screen, then tosses her phone into her purse. She smiles, but it's not as vibrant as before. She replies, "Usual stuff."

"Why don't I buy that?" I question, locking my gaze to hers.

She stays quiet.

My face falls, and my heart beats faster. "Zara, what's going on?"

"Nothing."

I study her closer.

"Really," she insists.

"Something's going on. I've known you forever," I remind her.

She hesitates, opens her mouth, then shuts it. She takes a deep breath and then slowly releases it.

Loud music fills the air, and I glance behind us. The few people outside disappear into the pub, and the song muffles when the door shuts.

I turn back to Zara. "It's just us, and I can keep a secret. Why do you look distressed?"

Tension grows between us, and her silence persists.

I wait her out, knowing I can usually get her to cave, but she doesn't.

"Is it about your latest boyfriend?"

She scoffs. "No. I don't have one right now."

4

Hope fills me, and I scold myself. I ask, "Since when?"

She shrugs. "A few days ago."

"What happened? I thought you and Zach were reunited forever," I tease, but I'm secretly happy. Zach's a good guy, but I never thought he was strong enough for her. They dated for a few years when they were in college. I was surprised when I found out they reconnected.

"Nope! Should have known once it's over, it's over," she states, not seeming crushed at the situation.

"So what's upsetting you if it's not Zach?" I push.

She taps her fingers on the table, staring at me.

"Come on. You can tell me. I promise it'll stay between us."

She looks away.

I stay quiet, wondering what has her so rattled.

She finally turns and speaks. "If I ask you a question, will you give me your honest answer and then promise not to dig further?"

My stomach flips. I knew something was going on. I nod and vow, "I swear."

She takes a sip of her drink and then sets it down. Her eyes turn darker.

A while passes, and I finally assert, "Whatever it is, you can ask me."

She blurts out, "If you could find out everything you wanted about your father, would you?"

Chills run down my spine. The anger, sadness, and loss I always feel when I think about my father ignites inside me. I don't hesitate, answering, "Yes."

She inhales deeply and nods.

I glance behind me again to ensure we're still on our own. I lean closer, confused but unable to keep my promise. My father's been dead since I was a child, so I need answers. "How could you possibly know anything about my father?"

She points at me. "I said no more questions. But for your information, it's not about yours. It's about mine."

A mixture of disappointment and relief fills me. If Zara did know something about my father that I didn't, it would surely be a situation that put her at risk with people she shouldn't be around. I point out, "Your father is inside. He's in your life. What am I missing?"

She shakes her head and looks at the sky, muttering, "You know he won't tell me the truth."

My chest tightens. Zara's always wanted to know more about why her father wasn't in her life until she was fifteen. Her parents told her it was to protect her from the Abruzzos, which is true, but she isn't stupid. She knows every family at this party is a crime family, and there's more to every story, even though Zara's not involved in our family businesses.

I carefully choose my words, knowing it's not fair, based on my lack of knowledge about what happened to my father. Yet there's no way I'd ever want Zara, my sister, or any of my female cousins involved in the family business.

My aunt Alaina is, but she was born into it and left her clan to marry my uncle Brody. She's as badass as they come, but it's not what most women would ever want. There's no way Zara comes close to Alaina's ability to rule a clan. It takes a level of calculated ruthlessness, and Zara doesn't have it in her.

"I know this isn't what you want to hear, but you have your father in your life. It's more than Fiona or I have. Sometimes, we have to be grateful for what we do have."

Her eyes turn to slits.

I toss my hands in the air. "What? You asked, and I told you what I think."

She clenches her jaw. "Fine." She finishes her drink, sets it down, then pushes her chair back. She rises.

I grab her arm and stand. "Don't stomp off like a little brat."

She smirks. "I don't stomp. I saunter."

I pin her with a sterner look.

She glances at my hand. "You can let me go now."

I don't. I step even closer. This question she asked me is loaded with too many red flags, the biggest one being that she could be in danger. If anyone is approaching her with details on her father, they can't be on our side. And that makes them our enemy. So I demand, "Who's telling you they have information on Luca?"

"No one," she lies.

I grunt. "Do you think I'm naive?"

"Let it go, Sean."

"Zara, certain things are meant to stay buried. If your father thinks his past should be—"

"But you'd dig into your father's past," she accuses.

I stay silent, my heart beating harder.

She huffs. "You don't see how hypocritical that is?"

"It's different."

"No, it's not," she spouts.

I stand my ground. "It's not the same."

"Just because your dad is dead doesn't mean it negates my situation," she claims.

Tension builds between us.

My worry turns to fear. I caution, "Don't step into a world you aren't meant for, Zara."

"What does that mean?" she hurls back.

I take a deep breath and try to stay calm, but the thought of Zara interacting with our enemies makes me ill. "Nothing is free in your father's world. If someone knows things, there's a price to pay to get that information. I doubt it's one you want to ante up."

"Why? Because I'm a woman?" she fumes.

"Yes."

She glares at me. "You're chauvinistic."

"Sue me."

She shrugs away from my grip and crosses her arms, claiming, "Alaina can run circles around any man in any of the families here. If you want me to prove it, I'll go in there and create a situation, then let her display her abilities."

I scoff. "You don't have to do anything of the sort. I don't disagree with you."

"Ha! See! Proved you wrong!"

I close the space between us, grab the back of her head, and lean over her face. "No. You're not Alaina. No one is Alaina, for that matter. So stop acting like you're someone you're not, because all you're going to do is get yourself into a situation you have no business being in."

She gasps, her eyes blazing with fire, her signature scent she makes with several perfumes, somehow growing more intense between us. She lowers her blues to my lips, pouting her own.

My pulse pounds between my ears. Her hot breath mingles with mine. The wind whips around us, and I circle my other arm around her to protect her from it, tugging her closer against me. I mutter, "Stop being a brat," even though her attitude is taunting my dick.

She swallows hard, her gaze pinned to my mouth, and states, "I've said more than I should have. Let's forget this conversation."

My erection throbs against her stomach, my veins burning with desires I shouldn't have. At least, not for her. But I can't stop myself. I suggest, "Maybe I need to put you over my lap and slap your ass until you tell me what this is all about."

She gapes at me, her cheeks burning and her chest rising and falling faster against mine.

Music blares, tearing us out of our trance. Fiona steps onto the patio with Shannon and some of their other friends.

My sister glares at me in disapproval. It's not the first time she's caught me and Zara in a moment with our hands on each other, even though nothing has ever happened. She beelines toward us, interjecting, "What's going on out here?"

I release Zara. "Nothing."

"Doesn't look like nothing," Fiona asserts, glancing between us.

"He's right. It's nothing," Zara agrees, then grabs her purse off the table, brushes past us, and adds, "I need another drink."

Fiona watches her leave and then spins on me. "What was that all about?"

"None of your business. Get over yourself." I tug Shannon into me and kiss her on the cheek. "Happy birthday! I couldn't get to you with all the people inside."

Happiness radiates from her. She hugs me back. "Thanks for coming."

"Like I would miss it."

"Well, I know you're busy with all your fights, Mr. Champion," she teases.

I groan. "Not you too."

"Don't make his head bigger than it is," Fiona adds.

Pride fills Shannon's features, reminding me of how Boris looked at her earlier. She says, "I need a favor from you."

"Anything for my favorite cousin," I reply.

Her face lights up more. She asks, "Then I shouldn't be ashamed to ask for four front-row seats to your next fight?"

I chuckle. "Nope. You got it."

She claps. "Yay! Thanks, Sean! You're the best!"

I hug her again. "Happy birthday."

"Thanks!"

I brush past them and go back inside, scouring the pub for Zara. Before I can find her, I run into Maksim Ivanov.

His thick Russian accent fills the air. "Sean, good fight the other night."

"Thanks."

Uncle Killian steps up next to him. He slings his arm around my shoulders, boasting, "Lad learned it all from the great one. Me."

Maksim snorts. "That's debatable."

Killian declares, "You got that jab down like I taught you!"

"You mean how I taught him," my stepfather, Dante, states as he joins us. Then he adds, "Your mother's been looking for you all night."

"Where is she?" I question, glancing around but freezing when I see Zara talking to a dark-haired guy I don't know.

"She's in the big front booth with the other women," Dante informs me.

"Thanks for letting me know. See you all later." I zig-zag through the crowd but stop when I get near Zara.

"I haven't made up my mind yet," she states.

The hairs on my arms rise.

The guy warns, "Time is ticking."

"Ticking for what?" I interject.

Zara freezes, then slowly meets my eyes. "Stay out of my business, Sean."

I refocus on the man. I hold out my hand. "Sean O'Malley. I don't think I've met you before. Who are you?"

He lifts his chin, squares his shoulders, and shakes my hand. He confidently announces, "John Smith."

"John Smith?" I repeat.

"Yep."

I arch my eyebrows at Zara.

"What?" she questions.

"John Smith?"

"What's wrong with his name?"

I grunt. "He just happens to have one of the most common names on earth?"

He chimes in, "Can't help it, man. Anyway, I'm late for another event. We'll talk later, Zara."

Like hell you will.

"Let me walk you out," I offer, but it's not a choice. I put my hand on his back to steer him toward the door.

"Sean," Zara snaps.

I turn my head and, in my sternest voice, warn, "You stay here."

She opens her mouth but immediately snaps it shut again, glaring at me.

I lead whoever this guy is through the pub door and into the cold. As soon as we get outside, I demand, "Who are you? And don't tell me John Smith."

He doesn't flinch, and something tells me he's not one to scare easily. It makes me want to keep him away from Zara even more. He replies, "Can't help it if my name is John Smith."

"Bullshit."

"Prove me wrong," he challenges, crossing his arms over his chest, displaying a mark near his thumb and index finger.

My gut clenches, as if I've been punched hard. I stare harder at his hand. It's not a tattoo but a branded skull. It has flowers and feathers around it, or maybe it's leaves. The nose is an upside-down heart. Something drips from the skull's chin, almost like it's blood, but there's no color to it, just the dead skin from whatever hot metal singed him.

For some reason, it seems feminine yet masculine at the same time. I peer closer, knowing I've seen it before. I rack my mind to figure out where, but I can't remember. It's too far away in my memories, but the sense of déjà vu is too strong to deny that this isn't the first time I'm seeing it.

Another chill runs down my spine when he lowers his voice and says, "You see something you like, Sean?"

I tear my eyes off the mark, threatening, "I'm only going to ask one more time. Who are you?"

"I told you. I'm John Smith," he answers with a cocky grin.

It's a rare occasion when I feel fear for myself, but it erupts within me, mixing with anger. And the overwhelming thought this guy is no good and needs to stay away from Zara consumes me. Whoever he is, there's evil resonating from him. I don't know how or why she's involved with him, but I need to find out.

I seethe, "What do you want with Zara?"

"That's between her, me, and The Underworld," he asserts.

"What's The Underworld?"

He wags his finger in my face. "You wish you knew, don't you?"

If anyone else responded to my questions this way, I'd turn them bloody before they could take their next breath. Something is telling me now is not the time for that, though. So, I use all the restraint I have in order to keep my curled fists at my sides.

I step closer and snarl, "Listen to me closely. You're not welcome here. You're not welcome near Zara. If you step within eyesight of her, the pub, our allies, or anyone else in my family, I'll make sure it's the last time you make a mistake. Are we clear?"

He doesn't flinch. My threat only makes him stand stronger. Amusement fills his expression. "You have a lot to learn, Sean O'Malley Jr. I promise you, the next time you want to make threats against me, you'll think twice."

How does he know I'm a junior?

"Yeah? Why is that?" I question.

His lips twitch. "I figured you were like him."

I freeze, my heart racing, blurting out, "Like who?"

He opens his mouth, but a woman's squealing voice interrupts him. "Sean O'Malley! You're here!"

I tear my eyes off him just as Shannon's friend, Milani, throws her arms around me.

"I'm in the middle of something," I tell her, but I can smell tequila on her. She's too unsteady on her feet for me to easily shrug her off without her falling.

"You did so good the other night!" she screeches in my ear.

I cringe and carefully push her away. "Thanks. Go inside, and I'll talk to you in a few minutes." I open the door and motion for her to pass me.

She puts her hand on my cheek as she strolls through the door, swaying her hips.

I turn to finish my conversation and then freeze.

I'm alone on the sidewalk.

John Smith has disappeared like a ghost, taking all the answers to my questions with him.

Zara Luciana Marino

Chapter TWO

There's no way I can stay at the pub. I don't know why John would come inside or how he even knew I was here. Yet I shouldn't be surprised. He always catches me off guard.

Six months ago, he appeared. I was coming out of my spin class at around six in the morning. The thick darkness had a bone-freezing chill. Sweat covered my skin, but I had welcomed the sharpness of the air.

I was still breathing hard, rushing out of the gym to get home so I could shower before work. My driver, Calogero, wasn't anywhere in sight, which was unusual.

My overprotective father gave him strict instructions to always be early and never make me wait. And it wasn't like some girls, whose fathers spoiled them and taught them to be demanding toward those on their payroll. Mine issued the orders due to his "safety" concerns. So every morning, Calogero was waiting on the curb for me when I exited my workout.

I was reaching into my bag to pull out my phone when I'd heard, "Ever wonder why you didn't meet your father until you were fifteen?"

My blood had turned cold, all the warmth in my body from my workout disappearing. I spun, realizing the only people who knew those details were those I was already associated with. But the dark-haired, fortyish guy wasn't anyone I had seen before.

He held up his hands and stated, "You don't have to be afraid of me."

"No?" I'd questioned, wishing my mace or the pocket knife my father insisted I carry with me at all times were more easily accessible. I always kept them tucked nicely inside the zippered compartment of my purse, thinking I'd never have to use them since Calogero was always waiting for me.

The stranger stepped closer, and I couldn't move, even though I should have backed up. Then he'd asked the one question my father refused to tell me the answer to, no matter how much I begged him. It was the sore spot between us, and as much as I tried to let it go, I never could. To this day, it nags me over and over on a daily basis.

John nodded and added, "Everyone has been waiting for you."

My heart raced and my mouth had gone dry. I'd barely gotten out, "Everyone?"

His lips twitched at my confusion, and his expression grew friendlier. "There's a world waiting for you, Zara, that few are allowed to enter. Once you're in, you'll have all the answers you've ever wanted at the tip of your fingers."

Goose bumps popped out on my skin, but Pandora's box had been opened. Curiosity flared in my cells, keeping me pinned to the cement, unable to move.

John continued giving me the same look, as if he knew he had me in a corner and that I wouldn't be able to resist whatever he offered.

I tried to appear unafraid and confident, lifting my chin, squaring my shoulders, and not batting an eye under his intense scrutiny when I'd declared, "If you're going to speak in riddles, I'm afraid I can't help you."

A gruff chuckle flew out of his mouth. It was as if he hadn't laughed in years and didn't know what to do with it.

"What's so funny?" I snapped, wondering again why my driver wasn't there.

Gathering his composure, he took a deep breath, assessed me further, and replied, "Everything will soon become clear. You'll vow to serve, and in return, all the things you've wanted will be yours."

"You don't know what I want," I spouted, then glanced behind me. My anxiety grew, knowing my driver was never late for any reason. My father would kill him.

Where was he?

A crooked smile formed on John's face. He stepped closer, leaning into my ear, murmuring, "You want answers. Riches. Power."

I blurted out, "I'm already rich," then my cheeks had heated. My father's wealth wasn't something I bragged about, and I didn't know why I felt it necessary to argue with this man I'd never seen until now.

He scoffed. "You don't understand rich yet. But unlimited knowledge gives you power. And power gives you control. And all the things you ever wanted lie within."

I took a few shaky breaths.

"You deserve to know the truth about why you never knew your father. And The Underworld will give it to you."

I should have run. Yet I couldn't help myself. I stayed, taunted by this dangling carrot of finally having the answers to the questions that burned within me for as long as I could remember. "The Underworld?" I asked.

He stepped back and put his finger to his curving lips with a harsh, "Shh!"

More confusion filled me.

"There is no speaking of The Underworld outside of us. You won't ever get access if you tell anyone about our conversations now or in the future. The truth you seek will stay hidden. The riches set aside for you will stay buried. And all the power and control you don't know you want will become someone else's. Do you understand?"

I gaped at him, a tidal wave of mixed emotions pounding me.

"There will be no other warnings. These rules aren't negotiable. I won't ever speak about them to you again, and before you vow, you'll get tested. The only time you'll hear them again will be on initiation night."

My voice was shaky when questioned, "What's initiation night?"

"You'll see," he replied, then glanced at his watch and back at me. "I suspect your driver will be here in the next minute. He may have had a flat tire. You might want to check your text messages."

I couldn't breathe. I watched him turn and stroll down the street. The moment he disappeared from sight, my driver pulled up.

Calogero jumped out of the SUV and, in disapproval, fretted in his Italian accent, "Ms. Marino, what are you doing outside in the dark? Did you not get my text messages?"

Still stunned by my encounter with John, I shook my head and said nothing.

Calogero put his hand on my back and led me to the vehicle, adding, "I texted you to stay inside. Your father would not approve of you standing out here by yourself." He opened the door.

"Sorry, didn't get it," I replied and slid inside.

He shut the door, got into the driver's seat, then pulled forward. He glanced at me through the rearview mirror. For several minutes, he lectured me on safety precautions and how I should look at my messages if for any reason he wasn't there.

I barely heard him, nodding occasionally and apologizing while reassuring him I was fine.

In a haze, I went through the motions, going through my day, wondering what this Underworld was that John had spoken of or if he really knew the truth about my father.

As hard as I tried to figure out how he would know my most intimate thoughts, there were no answers. The temptation to talk to Fiona about what had happened grew, but something about John's warning stopped me from confiding in her.

Several months passed, and John never reappeared. I began to wonder if I'd been delusional. Did I want to know the truth about my father's past so much I made the entire encounter up?

Then, out of nowhere, I ran into John. Or maybe I should say, he ran into me.

Fiona and a huge group of us girls were out for the night. A new club in town had opened. We were all on the dance floor, and I'd spun around right into his arms.

He leaned into my ear, demanding, "You've done well keeping our secret. Take the hallway past the bathroom to the exit sign. Go now and wait for me there. And smile so you don't draw attention to yourself with your friends." He spun me in a circle, released me, then stepped in front of Fiona and grabbed her to dance.

I didn't hesitate. I weaved through the sweaty crowd toward the bathroom and found the hallway. It took John ten minutes to arrive. Once he did, he swept me out the door and into the alley.

The conversation hadn't lasted long. He informed me, "The Omni think you're close."

I arched my eyebrows in question, clueless as to what the term "Omni" meant.

His stern voice sent chills down my spine. "Vows cannot be undone. They aren't reversible or revisable. Do you understand?"

I stayed silent, wanting to know everything about the vows he spoke of, but part of me had wanted to run.

"I need to know you understand," he demanded.

I squeaked out a "Yes."

"Good. Once you decide to enter The Underworld, you're pledging your life to the organization. Every task assigned to you leads you toward the truth. Each step you take moves you forward toward your destiny."

"What's my destiny?" I blurted out.

John's expression grew darker, laced with his crooked smile. He dragged his knuckles down my cheek and held his fist in front of my face. Then he turned it, displaying a mark.

The soft glow in the alley required me to look harder. At first, I assumed it was a faded tattoo, but then realized it was a brand, which horrified me but also electrified my curiosity.

Something about the skull adorned with flowers struck me—beautiful femininity mixed with bloody masculinity while hinting at love. Staring at it unearthed something deep inside me, something I couldn't explain. I wasn't able to look away. It held me in a trance, wondering what it meant and how he got it.

John's voice turned softer when he said, "Ah. You understand it." He then moved his hand away.

I slowly met his gaze, swallowing hard.

He continued, "There's only one way to get inside. You pledge your life to The Underworld, and there's no going back. Are you ready, Zara?"

Adrenaline and anticipation swirled within me, and a loud inner voice screamed at me with conflicting messages.

John lifted his fist again, seducing me with the skull to the point I almost agreed.

But then he pulled back and stated, "You're not ready. I'll return, and you will then be ready to pledge your allegiance and step into your destiny."

"I-I don't understand all this," I admitted.

"But you want it," he insisted.

I opened my mouth, my insides quivering, but nothing came out.

His expression went neutral. He patted my shoulder and then disappeared, leaving me in the alley.

That was three months ago. I hadn't seen him again until tonight, and he surprised me by showing up out of the blue.

"Another drink?" Molly asks, tearing me out of my thoughts.

I take my gaze off the front door, glancing around the pub at my family and friends, and know I need to leave. Who knows what happened between John and Sean? Knowing Sean, he's going to demand that I explain who John is, and I'm unprepared to answer his questions.

"No, thanks, Molly," I say, then push through the crowd to get to my father.

He stops mid-sentence when I approach, then he grins and tugs me into him. The creases in the corners of his eyes deepen, and his Italian accent is thicker than normal, which happens when he's drinking. He boasts, "There's my beautiful *figlia*. It's about time you came to see your mama and me."

Mom laughs. "Luca, she can't be expected to hang out with us old people all night."

He pulls us closer to him and says, "Ah, you speak the truth for me, but not for you, my *stellina*."

Mom beams brighter.

Dad refocuses on me. "Are you having fun?"

"Yes, but I have an early morning tomorrow. I came to say goodbye," I lie.

His expression falls. "Tomorrow is Saturday."

I nod. Out of the corner of my eye, I catch Sean's thick dirty-blond hair and tall frame step through the front door. He glances around and doesn't look happy. My gut flips, and I dig myself deeper. "Yes. We're very busy this time of year. If I stay any longer, I'll suffer tomorrow."

Dad glances at his watch. "It's only nine."

"Luca, she's being responsible. No one wants their attorney hungover and working on their case," Mom interjects.

Pride fills my father's face. He kisses the top of my head. "All right, smarty pants. Be responsible. But text me when you're safe in your apartment."

I groan. "My driver does that already."

He grins bigger. "Sue me for wanting my *figlia* to text me. Especially when she insisted on moving to Chicago and away from her mama and me."

"Dad," I moan.

He chuckles and turns toward Mom. "I'll return." He refocuses on me. "Let me walk you out to the car."

I open my mouth to object, but then shut it. Sean's pushing his way through the crowd with determination radiating off him. I quickly weigh my options and decide it's safer to go with my father. I'm ninety-nine percent sure Sean won't grill me in front of him.

Dad guides me toward the door, and we run into Sean halfway there.

"Zara. I've been meaning to find you," Sean states as he steps closer, his dirty-blond hair curling near his eyebrow and his tall frame looming over me.

"My beautiful *figlia* insists on leaving. She claims she needs her brains in tip-top shape tomorrow," Dad teases.

Sean pins his green gaze on me, then nods at Dad. "I was on my way out too. I have a few legal questions for Zara. Why don't I have my driver take her home on the way to my place?" He smiles, and his dimple appears.

Oh shit!

Dad's body stiffens, and his eyes turn to slits. He lowers his voice. "This is appropriate for Zara?"

Sean's expression goes as serious as my father's. He claims, "Of course. All legit. I just need some advice. Besides, you know I'd never cross the line."

Annoyance hits me. I spout, "Because I'm a woman, right?"

Dad and Sean give me the same exasperated look they always do whenever I ask why I can't know things or be the main attorney for the families.

Dad kisses my head again, asserting, "I'm your father. The safety of you and your mother is my top priority." He turns to Sean. "You'll walk her up to her apartment and make sure she's safe inside, correct?"

"Of course," he replies.

I groan. "I can walk to my apartment myself."

"But then I'd be worried. And you don't want that, right?" Dad says, flashing his intoxicated grin at me.

I sigh, sarcastically agreeing, "Nope! Wouldn't ever want that."

"See you later, Luca. Let's go, Zara," Sean says, then slides his arm around my waist to maneuver me out of the pub. Part of me wants to resist him and run, knowing that he'll grill me as soon as we're alone. But I can't. I sink against him, inhaling his toffee and bourbon vanilla cologne, and ignoring Fiona's disapproving glance from across the bar.

She's spoken her mind several times over the years, insinuating that Sean and I flirt with one another. We always deny it, but she's not dumb.

There is something between us, but we've never ventured down the path. We're friends, and that's how it's going to stay. It would be stupid to risk our friendship, especially when neither of us can seem to stay with anyone long-term.

One drunken night, we even admitted we get bored too easily with the people we date. So we pinky swore to never cross the line, and once we were sober, we never discussed our promise again.

We step outside, and his SUV pulls up to the curb. He doesn't wait for the driver, opening the back door himself and motioning me to get in.

"I have a driver," I object, trying to get out of the conversation I know is in front of me.

"Don't fight me on this, Zara. Now, get in," he commands, drilling his green gaze into me.

I cave, not having the energy to fight him. He usually gets everything he wants anyway.

He slides in after me and then shuts the door, ordering, "Zara's," to the driver. He hits the button, and the window between the front and back seats closes.

The SUV veers onto the road, and a tense silence fills the car.

I wait, hoping it's my lucky night and Sean will let me off the hook.

It's pointless, though. He leans close to my ear. His hot breath tickles my skin, and zings fly to my core.

I cross my legs tighter and shift in my seat.

He demands, "Tell me how you know John."

I close my eyes briefly, then slowly turn to him, an inch from his face. My pulse quickens.

He glances at my lips and then pins his authoritative stare on me.

My nipples harden. It only happens when I'm around Sean, and we have these intense moments. Yet I wish it didn't. I shouldn't react to him this way, but I can't stop it. All it does is remind me of the deep cravings I have but will never succumb to. It's not worth feeding my hunger only to get bored. At least, not with Sean.

"Don't make me ask you again, Zara," he warns, which doesn't help my itch. Something about how he assumes he's in charge and can order me around sets my veins on fire.

One inch closer and his mouth is on mine.

Don't go there with him, I remind myself.

"Zara!" he growls.

"I can't tell you anything," I insist.

"Bullshit!"

"I can't!"

"Why?"

I stare at him, my lips quivering, afraid to speak and risk losing my chance of gaining access to everything I've ever wanted to know.

My fear fights with my uncertainty. I couldn't tell John I'm ready to make whatever lifetime vow he was referring to. There are too many unknown details, and my gut tells me my father would never approve, and not just because I would find out the truth about his past.

Yet I still don't understand anything about this Underworld John keeps mentioning.

"What has he threatened you with?" Sean inquires.

"He hasn't threatened me."

"Then why did he come into the pub?"

I open my mouth and then shut it. No matter what Sean asks me, I can't tell him anything. There's too much to risk.

He slides his hand through my hair and palms the back of my head, like he did earlier.

I gasp, the butterflies in my stomach ferociously fluttering.

He leans over me, seething, "I saw it. Now, tell me."

"Saw what?" I whisper, my chest rising and falling faster.

He studies me for a moment, and I think he's going to kiss me, but he doesn't.

He takes several deep breaths, his exhales like fire on my lips, adding kindling to the flames scorching within me. He grits through his teeth, "I saw it, Zara."

"Sean, I-I don't know what you're talking about," I insist.

A world of turmoil explodes over his sharp features. The SUV stops, but he doesn't take his gaze off mine. He implores, "Don't lie to me, Zara."

I still don't know what he's referring to, so I just ask, "Sean?"

Neither of us moves, but it slowly hits me. Goose bumps pop out on my skin. Still, I'm too afraid to speak, but something in my expression must give it away.

He insists, "Tell me everything."

What does he know about it?

I try to inhale, but my lungs are already full of stale air. I murmur, "What did you see?"

Another moment passes before he finally answers, "I saw the skull."

Sean

Chapter
THREE

Zara's face pales, and her breaths come shorter and faster. There's no doubt she's seen the skull before too.

I wish I could place where I've seen the mark before. It's as if it's right there in my brain, teasing me, but I can't figure it out.

I demand, "Tell me what you know about it."

Zara shakes her head. "I have nothing to tell you. I saw it on John's hand. It's the first time I've ever seen it."

"You're lying," I declare.

"I'm not, and don't call me a liar."

"But you knew what I meant when I mentioned the skull.'"

"You were just talking to John outside. Yes, I know he has a skull tattoo. It's pretty obvious what you're referring to," she argues.

"It's not a tattoo. It's a brand," I inform her.

She shrugs. "Whatever it is, I don't know any more than you do."

I seethe, "Tell me who John Smith is, Zara."

"I've told you everything I know."

"Stop lying to me," I growl.

She glares at me and then jabs my chest, retorting, "Stop accusing me of things. I'm telling you the truth."

"But you're not telling me everything, are you?"

She shuts her mouth and then turns toward the window.

I study her for several breaths, then soften my tone, asking, "What are you keeping from me?"

She spins back to face me. "I've told you all that I can tell you. But what did John tell you? Why don't you share that information with me?"

"Nothing," I reply.

She tilts her head, glaring at me. "So I'm supposed to believe you when you claim he told you nothing, but you don't believe me that I don't know anything about the skull or more information about John?"

I cross my arms and sit back. "Yeah. You're the one who was being all secretive. There's more going on between you and John. So whatever it is, spill it. That man is not someone you should be associating with."

She scoffs. "How do you know? What did he do for you to make such a statement?"

"All I had to do was look at him from across the pub," I blurt out.

She smirks. "So this is a jealousy thing?"

"Don't go there with me, Zara. Not about him!"

"But I should go there with you about other guys?"

"Stop twisting this situation," I scold.

"Look, Sean, I don't know anything." She points at the door. "Are you going to open that and let me out, or do I have to exit on my side?"

I stare at her for a moment.

"Fine. I guess I'll get out on this side," she declares, reaching for the door.

"Don't you dare!"

She freezes and then slowly refocuses on me with her pouty lips and challenging stare.

I reprimand, "You know better than to get out on that side of the car. It's not the safest option. Your father would be livid."

"Well, I'll inform my father you didn't leave me much of a choice when your driver or you rat me out," she snaps.

"I wouldn't rat you out."

"Wouldn't you?"

"Have I ever?"

Her blue flames singe hotter in my direction.

I release a long breath and open my door. I exit and then reach back inside for her, but she ignores me, getting out alone and brushing past me into her building.

I follow her.

We step past the doorman, and she chirps, "Thanks for bringing me home. You can go now."

"I told your father I'd walk you to your apartment."

She sarcastically huffs. "Yeah, like I need you to do that. I'm in a secure building. Bye!" she says, waving, and then pushes the elevator button.

"Stop being a brat."

"Stop being a dictator."

I step closer to her and put my arm around her waist, gripping it firmly.

She tilts her head, looking up at me and fuming. "Really, Sean? Honestly, you can go now."

"Wouldn't you like that," I say.

The elevator opens. Nobody's on it. Zara steps in, answering, "Yeah, I would."

"No, you wouldn't," I declare, stepping beside her and pushing the button for the eighth floor.

The elevator doors shut, and we ride up in silence, with the tension growing between us.

Zara's stubborn, but I don't care what I have to do. I will find out what she's hiding from me about this John Smith guy.

The elevator stops, and the doors open with a ding. She stomps out of the elevator, and I follow. She gets to her apartment door and pulls out her key.

She quickly glances at me, waving again. "Bye! Time to go."

I stay planted.

She opens the door and tries to get in and shut it before I can enter, but I push it open farther and step in behind her.

"I didn't invite you in, Sean," she states.

I shut the door, announcing, "I'm not leaving until you tell me what you're hiding."

"Once again, I'm not hiding anything," she says, tossing her keys and purse on the table, and then saunters toward her bedroom.

"There is," I insist.

"No, there's not. Now, get out of my apartment."

"No."

She spins on me. "This isn't okay. I told you to get out, and I mean it. I won't have you sit here and grill me all night in my own house. Now, my father told you to walk me to my door, and you have. Thank you very much. You can leave." She crosses her arms and glares daggers at me.

I don't flinch.

"You're not going to learn anything here tonight, Sean. Please leave," she says in a softer tone.

"Zara, why was that man in the pub?"

She shakes her head. "Don't know." She turns and steps into her bedroom.

I follow her.

She unzips her dress, and it slides down her body, revealing her purple bra and thong.

I freeze. My cock hardens to the point it hurts. My voice cracks, "Goddammit. What are you doing?"

She glances behind her and tosses me a suggestive glance. "I'm getting ready for bed. What are you doing?"

My mouth goes dry.

Her expression turns stern. She continues, "Oh, you're still in my apartment, even though I've told you to leave. Sorry you didn't get the memo. Let me give it to you again. Don't let the door hit your ass on the way out." She strolls across the room, removing her earrings and putting them in her jewelry box.

I stare at her ass, swallowing hard, and accidentally murmur, "Jesus Christ."

I've seen Zara in bikinis before, but never like this. I've never been alone in her bedroom, pissed off and needing to release some steam more than ever while she's almost naked.

She reaches behind her, unclasps her bra, shimmies out of it, then crosses her arms over her chest. She turns to face me and arches her eyebrows. "Do you mind? It's my bedroom, after all."

My cock pulses against my zipper. I mumble, "Such a fucking brat."

"Are you looking to break our boundary or what?" she questions with a smug expression.

I don't say anything. I'm suddenly tongue-tied, staring at her hand, ready for her to drop it so her bra will fall to the floor.

"Eyes up here, Sean," she practically sings, tearing me out of my trance.

"Just tell me what you know," I roughly get out, trying to remember why I'm here.

"No. Now, get out."

I realize I'm dealing with the ultimate stubborn Zara. And it sucks. When she digs her heels in, there's nothing I can make her do. It's only happened a few times in our lives, but tonight, she's not caving. So I grumble, "I'm coming back tomorrow, and we're talking about this."

She rubs her thumb above her cleavage, sweetly chirping, "Okay. I'll make sure security knows not to let you up."

My gaze wanders, and I huff. "Like you would."

"Test me, Sean," she threatens.

I drag my gaze down her body and then back up, where I stare into her eyes.

Her cheeks blush slightly, but she's still as confident as any woman I've ever laid eyes on. The blood in my veins runs hotter.

Her challenging stare intensifies, as does her smirk.

I can't help myself. My pulse bangs between my ears. I warn, "You're being a bad girl, Zara."

"Oh?" she taunts, arching her eyebrow again.

I lower my voice, cautioning, "Yeah. Don't push me. I will put you over my knees and slap the shit out of your ass until my handprint is emblazoned on your skin for days."

Her lips curve. "Gee, don't tempt me, Sean. It's not fair to tease a girl like that."

I groan inside, trying not to salivate.

She points to the door. In a stern voice, she orders, "Out."

I decide it's best to leave before I do something I can't take back. As I step out of her bedroom, I shake my head and remind her, "Make sure you lock the door after I leave."

"Don't worry, Dad, I will," she sarcastically replies as she follows me to the door.

When I open it, I glance back, tempted once more to stay, to find out anything except what she sounds like when my hand connects with her ass cheek or when she comes.

She stares at me, almost as if she wants me to play out my dirty thoughts, but I decide it's all in my head. I warn, "I'm coming back tomorrow," then I step outside her apartment and shut the door. I ride down to the lobby in the elevator, leave the building, and return to my SUV.

I lower the glass between my driver, Conán, and me, directing, "Drive."

He doesn't ask questions. When I need to figure something out, he drives, and I think.

I roll the partition up and lean back, staring out the window, trying to forget about Zara and where I've seen the skull brand before tonight.

It's clear as day, and I can see it on a man's hand, but it's not John's. It's in the same spot, too, but I can't recall whose hand it is, even though it feels familiar.

The city lights flash past as we drive, and a few hours go by before things come together. I glance at my hand, make a fist, and turn it.

My stomach drops. The hand is familiar because it looks like mine. There's only one other man who had hands like mine.

My father.

A series of flashbacks attack me to the point I feel nauseous.

I'm seven, maybe eight, and I'm sparring with my dad. He grits his teeth whenever I hit the punching pad on his left hand. I don't take a lot of notice because I'm young. But once we get out of the ring, he removes the pad, displaying bloody white gauze wrapped around his hand.

"Stay here, Sean," he tells me, then enters the locker room and returns with a clean bandage.

By the time we get home, the red spot has returned.

My mom attempts to clean it up and stop the bleeding. She says, "This scab is nasty. Why did you feel the need to brand yourself instead of getting a tattoo like a normal person?"

Dad doesn't answer.

My father's hand is healed now. The skull with flowers is prominent against his skin, but there's no color to it.

I'm a year older. The mark has become more detailed. The flowers now tattooed pink.

The following year, I'm getting home from school and Mom asks him, "When did you add the shades of gray and black?"

He replies, "It was time."

I stand behind him and stare at it over his shoulder, unable to tear my eyes off it until he realizes I'm in the room. He rises, kisses me on the head, and says, "I'll be home later tonight."

I squeeze my eyes shut, beating myself up.

How could I not have remembered?

It's another thing I've blocked out.

It's a recurring problem I have. After my dad died, I blocked out memories of him. It makes me feel guilty, but I don't even know what I've forgotten until it reappears.

Why did I not want to remember his skull brand?

Anxiety and fear, along with a sense of urgency, plague me. I roll down the partition and bark, "Back to the party. Now."

Conán does an illegal U-turn across the median and heads back to town.

Why would that guy have the same brand as my dad?

Maybe it's a coincidence.

No, it's not.

What was Dad involved in?

Conán weaves through traffic, exits the expressway, and within minutes, pulls up to the curb in front of O'Malley's Pub.

I jump out and rush inside, glancing around the crowded bar. Only a few people have left, which doesn't surprise me.

I finally spot my mom sitting with Dante, Aunt Brenna, and Uncle Finn. They're laughing, and the table's full of drinks.

I ignore people trying to talk to me as I push through the crowd.

Mom sees me first, and her face lights up. "Sean, you're back."

"I need to talk to you," I assert.

Her face falls. "What's wrong?"

"Not here. In private."

Dante questions, "Everything okay?"

I don't look at him. "Now, Mom."

"Okay," she says, and rises.

"Sean, what's going on?" Uncle Finn asks.

Brenna gives me the same concerned look as Dante.

I shake my head. "Not now. I need to talk to my mom."

"Okay, honey." Worry fills her expression. "What's going on?"

"We have to talk," I repeat, putting my hand around her waist and guiding her toward the back, down the hallway, and into Nora's office. I shut the door.

Mom frets, "Sean, please tell me what's going on. You're worrying me."

I blurt out, "Why did Dad have a skull brand?"

Mom's head jerks backward a bit and then she freezes. "I don't know. Why are you asking?"

"What was it for, Mom?" I demand, harsher this time, my insides shaking. I'm on the verge of something, but I don't know what.

She pins her eyebrows together. "Sean, I don't know. It was just something he did. He used to draw it all the time on paper, even before we got married."

"Why did he do that?"

"I don't know. He would doodle it all over the place. I always thought it was a cool design, but I never thought further about it. Then, one day, he came home. You were, I don't know, maybe seven or eight, I don't remember, but he came home with it branded on his hand."

My chest tightens. "Why did he brand it and not tattoo it?"

She shrugs, and confusion fills her expression. "Honestly, Sean, I don't know. I never understood why he didn't just tattoo it."

"But then it was pink. I know that I saw pink on it. I was older, but I saw pink," I insist.

She nods. "Yeah, he added some pink to the flowers, and… I think, on some of the feathers. A year later, he went and had gray and black shadows added to it as well."

"Why?" I push.

"I don't know," Mom claims.

I scrub my face. "Please, think."

"Why do you need to know this?" she questions.

"I just need to know," I answer.

She puts her hand on her hip. "There's a reason you're asking this, and I want to know what it is."

"I don't know why. I just need to know," I insist.

She steps forward and puts her hand on my cheek. "Sean, if you're getting yourself involved in something that your father was involved in, then I need you to tell me."

I study her. "If you don't know anything, why do you seem so worried?"

"I don't know anything about whatever it is you're seeking answers to. If I did, I promise I would tell you, but I don't. That skull was just something your dad used to scribble on bar napkins, receipts, and any paper he had. I never thought anything of it besides the fact that he liked it. And I don't know why he branded it on himself, but your dad was unpredictable in lots of ways."

"Mom, if there was ever a time for you to think hard, it's now. I need to know what it represented."

Horror fills her expression. "Sean, I want to know what's going on."

"I don't know. That's why I'm asking you."

Her voice shakes when she says, "I don't know anything, but if you're getting involved in something your father was involved in, something that might've been the reason he was murdered, please, I'm begging you, don't."

I take her hand and pull it off me. "Is this like how you never told us why you kept us from our family for so long?"

She squeezes her eyes shut. "Sean, please, let's not open old wounds. I told you that I was threatened and had no choice. Your uncles confirmed that I had no choice. I thought I was forgiven and we were past this."

Guilt hits me. Something horrible happened to my mom when Dad was murdered. I've never found out the truth, but she's begged me to let it be, and my uncles also asked me to leave it alone. I know she feels guilty for keeping my sister and me from the O'Malleys for years, but she did what she had to do to protect us. So I reply, "I have forgiven you, but now I need to know why Dad had that brand, and I need you to tell me why."

"I don't know!" she shouts, tossing her hands in the air.

I step back.

She closes her eyes and softens her voice. When she opens them, they're full of tears. "Sean, I'm telling you, I don't know. I never thought anything of it. Honestly. I just thought it was a design your father loved. But please, tell me why you're asking about it."

I realize she's telling the truth, and I don't want to scare her, so I sigh and create a lie. "I don't know. For some reason, I thought about it today. Then, I thought about how he added color and shading over the years. It struck me as odd, like there has to be some meaning behind it."

"It was just a piece of artwork he was obsessed over. Nothing more." She blinks hard, looking defeated.

Guilt hits me. I know she loves Dante with all her heart, but she'll always love my father too. Losing him will always sting her. And I reopened that wound tonight.

She sadly states, "Sometimes we want something to have a reason behind it but there isn't one. I'm sorry that skull has been haunting you all day, but I can assure you it was just an image your dad liked and decided to put on his body, just like the art you tattooed on your arm sleeve. Really, it was nothing more."

Out of respect for my mom, and feeling remorseful that I brought up my dad while we're at a party, I step forward and hug her, offering, "I'm sorry. I shouldn't have bothered you with this."

She looks up, begging, "Sean, please promise me, if there's a different reason you're asking me this—"

"No, there's not," I interject.

She stares at me.

I continue to fib. "Honestly, Mom, I just had some flashbacks of the skull on his hand. I've never thought about it before today. I forgot he had it, and it's just... You know how I get when I block stuff out and then it comes rushing back."

A tear falls and she wipes it from under her eye. "Yes, I know."

"I'm sorry I bugged you with this, especially tonight."

"It's okay. We all have our moments."

I hug her again. "Thanks. I'll let you get back to the party, okay?"

She nods.

I guide her back to the table and then make small talk. Dante and Finn pin questioning stares on me, so I make my exit after a few minutes and get back into my SUV.

My driver pulls onto the road to take me home, and my phone dings. I look down and read the message.

> Unknown: Want answers to your questions? Then come ready to fight. Address to come.

I reread the message and then respond.

> Me: Who is this?

> Unknown: The Omnipotence has spoken. Your bid will be determined.

Zara

Several Weeks Later

Chapter FOUR

"Congratulations. It's now your business," I tell my clients.

Amy Eiden, a twenty-one-year-old social influencer, hugs her soon-to-be fifty-eight-year-old tycoon husband, chirping, "Thanks, so much for loaning me the money, Roy. I'm going to do well. I promise I'll pay you back."

"You don't have to pay me back. And you're going to do great, honey." He pecks her on the cheek, then hugs her.

She cringes, then puts her fake expression back on before he releases her.

Roy puts his hand out. "Zara, it's been great doing business with you."

"Thank you. You too. And best of luck to you, Amy." I shake their hands and then my assistant escorts them from the conference room.

I spend several minutes adding my signatures to a few documents and then hand over the pile of contracts to my paralegal. I return to my office and get lost in another client's issues.

My phone buzzes. I pick it up and glance at the message.

Fiona: You've been avoiding me.

> Me: Haha. No, I haven't. Work's been insane.

> Fiona: Tell me about it. Early dinner? I'm dying for some sushi.

> Me: Sounds perfect.

> Fiona: Meet you in 30 minutes at Forty-Five Degrees? The new sous-chef over there is pure eye candy.

> Me: What about Marcus?

> Fiona: Well, what Marcus doesn't know...

I laugh.

> Me: You're so bad. I'll see you soon.

> Fiona: Bye.

I finish the last of my work and then pack up for the day. I text Calogero that I'm ready, then make my way through the building. As soon as I step outside, he opens the back door to the SUV. I quickly get in and tell him, "Forty-Five Degrees, please."

"Seems to be your new hangout," he teases.

I exclaim, "It's so good! It never disappoints."

He shuts the door, gets into the driver's side, then merges into traffic. Five minutes later, I step out in front of the restaurant as Fiona's driver pulls up to the curb.

She exits the car, and we hug. Her eyes light up. "It's about time you returned my text."

I groan. "I'm sorry. You know how I am when I get caught up in work."

She wags her finger in front of me. "Uh, uh, uh. You can't use that excuse all the time."

"I know. I'm sorry. Maybe I should have brought you flowers," I tease.

"That would've been nice. Put it on the list for next time." She winks.

I pretend to be offended. "So much faith in me that there will be a next time."

"Yep. I know you well." She links her arm through mine, adding, "Let's go inside. I'm starving."

My stomach growls. "Me too. I haven't eaten all day."

We step inside, and Fiona points at the sous-chef. "See what I mean?"

I glance over the well-built, dark-haired twenty-something guy. "Not bad."

She wiggles her eyebrows. "You want to sit at the bar?"

I grin. "Lead the way."

We stroll across the restaurant, grab seats, and the server arrives. She pushes her red hair behind her ear. "Hey, ladies. What can I get for you to drink?"

"I'll have a prosecco," I state.

"Same," Fiona says.

"Great." She sets two glasses of water on the counter and grabs menus. She puts them in front of us and declares, "I'll be back with your drinks."

"Thank you," we both say.

Fiona turns to me. "So, work's been that bad, huh?"

"You have no idea. I swear I'm cutting my head off if I don't get this promotion."

She scoffs. "Yeah, well, Skyler's been on the rampage."

I tilt my head and furrow my brow. "Why? You usually don't have any issues with her."

"Not with me, silly," Fiona says, slapping my arm.

Relief hits me. "Oh. Well, what are you talking about?"

"It's intern season," she tells me in an annoyed voice.

"Ah, you got some good ones again, huh?"

She shakes her head. "Nope! Not one! I don't know why Skyler keeps bringing these interns in. All they do is screw up our stuff, year after year, and then I get to fix it before fashion week."

"She's lucky to have you."

Fiona shrugs. "I shouldn't complain. I have the best job on earth, and Skyler's such an awesome boss."

"Yeah. I suppose every job has its ups and downs. So, how are things with you and Marcus?"

The server sets our flutes down. "Do you ladies know what you want?"

"Same as usual?" Fiona asks me.

"Definitely," I concur.

She orders several rolls and a sashimi platter, and the server disappears. I hold up my glass and tap into my French roots, chirping, "*Santé!*"

"*Sláinte*," Fiona replies, giving me her customary Irish cheers.

I add my Italian roots, singing, "*Salute!*"

We clink glasses, take a sip, and set our wine glasses down.

"So don't leave me hanging. What's up with you and Marcus?"

"Not much. Same ol', same ol'," Fiona answers, rolling her eyes and taking a big mouthful of wine.

"That exciting, huh?" I offer.

She sighs. "You know, on paper, Marcus is everything."

"Is he?" I question, wrinkling my nose.

"What? You don't like him?" Fiona asks.

"Didn't say that."

"Then why the face?"

I shrug. "He's a partner at his dad's firm and head of the auditing department. You've got a good catch. What's not to love?" I tease, but deep down, I couldn't date him. Marcus is so vanilla. But Fiona's always gone for the "good on paper" guys.

She groans. "Maybe that's part of the problem."

"Since when don't you like CEO-type guys?" I question.

"I do, but...ugh."

"I thought you and Marcus were going strong. Besides, you know I'm just teasing about his job. It's good he's smart and successful, and I know you love that about him. So what's the problem?" I ask and take a sip of wine.

Fiona glances behind us and then leans closer. "Can't a girl be choked during sex or get a spanking once in a while?"

I practically spit out my wine and start coughing.

She rubs my back. "Sorry."

I take a sip of water, wait for my cough to settle, then lock eyes with her. "Is he that boring?"

"Eh..." She winces, then downs several mouthfuls of prosecco.

"So you need to spice it up, and it'll all be good?" I suggest.

Mischief fills her eyes. "I'm serious, Zara. If he doesn't choke or spank me soon, I swear to God I'm going to have to just cut off his cock and leave him to bleed to death."

"Jesus. That's pretty graphic," I say, but I can't help but smile. Fiona always cracks me up.

She adds, "I mean, you know how it is. You can't tell me you don't want a big palm on your ass."

"Your brother's into spankings," I blurt out before I can think about it.

Fiona goes quiet, her eyes turning to slits.

"Oh, geez. I'm just joking. You don't have to glare at me like that," I say.

"Out of all the men in this city, you bring up my brother? And how do you know he's into spanking?"

"I don't. It's just a joke," I lie.

"It doesn't sound like a joke. It sounds like you know more than you should," she reprimands.

"Ugh. Fiona, come on. I was joking."

She softens her tone. "Seriously, is something going on between you and Sean? If it is, will you tell me? I don't want to be lied to."

I groan. "I swear. Nothing is going on between Sean and me. You know we wouldn't do that."

She gives me a look like she doesn't believe me.

I continue, "It's true. I've never even kissed your brother, so don't worry. He's not spanking me anytime soon."

She cringes. "Ew. It's disgusting to even think about you two together."

"Is it?" I question, and once again, I shouldn't have opened my mouth.

She freaks out. "Oh my God. Please tell me you two are not hooking up."

"We're not," I reiterate, holding up my hands defensively.

She takes a sip of wine, then warns, "It's a horrible idea. You both get bored too easily. It's a total sinking ship!"

"I know. I know. Neither Sean nor I can maintain a relationship for very long. Trust me. We're never going down that path," I claim.

"You were with Zach for a while," she points out. "I thought maybe this time it would be for good."

I scoff. "I was eighteen when we started dating the first time. I definitely shouldn't have opened that door again. There's a reason people break up and the merry-go-round doesn't go anywhere. So my longevity with Zach when I was younger doesn't count."

She nods. "Okay. Zach aside, you and my brother don't keep anyone around. If you ever hooked up, you would have your fling, get bored, and then you two would never be friends again. I'd be in the middle and lose my bestie. It would totally suck!"

I lean closer, teasing, "Or, we could live a long, happy life, and I could be your sister-in-law." I bat my eyelids.

Her face falls. "You two are hooking up, aren't you?"

"No, silly." I slap her leg, then add, "Stop asking me if I'm hooking up with your brother. I'm not hooking up with him."

"Okay, because that wouldn't be good if you weren't friends anymore. You know that, right?" she frets.

"Yes, Fiona. I know the repercussions of wrestling naked with your brother."

"Ew," she spouts, wrinkling her nose.

I laugh. "Stop worrying about a situation that is never happening, and tell me more about what the issue is with Marcus. Is he that bad in bed?"

She puts her hands over her face, then widens her fingers to look at me. "He's not bad. He's just not..."

I toss out, "He's small?"

She lowers her voice, admitting, "He could be bigger, but his size isn't the main issue. I mean, a guy can be average and still rock your world."

"They can?"

She swats me. "Yes, Zara."

"Good to know." I finish the rest of my wine and motion to the bartender to bring another round.

Fiona continues, "He's not great, but he's not horrible. You know what I'm saying?"

"Unfortunately, I do."

"You know when a guy knows what he's doing and knows what to do with you?"

"Yes."

"Marcus doesn't have those skills."

My eyes widen. "That's not good."

"I know."

"But, I will admit, guys with grade A talent are few and far between."

"Right. And on paper he has everything else, so I thought I just needed to give him some time and maybe make some suggestions. So I asked him to hold my throat, and he got all freaked out."

I muffle a giggle with my hand just as the bartender refills our glasses.

She huffs. "It's not funny."

"Sorry. So, what are you going to do? Is it breakup time?" I question.

She sighs. "I don't know. It's so hard. My mom loves him. Hell, Dante even loves him, and that never happens."

"But do they really like him, or are they just putting up with him?"

"Why would they lie? If you didn't know about our sex life, you'd say we're perfect together, wouldn't you?" she inquires.

"Eh, I don't know. He doesn't fit into the family dynamics, does he?"

"Yeah, but we're not part of that world," she reminds me.

My mind quickly flashes to my conversations with John Smith.

"What's that look for?" she asks.

"What look? Nothing."

"Are you sure about that? I suspect you have something on your mind."

I hesitate, then answer, "No. Just a lot going on with work."

She studies me.

The last thing I need is another Sean situation. So I assert, "Don't read into my facial expression, Fiona. Work is crazy. That's it."

Thankfully, she changes the topic. "Okay. Well, are you dating anyone yet?"

"No, I'm taking a break. Zach wore me out."

"Lucky you," she says, nudging me.

"I wish it were that way."

"He's bad too?" Fiona asks.

"No, I wouldn't say bad. He's... You know, kind of like Marcus, but I'm assuming with a few more skills, based on what you're telling me."

"Did he wrap his hand around your throat?"

"No, he did not," I answer, then ask, "Do you really want to legit get choked?"

She tilts her head, peers at me closer, and in a shocked voice, questions, "Zara Marino, have you never been choked?"

"No."

Her eyes widen. "You're missing out."

"I am?"

"Yeah."

"So which of your boy toys introduced you to this little kink of yours?"

"Oh, it was a long time ago. Maybe like five years ago. God, what was his name?" She furrows her forehead.

I snicker.

"What?"

"You just admitted you slept with someone and don't remember their name."

She scoffs. "Don't tell me you remember every single person you've slept with?"

"I do," I claim.

"Really? Who'd you have sex with when you were twenty-six?"

"That was two years ago."

She nods. "In March."

I tilt my head. "You want me to tell you who I had sex with over twenty-four months ago?"

"Yep."

"I might not know dates, but I know the names of everyone I got busy with," I claim.

She swirls her wine in her glass, challenging, "Prove it. What about that guy from the club when we were twenty-three and on vacation in Spain?"

I cringe, admitting, "He was foreign. He had a weird name."

She laughs. "He did not. His name was Javier."

I put my hands over my face. "Oh, no. That's bad, isn't it?"

She laughs and takes another sip of wine.

A server arrives with our sashimi tray and sets down the soy sauce. "Your rolls will be up shortly. Can I get you anything else?"

I reply, "I'm good."

"Me too," Fiona says.

We fill our trays with soy sauce and wasabi, and I pick up a piece of salmon and pop it in my mouth. It melts right away, and I groan. "This is so good."

"Yeah, the sushi is the best here. I kind of hate going anywhere else these days," Fiona declares.

"Agreed." I take a sip of water, then ask, "So, are you breaking up with Marcus?"

She chews her fish and shrugs. "No idea."

"Maybe it'll get better," I suggest.

She winces. "Yeah. I thought that the first dozen times we had sex, but

I think it's him." She closes her eyes and shakes her head. "Man, why is it so hard to find somebody you're compatible with on all levels?"

"I don't know. You're asking the wrong person," I answer.

"Maybe we should start dating each other," she says, leaning closer.

"You're into women now?" I ask, amused.

"No, but we could figure out how to be and then we wouldn't have to deal with these men."

"I don't think it works that way," I reply.

She sighs again. "You're right. But I need to figure out how to get Marcus to become an animal in bed instead of a puppy."

"Woof! Woof!" I tease.

"Stop!" she orders, laughing.

"That situation sucks."

"Yeah."

We finish our dinner and discuss some family stuff, and then I head to my yoga class.

I'm feeling pretty Zen when my driver drops me off at my door afterward. I tell him for the millionth time, "You don't have to walk me to my apartment."

"Your father's orders," Calogero reminds me.

I roll my eyes. My father is overprotective, but I learned to accept it because fighting it only causes me stress. I groan. "I know. I know. All right. Have a good day." I step inside and shut the door. I shower, put on my pajamas, and go into the kitchen to get a glass of water. And I freeze.

I can hear soft music playing. It's barely audible, but I can tell it's coming from the family room.

My insides quiver, and the hairs on my arms rise. I grab a knife out of the wood block.

"You don't have to be scared," a woman's voice declares in a Greek accent.

I peek around the corner, gripping the knife over my head.

A petite woman in her late forties or early fifties sits in my chair. She has black hair with gray streaks running through it, and it's in a neat French twist. Her makeup is perfect, complete with dark-red lips and long, curled lashes framing her golden-brown eyes. She's dressed in a navy-blue skirt suit and conservative heels.

"Who are you?" I question, staying semi-hidden behind the kitchen wall.

She points at the couch. "My name is Sylvia Stevens. Sit down. Let's chat."

"Sylvia Stevens," I repeat, realizing that her last name is just as popular as Smith, and I think of Sean.

"Yes, Sylvia Stevens. I think you know my associate, John?" She arches her eyebrows.

"Yes," I reply.

"Then, you know I'm not here to hurt you. Sit down," she orders again, pointing to the couch.

I put the knife down and join her in the family room. I choose the cushion directly across from her and cross my legs. I tap my fingers on my thigh and stare at her. "How did you get in?"

"That's a dumb question," she replies.

"Why is it dumb? It's my house. It'd be good to know how you got in so I can fix the security issue so nobody else can intrude."

She scoffs and waves her hand in front of her face. "No one else is getting past your father's men. I'm the only one who can. Well, me or any of my associates." She smiles arrogantly.

A chill runs deep into my bones.

"Stop being scared," she instructs.

"I'm not," I claim.

She leans toward me, peering closer and asserting, "Really? You look a tad on the frightened side from where I'm sitting."

Annoyed and a bit freaked out, I question, "Why are you here?"

"Ah, don't worry. I come bearing good news from the Omni."

"The Omni? John used that word, but I don't know what it means," I blurt out.

"Omni is short for Omnipotence."

I cross my arms over my chest. "And why are you talking about omnipotence?"

"Well, the Omnipotence, or again, Omni for short, are our leaders. Their authority overrides all others in The Underworld. They're all-powerful, and they have no limitations. They are the ones we answer to. They are the ones we get permission from. They are the ones we go to when we need to seek truth."

I stay silent, processing what she's saying.

"You still want the truth, correct? About your father?" she questions.

I release an anxious breath. "Yes, of course."

"Great. Well, the Omni have decided to approve your bid for initiation."

"My bid? I don't know what you're talking about," I state.

"Yes, your bid to join. I'm sure John has talked to you about initiation, hasn't he?"

"Not really," I say, more confused than ever.

"Well, if you're going to join The Underworld, you must go through initiation. And, like I said, I have good news. The Omni has approved your bid."

"I didn't place a bid, nor would I know how. I don't even know if I want to be part of whatever this organization is," I claim.

Arrogance washes over her features. "You've already decided. There's no question you want to pledge. You just don't want to admit it yet."

"That's not true," I blurt out.

"Ah, but isn't it?" she asks, giving me a knowing look.

My stomach flips and my heart races.

She continues, "You have proved you're elite enough to have a bid for initiation. This is a good thing."

"It sounds like a snobby country club," I reply.

She snaps, "Don't ever disrespect The Underworld. Never, never, never. Do you understand me?"

I put my hands in the air defensively. "Sorry."

Tense silence fills the air between us, and goose bumps break out on my skin.

She finally speaks again. "I thought you wanted answers, Zara."

I choose my words carefully. "I do want answers, but I don't understand all this Underworld stuff. I'm not looking to get involved in something I don't know all the details about."

"You've not told anyone about your encounters with John," she states.

"No."

"That's because you want in."

"Not true," I insist, but I wonder if she's right.

She studies me until I feel uncomfortable, but I don't flinch. She asks, "Don't you want better for your children someday?"

I jerk my head backward. "My children? I don't have children. I don't even know if I'm ever getting married."

She purses her lips, then cautions, "Don't speak such foolishness."

"I'm being honest. Besides, women don't have to get married these days. I have a career. I can get married later. And who says I need to have kids?"

She keeps the same expression on her face, and I realize I'm saying the wrong things. She returns to her friendly smile. "Zara, I come bearing gifts, and you should be excited about this."

I glance around. "I don't see any presents."

"Ha-ha. You're a funny one, I see," she says.

I tap my fingers on my thigh. "If you don't mind getting to the point of this, I have to work early in the morning," I say, ready to have my apartment back to myself, and still freaked out that this woman is in my living room when my dad has top-notch security on me at all times.

"Fine." She lifts her chin and stares at me momentarily, then reveals, "I came to show you who you'll be paired up with should you prove your worthiness to get through initiation."

"Paired up with? Worthiness? Once again, I'm lost," I admit with annoyance.

She glares at me.

The hairs on my arms rise. I stay silent, afraid I'll say something that will upset her again.

She continues, "It's an important decision." She grabs a thick binder off the table I hadn't noticed before and holds it toward me, adding, "This is for you."

I cautiously ask, "What's in it?"

"Pictures of men," she states.

My heart races faster. "Why do I need to see pictures of men?"

She rises. "If you're lucky, one of these men will be given the authority to choose you. You can choose them and move forward, or the opportunity will disappear. And then..." Her voice trails off. She looks away and swallows hard.

A shiver racks my body. I sternly ask, "The opportunity disappears and then, what?"

She takes a calculated breath, refocuses on me, and her lips tighten into a thin line.

I tense at the look she gives me.

"You'll soon find out. And trust me, you don't want to be on the unchosen side."

Sean

Chapter FIVE

*E*very day that goes by, I grow antsier. I've been having dreams about my father. I see his face, and his hand with the skull. He never says anything, and I always wake up sweating.

I've barely spoken to Zara, or anyone for that matter, since Shannon's party.

I've blown off my uncles' and my cousins' text messages, as well as those from my friends. I've only replied to necessary work issues, but I've especially avoided Uncle Finn. He wants to talk to me about what happened at the party between my mother and me.

Dante won't get off my back either. He keeps sending me text messages and leaving me voicemails. But he and my mom are back in New York. So, I'm more worried about Uncle Finn.

I can't be sure, but my gut tells me that the skull needs to stay between myself and Zara. I shouldn't have brought my mother into it, but I was desperate for answers.

I still am.

Every time a text message comes in, my anxiety grows.

Why haven't they sent me any more messages?

When and where is this fight, and who do they want me to beat up?

Who are these people and the Omnipotence?

What is all this talk about a bid?

I search and search for answers, but they're nowhere, and I never receive the text message they warned is coming.

I've been working out every morning in my building, avoiding the family gym where I normally box. I spend my days getting the information I need that Uncle Nolan and Declan request from my job at O'Malley Cybersecurity. Other than that, I'm diving into the Darknet. I'm searching for anything about The Underworld or skull brands. I've searched photos and looked for any chatter about discussions of the Omnipotence.

I've even been searching for John Smiths, which I know is a waste of my time. There are thousands of them on different threads.

Today, I went deeper, even though I shouldn't have. I searched for my name, Zara's, and the rest of our family members. There's nothing besides the typical chatter about our crime family activity. It's a dead end, and it's driving me crazy.

Now, it's Friday night, and I should be out. But I'm obsessed with finding something, so weekend or not, I'm committed.

I get up to make a cup of coffee. I put in the pod and hit the button when my doorbell rings.

I groan. Only a few people have clearance to come up without security notifying me. I consider acting like I'm not here, but my family members would find a way to get in, so I open the door.

My best friend, Brax, says, "Mate. Where the fuck have you been?"

"Oh, it's you."

"Gee, thanks for tossing out the welcome mat," he teases.

"Sorry. Come in," I invite, opening the door wider.

He steps inside and pins his eyebrows together. "Who did you think it was going to be?"

I shrug. "I don't know. Somebody in my family."

"Since you've been hiding out and we're about to put you on the missing posters at the post office?" he offers.

"I've not been missing."

"You might as well be. Why haven't you been in the gym? It's not fun for me to box the old geezers, you know," he whines.

I grunt.

The days of my uncles ruling the O'Malley gym are over. They're better off as trainers now, and they spend their time helping all my cousins and me.

Uncle Liam, Finn, Killian, Nolan, and Declan still work out. They can't go as hard as they used to, but they could still take out any guy twenty years younger than them. So I take all the advice I can get from them regarding fighting. But I understand Brax's frustration, so I say, "Sorry, I've been busy."

He studies me. "Doing what?"

"Nothing," I lie.

"Something's going on if you're holing yourself up in here. And, Jesus"—he inhales deeply—"your place stinks. Why don't you let some air in and clean up a bit?"

I glance around my house. There's an empty pizza box on the table, but that's it. I claim, "My house isn't that dirty."

"It's going to be if you continue to hole yourself up and jack off all day. Now, go get changed."

"Nah, I'm good. I can't go out tonight," I say, glancing at his outfit of sweatpants, a hoodie, and sneakers. I add, "You don't necessarily look like you're trying to woo the ladies."

He crosses his arms. "Sorry, we're not going pussy hunting. At least not right now. We've been summoned."

"Summoned?" I question, my gut sinking.

His expression turns serious. "Yeah. Liam ordered me to personally escort you to the gym. So go get changed, or we'll be late."

I groan and scrub my hands over my face.

"Come on. Don't get me in trouble, man. You know what happens when we keep Liam waiting. I don't need another round of grave duty all week," Brax adds.

I scoff but can't argue. So I turn and go into the bedroom. I toss on some workout clothes and then grab my keys. I step outside my bedroom.

Brax points to my hand. "Put your keys away. I just told you Liam said I have to escort you there."

I groan again. "My family's ridiculous sometimes."

"Yeah, well, at least you have a family."

I feel bad for a moment. Brax is an orphan, and I remind him, "You're an O'Malley through and through. You know that."

He has a strong connection with Finn and Aunt Brenna. Maybe it's because they never had kids and Brax needed parental figures. He's even lived with them at times.

Something flashes in his eyes, but it doesn't linger. "Yeah, no shit. You guys are lucky to have me."

I chuckle and pat him on the back. "Yep. Come on. Let's get this over with."

We leave my building and head out to his rebuilt 1982 Mustang.

Finn and Brax are always buying old vehicles and restoring them. And Brax likes to drive them around even in crappy Chicago weather. It's like he has to prove the car can withstand the horrible weather conditions.

The snow's falling, and I get into the Mustang, suggesting, "Maybe it's time to upgrade your vehicle to an SUV in the winter."

He grunts. "No need, man.

"Suit yourself."

He turns on the engine, and Led Zeppelin blares at full blast. It's another thing he's taken on from Finn. They listen to the same music. Sometimes, I wonder if Finn's his blood dad, even though I know it's impossible.

I turn the volume down and question, "Did Liam say why he's calling a meeting on a Friday night?"

Brax glances quickly at me before turning his attention back on the road, and answers, "Does he ever?"

"Yeah. Good point," I say and then lean back in the seat, glancing out the window at the lights on the buildings. I mutter, "I thought the snow would be gone by now."

"Yeah, me too. I'm over it. We need to get some ladies and fly off to the Caribbean for a week. We're way overdue, don't you think?" Brax suggests.

I nod. "Sea, sand, and sex. Sounds good to me."

Brax holds his fist out, and I bump it with mine. We turn the corner, and he pulls up to the curb. "Let's get this over with. Then, we're going home and showering, and you're putting on some nice clothes. There's pussy to be had tonight."

I shake my head. "I got shit to do, man."

"Jesus. Sean, whatever's going on, you need to tell me."

"Nothing's going on," I lie.

He grunts. "Bullshit. Since when do you pass up pussy?"

"I'm just busy," I claim as I get out of the car.

He follows, and before I can step into the gym, he puts his hand on the front door so I can't open it.

"What are you doing?" I question.

His eyes turn to slits. He glares down at me. There are few men taller than me, and Brax is one of them.

He asserts, "You're hiding something, Sean. I know it, and they know it. The longer you've stayed away, the more the old geezers have recklessly gossiped like little old hens. Even Finn's asking me what I know."

"They're getting soft, aren't they?" I tease.

He chuckles, but then his expression sobers. "They'd only do that if they're super worried, so why don't you cut the shit and tell me what's going on?"

I clench my jaw.

He lowers his voice. "Does it involve ratting someone out?"

"Fuck no. You know I'm not a rat," I spout.

Relief fills his face. "Okay. Then what is it?"

"I can't discuss it, Brax."

Anger flares in his eyes. "I'm the one person you tell me you always trust."

"I do trust you, but I can't tell you this right now. I'll tell you later, though. I promise. Just... I can't right now. Okay?" I give him a look, silently begging him to let me off the hook for the time being.

"Is it because I said Finn is asking questions? You know I won't speak a word," he states.

"No. It has nothing to do with Finn, and I know you're not a tattler," I assure him.

He finally sighs and yanks open the door. "Fine. Let's get this over with. But you're going out with me tonight. I need my wingman. I'm not taking no for an answer."

I realize I need a break away from my computer, so I agree. "All right. I'm game."

He looks up and presses his hands together, as if in prayer, saying, "Thank you, pussy gods!"

I chuckle.

We walk inside the gym, and I freeze. "What are you doing here?"

My mom's brothers are all here. Brody, Aidan, Devin, and Tynan are lined up next to my O'Malley uncles.

Brody turns his head to the others. "That's the welcome we get."

Brax and I cross over to them. "No, but you were in town a few weeks ago. Why are the four of you here? That never happens unless there's something special going on."

Brody's eyes darken. "Time for a workout, Sean. Brax, get into the ring. Work off some steam. We'll talk about business later."

My chest tightens. While I love a good workout at any time of the day, I hate it when I know something's looming and I don't know what.

Uncle Aidan takes a lighter out of his pocket and starts flicking it. It's something he always does, and I'm usually mesmerized by how he can let the flame burn practically on top of his fingers. But for some reason, today it makes me antsy.

I ask, "Can you stop doing that?"

"Why? What's it to you?" Aidan says, flicking it faster.

"Maybe he's worried the place will go up in flames," Tynan jabs.

"Shut up," Aidan orders.

I get in the ring.

"Come on, now," Liam says, nodding toward the ring. "Make the fight good."

"Yeah. We've been bored the last few weeks," Nolan calls out.

Finn goes over to Brax and helps him lace his gloves, and Killian helps me with mine. They both talk to us, giving us their coaching advice. And then Declan rings a bell.

Brax and I practice in the ring for the next hour, tossing punches at each other until we're covered in sweat, a bit of blood, and out of breath.

"That's enough," Liam calls out.

Uncle Killian comes over and helps me remove my gloves. I take my hand out and get a flashback of my dad's hand flexing just like I'm flexing mine now. I grab the top rope of the ring and close my eyes, feeling slightly dizzy.

"What's going on, lad? Are you all right?" Killian questions.

I steady myself. "Yeah. I just haven't eaten a lot today."

Killian says, "Devin, grab a protein bar and some electrolytes."

Devin brings it over and hands it to me.

I guzzle the drink and then rip open the protein bar. I down it in two bites, realizing I'm starving.

Declan jumps up and holds his hands to his mouth, shouting, "Everyone get your fucking asses out."

The gym erupts in loud grumbles, but they all listen. That's the rule. When an O'Malley speaks, you don't question it. You listen and do what you're told.

"You too, Brax," Finn orders.

His face falls. "Seriously?"

"Yeah. Get your arse out," Declan follows up.

Brax gives Finn another look, pleading to stay.

Finn shakes his head.

"I'll be in the car," Brax huffs as he exits.

When the gym is clear, I feel outnumbered. My uncles are the only ones left, and all nine men are staring at me.

Liam starts. "What have you been up to lately, Sean?"

I shrug. "Not much."

His eyes narrow. "Why have you been staying away?"

"I've just been busy," I say, singing the same song and dance I gave Brax earlier.

"That's a great way to put it," Nolan says.

"What does that mean?" I snarl.

"Sounds like you've been digging into a lot of stuff and going places you shouldn't," he declares.

Anger hits me. I accuse, "You hacked into my computer?"

Nolan grins. "Nah, it wasn't me."

I spin. "Fuck you, Declan."

He chuckles. Then innocently asks, "Why am I to blame?"

I point between him and Nolan. "You two are the only ones who know how to hack into my system."

"Maybe Simona did it," Brody suggests.

I glare at him.

"Don't bring Simona into this," Declan protectively asserts.

"Well, she is smarter than both of you," Killian states.

"Enough," Liam says in a stern voice. He's the head of the O'Malleys, just like Brody's the head of the O'Connors. When either of them say to knock it off, we all obey.

Brody says in his thick Irish accent, "All of ya watch your mouth, or I'll smack it off. Don't let me remind any of ya again."

I stand there, waiting and hoping they don't have any idea what's going on. And I still don't understand why I need to hide it. But if Zara's hiding it, it tells me I need to too.

And I don't know why my father had that skull on his hand. Maybe I'm staying silent as some sort of loyalty toward him. Whatever it is, I keep my business to myself.

Finn steps forward. "Why were you questioning your mom about your dad's tattoo?"

"It wasn't a tattoo. It was a brand," I blurt out, then remind myself to step carefully in this conversation.

Finn's eyes grow darker. He nods. "Yeah, it was. And then ink was in several stages. And you know that. So why were you questioning your mom about it?"

I'm more determined than ever to find out the truth and keep my business to myself at the same time. "Why does it matter? My mom said she didn't know anything about it, that it was just something my dad doodled. So why are you asking me questions about it? Is there something you want to tell me?" I toss back at him.

Nolan states, "Your father was a dreamer. He had unrealistic ideas about a world where we could coexist with our enemies and there would be a place where there would be peace for you kids in the future. But we all know that we can't trust our enemies. There is no real utopia."

I take a moment to process everything he said, then charge, "So there was meaning behind the skull, and you know about it?"

"Meaning is different from reality," Declan states.

I stand taller, demanding, "I want to know what my father was involved in."

Brody warns, "He wasn't involved in anything. Stop looking for things, Sean, or it'll ruin your life."

"If there's nothing there, then why would it ruin my life?" I retort.

Liam steps up and points at me. "Look at you. We haven't seen you for weeks and then we find out you've been searching for pictures of skull brands and everyone's names all over the Darknet. That's reckless, and you know it."

I stay quiet. It is risky, and I can't deny it.

"What do you have to say for yourself?" Liam questions.

Before I speak, I think. Then I slowly state, "You're right. I shouldn't be searching anyone's names. But I'm trying to get to the truth, so please tell me everything you know about my father and that brand. I'm not a kid anymore. I'm not someone who has to be hidden away or taken away from his family or not know what really happened to his father."

Killian groans. "We've gone through this before. You know what happened and why your mother had to keep you away from the O'Malleys for several years."

"No, I don't. I thought you guys didn't know the whole truth either. But I'm getting the feeling you do, which means you've lied to me. And it's my father we're talking about. So I have a right to know," I declare.

Aidan scoffs. "No one's lying to you. Stop feeling sorry for yourself."

"Sorry for myself? Your father's still alive. You aren't searching for answers. But why does that mean I feel sorry for myself? Just because my father's dead and I want to know the truth, that means I'm some pussy feeling sorry for myself?" I sneer.

Brody steps forward next to Liam. "Listen, Sean, and listen closely. Do not go all over the Darknet searching for your father's mark. It was just an idea. And when he died, so did his imaginary utopia. But it's buried. Let it lie. Looking for something that doesn't exist will only cause problems for everyone in the family. And not only ours but the Marinos as well as the Ivanovs."

I don't reply.

Liam adds, "You're going to drive yourself nuts looking for something imaginary. Don't put the families at risk. And that's an order."

I blurt out, "But what if it does exist?"

Liam's gaze burns. "It doesn't."

"What if it does?"

"Is there something you know you're not telling us?" Finn interjects.

I sigh. "I'm just asking, what if the world my father wanted to create did exist? Then what?"

Killian shakes his head. "Then, it'll be nothing like what your father intended it to be. There's no way on earth O'Malleys and O'Connors can ever exist and play nicely with Baileys or O'Learys."

"Alaina's an O'Leary," I point out.

Brody crosses his arms and barks, "Not anymore. She's an O'Connor. She left them."

"I'm only going to tell you one more time, Sean. Let it lie," Liam threatens. "As much as we loved your father, we can all agree on one thing."

"What's that?" I seethe.

"There's no way we would ever get into bed with our enemies. He was a fool to ever think that we could," Liam snarls.

Zara

Several Days Later

Chapter
SIX

Twelve men of all shapes, sizes, and colors stare back at me from the photos. It's Sunday night, and I spent the weekend fixated on the images to the point I've memorized things others probably wouldn't ever notice about them.

Each man has a set of seven photos, spiral bound together. The first is a close-up of their face. The second and third are photos of their naked bodies, both front and back. The fourth is two side-by-side images of their ears. The fifth is the bottom of their feet. The sixth is the inside of their mouth. In the seventh photo, their cock stands at attention, hard as a rock.

Their features are all different, but each man has the same evil glint in their eyes. It draws me in while sending chills down my spine.

No matter how many times I tell myself to close the binder and toss it in the trash, I can't. I study every man until I know every mole, tattoo, scar, and imperfection. If I were blind, I could feel their sharp or rounded features in the dark and know which one is which.

Well, I'd know their number.

There are no names on the photos, only one through twelve. I'd be attracted to half of them if I saw them on the street. The others, I'd never give a second glance.

I still don't know what Sylvia meant when she stated one of them would choose me and I would choose them. Yet the fact these men are naked in their photos, and one displays their erections, gives me the impression she's insinuating I'll be sleeping with someone in this binder.

That's not happening.

Number six, a Middle Eastern man who's one of the most well-endowed, stares back at me with his hazel eyes glowing, a confident expression, and a thin scar running from his eye to his chin.

I study the photo for several minutes, then mutter, "Gotcha!"

The end of his scar widens, and it's a new detail I hadn't noticed before. I study it another moment and add it to my mental list about number six.

My heart races faster, and I flip to the next man, unsure why I'm trying to memorize everything about these men.

I've already decided that I'm not going through with this bid or initiation ritual. As intrigued as I am, it sounds like a cult. Besides, there's no proof they know anything about my father.

How did they know I want answers I can't get from my dad?

It's the lingering question I can't figure out. No matter how hard I try to let it go, it's the thing that keeps bringing me back to the photos.

Number seven's Asian. His eyes hold a dark mystery. Evil flirts with his expression, but it's borderline soft, as if he's a bad boy but could be a true friend.

Don't kid yourself, I scold myself.

I stare at his torso, then pick up my pen. I draw the shape of his birth-mark, weaving around his abs as best as I can. I make several attempts to get closer to the one on him and finally move on.

Eight steals my breath. He always does. Everything about him reminds me of Sean. He wears his dirty-blond hair the same way, just slightly over his eye. I can almost see him shoving it to the side the way Sean does. His crooked nose screams it's been broken, possibly multiple times. I smile every time I see it. Over the years, I've witnessed several of Sean's fights where his nose has gotten smashed. It's a fighter's risk, and the scars on eight's knuckles tell me he's no stranger to landing punches on men.

I pause longer than I should on him until the butterflies in my stomach need to stop. To make myself suffer further, I pick up my phone. I scroll to Sean's name and click on his picture.

My eyes drift from eight to Sean, over and over. I make mental notes on the differences between the two men, about things I can see in the photos and things I know about Sean without seeing a picture.

Eight has a scar on his chest, ripping through his nipple and stopping an inch from his belly button.

I've seen Sean shirtless enough to know he has a scar on the back of his shoulder in the shape of a half-moon.

Eight has a mole near his lip.

Sean has a mole on the top of his foot.

Eight's arm sleeve is on his right arm.

Sean's is on his left.

Eight has a snake tattoo on his lower back.

Sean has the O'Malley family cross across his entire back.

Eight appears tall but smaller than Sean.

81

Sean's feet and hands are bigger, and I assume so is his cock. Not because of the stereotype about big hands and feet but because his erections have been pushed against my stomach too many times for me to count. And eight doesn't have anything above average below the waist.

My eyes turn blurry from studying the binder, yet I can't stop. I turn the page to number nine.

The doorbell rings, tearing me out of my haze. I turn and stare at it, frozen, unsure if I should let anyone in.

Is it them?

No, they would just let themselves inside.

It has to be family or a friend who has unannounced access.

There's a loud knock. Sean's voice rings out from the other side. "Zara, let me in."

My pulse skyrockets.

What's he doing here?

"Zara!" he orders, banging again.

I shut the binder, get up, and open a drawer. I shove the binder inside, shut the drawer, and step in front of the mirror.

I wince at my reflection. I showered in the morning and my hair air-dried. It's a frizzy mess, and I have no makeup on.

It doesn't matter.

"Zara!" Sean shouts.

"Hold your horses," I reply, running my fingers through my hair before I step in front of the door. I fling it open. "What's the emergency?"

He shoves past me, shuts the door, and locks it.

The hairs on my neck rise.

Sean grabs my hand and leads me to the sofa. "Sit."

I obey, unsure what is happening.

"Is anyone else here?" he asks.

"No. Why?"

"Stay here." He gets up and searches my bedroom, then returns.

"Why are you searching my house?" I ask.

He releases a big breath. "Did you get any gifts?"

The binder flashes in my mind, but I lie. "Gifts? No."

He clenches his jaw and goes to the window, staring down at the street.

"Sean, you're acting paranoid. What happened?"

He spins to face me. "John must have been in my apartment."

My insides quiver. I ask, "Why do you believe that?"

"There was a box with a bow left on my bed. This was in it." He comes over, pulls a piece of paper out of his pocket, unfolds it, and hands it to me.

A drawing of the skull branded on John, but with some flowers and feathers, along with gray and black shading, fills the sheet. The initials S.O. are on the corner.

My mouth turns dry. I glance up, unsure what this means.

Sean blurts out, "My dad drew it."

"How do you know?"

He points to the corner. "S.O. Sean O'Malley."

"That could be anyone," I declare.

He shakes his head. "No. It's not. My mom and uncles confirmed my dad used to doodle this everywhere. He had this branded on his hand, in the same spot John has his. Except, before he died, his had colors just like this one."

My stomach flips. I process what he's saying, trying to understand it all.

Sean adds, "My dad used to sketch this everywhere he went. My mom and uncles wouldn't lie about it."

Why would his dad have the same mark as John?

Sean plops down next to me. "When did you talk to John last?"

"Why?"

"Don't ask questions. Just answer mine, please," he pleads.

"I haven't had any contact with him since Shannon's party."

He assesses me.

"Sean, what's going on?"

"What did he promise you?"

My chest tightens. I open my mouth, and Sean puts two fingers on my lips. He orders, "Don't lie to me, Zara. Please. Just don't lie." He slowly removes his hand.

My heart beats harder. I swallow hard and answer in a low voice, "Sean, I can't discuss anything about my conversations with John."

"You can tell me," he insists.

I grapple with what my heart wants to do, but my fear leads. I insist, "I'm sorry, but I can't discuss anything with you."

"You have to!"

"No, I don't. I can't. I want to, but I can't."

"Zara—"

"You tell me everything you know, and I'll reconsider telling you what you want to know. But until you go first, I'm not budging," I assert.

He grits his teeth.

I point at him. "See. You won't talk either, will you?"

He takes long breaths, keeping his challenging stare pinned on me.

Tense silence builds between us. The air turns thick from his toffee and bourbon vanilla cologne. I break the stare, lean closer, and grab his hand.

He glances down at it.

I scoot closer, softening my voice. "Tell me what your dad has to do with this."

His eyes dart to my lips, then he sniffs hard. His expression reveals no emotion.

I put my hand on his cheek. "Sean, you can trust me. I won't say anything to anyone. I promise."

He snorts. "That's rich, coming from the woman who won't answer anything I ask her."

"Sean—"

He grabs my hand and pins it behind my back, then lunges forward.

I fall back on the couch and stare into his blazing greens.

He positions his face an inch from mine. His hot breath laces with mine, teasing me. His legs straddle my waist.

He yanks my hair with his other hand.

My breath catches. I can't breathe, and adrenaline burns through my body.

He growls, "Don't be a brat, Zara. I need you to tell me everything."

I stay silent, unable to move, except for the butterflies in my gut waking back up and tormenting me.

"What's it going to take to get you to talk, Zara, huh?" he murmurs in my ear, his lips grazing my lobe, sending a shock wave down my spine.

I shudder beneath him, my chest rising and falling faster.

"Tell me everything, and I'll give you whatever you want," he adds.

I've never felt so tempted in my life. The ache in my body grows to the point I feel dizzy. His scent somehow intensifies, flaring into my soul.

I open my mouth, but John's voice comes at me from nowhere. *There is no speaking of The Underworld outside of us. You won't ever get access if you tell anyone about our conversations now or in the future. The truth you seek will stay hidden. The riches set aside for you will stay buried. And all the power and control you don't know you want will become someone else's.*

Sean's tongue teases my lobe and then he seductively asserts, "Don't be a little brat. I'll do multiple things if you want. Whatever you want. Just talk to me."

"I can't," I manage to get out.

Sean tenses, putting his face over mine again, scowling with a rage I've only seen on him in the ring.

It scares me, and I take my free hand and push against his chest. "Get off me."

He hesitates for a moment, then releases me, rolling to a seated position.

I rise and walk to the kitchen, needing some distance. I fill a wine glass with Merlot and take a long sip.

Then I open the fridge and take out a beer. I open it, then take it to him, suggesting, "Have a drink and relax for a minute."

He glances at the bottle, then me, and stands. In a betrayed voice, he declares, "I thought we were friends."

"We are friends. Always have been, always will be."

He shakes his head. "No. If you can't tell me what I need to know, then we aren't friends, Zara."

My insides tremble. "Don't say something so horrible."

He cries out, "Then don't keep things from me! Things I need to know, not just for me but for you!"

I rarely hear Sean raise his voice, and I'm momentarily taken aback. I find my voice and ask, "What does that even mean?"

He steps forward, and I take several steps back until I'm against the wall. He pushes his body against mine and leers down at me, but worry laces his expression. His voice turns low, and he questions, "What do you think they want with you, Zara? Hmm?"

I open my mouth, but no words come out. It's something I've never asked myself. I suddenly feel foolish for not considering it.

"Ah. You can only think about whatever it is that they promised you," he states.

I shake my head. "No. I-I..." I release an anxious breath.

His voice turns stern. "What did they promise you?"

I bite my lip to keep from speaking.

He drags his knuckles down the side of my arm, and I shiver. He murmurs, "Do you think they'd take a girl like you and not have any plans for you?"

The binder in my drawer pops into my mind, and I glance over at it.

Sean freezes.

My pulse pounds between my ears.

"Why did you look over there?" he questions.

"No reason," I lie, but it comes out flat.

He stays planted against me, then turns his head, assessing the room.

My heart races so fast, I think I might faint.

He releases me and races toward the drawer.

"Sean!" I cry out.

He doesn't stop. He yanks the drawer open, then goes still.

I chase after him, dropping the beer on the carpet, but I'm too slow to react.

He grabs the binder, flips through it, and his face pales, then turns bright red. He gets through several pages and then sets it down. Horror fills his expression.

My voice cracks. "It's not what it looks like."

In an angry voice, he admits, "I'm not sure what this is, but it's nothing good."

I grab the counter to steady myself, focusing my gaze on the pattern of the stone, unable to look Sean in the eye. Shame fills me, and I don't know why. I've not done anything wrong, but the disappointment in his expression makes me feel like I have.

He softens his tone, ordering, "Tell me everything, Zara."

Tears fill my eyes. I want to so badly, but the promise of things I don't even know really exist keeps me from it. The quartz under my fingers turns blurry, and I reply, "I'm sorry. I can't."

Silence builds between us, and it tears at my heart. I still can't look at him.

He finally warns, "Last chance. Tell me, and I'll make sure you're okay."

For some reason, I laugh. It's emotion-filled, crackling with tears.

He barks, "That's funny?"

I stop laughing and force myself to look him in the eye. I shake my head and declare, "It's hard for you to promise you can make sure I'm okay when you don't even know what it is your father was involved in."

Hurt fills his sharp features. His eyes turn to slits. He glares at me until I feel like I'll melt into a puddle on the floor. Then he turns and goes to the door. He reaches for the doorknob.

I blurt out, "I'm sorry. I didn't mean for my statement to hurt you."

He huffs. "Sure you did. But don't worry. From here on out, you're on your own."

Sean

Two Weeks Later

Chapter

SEVEN

L iam has kept me from focusing on anything but work since our meeting a couple of weeks ago. I only get to think about The Underworld or my father's involvement when lying in bed. And Liam hasn't given me much time to do that lately either.

All O'Malleys go through specific training, so I'm used to running on no sleep. It's important we can function without it at any time. So, while it's annoying that Liam's keeping me on a short leash, the lack of sleep isn't affecting me.

The first few days, his jobs bored me to death. Brax wasn't happy he got chosen to be my sidekick, claiming it wasn't fair he was in trouble when I wouldn't tell him what the meeting was regarding. But I stood my ground, maintaining my silence.

Mid-week, Brax caught one of our enemies attempting to hack into our gambling operation. He tried to figure out who it was, but it wasn't clear who had the balls to fuck with our business. So we moved most of the money out and left a few million.

Declan instructed Brax to install a bug on the remaining assets. Then, he reduced the level of security and made it easier for the hacker to access our account.

Once he was in, the bug traced the money to an account owned by the Baileys. As soon as the first transfer hit, it was all hands on deck at O'Malley Cybersecurity.

It took me two days to hack into the account and determine the culprit behind the novice operation. And it was so weak, I kind of felt bad for the guy. Only an amateur would move the money directly to the real account instead of several ghost ones.

Paddy Bailey's only saving grace was he hid pretty well. Except he wasn't that good. It only added ten days to his freedom.

Yesterday morning, Brax and I picked him up. The rodent-infested, crappy apartment in a beaten-down building on the south side of Chicago showed how low he was on the Bailey totem pole.

We took the skinny computer geek to headquarters. Decades ago, Liam's father, Darragh, transformed an empty warehouse space into a combination storage unit and torture chamber. We keep enough ammo and firearms to take out the entire state of Illinois if needed, along with fleets of vehicles and other items. Any device you can think of to make someone suffer is in a separate section. And a huge room full of screens allows us to hack into any security camera or public footage as needed.

The first thing we did was tie rope to Paddy's wrists and ankles. Then we got rid of all the slack. For the last twenty hours, he's been hanging in the air, stretched out in the shape of an X.

Once we had him shackled, I made sure there wasn't a bug on the money. When assured, I transferred our money back into our account, along with another four million of Bailey assets. Brax erased their account and the digital trail the second the money moved out.

On Liam's orders, we programmed the thermostat to rotate every two hours between forty degrees and one hundred ten. We turned on a recording of several men screaming from our past torture sessions, shut all the fluorescent lights off, then left.

Today, around noon, Brax and I were called to the warehouse. It's now time for Paddy to pay for his sins.

When we arrive, Liam's sitting in a metal chair, wearing a thick winter coat. He presses his gloved palms together, his lips pursed and eyes blazing at Paddy.

"P-please," Paddy cries, covered in sweat but shaking from the cold, his breath coming out in a fog. Crystalized frost covers his nipples. His nose, lips, fingers, and toes are dark purple.

"Fucking cold in here, what temperature is it?" Brax questions.

Liam's lips twist. He casually glances at us. "Thirty-three. Go bundle up."

Brax and I don't question our orders. It's one degree above freezing, and our egos aren't big enough to want to fight the chill. We go into the closet, grab coats and gloves, and put them on.

Liam rises and pulls out his pocket knife. He approaches Paddy, puts the blade against his throat, and snarls, "You think you can take what's ours?"

"P-please. I d-didn't. It w-wasn't m-me," Paddy claims.

It's a lie. We all know it, and nothing Paddy says will stop his fate.

Liam slowly drags the knife across his throat. A thin line of blood appears, and Paddy sobs. Liam murmurs, "While I'd love to do the honors, I allow those who do the work to have the fun." He turns to Brax and me and nods his head toward Paddy. "Finish him off, boys. I have to get to Hailey's school. It's teacher appreciation day. I'm bringing cupcakes."

"You could have brought us some," Brax whines.

"Send me some videos of the next few hours, and I'll have some sent to your house. They're from Sullivan's," Liam replies with a twinkle in his eye.

"Are you getting the strawberry champagne ones?" I ask.

"Of course," Liam affirms.

Braxton adds, "Toss in some peanut butter cup ones in my box."

"Footage better be good, or you're just getting vanilla," Liam warns.

"Don't worry. Watch your secure app," I state.

Approval fills his expression. He walks out, and the door slams shut behind him.

I study a distressed Paddy, asking, "Should we bring out the torch or the fire extinguisher?"

A tear falls down Paddy's cheek.

Brax's smile twists. He walks over to the bench, picks up the torch and the fire extinguisher, and answers, "I say we do both. I'm feeling like being on flamethrower duty, though." He hands me the extinguisher.

I chuckle.

Brax steps in front of Paddy and turns on the flame, holding it close to Paddy's lower body.

"P-please don't," Paddy cries out.

Brax scowls. "Did you think you could hack into our system and take what's ours? It doesn't work like that, and you should know better. There are consequences, and now it's time to pay the piper."

"Make sure you only sear him; don't kill him yet," I remind Brax.

Paddy starts to sob, begging, "Please. I have ch-children."

"You should have thought about that before you stole our money," Brax states, moving the flamethrower close enough so that his pubic hairs singe into black ash.

Paddy's whine fills the air.

"He's just getting started," I taunt, and step beside Brax. I take two nails out of my pocket and run them down his cheek as lightly as Liam did his knife on his throat.

A whimper falls from Paddy's lips as blood seeps from the wounds.

"Come on now. This is nothing compared to what you're going to feel," I inform him, then dig the nail deeper over the same spot.

He wails as blood coasts down his face and drips onto the floor.

Brax suggests, "Maybe we should collect his blood. I heard they're low at the blood bank, and there's going to be a lot of it tonight."

I leer at Paddy. "Nah, no one wants tainted donations."

"P-please, it wasn't m-me," Paddy cries out.

"Your nipples look cold," Brax states, then takes the torch to each side of Paddy's chest.

A screech rings through the room.

Brax's eyes light up as hot as the flame in his hands. "The Baileys should have taught you better about what happens when you fuck with O'Malleys."

Paddy gets a kick of courage and spits out, "What would you know? You're not an O'Malley. You're a wannabe O'Malley."

Brax's expression turns angry, but I put my hand on his chest. "Hold on, brother. I think I'll handle this one." I take the fire extinguisher and step behind Paddy. "Lean him over," I instruct to Brax.

Brax gives me a satisfied look. We've partnered on torture sessions too many times over the years. We can foresee each other's moves.

He goes over to the wall and hits a button. The tension loosens on Paddy's wrists and his body slumps forward. Brax hits another button, and Paddy's legs stretch farther, spreading his ass cheeks.

I take the fire extinguisher and blast it at his cheeks and balls.

His shrill scream would haunt a normal man. Not us, though. It only encourages us to keep going.

I walk around his body and tug his head up. I lean toward his ear and ask, "Do you have anything else you want to say about my brother?"

He hysterically sobs.

We torture him for a few hours until his body can't handle it anymore. When he hangs lifeless, his corpse burnt, bloody, and frozen, we call it a day.

Brax points to the cameras. "Don't forget the video so we get our cupcakes."

"Good call." I take off my gloves and sit in front of the computer.

Brax takes the seat beside me, and we spend another hour splicing and editing footage. We send the videos to Liam via our secure app, and he replies with photos of cupcakes.

Brax grins and holds out his fist, and I fist-bump him. "Let's get the cleanup crew in here."

It's good to have so many younger cousins who still need to prove themselves to the clan. Brax and I spent years on cleanup duty.

He adds, "Which ones should we bestow the joy on?"

I reply, "I saw Mikhail with L.J.; I'm sure their fathers will approve."

His grin widens. Mikhail is Dmitri and Anna Ivanov's son. Liam's son, L.J., short for Liam Jr., and Mikhail are thick as thieves. They're twenty-six and just as cocky as Brax and I were at that age. But they still have a lot to learn, especially L.J., who by birth is expected to someday take over the clan. And Liam doesn't show him one ounce of favoritism.

Brax pushes the button on the speaker and orders, "L.J., Mikhail. Get your asses in chamber three."

In less than a minute, the door opens and they stroll in.

L.J. asks, "What's up?"

"Looks like you two had a fun day," Mikhail mutters, staring at the corpse.

L.J. glances over at Paddy, then walks around him, assessing our work. He affirms, "Sure does. Thanks for not including us."

"Oh, we're including you," Brax states.

"He's dead," Mikhail points out, as if we're stupid.

I smack him across the head.

"Ouch!" he cries out, jumping back.

"No shit, he's dead. Clean it up," I order.

"But I was on cleanup duty for your last guy," L.J. whines.

"So?"

"So why don't you call someone else? The warehouse is full of O'Malleys."

"I'm an Ivanov. Why do I have to do it?" Mikhail questions.

Brax wags his finger in front of them. "Tsk, tsk, tsk. You know the rules."

They freeze.

"I was just joking," Mikhail states.

"Me too," L.J. quickly adds.

"You sure about that?" I ask, crossing my arms.

They nod and move toward the closet, knowing you don't break the rules. You obey whoever has a higher status than you. Right now, that's Brax and me. As far as Mikhail is concerned, if you come into O'Malley territory, you don't get to pick and choose your role. It's the same if we step into the Ivanov garage, which is their version of our warehouse.

Brax shakes his head at me. "Young lads. They're so naive, aren't they? Thinking they don't have to put in the time..."

"Agreed. I'm going to go shower. You two know what to do," I add, then exit the room as they grumble behind me.

Brax follows, and we go into the locker room. We remove our pants and shirts, disposing of them in the incineration can. We shower and grab new clothes off the shelf.

As I'm putting my head through the T-shirt, my phone buzzes. I pull the cotton over my abs and then grab my phone.

The hairs on my neck rise. There's an address on the lower East side of Gary, Indiana. It's a town about forty-five minutes from Chicago, known for its abandoned factories and high crime rate.

Another message comes in right after it.

> Unknown: Be there in an hour, and don't be late.

I glance at the time on my phone and curse. It doesn't leave me a lot of time.

I don't have to go. Who are these people to dictate to me what I need to do?

If I don't show up, I won't get any closer to the truth about my father.

My phone buzzes again.

> Unknown: Come alone.

Brax interrupts my thoughts. "Which club are we hitting tonight?"

My chest tightens. I glance at him. "Sorry, I can't go."

"What are you talking about? We always go celebrate after we take our enemy out."

"Sorry, I can't. I have somewhere I need to be."

"Why? Where are you going?" he asks.

"It's personal," I reply, then move toward the other side of the warehouse.

Brax follows on my heels. "Sean, stop bullshitting me. What's going on with you?"

"Nothing. I've just got something I've got to do." I jump in one of the dated Jeeps from the early 2000s.

The fleet of cars Liam stocks in the warehouse is an assortment of vehicles. Some are nice and fancy, like the Range Rovers. Some are old and beat-up but have engines that can outrun a sports car. Since Gary tends to be rough, flashy isn't a great option.

I open the garage door and leave. I glance at the rearview mirror. Brax stands outside with his arms crossed and a scowl on his face.

I feel bad. I hate keeping secrets from him, but I don't know what to tell him. I don't know what I'm stepping into anyway.

It's early evening, and the sun is starting to set. I follow the directions on my phone and then pull up to a warehouse. There's no glass on the windows and no other cars in sight.

My heart races. The last thing I want to do is put myself in an unknown situation, but that's exactly what I've done.

I reply to the text.

Me: I'm here.

Unknown: Walk in the door.

I should insist they tell me what this is all about, but I know they won't. And I assume it's about whatever fight they referred to in the text that was sent weeks ago. So I grab the gun from the glove compartment just as another text comes in.

> Unknown: Don't bring any weapons. If you do, I'll confiscate them. And it'll be a penalty against you.

I think about what I want to do. I consider putting a knife in my boot, but I decide maybe it's best if I don't. And then I get another text.

> Unknown: You can't hide anything, Sean. We're waiting, and you have two minutes to get inside or you're late. The window of opportunity shuts.

"Dammit!" I slam the glove compartment closed and then exit the vehicle, glancing around and muttering, "This place is a fucking shithole."

I walk to the only door in the building, turn the handle, and push the heavy metal door. It opens with a creak.

The only thing in front of me is a staircase leading down. I step inside and turn on the flashlight on my phone.

The door slams, and the sound of an electrical bolt locking fills the air. It makes me hesitate, and I wonder again what I'm getting myself into.

It's now or never.

I walk down a flight of stairs, then turn and descend another. Four floors down, another door appears.

Muffled sounds come from the other side. I take a deep breath, push it, and stale air hits me. Loud shouts deafen my ears.

I step inside, shocked. The room is dim. Light bulbs hang from the ceiling, and there's a dirt floor. A massive crowd fills the room from wall to wall.

Women, men, and even some children make up the group. They scream insults and cheer with joy. There are so many people, I can't see past them to know what causes them to yell.

From the shadows, John steps out. He pats me on the back and says in an Irish accent, "Made it with ten seconds to go. Well done."

The crowd roars louder, and I realize it's the same as when I'm fighting, but I can't see any fighters. There are just too many people.

I question, "How did all these people get here? There are no vehicles anywhere."

John taps his head. "Aye. That's for me to know."

I glance between him and the crowd. "What is this place?"

John's lips twist. "It's something you're going to love."

"Yeah? Why is that?" I ask doubtfully.

"Because your father imagined, designed, and loved it," he informs me.

Adrenaline rushes through me. I hate that it does. I don't want John to predict how I'll think or feel, yet he's correct.

It's only one reason I don't like him. I've loathed him since the minute I saw him talking to Zara. I hate how he's mysterious and only gives me little tidbits of information. I can't stand how he has the same brand as my dad, when I don't even understand what it truly represents. And I detest that he seems to hold the keys to a world my father took part in, and that the rest of my family doesn't know about it, or does and wants to keep me in the dark.

He steps beside me, puts his arm around my shoulders, and leans into my ear. He declares, "It's time to see if you're meant to follow in your father's footsteps."

My gut flips. "What are you talking about?"

He points around the room. "No one could beat him."

I blurt out, "My father was an amazing fighter. Nothing scared him."

"Aye, he was, and you're right. He was braver than most men."

"Why do you have an Irish accent tonight? You never have before."

John's lips twitch. "I have many accents, son."

"I'm not your son."

"Aye, you're not, but this is your destiny. But first, you must prove you're as worthy as your father was, as blood doesn't give you an automatic seat on the throne," he asserts.

My pulse races, and my mouth turns dry. I don't understand what the throne is, and I'm pretty sure why he summoned me here, but I still ask, "Doing what?"

John smiles.

It's eerie, and goose bumps erupt over my arms.

"When that man in the ring dies, you will step forward. Whoever stands at the night's end, still breathing, wins the bid."

"You keep talking about this bid, but I don't know what you're referring to," I remind him.

"You will when it's time. But trust me, you want to win the bid. And especially tonight, because if you don't, you'll die." He grins wider.

I tear my eyes off him, staring at the crowd dressed in street clothes. They look like normal people, but I still don't know how they got here.

The crowd erupts with louder shouts, and within several seconds, I wince from the ear-piercing screams.

And a chill runs down my spine when I notice many men with the same brand my father had. Some have no color. Some have light pink in them. Some have other colors of the rainbow. Some have shading while others have none.

"Aye. You're up." John nods and steps toward the crowd. Then he stops and turns his head. "Are you coming?"

Without hesitating, my feet move. It's as if something takes hold of my body, and I couldn't stop myself if I tried.

John pushes through the mass of bodies until we're at the center, and there's a bloody, unrecognizable dead man lying on the ground. Another man's barely able to stay on his feet as he holds up his arm in victory.

A bald, stocky man with three hoops through his nose and tattoos all over his face jumps into the circle and makes an X with his arms above his head.

Two men grab the corpse's legs and arms and cart him to the edge of the circle. The crowd parts, and they disappear.

The fighter who won gets led to a metal chair. A woman holds a bottle of water to his lips, almost as if it were a fight in the ring.

But it's not.

The ring has rules and structure. There's a referee to ensure people can breathe at the end, even if barely. That's not the situation here.

John orders, "Drop your pants."

"What?"

"Drop your pants," he sternly orders.

I glance at the fighter sitting down. He's in a pair of red silk boxer shorts. I do as instructed and strip out of my jeans.

A woman with long blonde hair approaches me. She bats her lashes and holds out a pair of green silk shorts.

I take them and put them on.

The crowd cheers, "Fight! Fight! Fight!"

Adrenaline courses through me as my fighter instincts turn on.

John directs, "Take your shirt off. Shoes too."

I obey.

He points to another chair someone moved into the circle. I take two steps and sit down.

A man with reddish-orange hair steps in front of me. He's older, probably the age my father would've been. He peers at me closer, and something washes over him. He says, "Aye, you look just like him." And I realize it's nostalgia he's feeling.

Emotions fill me, but I don't have time to think about my father and what I lost when he was murdered. I'm in a life-or-death situation. I'm not stupid. I understand what this fight is meant to be.

The man states, "I'm Byrne." He holds a bottle of water to my mouth. "Drink it. You're going to need it."

I don't question him, and guzzle the entire bottle.

A woman in electric-blue lingerie screams in the center of the ring, "Bets! Bets! Place your bets! You have one minute."

The crowd turns more chaotic. Then, a bell rings.

"Up," Byrne instructs.

I rise.

He steps forward, puts his hands on my cheeks, and tugs my head down. His green gaze bores into mine. He sternly orders, "Go step on the line. And, lad, forget the rules. There are none here. It's fight or flight. Understand?"

I nod, stepping up to the line.

The man who just killed the last guy steps forward. His swollen face is covered in blood. One eye is completely swollen shut. He's still breathing hard, and the look he gives from his one partially good eye tells me two things.

He wants to kill me, and he'll do anything he can to make sure it happens.

Zara

Chapter

EIGHT

Work kept me busy the last few weeks. I've resisted texting or calling Sean. I want to make things right between us, but I don't know how. He wants answers I can't give him, and he won't let it go.

My parents texted me this morning that they were flying in and wanted me to come for dinner. It was a welcome invite, and I'm excited to see them. They bought a condo in Chicago when I took a job here, and they only stay away for a short time without visits.

My last appointment ran late, so I rush to get ready. Mom's making her veal osso buco, and it's my favorite. I pick up my hair dryer, and my phone rings. The caller ID says it's the reception desk.

I answer, "Hello?"

"There's a delivery for you, Ms. Marino. Should I bring it up?" the receptionist says.

"Sure. Thank you." I remove my towel, put on my robe, secure the belt, and go to the front door.

Richard arrives shortly after, and as soon as the doorbell rings, I open the door.

He holds out a yellow envelope. "This is for you."

"Thank you, Richard." I take it from him.

"You're welcome, Ms. Marino."

I shut the door and glance at the envelope. Nothing but my name is written on it.

My pulse quickens. I debate opening it as I return to the bathroom. I set it down, then turn on the hair dryer. Less than a minute passes before my curiosity gets the best of me. I turn off the dryer, pick up the envelope, tear it open, and pull out a stack of photos.

My gut churns so fast, I feel nauseous. I grab the counter to steady myself and then turn to lean against it.

Each photo is of my father when he was younger. He's with men and women I don't recognize. He looks happy in most of them. He's laughing, smoking cigars, drinking what I assume is scotch, and always dressed in his suit.

I thumb through the stack several times, staring at them and realizing the photos were taken over a fifteen-to-twenty-year span based on how my father looks in the photos. I turn them over and discover writing on the backs.

Names and dates are written neatly on the bottom corner of each one. Names like Jacopo Abruzzo, Biagio Abruzzo, Leo Abruzzo, and Uberto Abruzzo. And it only makes me feel sicker.

While I've never met or heard of these men, their last name is the only thing I need to see. They're enemies of the Marinos.

Why would my father be with them and look so happy?

I flip the photos back around, confused, staring at them and studying each one the same way I assessed the binder full of men.

One in particular makes my gut sink to the floor. There's a beautiful woman in it. She has long, dark hair, stunning eyes, high cheekbones, and a killer body. She's holding a baby and looking at my father like she adores him. Or maybe she's in love with him? And he's touching the baby's head.

My hands shake as I turn the photo to read the back of it. *Finzia and Aurora.* No last name or date like the others.

Who are they?

Is the baby my father's?

Was that his wife before he married my mother?

Is it still his wife?

Do I have a sister?

Questions spin in my mind, making me dizzy. I glance at the dates on the other photos and see they were all taken between when my mom would've been pregnant with me to when I was fifteen, which was before my father came into my life.

I don't finish drying my hair. I go into my closet, put on a pair of joggers, and toss a sweater over my head. I slide into a pair of sneakers and return to the bathroom. I shove the stack of photos back into the envelope. Then I text Calogero.

> Me: Pull the car up, please. I'll be down in a moment.

> Calogero: I'll be waiting.

I take the envelope and put it in my oversized bag, then slip on my coat. I make my way through my building and step outside.

Calogero is waiting on the curb. He stands next to the back door of the SUV and opens it, nodding. "Ms. Marino."

I blurt out, "I need you to take me to my parents' house, please. Quickly."

His expression shows concern. "Yes, ma'am. Is everything okay?"

"Yes. Please, just hurry." I slide into the back, and he shuts the door.

He hurries to the front, gets in the driver's seat, and veers into traffic.

I put up the partition, not wanting to talk. My insides quiver. A million scenarios race through my mind, but confusion plagues me.

Calogero pulls up to my parents' building and gets out. Before he can come around to my door, I open it.

"Ms. Marino," he frets, following me.

"You don't need to walk me up," I call back, but like always, he doesn't listen.

It's my father's rule, and I know it. Calogero will always walk me anywhere I go unless my father or someone like Sean is with me.

The ride up in the elevator is excruciating. It takes forever before we get to the penthouse, and the elevator opens.

"Thank you," I say to Calogero as I step out. I quickly reach over and hit the button so the doors close before he can follow me.

The house smells delicious. The rich, deep scent of Mom's veal osso buco hangs in the air.

Normally, I'd be excited to be here. I love visiting with my parents. But my emotions are hitting me hard, and I don't know what to think.

I walk through the penthouse and into the kitchen. Mom and Dad stand side by side, cutting up vegetables for a salad. Slow music plays in the background, and glasses of red wine are in front of them.

Mom sees me first, and her eyes light up. "Ah, Zara, you're here."

She comes over to hug me.

I hug her hard, and she pulls back. She tilts her head, asking, "Zara, is everything okay?"

"I need to speak to Dad alone," I tell her.

She wrinkles her forehead. "Why?"

"I just do. Please, Mom." I blink hard, and my eyes well with tears.

"Zara, what is wrong?" she repeats.

"Mom, please let me talk to him alone," I beg.

"My precious *figlia*, what is going on?" Dad inquires, stepping up to us, concerned.

"Please go, Mom," I plead.

She looks at Dad.

"Zara, whatever you have to say, you can say in front of your mama. We don't have secrets between us. You know that," Dad asserts, and puts his hand on my back.

I shrug it off.

He tosses his hands in the air. "Whoa. What's going on?"

The worry in Mom's expression deepens. "Zara, please. Talk to us."

I realize I'm not going to get my father alone. I hate that I'm going to hurt my mother, but I lift my chin and meet my father's eyes. I step backward to put some distance between us, then accuse, "What have you done? Who are you?"

Shock and hurt fill his features. He peers at me closer, asking, "What are you talking about?"

I pull the envelope out of my purse and turn to Mom again. "Mom, please go."

She glances at my father, then at me.

He steps next to her and puts his arm around her. "No, you stay. We don't have secrets."

"But you do. I know you do," I say, my voice quavering.

"Zara, what is going on?" Mom asks again.

My father grabs the envelope from me. He opens it, pulls the stack of photos out, and tenses.

Mom glances at them, and her face turns pale.

I blurt out, "Why are you with the Abruzzos?"

Dad's gaze, dark and penetrating, meets mine, and he sternly says, "These are not photos you should have. Who gave them to you?"

I huff. "Does it matter?"

"Yes, of course it matters. Where did you get these?"

"It doesn't matter. Why are you with enemies of our family?"

"I want to know right now, my beautiful *figlia*, who gave you these?" he asks, his tone commanding.

I cry, "What are you hiding from Mom and me?"

Mom steps forward and puts her arm around me. "Zara, I know all about your father's past. I don't know where you got these, but this isn't your business."

Dad interjects, "These photos are dangerous for you to have. I want to know who gave them to you."

I shout, "I want to know why you're with Abruzzos!" A tear drips down my cheek, and I'm so tired of my father not being able to tell me the truth of where he was for fifteen years of my life. And I can't stand how my mom thinks it's okay. It's not enough to tell me he did it to protect us.

He replies with the same thing he always does. "We've gone over this multiple times. Your mother hid her pregnancy, and you, from me because she didn't think it was safe. I agree with her decision. So I was away and you were protected."

"It's true," Mom insists.

I shake my head. "It's not a full answer. I want to know the whole truth!"

"Zara," Mom warns.

"You're laughing and happy in those photos," I shriek at Dad.

My father fumes, "You should not have these. Whoever gave them to you is dangerous. I'm not going to ask you again, Zara. This is not a request. Who gave these to you?"

"They showed up on my doorstep."

The color drains from his face. "Someone knows where you live."

"It doesn't matter," I claim.

"Of course it matters!" Dad cries out.

Mom puts her hand on my arm. In a soft tone, she requests, "Please answer your father."

I shake my head. I know where they came from. John, Sylvia, or somebody associated with them left those photos at the front desk. But I'm not telling Mom and Dad anything.

"Think, my precious *figlia*," Dad insists.

I don't answer him. Instead, I question, my voice cracking, "Who's the woman and the baby?"

"None of your business," he replies.

Mom looks surprised. She blurts out, "What woman and baby?"

Dad hadn't gotten to that photo yet, but he didn't even flinch when I brought them up.

My gut spins. I put my hand over it, feeling ill. "Do I have a sister? Are you married?"

His eyes turn to slits. "I will not answer questions about my past. It is not your business, and it is unsafe for you to know."

"Luca, what woman and baby?" Mom repeats.

"Show her," I demand.

Dad scowls at me.

I reach for the photos.

He shoves them back in the yellow envelope, demanding, "I want to know who gave these to you."

"Luca," Mom says, more emotion filling her voice.

"Tell us. We deserve to know," I order.

Dad's face goes red with anger. He puts his finger in the air, pointing at me. "You aren't entitled to anything. This is not your business."

"It is! And I want to know why you look like you're besties with the Abruzzos and if you have another family!" I hysterically shout.

Deafening silence fills the air.

Mom's lip trembles. She glances between Dad and me.

I glare at my father, seething. "Tell. Me."

He refuses. He steps in front of the fireplace and then tosses the photos onto the fire.

"What are you doing?" I cry out as the edges curl and the pictures erupt in flames.

He spins to face me, his cheeks maroon, eyes wild. "This is not your business. There is no reason to dredge up the past. Whoever decided to do this has nothing good up their sleeve. So you will tell me right now who brought these to you."

I lie again. "I told you, I don't know."

He steps closer to Mom and puts his hands on her cheeks. "We will talk about this later."

She stares at him, blinking hard.

He vows, "I promise we will talk about this later."

She swallows hard.

He turns back to me. "Zara, everything I do is to keep you safe. If you are involved with people you shouldn't be—"

"Like your buddies, the Abruzzos?" I hurl.

"Zara!" Mom chastises.

I turn on her. "How can you stand there and be okay with his lack of answers?"

She stays silent.

My eyes overflow with more tears.

My father kisses Mom on the forehead and sternly states, "We will not speak anymore of this. I will find out from security who brought you the photos."

"You do that," I sarcastically fume.

He points at me. "We are done discussing this, Zara. Chanel, we will talk more about this later. Now, let's go back to making dinner." He walks over to the bar, picks up a glass, and fills it with wine. Then he returns and holds it toward me. "Have a drink, Zara. Tell us what you've been up to since we were last in Chicago."

My insides quiver harder. I glance between him and Mom.

How can she stand there and not ask questions?

How can she trust that he'll tell her the truth about whatever this is, whatever he's done, and whoever in the world may be linked to us?

Was he with that family instead of us? How can she be okay with the secrecy?

115

"Zara, here." He motions with his head for me to take the wine.

I briefly glance at it and then at him. "No, I'm not staying for dinner."

"Zara, don't leave," Mom begs.

I refocus on her. "I'm sorry, I can't stay." I brush past her toward the elevator.

They follow me.

Dad calls out, "Zara!"

"Please, don't go," Mom pleads.

But I can't stay. I can't continue to not know the truth about why I spent the first fifteen years of my life without a father, with my mother telling me she didn't know who he was when she knew the entire time.

I'm tired of lies and deceit and the questions I never get answers to. Now, there are even more.

Dad puts his hand on my arm. "Zara—"

I shrug away from his hold. "Do not touch me. Do not touch me, and do not talk to me until you're ready to tell me the truth."

I hit the elevator button.

"Zara, you have to trust me," he claims.

I shake my head. "Do you know how tired I am of hearing you say that I have to trust you? Well, guess what, Dad? I'm tired of trusting you."

Mom snaps, "Zara—"

"No! You both ruined the first fifteen years of my life! Now, this new information comes to me, and he won't explain it. And you're going to support him? Sorry, but I'm thirty years old. I'm not a child," I point out.

Dad declares, "No, you're not a child, but you're still my precious *figlia*. I don't want anything to happen to you, so you have to trust me."

"Dad, please. Enough with all the protection excuses." Tears fall, and I swipe at them.

"They aren't excuses," he claims.

"I'm sorry, I can't stay." The elevator door opens, and I step inside. I push the button, not looking at my parents.

The door shuts, and I make a decision.

If given the opportunity, I'll go through initiation. I'll do it no matter what it involves because I need to know the truth—the truth I'll never get from either of my parents.

Sean

Chapter
NINE

Killing isn't something new to me, but ending a man's life during a fight isn't part of the sport I've spent my life perfecting.

I'm a champion boxer. I respect the rules and structure. I thrive within them.

Here, none of that exists.

The beaten, bloody man who's ready to kill me stands on the other side of the line. He's a few inches shorter, a bit more muscular, and has snake tattoos all over his chest.

He's exhausted and struggling for air, yet there's no doubt he'll do everything he can to make sure he's the one standing at the end of our encounter.

A shrill whistle is blown, and before I can even comprehend what it means, his fist slams into my jaw. His other one pounds into my belly, knocking the wind out of my lungs.

I stumble back and almost lose my footing. I regain my balance, and he charges at me, but I step out of his reach at the last second.

My father's voice fills my head. *"Forget the rules."*

The animal within me wakes up. This isn't a boxing match. This is a fight. The only way to win is to shed as much of your enemy's blood as possible.

I crouch down, assessing him, attempting to anticipate his next move. He roars while lunging at me.

I swing as hard as I can, landing a punch on his jaw. His head whips to the side, and his blood sprays across the floor. I follow up with another swing to his gut, making solid contact.

He gasps and leans over.

I grab his head with both hands and then shove my knee into his face, and his nose cracks.

The excitement in the crowd grows. It feeds my adrenaline, pushing me to not think about anything but survival. I jab my fingers into his eyes, and a painful sound flies out of him.

"Kill him! Kill him! Kill him!" the crowd chants.

He falls to his knees, and I kick him as hard as I can in the temple.

His body goes limp, and he thuds to the ground. Dirt flies into the air.

The audience gets louder.

"Get up!" I order, ready to pounce on him again, but he doesn't move. I remain in fight mode until I realize a new chant fills the room.

"One! One! One!"

Byrne rushes out and grabs my arm.

I shove him, unable to let anyone touch me. Right now, everyone is the enemy.

"Sit!" he screams over the crowd, and points to the metal chair.

I snap out of it and obey, grateful for the moment to rest.

The same woman who gave me the pair of shorts holds a water bottle to my lips.

Byrne instructs, "Drink it!"

I don't argue, and the liquid slides down my throat.

Byrne screams in my ear, "One down. Don't let up, Sean. Whatever you do, don't let up."

The air's so thick, I can barely breathe. My hand has started to swell, but I can't worry about it now.

Byrne shouts, "Two's ready, lad."

I glance over at my new opponent and try not to freak out. He's huge. I assume he's 350 pounds of muscle and eats children for breakfast.

Jesus. He looks like Goliath.

He drops his pants, and a woman hands him gold shorts. He puts them on and then tears off his shirt and shoes.

His face and chest are covered in burn scars, and what look like healed-over claw marks run down his legs. He roars and pounds his chest, pinning his scowl on me.

The crowd goes crazy, chanting, "Fight! Fight! Fight!"

The bell rings.

Byrne slaps my cheeks. "Stay focused, lad. Don't let him intimidate you."

I jump up, crack my neck, and step to the line.

The shrill whistle explodes in the air. My enemy pounces toward me, but I'm faster than him.

I duck out of the way and sweep my leg against his shin, catching him off guard.

He falls to the ground face-first, and a dust cloud rises three feet in the air.

The audience yells louder and claps.

I jump over the beast, and grip his ponytail as tight as possible. I slam his head into the dirt, slide my hand under his chin, and yank it toward me as fast as possible.

A crack fills the air, and his eyes roll. His heavy head goes limp in my hold.

I release it and jump up, pumping my fist in the air.

"Two! Two! Two!" the crowd screams.

Byrne pulls me to the chair as six men work to remove the mammoth corpse. When they finally get him up, the crowd parts, and then they all disappear.

The woman gives me more water.

Byrne rubs my shoulders and shouts in my ear, "Two down! Eleven to go!"

I move my mouth away from the bottle. "Eleven?" Water drips down my chin.

"Drink," he orders, pointing.

I repeat, "Eleven?"

"Aye. Your bid number is thirteen. We never have thirteen. No one makes it. But you're going to, lad. Now, drink," he demands.

The woman moves the bottle back to my mouth.

My chest tightens, but I drink.

The crowd chants, "Fight! Fight! Fight!"

I try to take a few deep breaths as I glance over at my next victim.

He's shorter than me, and I suspect he's faster. He's a pretty boy with blond hair and blue eyes. He's muscular, but it's from gym equipment, and I suspect he spends most of his days at the country club.

The bell rings, and we step to the line.

It's not even a battle. One hit, and he falls on his hands and knees. Within seconds, I end his life.

Over and over, I kill each of my opponents until Byrne finally states, "Twelve. Ya got one left, lad."

Out of breath, swollen, and low on energy, I drink some water and stare at the final man who stands in the way of my life.

Blood and sweat drip off me. My knuckles are split open, and my foot is shaking from kicking hard without a shoe to protect it.

My opponent's back is toward me. He drops his pants, puts on a black pair of shorts, removes his shirt and shoes, then spins toward me.

We lock gazes, and my pulse skyrockets. Diesel Conway, a boxer I've fought too many times to count, clenches his jaw in recognition. His dark eyes glow with the same killer instinct I'm sure I have in mine.

Over the years, we've traded wins and losses against one another. His skills match mine, but we've always stuck to the rules and structure of the boxing world.

Now, none of that matters. Diesel clearly wants to be the one breathing when this is over. And he's fresh, while I'm exhausted from killing twelve other men.

The bell rings, and we step to the line. Neither of us tear our focus off the other.

The moment the whistle sounds, we fall into a familiar rhythm.

We each get a few punches in, but then I hear my father's voice again. *"This isn't a boxing match, Sean. Time to fight dirty."*

I lunge at Diesel and grip his throat, squeezing as tight as I can.

He tries to pull my hands off him, and I knee him in the groin. He sputters, but I don't let up. I keep my grip tight, then headbutt him in the temple.

His body goes limp, but I don't release him. I can't take any risks. The weight of his body becomes too heavy, and we slump to the ground, but I maintain my hold on him until Byrne tries to tear me off him.

"No!" I shout, staring at Diesel's wide, dead eyes.

"It's over, lad! He's gone!" Byrne insists.

Another guy steps on my other side, and he and Byrne eventually pry my hands off Diesel.

The crowd turns deafening again, chanting, "Thirteen! Thirteen! Thirteen!"

Byrne hauls me to my feet and holds up my arm. It's only when they remove Diesel from the circle and a chair is brought behind me, that I realize I killed thirteen men.

Sweat and blood pool at my feet. I don't know how many hours I've been here. The woman holds water for me to drink while Byrne massages my shoulders. Exhaustion and inflammation take over my body in a matter of minutes.

Relief mixes with dread. I made it, but what's next? Nothing ever seems straightforward with The Underworld.

Byrne hands me another bottle of water, and my ears ring. The crowd's cheering intensifies, and no one leaves. The energy in the room is as electric now as when I was fighting.

Byrne's face is full of pride. He pats me on the back. "Your dad would be proud, lad."

An alarm goes off. It's four quick bursts. The crowd goes silent.

A voice comes over a microphone, announcing, "The bid is granted."

The crowd shouts in jubilation.

Adrenaline fills me, but I still don't know what the bid means. Yet I'm not dead, and this test is over.

The scent of blood, sweat, and beer swirls around me, making it harder for my lungs to draw in breath.

I assume it'll be time to leave, but another alarm sounds.

Three long beeps blare through the room, and the crowd quiets again.

My sweat cools on my skin, and I shiver. The hairs on my arms rise, and I glance at Byrne in question.

His forehead creases in worry.

The crowd parts.

Four men drag Brax into the ring. He tries to fight them, but it's only making it worse.

One pulls a knife out and holds it to his throat, and he immediately freezes. We lock gazes and my gut sinks.

What the hell is he doing here?

He gives me his I'm-sorry look, and I curse myself. I never once made sure he, or anyone else for that matter, wasn't following me. And I know this isn't good. They told me to come alone.

John steps forward. The silence in the room is deafening until he breaks it by saying in his Irish accent, "You were told not to bring anyone here."

"I didn't bring him," I carefully state.

"Then how did he get here?"

I don't say anything.

"You weren't careful," John accuses.

I continue to stay silent.

He takes a pocket knife out of his jeans and opens it. He steps before me and holds it in front of my face. "You do the honors."

"The honors of what?" I question, even though I know deep down what he wants me to do.

John orders, "If you didn't bring him, and you don't want him here, then get rid of him. Slit his throat."

My insides quiver. I don't look at Brax.

As beaten as my body is, I square my shoulders and lift my chin, standing as tall as possible. I step closer to John. In a loud voice, I declare, "No. I vouch for this man."

A gasp fills the crowd.

John sarcastically chuckles, "You vouch for him?"

"Yeah. I vouch for him," I repeat.

Tense silence fills the air between us.

Byrne interjects in a stern but respectful voice, "He hit thirteen. He won the bid."

John snaps his head toward him. "He didn't follow directions."

"I did," I insist.

John jabs me in the chest. "You were careless."

"He still hit thirteen," Byrne states.

The crowd starts chanting "Thirteen! Thirteen! Thirteen!" so loudly, I don't know what to make of it.

Another alarm sounds. This time, it rings for five full seconds.

Another hush falls over the crowd, and a different section parts.

A tall woman with curled long, dark hair and a ruby-encrusted red mask over her eyes and nose steps forward. She wears a matching strapless cocktail dress and stilettos. She confidently struts toward us and glances up when she stops in front of me. She reaches for my chin and holds it authoritatively so I'm forced to look at her.

I stare silently into her hazel eyes, unsure who she is but understanding she has power. And I'm not a God-fearing man, but I pray she'll give me some mercy. There's no way I'm killing Brax, but I'm unsure how we'll get out of here alive if I don't.

She tilts her head, studying me. Then she says with an Italian accent, "You're the spitting image of him."

My heart beats faster. It's surreal to be in a world where so many people seem to know my father. It makes me feel like I barely know him. I didn't used to think that, but I'm starting to question everything I did know.

I ask, "You knew him?"

She shakes her head, replying, "No. It was before our time. But my parents did, and I've seen photos."

"Who are your parents?" I question.

Her lips curve slightly. "That's not a question for you to ask."

"What question should I ask?" I retort.

Another moment passes before she replies, "They said you have your father's humor. I guess they were right."

I don't know what I said that struck her as funny, but I say, "Some say I do."

She nods. "I suppose you do."

Silence ensues, and my chest tightens.

She steps closer and curls her finger. I lean closer and she whispers in my ear, "Do you think your father's position allows you to not abide by the rules?"

I pull back so my face is in front of hers, answering, "No. I do not. I was careless coming here. I admit it. I was thinking about making it on time, and I apologize. It will never happen again. But I can assure you, I can vouch for this man."

She tilts her head and inquires, "Why do you have so much loyalty for him?"

I sternly repeat, "I vouch for him."

She steps back and glances over at Brax. Her gaze travels from the top of his head to his feet and back up. She smirks. "Granted, he's sexy in a rough way, but so are others. Why are you vouching for him?"

"I know who he is," I say without hesitation.

She raises a brow. "You know who he is?"

"Yes."

"Ah. You're a foolish one."

"Why is that?"

She glances at Brax again, then pins her gaze back on me. "You think you know people, but I can assure you, you do not."

My mouth turns dry. Before John entered the scene, I would've said I knew everybody close to me, but now there seem to be secrets, possibly lies, and I don't know what to think.

Her eyes brighten, but sadness laces her voice. "Ah. I see. I've spoken a truth, and you're unable to deny it."

I stand straighter. I assert, "I can vouch for this man, and I will not kill him. If you must, take my head and let him go."

"You would rather be killed than kill him?" she questions.

My heart beats faster, my pulse pounding between my ears. I nod, affirming, "I would rather you attempt to kill me."

Her lips twitch. "Attempt?"

"Do you believe I'd go out without a fight?"

She studies me for a long time, and the crowd circled around us deathly quiet.

She finally smiles, then warns, "Those who vouch for the uninvited choose a different path."

It's another riddle full of confusion. I admit, "I don't understand what that means."

She glances again at Brax, then turns her attention back to me, challenging, "Are you sure you want a different path, Sean O'Malley Jr.?"

I don't know what the different path means. All I know is there's no way I'm killing Brax. So I nod, and in a loud voice shout, "I vouch for this man."

The crowd gasps.

A look of approval crosses her expression, along with something else. But then it dawns on me what it means. Maybe it's the mask hiding part of her face, but I didn't immediately see it. Yet I know what it is. It's pure sadistic evil. I've seen it before on men, and a few women, but she surely has it.

She snaps her fingers toward Brax.

The men release him and push him toward me. He stumbles, finds his footing, then stands next to me.

She gives him another once-over and praises, "At least you vouch for a man who seems to have..." She tilts her head, looking him over again, and continues, "Shall we say, benefits for the ladies?"

I try not to smile. Part of me wants to laugh as I strike her comments as odd for the situation. Instead, I reiterate, "I vouch for him."

She steps back farther. "Then he's your responsibility. Go home, Sean O'Malley Jr. Heal. Your bid is secure. But remember, you've selected another path."

She turns to the crowd and shouts, "He will now compete for an initiation with rings."

The crowd erupts, deafening my ears once more. This time, a chill consumes me, digging deeper into my bones than ever before.

Zara

Two Months Later

Chapter
TEN

*T*he room buzzes with excitement. Every Ivanov, Marino, O'Malley, and O'Connor fill the room, including the members who live in Ireland.

I fight the crowd, engaging in small talk, until I step in the line of people waiting to offer congratulations to Kinsley and Kylie Ivanov. They're Sergey and Kora's identical twenty-one-year-old twin daughters. It's their college graduation party, and they both decided to follow in their mother's footsteps. They selected a prestigious school in New York and will attend law school in the fall.

"Congratulations. I'm going to miss you when you leave for New York," I tell them as Obrecht and Selena Ivanov step aside, allowing me to embrace the girls.

"Thank you. I'm excited to get out of here," Kinsley states, tossing her long dark hair over her shoulder and glancing across the room at Killian's oldest son, Kian.

Kylie elbows her.

"What?" Kinsley bursts out.

"Don't be so obvious," Kylie reprimands.

I lean closer to Kinsley, teasing, "I thought you gave your ring back to Kian."

She smirks. "I did. He cried, remember?"

I laugh, recalling how they made rings from pipe cleaners when they were five. At ten, they fought over something silly, and Kinsley dramatically returned her ring during a Christmas party.

Since then, they've seemed to have a love-hate relationship, always fighting and flirting.

I suggest, "You two should try being nice to each other all the time, not just every now and then."

Kylie scoffs. "She's been way too nice to him lately."

Kinsley's face heats. She mutters, "Shut up."

I lean closer. "What did I miss?"

Kinsley rolls her eyes, stating, "Nothing," and giving Kylie a look of warning.

Kylie just grins.

Kinsley changes the subject, suggesting in a mischievous tone, "Maybe we should play switcheroo and see how long it takes him to figure it out. That always annoys him."

I arch my eyebrows. "You two are still tricking people?"

"Sometimes," Kinsley admits.

Kylie shrugs. "There's nothing else to do around here. It's boring."

I jerk my head backward. "We're in Chicago. How is it boring?"

Kinsley says, "New York will be so much more fun. There's so much more to do there."

"I don't know. I grew up there, and I prefer Chicago," I tell them.

"Kylie. Kinsley. Over here," Gianni Marino's oldest son, Romeo, yells. He stands next to Kian, and they look like they're up to no good.

The girls glance at each other, then at me.

"Well, don't stand around because of me. Go," I order.

"Thanks again for coming. We'll talk later," Kinsley says, hugging me.

Kylie follows, and I watch them disappear into the crush of bodies.

There's a huge crowd at The Aspen, Maksim Ivanov's newest restaurant, which he named after his wife. He spared no expense, and worked with Dmitri's wife, Anna. She designed the space into one of the most luxurious restaurants in Chicago, and every time I'm here, I'm awed by the intricate details and things I didn't notice before.

I glance around to decide who I should talk to, then turn right into Aspen. I gasp, "Sorry!"

She beams. "Me too. I'm so glad you made it."

"I wouldn't miss it," I reply, and we hug.

She asks, "Are your mom and dad here yet?"

My gut drops. I've barely spoken to my parents in the last few months. My plan for the evening is to avoid them at all costs.

"Not yet. I was just admiring the restaurant. It always stuns me."

With bright eyes, she says, "Thanks. Maksim always goes overboard with his gifts, you know." She smiles, and it's full of love and appreciation for her husband.

"Zara." My father's voice comes from behind me, and my pulse quickens.

Aspen glances between us and chirps, "Chanel. Luca. Good to see you."

They hug, and I try to figure out how to escape without being too obvious, but I have no options.

I might as well deal with this situation now.

The tension I've felt anytime I speak to my parents heightens. The day after I left their condo, Mom called. She claimed my father told her everything she needed to know and that they have no secrets. Yet she wouldn't tell me what he said.

I'd asked if Dad had another family and if I have a sister somewhere out there.

She'd said I'm his only child.

Then I'd demanded to know who the woman and baby are.

She'd told me it's not my concern and that she wouldn't be discussing this further.

I got angry, and she demanded that I tell her if I knew who'd given me those photos. Like my father, she fretted over my safety.

I once again denied knowing anything, and our conversation stalled after that.

I'm still in the dark. Anytime they contact me, I insist they tell me the truth.

It's always the same.

They refuse to tell me anything, and I stay angry.

For the first time ever, I don't know if I believe my mother. Did my father really tell her everything? Or did he lie to her? If the woman and baby in that photo aren't his other family, then who are they and why can't he tell me? And why did he look like he was friends with the Abruzzos, people I've been told to stay away from my entire life?

The secrecy is killing our relationship. And the longer they've let me stew about it, the more I'm convinced that I don't know my father at all. Who knows if my mother does either? Is she just a naive woman whom he's deceived all these years?

That realization hurts worse than I ever anticipated.

Dad tugs me into an embrace, but I don't return any of his affection. He murmurs in my ear, "Zara, it's time to let it go."

I don't reply. We've been through this, and I'm tired of fighting, but I'm not giving him a pass. For fifteen years, I wanted to know who and where my father was and why he wasn't in my life. When he finally entered it, I loved him unconditionally. I forgave him and trusted he stayed away for my safety. I gave the benefit of the doubt to my parents and their story. But after seeing those photos, I realized there's no way I can return to the way things were without explanations.

Dad's face falls when he realizes I'm not budging. He orders, "Hug your mother. She's been upset that you're treating her this way."

"She's not a victim. Neither are you," I point out.

"You're shutting us out," he accuses.

"Luca, not now," my mom states as she steps up before me.

I go through the motions.

She hugs me, and I give her a small hug back.

In some ways, I'm angrier at her than my father.

"How have you been, sweetie?" she asks.

"Fine, working a lot."

"Are you dating anyone?"

"I'm sorry, I see someone I need to talk with," I lie, exiting the conversation and cursing myself for coming.

I thought about staying away but didn't want to disrespect Kinsley, Kylie, or any of the Ivanovs.

Kora stepped up and helped me with my law career. She mentored me and gave me a job at her law firm. I'm a better attorney because of her guidance.

Also, I babysat the girls and their younger brother, Dion, when Kora and Sergey would go out of town for their adult getaways. It wouldn't be right to have skipped their big day. And I'm proud of them. Yet, right now, I'm regretting my decision to come.

I get closer to the bar, and a server steps in front of me with a tray of champagne. I grab two glasses, downing one and then setting it back on the tray.

The server, who's probably the girls' age, chuckles. He wiggles his eyebrows and asks, "Bad day?" He glances at my cleavage with a cocky expression.

"No," I reply, then weave through the crowd, engaging in surface-level conversations.

"There you are," Fiona chirps, appearing at my side with a martini glass semi-full of a blue drink.

"Thank God I found you. My parents are here," I say.

"Are you still fighting?" she questions.

"Yeah."

"And you were saying it's about..." She smiles bigger, arching her eyebrows.

I take a long sip of champagne, scolding myself. Fiona doesn't know anything about The Underworld. I've not told her anything except that I'm at odds with my parents. We got drunk one night, and I admitted I was avoiding them, but I went tight-lipped when she asked for details.

Her expression takes on a concerned note. She steps closer and lowers her voice. "Are the issues between you really that bad?"

I mutter, "You have no idea," and finish the flute of alcohol.

"Maybe we should sneak out in a bit," she suggests.

"Please," I say.

She grins. "There's that new club in town. We should go check it out."

"Sounds good," I say, just as Sean walks in.

Our gazes collide, and he scowls, burning me with his disdain from across the room.

My stomach flips. He won't talk to me. He's sworn me off, and any attempt I've made to get back into his good graces has failed. Whenever I try, he reminds me we're no longer friends unless I tell him what I know. I refuse and then he tells me to stop talking to him.

He claims I'm a hypocrite since I want answers about my father.

He's right. I am a hypocrite, and hate myself for it. Yet I won't disobey John's orders. I can't jeopardize whatever is in front of me. The promise that The Underworld holds all the answers I want, is the answer to my lifelong questions.

"Sean's here. Let's see if he wants to come with us," Fiona says.

It's a welcome excuse to talk to him. We make our way through the crowd, getting into several small conversations. When we finally get to him, he's with Brax and L.J.

Fiona questions, "You guys want to go to the new club tonight?"

Sean glances over at me, then replies, "No."

"Why not? We haven't been there yet," Brax questions.

Sean asserts, "It'll be boring."

"Says who? That place is hopping," L.J. interjects.

Sean turns his head and locks eyes with him. "Who asked you?"

139

"Why are you being such a dick?" L.J. asks.

"No reason," Sean says and then walks away.

"Excuse me," Brax says, then follows him.

My insides shake. I don't know how to get us back to how we were. I'd do anything except tell him what he wants to know because I can't.

"What the fuck's up his ass?" L.J. questions.

"Language," Fiona scolds.

L.J. grunts. "Whatever. But seriously, what's his deal?"

She shrugs. "Why should I know? I'm not his keeper."

L.J. states, "He's your brother."

"Like I said, I don't claim responsibility for him," Fiona declares.

"I have to go to the restroom," I lie, and force my way out of the conversation.

The room is suddenly too hot. The air in my lungs has become stale. There are too many people here who I'm currently at odds with. Normally, every person in this room is my family or good friend. Tonight, I don't feel the love. My insides buzz with anxiety and anger.

I push through the crowd, down the hall, and into the bathroom. I put the lid down and sit on the toilet, hiding. I rest my elbows on my knees, my hands over my face, and close my eyes, reprimanding myself for coming. I should have known better. I should have said I was sick, and sent the twins' gifts to them. I could have taken them out to dinner on a different night.

My phone blares a French song my mom's dad used to play all the time. Growing up, I was close to my grandparents. In some ways, they helped my mom raise me. When my grandfather died, I added the song as my text alert.

I open my purse and pull out my phone.

Unknown: Go to the alley.

My chest tightens and my pulse increases. I leave the stall, wash my hands, and stare at my reflection. I take several deep breaths.

Maybe I shouldn't go.

I have to.

My phone buzzes again.

Unknown: Come alone.

It's now or never.

I exit the bathroom, move toward the exit sign, double-check that nobody's following me, and push open the door. I step out into the alley.

There's a man on a motorcycle. He's dressed in all leather and has a helmet on. He holds another helmet out to me. "Put it on."

"I'm in a dress," I state, glancing down at my black minidress and stilettos.

He grunts. "Make a choice. Do you want answers or not?"

I stare at him.

"Times a-ticking, sunshine. Three, two..."

I grab the helmet, put it on, and lift my leg over the bike's seat. My dress bunches to my waist, but there's no time to worry about it.

He takes off as soon as I wrap my arms around him.

I lean into his shoulder and close my eyes. I hate motorcycles. Dad warned me to stay off of them, claiming they were dangerous. Pina and Tristano Marino got into an accident on one, and she lost her memory for a while. It happened before Dad entered my life, but he didn't have to warn me too much to convince me to stay off bikes.

Thankfully, we only go several blocks. He pulls into a parking garage, and I'm relieved. But then, I realize we're next to a blacked-out SUV. The door opens.

Another man orders, "Get in."

My uneasiness reignites. Yet I don't question anything. I slide inside and shut the door.

The window between the driver and the back seat is closed. The driver accelerates, and I turn toward the man.

He has dark hair, and sunglasses cover his eyes. He reeks of danger, and everything about him makes me shudder. A scar runs from under his sunglasses to his ear, and it looks fresh.

He scowls at me.

I blurt out, "Who are you?"

"Matt Johnson."

"Another common name, which means it's not your real one," I mutter.

His lips press into a thin line.

I glance out the window as we pull out of the parking garage. The SUV increases speed, and we race down the side streets faster than we should.

"Where are we going?" I question, my heart beating against my chest.

"You'll find out," Matt states.

"Please tell me," I beg.

He sits back, folds his hands on his lap, and says nothing else.

I decide not to ask any more questions. What's the point? It's clear he's not going to answer any of them.

We drive and drive until we get to a private airport. There's a jet on the runway.

The car stops. A moment passes and then the driver opens the door. He points to the staircase on the plane.

I don't ask questions. I stay silent and get out, then carefully make my way up the staircase, my pulse skyrocketing.

A bit of relief hits me when I get past the door and turn the corner. Sylvia sits on a plush leather chair. In a sweet tone, she says, "Zara, it's nice to see you again."

"You too," I reply.

She pats the plush leather next to her. "Sit, darling."

I don't argue. I sit down and wait for her to speak.

It doesn't take long before the jet's door closes, and we're in the air. Anxiety electrifies my veins, intensifying every minute she remains silent. I finally blurt out, "Where are we going?"

Sylvia puts her hand on my thigh, replying, "I can't tell you, but don't worry. You'll be safe."

"Why can't you tell me?"

Amusement fills her expression. "You seem so naive, Zara, but I know you're not."

"No?"

She shakes her head. "No. And it's time for you to make a forever choice."

Fear hits me. The word forever scares me for a lot of reasons. I admit, "I don't understand."

She smirks.

I add, "I hate it when you talk in riddles."

"Everything will soon make sense." She hands me the binder that was in my house.

I gape at it, then ask, "How did you get this?"

She raises an arrogant brow.

"Never mind, that was a stupid question."

She softly laughs. "Ah, now you're seeing how this works." She points to the binder. "Which one do you prefer? I've been wondering since we last met. I know you've been studying them."

My face heats. I hate the fact that she seems to know what I'm doing. I searched my entire apartment for cameras or microphones and found nothing. But she and John seem to know everything about me. I don't like it. I don't understand it. It makes no sense to me, no matter how hard I try to figure it out.

When I don't answer her, she adds, "Don't worry, Zara. It doesn't matter who you select, so stop stressing over it. Whoever you end up with will be the right one."

The hairs on my arms rise. "Why is that?"

She flips through the book slowly, so every man appears, and then shuts it, pinning her challenging stare on me. "They have to choose you first before you choose them. So whoever you commit to, will be the correct one."

Commit to.

My stomach flips faster. "Choose me for what?" I demand, but I'm scared of the answer. It's another mystery that has kept me up at night. I can think of too many bad things about what these men choosing me might mean.

She doesn't respond.

"Please, I want to know. Answer my question."

She leans closer, her lips twitching.

Tension builds between us, and my heart races.

Her cocky expression intensifies.

"Tell me," I demand.

In a confident tone, she answers, "You're going to marry one of them."

I start laughing. It's full of nerves. Then I declare, "No, I'm not."

Her features go stern, her voice equally so as she insists, "You will. The choice will be yours, but you will go through with it."

"And why is that?" I question, pissed off and not wanting to do anything of the sort.

She claims, "You want the truth."

I dig my heels in, restating, "I'm not marrying one of them."

Sylvia smirks. "You will. The truth is in front of you, so when it comes time, I'm one hundred percent sure you will say 'I do.' And vows in The Underworld aren't like out here, so know that going in."

My mouth turns dry. I snap, "What do you mean?"

Her smile turns cold. Her eyes burn with something that scares me even more.

A wave of nausea hits me, and I swallow hard.

She replies, "There is no separation. There is no divorce. It's your blood, their blood, and a lifelong commitment that can never be undone."

Sean

Chapter

ELEVEN

My lungs work to expand with stale breaths. They got like that the minute I spotted Zara across the restaurant. Then she had to approach me and suffocate me with her floral perfume and begging eyes.

But I'm not giving in. She has information I need. She might as well be my enemy if she won't disclose it.

I shove through the crowd and step onto the rooftop deck, but the warm, early summer air is just as claustrophobic. There's a handful of others out here, but I ignore everyone, grabbing a beer from the bartender and stepping over to the corner. I stare at the twinkling city lights, wishing my father was still alive so he could answer all the questions I have.

I feel Brax's presence next to me but don't look at him.

He questions, "When are you going to tell me why you're upset with Zara?"

"I'm not," I claim, and take a big swig of my beer.

"You are," he insists.

"I'm not," I repeat, turning away from him.

His voice grows angry. "Sean, I'm getting sick of being in the dark."

I turn back to him and grit through my teeth, "If anyone should be upset with anyone, it's me with you."

He grinds his molars. Things have been off between us since he showed up at the fight. He was trying to protect me, but he's gotten us both into a situation where I don't know who the players are or what the possible outcomes could be.

There are only a few things I do know. Dangerous people hold the cards in whatever game we're in. We're not privy to the rules. Plus, Brax almost got us killed.

He adds, "That wasn't just a normal underground fight, Sean, and you know it."

My pulse bangs between my ears. Nothing he's saying is incorrect. It took me a month to heal after I killed all those men. A few times, I've woken up in a cold sweat, hearing their bones crack.

I finish the bottle of beer and set it on a table. I motion for the bartender to bring me another one.

He quickly opens two and then hands one to Brax and one to me.

"Thanks," I say.

He nods and leaves.

"Well, don't just go silent on me. Say something," Brax orders.

I drink a third of the bottle, then step back against the ledge, staring at the city, wishing I could tell Brax the little I know about The Underworld, yet I can't.

Before I left the building, the woman with the mask warned in my ear, "You tell him nothing."

"Okay, fine. At least tell me this. If you're not upset with Zara, why are you avoiding her? Every time she comes near you, it's obvious you're mad. Did you two finally fuck or something?"

"Stop talking about things you know nothing about," I reprimand, then drink another large mouthful.

He eyes me over.

I shake my head. I'm angry at so many things. The thought that I might have been in a situation where Brax and I died because I refused to kill him makes me ill. We don't get into those types of situations. We were taught better than to take uncalculated risks. But in fairness, I've never been in a situation like this.

Brax's expression turns sour. He crosses his arms over his chest, scowling, his anger matching mine. He asks, "When will you remember I'm your best friend and you can trust me?"

I stay silent.

He continues, "I want to know what we got ourselves into."

"I told you it's just an underground fight. Stop making it more than it is, and remember that you're in it because you inserted yourself into a situation you had no right stepping into!" I snap.

His eyes darken, and he snarls, "What did she mean when she said 'initiation by rings'?"

My insides tighten, and I shrug nonchalantly. It's a question that's haunted me ever since that night. I don't know what it means. The more Brax questions me, the more dread fills me.

"Tell me what you know," Brax pushes.

My anger boils over. I grab his shirt and tug him toward me, catching him off guard.

His eyes widen.

"Let it go," I seethe.

His expression hardens, and he pushes against my chest.

I release him.

He fumes, "I can't, man. You're involved in something, and I know it."

I blurt out, "Yeah, well, it looks like you stepped into it as well."

"What does that mean? I think I have a right to know," he barks.

I grunt. "There are no rights in this world, and you know that as much as I do. It's an underground fight. That's it. Leave it and move on."

He ignores me. "They said you won the bid. What does that mean?"

I rub my hands over my face, groaning. "Let it go, Brax."

"I can't. We're both involved in something, and you know it."

"Yeah, and whose fault is that?" I accuse, a little too loudly.

Others on the roof turn toward us.

I release a pissed-off breath, and my phone buzzes. I step over to the corner and pull my phone out. I read the text, and my heart rate ratchets up.

> Unknown: Go to Ivanov gym. Leave your driver.

My throat turns dry. I swallow, and it hurts. I stare out at the city and contemplate staying, forgetting I ever saw the skull or heard of The Underworld.

"What's that about?" Brax questions.

I put my phone back in my pocket, lying, "Nothing. I have to go."

"Where?" he insists.

I spin to face him, sternly asserting, "Nowhere. Enjoy your night,

Brax." I turn to leave and push through the crowd. I get through the restaurant, walk down the block, and find my parked SUV.

Conán steps out, fretting, "I didn't get a text from you. Did I miss it?"

"No. Go inside and have some drinks. Take the night off," I instruct.

He furrows his eyebrows. "Why would I do that?"

"Just go inside and mingle. Have some drinks," I restate in a non-argumentative tone.

He finally caves. "All right. Thanks."

"Sure." I get to the driver's door, and my phone buzzes again. I pull it out.

Unknown: Leave Brax. If he comes, he's dead.

My gut sinks. I reprimand myself for not checking to see if he's following me. Sure enough, he's walking right toward the SUV. I get out and meet him on the sidewalk, jabbing him in the chest, ordering, "Do not follow me. Go back inside, Brax, and this is an order."

Amusement lights his eyes. "An order? I don't take orders from you."

"You do tonight," I state.

"No, I don't," he insists.

More anger fills me. The last thing I want to do is get into another shitty situation. I also don't want my best friend dead. Everything inside me tells me that these people are more than capable of killing us both.

"When are you going to listen to me? I vouched for you. So, as of now, I am in charge. Get your ass back to the party and have fun. Forget about me tonight. Understand?"

He clenches his jaw, not moving.

I step closer, lowering my voice. "I mean it, Brax. We're both dead if you come, so I need you to do what I say. Can you trust me on this?"

He doesn't flinch.

I think he's not going to drop it, but he finally does.

He holds his hands in the air. "Fine. But what are you getting yourself into, Sean?"

For a moment, I let my guard down. I admit, "I don't know, but I need to ensure you're safe. I can't worry about you and whatever is going on."

"Which would be what?"

"I don't know. And that's the truth."

Another tense moment passes.

He asks again, "Who are they?"

I shake my head, pleading, "Please. I can't talk about this right now. I need you to go inside and stay there."

Something in my voice must convince him. He finally nods. "Okay, but Sean..."

"What?"

"Don't make me regret not coming with you or following you," he warns.

"You won't," I insist, standing taller.

He hesitates a moment. Then, finally, pats me on the shoulder, turns, and disappears inside the restaurant.

I slide back into the SUV and go through town. It takes twenty minutes to get to the Ivanov gym.

It's not in a great part of town. Over the years, they've rebuilt several blocks around it, but there's still a lot of crime.

Still, I've never been scared to go there. Tonight, I'm uneasy.

As soon as I turn onto the street, I get a text.

> Unknown: Park three blocks away.

I mutter, "Great. I get to tour the fucking city." I drive several blocks and park. I get another text.

> Unknown: Go in through the alley.

"Of course. Dark, garbage-smelling roads," I mumble but obey.

I stay in the shadows, hustling down the street and into the alley. When I reach the back of the Ivanov gym, the door opens.

There's barely any light, but Byrne's flame-colored reddish-orange hair peeks out from his worn, brown tweed paddy cap. His green eyes glow. He doesn't say anything, just motions for me to come in.

I step inside, and we don't go farther than the hallway. I demand, "Why am I here?"

"Before you make your decision tonight, I need to give you information," he replies.

"My decision?" I question.

He nods. "Aye, lad. Your decision."

Something about Byrne comforts me. At the same time, I still don't know who he is, so I ask, "Who were you to my father?"

A soft look of nostalgia washes over him. He answers, "We were best friends."

My heart pounds harder. "Best friends? Why have I never heard of you?"

"I'll clarify. We were best friends in The Underworld."

"You weren't friends in the real world?"

His lips twitch. "The Underworld *is* the real world. You'll soon understand."

I stare at him.

He chuckles. "You got more questions, son?"

A million race through my mind. But the one I ask is, "What about my mother?"

Surprised, he asks, "What about her?"

"I questioned her about the skull brand, but she didn't seem to know anything about The Underworld. But it wouldn't be the first time she lied to me."

Disapproval replaces his surprise. He asserts, "Answers will come to light when you step into your inherited role."

"More rhymes, no answers," I spout.

He sighs and pats me on the shoulder. "Sean, I know this is bothering you."

"Do you know?" I sarcastically ask.

A loud chuckle erupts from him.

I sneer. "What's so funny?"

Tears fill his eyes, and he swipes at them. He stops laughing and answers, "You're so much like your father."

Grief fills my chest, catching in my lungs. It happens whenever I think about my dad. But there's no time to dwell on it, so I force myself to take a deep breath. "Were you there when those thugs murdered him?"

Byrne's face falls. "No. I would never have let that happen."

"Why did they do it?" I question.

Byrne closes his eyes, as if in pain, then opens them. He releases a stress-filled breath. "As I said, lad, answers will come to light when you step into your inherited role."

"I don't know what that means," I admit.

"You have to commit to The Underworld. You have to accept your bid and complete initiation."

"Gee, sounds easy."

"Don't get smart with me, lad. I'm the messenger and your friend. Remember that," he warns.

Something in his tone tells me to back off a bit. So I confess, "I keep hearing about initiation, but I have no fucking clue what it is or means."

He nods. "You aren't supposed to, but it'll all make sense in due time."

"Sure it will," I grumble, pissed off with all his answers that seem to go nowhere.

His face lights up. He holds a finger in front of me. "Let's not forget why I'm here, lad."

I arch my eyebrows in question.

"Tonight is initiation. It's the end of one era and the beginning of a new one. All you have to do is embrace it." His voice drops when he continues, "But if you don't, there won't be any other initiations."

Goose bumps cover my arms. I ask, "End of what era?"

"I can't tell ya."

"Of course you can't," I sneer, my heart racing faster.

He studies me, then declares, "Your chosen path is the initiation of rings."

In a sarcastic tone, I jeer, "Am I going to have to jump through hoops of fire?"

His lips twitch.

"Or maybe play a few rounds of ring toss?"

He ignores my taunts and informs me, "Everyone's initiation is different."

"And?"

He gives me a stern look. "You've been chosen for rings. Twelve women will stand before you. One of them is yours to take."

My stomach drops. I growl, "I don't rape women."

He holds his hands in the air. "Whoa, whoa, whoa! There'll be no rape. Who said anything about rape?"

I point at him, arguing, "You just said there's twelve women and one will be mine."

"Aye. You'll choose her."

"Choose her for what? Ring around the rosie?" I question, my stomach dropping further.

He snaps, "Choose her to be yours. Forever."

I snort. "Sure."

With an angry tone, he announces, "You will marry her. You will make blood vows, and there will be no going back."

"You're joking."

"I'm not. And nor should you be at this moment," he warns.

I curl my fists at my sides with a new round of rage filling me. I insist, "I'm not marrying any woman tonight, especially one I don't know."

"Aye, but you will. And you'll know which one is your bride when you step in front of her. But be careful."

"Of what?"

He glances behind us, even though no one else is here. He continues, "You'll only secure her as yours if you have a reason for her to accept your bid. And it has to be compelling enough because one man will be out. Son, you don't want to be that man."

A chill runs down my spine. I try to take in everything he says, but the more I absorb, the angrier I become. I hurl, "I'm so tired of these answers that aren't answers. They just lead to more questions."

He puts his finger in front of my face, boldly ordering, "Listen to me, lad. You have an inherited right to sit on the throne, but your spot at the table isn't guaranteed. It's meant to be yours, but you have to grab it."

My head buzzes with too many questions.

Fear laces his tone when he says, "Sean, it was your father's place, and now it's meant to be yours. But there's always a fight, and you can't let anyone else win. Am I being clear?"

"No. I don't understand any of this. I don't know what my father was involved in. And I'm not marrying some woman tonight, no matter who she is," I state.

He points up at me and insists, "You *will* marry her. You will. When the moment comes, you will. If you don't, your seat will go to someone else and then we're in trouble."

"What kind of trouble?"

"The kind your father wouldn't want," he answers.

A lump forms in my throat. I try to swallow it down, but it seems impossible.

He softens his tone, but it reeks of desperation. "Sean, they took everything away from your father. I've suffered through it and waited for decades for this moment. You have to take his place."

My voice cracks when I go to speak. I clear my throat and try again. "What happens if I don't?"

"Like I said, someone else will take his seat, and we can't have that."

"Why? What will happen?"

He closes his eyes and shakes his head. The wrinkles around his eyes deepen. "We can't have that, Sean."

The blood in my veins turns cold. None of this makes sense, but there's one thing tying me to it.

My father.

Byrne adds, "Choose your bride carefully."

I grunt. "You're speaking ridiculous things."

"I'm not. There'll be twelve to choose from. There's a redhead. She's the one you need to pick," he instructs.

"So just go in and tell the redhead we're getting hitched? Yeah, okay," I scoff.

He slaps my cheek.

A sting rises where he struck me, and I clench my fist, but the glow in his eyes stops me from striking him back. He barks, "Don't take this lightly! There are thirteen men. Do whatever it takes, but convince the redhead to accept your bid. One man will be out. If you listen to anything I say tonight, listen to me now. You do not want to be the man without a bride. Understand?"

"Yeah," I answer, still pissed off he slapped me.

In a threatening tone, he asks, "Do you think this is funny, Sean?"

I curl my fist tighter. I like Byrne, but I wonder if I should trust him. Was he best friends with my father, or is it another lie?

"Time's up. Our ride is waiting," he announces, opening the door.

Headlights flash in the alley, and I put my hand over my eyes.

Byrne opens the back door of the car and motions for me to get inside.

I hesitate.

"Everything you've ever wanted to know lies in front of you," he taunts.

It's the final push I need. No matter what he says, I'm not marrying anyone tonight. I'll learn more about this Underworld and what my father was involved in, but that's it. Somehow, I'll figure out how to change my initiation to something else. If, and only if, I decide I truly want to step into this secret world.

Zara

Chapter
TWELVE

It feels like we're in the air forever. Sylvia told me to sleep, but I couldn't shut off my mind. She's been beside me with a mask over her eyes, peacefully sleeping for hours.

The shades over the windows are locked, so I can't lift them to know if it's nighttime or daytime.

Destiny, the flight attendant, approaches with a smile. She softly shakes Sylvia, cooing, "Time to wake up," as if they're longtime friends, and she's used to being her alarm clock.

Sylvia stirs, then removes her mask, blinking a few times.

Destiny chirps, "We're landing shortly."

"Thank you," Sylvia replies, and puts her seat upright.

Destiny disappears behind the curtain.

The landing gear squeaks, and the plane descends.

I ask, "Where are we?"

"I already told you it's classified information," Sylvia reprimands.

I roll my eyes and turn toward the window, then get more frustrated from the reminder I can't see out of it.

The wheels hit the ground, and the bins rattle. The pilot hits the brakes, and we slow down to a stop.

Sylvia stretches her arms over her head, yawning.

The door to the jet opens, and Destiny slides the curtain back. "All safe to deplane."

Sylvia gets up and steps behind her seat. She motions for me to go first.

My stomach flips. I walk down the aisle, pass Destiny, and enter the jetway.

It, too, has no windows. The air is warm and borderline humid, so I'm guessing we're somewhere tropical, but I could be wrong.

Soft light flickers from candles inside sconces. A dark hardwood floor and black painted walls surround us.

Sylvia keeps her hand on my back, guiding me forward. A door opens, but it looks the same as the jetway. We travel down several more hall-ways until we finally enter a high-end locker room.

It reminds me of a spa, but a very intimate, personal, and luxurious one. Plush cream-colored couches and chairs line the room. The center has a massage table with an infrared light hanging above it.

One side of the room has a marble counter. Water infused with lemons, limes, oranges, and basil fills glass jugs. Nuts, dried fruit, and dark chocolate heap out of bowls.

Similar to the hallways, the room is light by candles in sconces. The scent of roses fills the air, mixing with some earthy oil, which I assume is sandalwood.

Sylvia points to the corner of the room. There's a toilet room with a door, and a huge, open shower fills the rest of the space. An oversized vanity with tons of cosmetics, hair tools, brushes, and other toiletries is situated across from the beverage station.

Sylvia states, "Renzo and Mila will give you a massage before they help you shower. They'll also do your makeup, hair, and nails, and ensure you're freshly waxed."

Renzo and Mila?

Massage?

Help me shower?

Wax?

My chest tightens, and my heart races. I glance around.

A tall Italian-looking man steps into the room, followed by a beautiful Middle Eastern woman. Her long, dark hair reminds me of silk. They both have warm brown eyes and perfect skin. Her makeup is flawless, and she offers a kind smile.

I freeze. My eyes dart between them and Sylvia, still unsure what's happening.

She strokes my hair and smirks. "Ah, yes. I know you want to run, but that's not the smart move."

I admit, "I don't understand why I'm here."

Sylvia arches her eyebrows, as if she's convinced I have no reason to be confused and made a silly statement. "Darling, it's about getting you ready for initiation. It is what you said you wanted, correct? To know all the answers?"

I bite my lip, the thumping in my chest growing louder, wanting answers but unsure what I'm getting myself into.

Sylvia orders, "You will do everything Mila and Renzo instruct you to do so you are fully prepared. Do you understand, Zara?"

I glance again at Mila and Renzo. They seem harmless enough, but I'm unwilling to trust anyone I don't know.

"If you fight them on anything, showering, waxing—"

"What do you mean?" I interject, her words sinking in. "I don't need to shower. And I had my wax last week. Not that it's any of your business."

Anger and authority fill Sylvia's voice as she declares, "You will do everything they say and not argue or fight them. If you make any trouble, you will not take part in initiation. The choice is yours. Do I make myself clear, Zara?"

My heart beats faster. I glance around the room. On any other day, it'd be every girl's pampering dream, but everything feels off about this situation. Besides, I'm not marrying someone. Sylvia can be as insistent as she wants, but there's no way I'm marrying any of those men in the binder.

Sylvia tilts her head, arches her eyebrows, and softens her voice. "Didn't you promise yourself you would do whatever it takes to find all the answers?"

My insides quiver. I'm shocked once again. It's like she can read my thoughts, but I don't understand how she can. It's a vow I hadn't spoken to anyone.

She steps closer, taunting, "Didn't you stand in that restaurant tonight, reaffirming that you would learn the truth about what your parents are hiding from you?"

My pulse quickens even further. The quivering intensifies, making me feel slightly ill.

She puts her hand on my cheek in a motherly way. "You deserve to know the truth, don't you?"

"Yes," I say without hesitation.

"Then initiation is the only way. But you must choose it," she reiterates.

Everything around me seems to amplify. The smell of the roses, the dim lights, and the strangers who study me with a sultry expression, all make my conscience tell me to run.

Sylvia's voice sharpens. "It's yes or no. You can either let Renzo and Mila help get you ready or not."

I remain silent, unable to say I'm willing to walk away from learning the truth.

Sylvia adds, "When you're done, they'll help you dress and offer you to the bidders."

A chill flies through my bones. My voice cracks when I say, "O-offer me?"

Her challenging smirk reappears. "Yes. Initiation will begin. You will continue to secure your place at the table."

More confusion floods me. "My place at the table?"

She laughs, as if once again she can read my mind. "Darling, your spot at the table gives you all the answers. That is still what you want, correct? No more secrets regarding your family members?"

I lick my dry lips and nod, unable to stop myself.

She looks satisfied with my answer. "Good. You'll be a married woman the next time you see me."

A new round of fear fills me. There's no way I'll ever commit to marrying one of the strangers in the binder. I blurt out, "I'm not marrying anyone."

She scoffs. "Of course you are. That's the only way to get through your chosen initiation ceremony."

"Chosen?"

"Yes. The Omnipotence has selected this as your initiation."

"So others get in with a different task?"

She shrugs. "Sure. We wouldn't want things to turn stale."

Relief fills me. "Great. Give me something else to do."

Her eyes turn to slits. "You don't get to choose your initiation."

"Why not?"

Haughtiness fills her expression. "Oh dear, naive woman. Until you are at the table, there is no power. No control. If you wish to have it, you must be brave and take your seat. The table is not for the faint of heart, is it, Mila?"

Mila looks at the ground and shakes her head.

"How many chances do you get?" Sylvia asks her.

Mila doesn't look up, quietly answering, "One."

The disappointment in her tone makes me feel sorry for her.

"There will be no more disrespect toward your initiation or marriage. Do I make myself clear, Zara?" Sylvia says coldly.

The hairs on my neck rise.

She glares at me.

I lift my head higher and square my shoulders, trying not to let her intimidate me.

She smiles, her voice softening. "The time to make a choice is now. Decide to step into the world of knowledge and everything you've ever wanted, or don't. But you have two minutes to decide. Stay or leave." She points to the door.

Everything seems to stand still. It's excruciating, and I tell myself to leave, but I can't seem to get my feet to move.

Sylvia's cocky expression returns. "Good." She leans forward and whispers in my ear, "I suggest you stop fighting things and enjoy every moment tonight will offer. There are a few times in our lives where everything is all about us."

My blood runs cold. I open my mouth, but nothing comes out.

"Renzo and Mila are now in charge. You will allow them to do their job and not fight them. If you fight, the Omni will revoke your initiation. Do you understand?"

Let them revoke it. I need to leave, I tell myself, but once again, I can't seem to move.

"I'll take that as a yes. Now, strip," she orders.

My head jerks backward. "Strip? As in, take off my clothes?"

"Yes. Strip," she repeats, and points at the massage table.

"Can you leave the room?" I question.

A sarcastic laugh fills the air, as well as a giggle. My head whips toward Renzo and Mila. She has her hand over her mouth.

Sylvia suggests, "You might as well get used to others seeing your body. Now, get on the table."

I glance at it, telling myself, *It's just a massage.*

I slowly undress, feeling self-conscious, even though I don't normally feel that way when I'm naked. Though I'm not usually naked in front of strangers.

"Lie face down," Sylvia directs when I drop my panties.

I obey, realizing there are no covers, but the heated pad on the table and red lights provide an instant warm feeling.

Sylvia leans down and pets my hair, cooing, "Enjoy your pampering. If you don't allow yourself to, you'll regret it. I'll see you when you're a married woman."

My fear blossoms again. Someone touches me, and I jump.

Renzo declares in an Italian accent, "Easy. We're just going to give you a massage."

I take a deep breath and slowly release it.

Four hands glide across my skin, kneading my muscles. At first, it's nice, like an upscale massage. Within a few minutes I relax, enjoying it as if I were at a spa.

Then things take a turn. Someone's hands, I don't know whose, move closer toward my breasts as two other hands reach between my thighs and widen them.

I inhale sharply.

Mila's voice murmurs close to my head, "Don't tense up. This is a massage."

I try to relax again, but it soon becomes clear this is not like a normal massage.

Someone's hands, I believe they're Renzo's, glide upward, stopping an inch from my pussy, teasing the skin until my blood runs hot.

Another pair of hands trails the sides of my breasts, sliding between the sheet and my skin, getting closer to my nipples.

I try to squeeze my legs together, but I can't. Renzo's hands hold them apart as his thumb circles right next to my growing dampness.

I open my eyes, staring at the floor, my breathing ragged.

Hot breath hits my pussy, and I lift my head off the pad, but someone pushes it back down.

"Relax," Renzo orders in an authoritative tone.

"I can't," I admit.

Hands rub my neck behind my ears.

Tingles race down my spine.

Another breath of air teases my most intimate parts, but nothing touches it.

Renzo declares, "Her pussy's hot. Her husband will approve."

Panic slaps me. I try to lift my head again, but a palm quickly presses it down, keeping it in place.

Mila's hot breath tickles my ear. Her hand travels down my spine, and she murmurs, "Relax, kitten. No one wants a dry bride."

The more I fight, the more they warn me.

Renzo asserts, "We have a deadline to meet. The longer we're here, the more they know you're resisting. I suggest you relax and let us do our job."

I finally cave, and I hate myself for it. My juices pool on the table without anyone touching the parts that normally make them wet.

Renzo lowers his head and sniffs near my ass, rubbing my upper thighs, close to being sexual but never touching my pussy.

Heat courses through my body, and I feel slightly dizzy.

"Time for your wax," Mila softly states as something hot drips all over the back of my thighs and buttocks, then the strip is applied.

Someone pulls it, and I yelp, unprepared.

Within a minute, they're done.

"Get on all fours," Renzo orders.

Horror fills me. I've had Brazilian waxes before, but it's always been by somebody I know, and never a man.

"Don't make me repeat it. They're watching," he threatens.

"They?" I question, moving my head out of the headrest.

"They know everything," Mila says, as if it's not a big deal. "Now, get on all fours."

I decided it's best to obey. I lift to my hands and knees, and they finish waxing the back part of me.

Renzo snaps, directing, "Flip over and put your heels together."

My heart races. I turn over, and soon have no hair except for the locks on my head.

Mila's lips twist. She glances over my naked body and then meets my eye. "Time to shower."

Adrenaline rushes through me again.

Renzo holds out his hand. "Come on, *il fiore*. Let's go."

Within moments, I find myself under a hot shower.

Renzo warns, "Don't argue about anything. Sylvia will make good on her threat to revoke your initiation. So behave. Put your hands on the bar."

I hesitate, staring at the gold rail in front of me.

"Do you want to know the truth or stay in the dark? Because this is the only option," Mila reminds me.

I take a deep breath and grip the bar.

Renzo puts a cold mask over my eyes. They're like a pair of sunglasses, and they hook behind my ears.

Mila states, "The puffiness will be gone by the time we're done cleaning you. They're amazing, trust me."

I don't reply, and I'm unable to see anything. I find it odd that she's acting like this is some beauty hour. And the lack of sight intensifies all my sensations.

They rub soap all over my body, then shampoo and condition my hair. Once it's rinsed, they add a hair mask to my strands and turn off the water. They wrap a towel around my head.

They continue to massage me until every part of my lower body aches with need, wanting to do things I wouldn't want to normally do with either of them. And I don't understand what's happening. It's like I've taken a drug, because I feel relaxed, but I know I haven't.

"Time to rinse," Mila chirps and turns the water back on. They carefully rinse the mask from my hair and then reposition the towel around my head again.

Renzo diligently dries my body off with another towel.

They lead me to the vanity, grooming me while I sit naked. Oddly, I'm not cold. There's another red light heating my skin.

Luxuriously thick lotion is rubbed into my skin until I'm glowing. My nails, makeup, and hair all receive five-star attention.

The entire time, Renzo and Mila rave about every part of my body and how perfect or amazing it is, making me more uncomfortable but eventually almost immune to it. They continuously touch and massage me, keeping me on edge with a pool of wetness soaking the chair.

Renzo drops to his knees, puts his hands on my thighs, and leans toward me.

"What are you doing?" I nervously ask.

He inhales deeply and then looks up at Mila, declaring, "She's ready."

My pulse goes haywire, and a chill runs down my spine.

He disappears while Mila finishes curling my hair.

Renzo returns, holding a corseted white-lace minidress, announcing, "Time's a ticking."

My butterflies go crazy to the point I feel nauseous. I put my hand over my stomach.

Mila pouts. "Aw, don't be like that. This is your big day."

Renzo adds, "This is the day every girl dreams about her entire life!"

My heart races so fast I think it's going to explode.

They're crazy.

This entire situation is fucked-up.

There's no way I'm getting married.

Mila grins, chirping, "The truth is right around the corner."

Get out of here, I tell myself, but once again, I'm unable to make myself leave.

I let them help me into the corset. There's luxurious boning all around it, pushing up my cleavage. It tapers to my waist, then stops before a detailed see-through lace floral design barely covers my pussy. The back is just as transparent as the front, and the bottom of my ass cheeks peek out from under the delicate lace.

Renzo and Mila fuss over me and then she attaches an elegant train at each side of my waist. It falls several feet behind me, and Renzo pulls it out.

They guide me in front of the floor-length mirror.

Renzo whistles.

Mila claps. "The perfect bride."

"Almost. Don't forget her veil," Renzo says.

"Oh, duh," Mila says, grabbing a tiara with lace attached. She secures it at the back of my head.

I stare at myself in the mirror. My makeup is flawless, and I look more exquisite than ever. I'm in an outfit that should only be worn in the bedroom, yet it has a train, as if it's an actual wedding gown.

My cheeks heat at first, but then something strange happens.

The more I stare, the calmer I get, and I don't understand why.

"Ah, there it is," Renzo coos, pointing at my reflection.

"What?" I question.

Mila slides her arm around my shoulders and gives me a small hug. "You've accepted it. You really are ready."

I gape at them and then at myself.

Have I accepted this?

Another shot of panic shoots through me, and I shake my head.

Mila puts her head right next to mine. "Don't do that. You're too close to the truth."

I freeze.

Renzo cocks his elbow and holds out his arm for me. He gives me a fatherly smile and declares, "It's time to take your seat at the table. Let's go, *il fiore*."

Sean

Chapter THIRTEEN

*H*ours pass and I have no idea where we're going. Byrne took my phone and locked it in a cabinet. He's dozed on and off since then, snoring loudly.

All I can seem to do is pace the plane, wondering how to enter The Underworld without taking a bride.

There's no way I'm getting married.

The flight attendant steps through the curtain. "We're about to land. I'm going to need you to take your seat now."

My pulse increases. I'm one step closer to learning more about The Underworld and getting answers about my dad.

I sit down in a seat across the aisle from Byrne, ordering, "Wake up."

He blinks a few times, then stares at me as the wheels lower, stating, "Oh, good. We're almost there."

"Where exactly are we?" I question.

He gives me the same look whenever I ask most questions. "I can't tell you that, lad."

"Of course you can't," I retort, sulking in the chair and adding, "It's getting old, not being told things."

"Don't worry. You'll know everything soon enough."

"You said my father created The Underworld?"

"Aye, he did," Byrne says with pride sweeping across his expression.

"Then I should be privy to everything," I declare.

He snorts. "Your father wasn't into entitlement. I'm pretty sure you know that already."

My gut sinks. I'm not into entitlement either, but I'm over the secrecy.

Byrne says, "Once you choose your bride, things will start to come to light."

I chuckle.

He tilts his head. "What's so funny?"

"There's no way my father would do anything like this. The crazier this gets, the more I'm convinced he didn't have anything to do with this Underworld, whatever it is."

Byrne's eyes turn to slits. "Don't disrespect your father. There are reasons he created The Underworld the way he did."

I scoff. "There's no way he'd want me to walk into a room and marry a stranger. I—"

"He did. And he thought ahead. Years ahead. Why do you think I'm telling you to pick the redhead?"

My heart beats faster. "What are you saying? And be clear. Don't speak in your riddles," I warn.

The plane makes contact with the ground, and the pilot applies the brakes. We slide across the runway.

I demand, "Answer my question."

As the plane rolls to a stop, the flight attendant gets up and moves the curtain.

Byrne waves his hand at her.

She shuts it again and disappears.

He slowly rises and sternly gazes down at me. "It's part of your birthright to marry the redhead. And, yeah, your father knew about it. He set it all in motion, so don't fuck it up today," he threatens and then walks to the curtain and opens it.

My pulse pounds through my veins.

Is it true?

Did my father pick this redhead for me to marry?

Why would he do that?

It's not uncommon in crime families to have arranged marriages, but there's always a reason for it. So I want to know why.

Byrne turns. "Lad, are you coming, or are you going to sit there all day?"

I get up and follow him off the plane. Everything's dark. I can't tell if it's night or day. The flickering of candles against the wall is the only way to see. Once we're far from the flight attendant, I ask, "Why would my father arrange for me to marry this redhead?"

He stops walking and crosses his arms over his chest. "You ask a lot of questions."

"Should I not?"

He leers at me.

"I want to know," I insist.

"Alliances were made so everyone could live harmoniously."

I huff. "Jesus. Not more riddles."

"That's all you're getting from me now," he adds, continuing down the hall.

Frustrated, I follow him, not seeing any other choice.

Byrne finally opens a door, and when I step inside, I freeze.

It's a plush locker room. There's a shower and a bathroom, a vanity with toiletries, and some overstuffed furniture.

I ask, "Why am I here?"

"You have thirty minutes. Take a shower, shave, and put on the clothes in the closet. I'll meet you back here," he answers.

I don't move.

"You don't have time to dawdle," he instructs and then leaves.

I glance around the room, taking it in again, and for some reason, I do what he said. I get undressed and shower. I shave. I use the toiletries, brush my teeth, and comb my hair. Then, I pick up the same brand of cologne I normally wear, and spray it over me.

I step over to the closet, open it up, and the hairs on my neck rise. The only outfit in it is a black tuxedo. There's a white shirt, a black bow tie, cummerbund, underwear, socks, and shiny leather shoes.

A debate about whether to get dressed plays out in my head. I decide this is insane, and that it would be best if I don't put it on and give anyone the notion I'm getting married.

I turn to find my clothes but realize they're gone. Someone must have come in and taken them when I was in the shower.

"Fuck's sake," I mutter, and realize I have no option but to put the tuxedo on. I get dressed and pace the room, wondering what comes next.

Byrne walks in with a large wooden box. An image of the skull is burned into the lid, and I notice he has the brand with the same pink in it my father had. It's in the same spot as my father's and John's.

He beams at me. "Aye, look at you, lad. Your father would be proud."

"Stop talking about my father that way," I state, not wanting to feel the turmoil in my stomach. I don't think I'll ever get married. Like Zara stated, I get too bored with women. But the thought that my father would miss my wedding, should I have one, still stings after all these years.

Byrne scowls. "You need a better attitude before you go in there."

I stare at the ceiling and sigh.

"Come sit down, lad," he directs, and sits on the couch.

I follow him, figuring I should engage in the motions, and plop down on the other side.

"Now, this is an important decision. It's forever," he starts.

My chest tightens.

He opens the box, revealing a dozen stunning rings in various shapes. Pear, princess, emerald, marquise, Asscher, radiant, heart, round, oval, and cushion cut diamonds shine in the dim light. Different plain metal bands of white gold, yellow gold, rose gold, and platinum are nestled on the bottom row.

I shift in my seat.

He's actually serious.

He thinks I'm getting married today.

"What is this?" I question, but I don't need to.

"You have to pick the ring, son. Which one's it going to be?"

I stare at the rings.

He picks up a pear-shaped one. "May I suggest this? The redhead loves pear-shaped diamonds."

"No," I state.

He wrinkles his forehead. "Why? What's wrong with it?"

I shake my head. "I don't know. I don't like it."

"Why don't you like it?"

"I don't know, but I don't."

"Happy wife makes a happy life. I highly suggest you take the pear one," he pushes.

"No. I'm not looking at that forever," I insist, then wonder what the hell I'm saying.

I'm not getting married.

Byrne sighs. "Well, you've got to pick one, son. It'd be better that your bride likes it."

I grunt and then pick up a radiant cut diamond. It's not a square. It's more of a rectangle of at least four karats.

He whistles. "That's a big ring. She's got petite hands. I don't think that's going to look very good on her. It's going to be overpowering on her slender finger."

I shrug. "So what?"

He glances at the box and then picks up a smaller Asscher cut option. "This might be better since it's more of a square, but it's still similar to the radiant."

I shake my head and then rise. "Nope. It's the radiant." I go to put it in my pocket.

"Wait."

I glance at him. He holds his hand out. "Give me the diamond."

"I thought I had to take it with me," I say, telling myself I'm just playing his game.

"No. We'll bring you one in her size when the time comes to say your vows."

Vows.

My stomach flips.

"Come on. I don't have all day," he says, impatiently bending his fingers.

I hand him the ring, and he puts it in the box and shuts it.

I stare at the box. "You seriously just have a ton of rings sitting around for twelve women?"

He nods, his face serious. "Aye, we know all their sizes. We make sure we have everything prepared for tonight. It's a special night, and it only happens when there's a full moon, so it's special for many reasons."

"What does the full moon have to do with it?" I question.

Nostalgia lights up his expression. "Your dad loved full moons."

That feeling in the pit of my stomach claws at me again. I grind my molars.

Byrne looks at his watch. Excitement grows on his face and matches his voice. "It's time. Now, look for the redhead as soon as you enter the room. Make sure you convince her. She has to choose you as well."

"What if I want another one?" I ask, not that I'm going to go through with this crazy charade.

Byrne's eyes turn to slits. "You can't choose another one. The redhead is the one."

"But what if someone else catches my eye?"

His tone turns stern. "They won't. It's meant to be the redhead. Your father already promised you. This is your destiny."

"Promised me to whom?"

"To her parents. And they promised your father she was to be yours."

"What about my mother?" I question.

He gives me more of his silent treatment.

I scowl.

He offers, "I won't have to stay silent forever, son."

If anyone else called me son, I'd tell them not to. I don't know why I don't with him, but I let it go.

He pats my shoulder. "Come on now. It's time."

Part of me wants to turn, leave, and not go any further with this debacle, but I still want inside The Underworld. If this was my father's secret world, then I'm supposed to be part of it. I'm sure of it.

And I want to find out everything he had planned. I know there's a reason for it. He couldn't see it through, but surely I'm supposed to if it was his doing?

But I'm not marrying anyone, especially this redhead, whoever she is. And I don't care about her parents either.

Byrne leads me down more dark hallways and then when we turn the corner of the last one, I hear music with deep drum rolls. Something about it is terrorizing. It's so strong it sends a shudder down my spine.

He gets to the door, puts his hand on the handle, and glances up at me, warning, "Make sure you choose the redhead."

I don't reply.

He opens the door and motions for me to step inside.

I take three steps and freeze.

We're somewhere outside. It's warm, and we're in a huge arena. The sky's clear, dotted with stars and a full moon, but it's unlike anything I've ever seen. It's as if I can reach up and touch it.

Just like at the underground fight, people are everywhere. This time, it's not chaotic, though. The men wear tuxedos and skull masks. The masks are the same design as the brand.

Women wear pink from head to toe. The gem-encrusted eye masks are similar to the one lady at the fight wore. Their strapless evening gowns dip low in the front, have low backs, and slits to their upper thighs. Their stilettos have diamond-encrusted heels.

The crowd stands shoulder to shoulder, like at a sold-out event. The women hold candles. The men hold long wooden torches with flames burning toward the sky. A pink carpet stretches down all the aisles, leading to a huge stage.

Twelve women stand in a row, turned away from the crowd. They wear white, lacy lingerie. There's a long train attached to their "dress," and veils cover their faces.

"It's time to go, son. Whatever you do, don't be the one without a bride," Byrne warns, pointing to the stage.

My heart beats faster, as if in tune with the drums. I move forward, and as I get closer, I realize other men are walking down the other aisles toward the stage.

My pulse skyrockets. I count twelve of them, and Byrne's warning screams in my head. It sets in that one of us will receive a bad consequence, and I don't know what it'll be, but I don't want to find out.

I'm not marrying one of these women.

But I don't want to be at the tail end of their consequence.

Jesus. How do I get out of this?

I'll pick a bride and find a way not to marry her.

183

Will it even be real?

I'm sure it's not a legal wedding.

What if it is?

My aisle ends. Thirteen pink X's mark the ground at the edge of the stage, facing the crowd. A man directs me to the thirteenth one, and I take my spot, with my back to the women.

When all thirteen of us stand shoulder to shoulder, the music stops. A woman comes forward, in the same dress as the others, but her mask is adorned with diamonds instead of pink gems. I realize she's the same woman from the fight.

The crowd chants, "Valentina! Valentina! Valentina!"

She throws her hand in the air, and the arena turns silent. She roars, "We have thirteen men tonight. One will not have a bride."

Ear-deafening cheers explode around me. Everything about it makes my blood turn cold. Their excitement reminds me of the under-ground fight and how they cheered when men died.

Byrne's warning plays over and over in my mind.

Valentina silences the crowd and explains, "Here's how it's going to work." She walks down the line of men, running her gaze from the top of our heads to our feet and back up before going on to the next one. When she gets to me, she stops longer than she did with the others.

I hold her gaze, wondering what she's thinking.

She reaches up and puts her hand on my cheek.

A wave of coldness flies down my jaw, through my neck, and into my heart. I clench my jaw.

Her lips twitch. "Ah, you came to take your rightful place, but there's no seat at the table for free. Your dad didn't agree with anyone not earning their spot."

A claw scrapes into my gut. I wish everyone would stop talking about my father. I hate how they all seem to know more about him than I do.

Yet he's the reason I'm here. I might not understand this world, but I'm determined to get to the place where everything makes sense.

Valentina smirks. "I assume you were told who you will choose?"

I stand taller, staring at her, not answering. If I speak, then I'm telling her to go fuck herself. I'm not marrying anyone. And I don't think this is the right moment for that conversation.

She laughs. "Ah, I see. Okay then. Let the games begin." She walks back and forth a few more times, past every man, closely studying them. Then she steps back in front of me and turns to the crowd, tossing her arms in the air and shouting, "Who's ready for the ceremony to begin?"

The crowd stomps in unison until it's so loud my ears ring with the beat. The dark music slowly starts again.

Valentina spins toward us and silences the crowd. She informs us, "You have two minutes to convince your bride that she should choose you. If she doesn't, you're out. If there's more than one man standing, they're all out. If a bride doesn't choose a groom, she will escape her vows until a later date. At that point, we will choose one for her."

Horror fills me. I don't understand how my father would ever condone this.

Valentina booms, "I pity those of you who can't secure your bride."

A horn blows, and there's a moment where everything goes still.

She looks at her watch. "Time's ticking, boys."

Suddenly, everyone understands. Chaos erupts, and men run over to the women. Several of them talk over the other. A few take the brides and move them forward.

185

I find the redhead. She's stunning, with shiny hair to her mid-back, porcelain skin, a pouty mouth, and bright green eyes. I almost step in front of her but then freeze.

What is she doing here?

My heart races, my pulse pounds between my ears, and my mouth turns dry.

It can't be her.

It is.

Another man tries to convince Zara to marry him. I take a step toward them, and the redhead grabs my wrist.

I glance at her.

In a thick Irish accent, she frets, "What are you doing?"

"I'm sorry. I can't," I reply, shaking out of her grasp, then rush over to Zara. I bark, "What are you doing here?"

She tears her eyes off the man, and her face fills with shock. "Sean?"

Maybe I should have expected her to be here, knowing she had something to do with The Underworld, even though she wouldn't tell me what.

She would never agree to this.

Would she give herself to a stranger under these terms?

The man beside her says, "I don't know who this guy is, but I'm choosing you. I'm asking for you to choose me back."

She turns toward him and opens her mouth, but nothing comes out.

"Get the fuck out of here," I bark at him.

He scowls at me, and I get an eerie feeling. There's something familiar about him.

"She's my chosen one," he declares and then looks at her. "I'm the one you studied the most, aren't I?"

Jesus. He was in her binder.

"I said to fuck off," I demand.

"I'm your chosen one, and you know it. Now, take my hand," he orders, holding his out toward her.

Zara gazes at it and then back at me.

The bell rings. I glance around us and realize that the others are all paired up. We're the only three left.

The crowd's deafening roars get louder until Valentina steps forward and puts her hand in the air. Silence fills the arena.

She glares at me, snarling, "You did not choose the redhead."

"No. I choose Zara," I declare.

She snaps, "That is not in the cards for you. I will give you one more chance. Choose wisely."

Zara

Chapter
FOURTEEN

It takes everything I have to stay on my feet. My insides tremble as Valentina sears her fiery gaze into Sean.

He grabs my hand, lifts his chin, and confidently announces, "I choose Zara."

Relief and fear hit me at once. I don't want to marry the stranger next to me, even if he did remind me of Sean in the photos.

He isn't anything like Sean.

I clutch Sean's hand as anger floods Valentina's expression.

Tension grows, and the entire arena sits on pins and needles, waiting for her reaction.

She steps closer and murmurs in his ear, "I'll deal with you later." She spins and saunters over to the bald man.

I glance at Sean, and he tugs me closer to him.

Valentina steps beside the redhead. She asks the bald man, "Why did you choose her? Were you not directed to choose Zara?"

He looks nervous. My guess is he's normally a man who'd step into a dark alley with no qualms and come out alive. Right now, he looks scared to death.

He replies, "There were already two men going after her."

Valentina arches her eyebrows. "So? Are you a coward?"

He swallows hard and doesn't speak. She steps forward, takes her ring finger, and lifts his chin higher so he's looking at the sky. She coos, "Do you see the moon?"

"Yes," he replies.

"Good." She releases him, and he looks at her. She states, "It's the last time you'll see it."

Confusion fills his expression. He blurts out, "Why would you say that?"

She points to a man on the side of the stage. Like all the men in the crowd, he's in a tuxedo and wearing the same skull mask. He comes on the stage, steps next to Valentina, and pulls a gun out of his pocket.

The crowd begins to stomp their feet again, chanting, "Kill him! Kill him! Kill him!"

The bald man shakes his head. He holds his hands out in front of him, begging, "Valentina, please."

"You were given a direct order. You were supposed to pick Zara, not a woman who was promised to another man. Instead, you defy your orders and attempt to break the promises our families made. Now look at the mess you created for them," she spouts, and points at the redhead and then me.

My insides shake harder.

Sean releases my hand and secures his arm around me. He murmurs, "Everything is going to be okay."

I lock eyes with him.

He squeezes me tighter and refocuses on Valentina.

The bald man declares, "There were two men going after her."

Valentina argues, "Like I said, that makes you a coward." She holds her hand out, and the man in the tuxedo gives her the gun.

"Please, Valentina. No," the bald man pleads.

Her lips twist. She studies him for a moment, then announces, "Don't worry, I'm not killing you."

He sags in relief. "Thank you."

She holds the gun out in front of the redhead, asserting, "You derailed her promised future. So she's going to be the one to kill you."

My stomach flips.

The bald man implores, "No, please."

The redhead's eyes widen. She shakes her head. "No. I—I can't."

Sean tightens his grip on my waist, and the other man who wanted me to choose him takes a few steps away from us.

Valentina continues to hold the weapon, asking the redhead, "Are you not able to follow orders either?"

She glances between the gun and the bald man, stuttering as her face pales, "I-I-I—"

"Kill him! Kill him!" the crowd chants louder and louder, stomping their feet.

"Go on," Valentina urges.

The redhead slowly takes the Glock. Her hand shakes so hard, the barrel's moving all over the place. She holds it out in front of her, but then shuts her eyes and puts her arm down. "I can't. I'm sorry. I just can't."

Valentina nods to the man next to her.

He grabs the gun, shoots the redhead in the chest, then turns and fires another shot at the bald man. There are two loud thumps as their bodies fall to the ground.

The women on the stage scream, and a few of the men as well. The crowd goes wild as blood pools between the two corpses until it circles Valentina. Only a tiny area around her shoes isn't coated by blood.

Two men come and hold their hands out to her. She takes them, and they put their other hands under her armpits and lift her over the blood.

As soon as she's in a clean area, the men disappear off the stage, as does the one with the gun.

She holds her hand in the air to quiet the crowd, then pins her gaze on me.

A whimper flies out of me. My knees buckle, but Sean holds me against him as close as possible.

The stranger who wanted me to choose him takes another step away from us.

Valentina struts across the stage, stands in front of us, and focuses on Sean. "You were told to choose the redhead."

He stands taller and scowls at her, stating, "If you're told to do something and you do it, it's not really a choice, is it?"

The crowd gasps.

Valentina doesn't flinch, drilling a glare at Sean until a smirk forms on her lips. She says, "Always the wise guy, I see."

He retorts, "I only speak the truth."

She glances at the other man, declaring, "It appears she has not chosen you."

"She hasn't chosen anyone yet," he quickly informs her.

She arches her eyebrows and curls her finger, ordering, "Zara, step away from him."

I don't move.

Sean pats my ass, encouraging me, "Go on. I'm right here."

I glance at him.

He nods.

I step toward her.

Valentina asks, "Have you decided to obey this man, or have you chosen him?" She points to the stranger who's moved another three feet away.

My heart races so fast that I fear I might faint. I pin my eyebrows together and open my mouth, but nothing comes out.

Valentina steps closer.

My tremors intensify.

Sean reaches for me and tugs me back into him, claiming, "She chose me."

Valentina doesn't look at him. She keeps her focus on me, asking, "Do you choose Sean or Antonio?"

I bite my tongue, afraid I'm going to get Antonio, Sean, or all of us killed.

Sean squeezes my waist.

"Speak. I know you're not mute," Valentina snaps.

"I... I..." I glance between the two men, then meet Valentina's gaze, admitting, "I don't want anyone dead because of me."

Valentina purses her lips and then looks at the crowd.

"Kill! Kill! Kill! Kill!" they start chanting again.

Sean steps in front of me and snarls, "Don't touch her."

Valentina puts her hand in the air, and the crowd goes quiet. She seethes, warning, "Step away from her and do not try to shield her again."

Sean doesn't move.

"Do you dare disobey me right now?" Valentina barks.

He clenches his fist at his side, then slowly steps to my left but tugs me into him.

She questions, "Were you not told to choose the redhead? Or do I need to go find Byrne and make him pay for not giving you the message?"

"No, he told me," Sean affirms.

She tilts her head, studies him, then continues, "So you know your father made a pact, and you were to choose the redhead? Yet you didn't?"

He tightens his grip around my waist, claiming, "My father's pact was not from blood."

She arches her eyebrows. "How do you know it wasn't?"

Sean strokes his thumb over my waist and states, "It wasn't. I know it wasn't."

Valentina is eerily calm, asking, "So you believe that gave you the right to not choose the redhead?"

Sean answers, "I was told vows were a blood oath. Are they not?"

"Yes. Of course they are," she replies.

"So blood is more powerful than words?" Sean challenges.

She glances between us. "Of course it is, but why are you asking such a thing?"

Arrogance fills Sean's expression. He leans down, tilts my chin, and gives me a chaste kiss on the lips.

I inhale sharply.

He tears his gaze from me, squares his shoulders, and leers at Valentina. He announces, "Zara and I already have a blood oath."

The crowd gasps.

Valentina's head jerks back just a tad. She recovers and hurls, "You dare stand on the stage and lie!"

"It's not a lie," he states.

"Of course it's a lie!"

"It's not," I blurt out.

Her head snaps toward me. "You speak lies too? And to my face?"

Sean interjects, "We have a contract. We signed it in blood."

She scoffs and then points her fingers between us. "You two... You try to cover each other's tracks. Maybe you *should* be married."

"We're not lying," I say, finding my courage.

"I should kill you now," she snarls.

Sean steps in front of me again and warns, "You won't threaten Zara ever again. She will be my wife, and you will respect her at all times." He looks past Valentina and shouts, "In the name of my father, Sean

O'Malley, you all will adhere to my rules regarding my bride—my wife! Is it understood?"

Silent tension fills the arena.

Valentina steps so close, her scent flares in my nostrils. She seethes, "If you're lying to me, the penalty is death. It's always death if you lie to me. Not just tonight. And it doesn't matter who your father or wife is."

I blurt out, "We're not lying! You want me to choose someone, well I've already chosen him! And he's already chosen me. We did it on my twenty-first birthday!"

"I would've known about this," she claims.

"Apparently, you don't have as good of spies as you think you do. You might want to look into that," Sean taunts.

Anger floods her expression. "You're lying. Both of you."

"We're not. I can prove it," I insist.

She points to the sky, ordering, "Look up."

I obey.

She threatens, "Maybe this should be your last full moon."

"I won't warn you again about threatening Zara," Sean snarls.

Two men race across the stage and step next to Valentina. One barks, "Do you dare make a threat against our high empress?"

I repeat, "I have proof we're not lying!"

Valentina licks her lips and asks, "What proof is this you have?"

"A contract. We signed a contract."

She laughs. "A contract? I would've known about a contract."

"I have it. It's in my jewelry box. Under the lid, there's a removable compartment. It's in there. I can get it and show you."

A new wave of gasps rolls through the crowd.

Valentina questions, "How would I not know about this?"

I continue, "I don't know. But I was twenty-one. We were coming back from the club. Fiona passed out in the car, and Sean helped me upstairs. I got sick. I had just broken up with my boyfriend and drank too much. I cried to Sean and told him I didn't think I would ever get married. He said he wasn't going to either. Then we made a pact that when we were older, we would marry each other."

Valentina's face goes pale. She's as silent as the crowd.

Sean interjects, "I wrote the contract. Zara said we needed to sign it in blood for it to be real. So I pricked her finger with my pocket knife and then my own."

Valentina hisses, "Stop lying! I would know about this!"

My chest tightens. I cry out, "It's in my apartment. In the jewelry box. His signature is in blood on top of mine! I swear to you."

The silence is deafening. The moon seems to shine brighter, and my heart beats faster. I reach for Sean's hand and grasp it as tightly as possible. He puts his other arm around me, and I put my hand on the front of his thigh to steady myself.

Valentina turns and snaps her fingers in the air.

Another man comes on stage. He hands her a phone.

She hits a few buttons and holds the cell to her ear. After a few seconds, she orders, "Go into Zara's apartment. There's a jewelry box. I'm told there's a contract there. Call me back." She hits a button and turns back to us. "If this contract is real, we should have known about it."

Sean scoffs. "Your problems aren't our fault, are they?"

Her eyes turn to slits. "This is not the time for you to get smart, Mr. O'Malley."

197

He stands taller. "Well, it seems to me like you have some issues with your surveillance, doesn't it?"

She opens her mouth, but the phone rings in her hand. She puts the cell to her ear, staring at Sean as if she wants to kill him, and fear runs through me.

She demands, "Did you find it? Is it true?"

Time seems to stand still as the blood drains from her face. "Send me a photo."

She holds the phone away from her and stares at the screen. Several minutes pass as the last of the color drains from her cheeks.

She snaps back into the phone, "I'll deal with you later." She hands the phone back to the man who gave it to her.

He scurries off the stage.

She faces the crowd. "It seems we have a contract we didn't know about."

More gasps fill the arena.

She nods over to the side of the stage, and another man walks over.

He hands her a knife.

She steps up to me and holds it out. "Take it."

My hand shakes, but I obey.

She points to the other man, who looks like Sean, the one I studied for too many hours. She orders, "Slit his throat."

My knees almost buckle, but Sean holds me tight to him.

He says, "Give me the knife, and I'll do it."

Valentina spouts, "No, you will not pay for her sins. You will not pay for the debt that she owes us."

"Her debt? She doesn't owe you anything," Sean claims.

My hand continues to shake.

She declares, "It's a debt. You both made a contract you had no business making."

Sean scoffs. "How were we supposed to know about this?"

"You were supposed to marry the redhead," she seethes.

He tugs me closer to him. "No, I'm supposed to marry Zara," he tells her, then turns to me. "Give me the knife."

"If you kill that man, Sean, Zara's next," Valentina warns. She slowly meets my eye. "Decide. Choose your man. If you want the blood contract to be over, then slit Sean's throat. It's your choice at this point."

My insides quiver harder. A chill runs through my blood. I can't seem to make my feet move.

"Let me do it," Sean pleads with her in a confident voice.

Valentina won't have it. She doesn't tear her gaze off mine. "I won't tell you again. You have a choice to make. Who's it going to be?"

I slowly push away from Sean.

"Zara," he says under his breath.

I don't look at him. I go right up to the man whose picture I studied and felt so many things for because he reminded me of Sean. A tear falls down my cheek. I mutter, "I'm sorry."

He looks at me in horror, then begs, "Choose me instead. I'll give you a better life."

I can't. I don't know where it comes from, but in a quick move, I take my hand with the knife and slash it against his throat.

A look of surprise fills his eyes. He places his hand over his throat, and blood seeps all over it.

Valentina orders, "Now, stab him in the heart."

I don't think about it. I jam the blade into his chest and then let go, not having any more strength to pull it out. I step back with tears streaming down my cheeks, staring as he falls to his knees.

Sean steps behind me, wraps his arm around my waist, and tugs me into him. He spins so we're facing Valentina. "You got what you wanted. The debt is paid."

She arches her eyebrows. "You think the problem you created by breaking your father's promise frees you?"

The air turns stale.

She points at Sean. "You don't know what you've done."

He clenches his jaw.

She glares at me, cursing, "The mistake of your blood oath will loom over you and your children."

I shudder, not knowing what she means, and look over at the pool of blood filling the stage from my actions. More tears fall down my cheeks.

Sean holds me tighter, pulling my head to his chest.

I weep, not understanding how I could kill a man, the realization of what I've done sinking in.

Valentina shouts, "The other ceremonies are off! We will only have one set of vows tonight. And it will be with full exposure!"

The crowd cheers so loud it vibrates through my body, filling me with more fear.

Valentina silences the crowd. She roars, "Brides don't cry! Those who do choose to die!"

A loud, chaotic din rumbles through the arena.

Sean leans into my ear and yells so I can hear over the crowd, "You have to stop crying. We'll talk about it later."

I glance up at him.

He swipes my tears and kisses me on the lips. He holds my cheeks in his palms, instructing, "No more tears, Zara. Right now, you have to become my bride."

Sean

Chapter

FIFTEEN

Zara's fear is palpable. She swallows hard.

My mouth brushes her ear when I shout over the crowd, "It's the only way we're leaving this place alive." I move my face in front of hers.

Her eyes meet mine. The fear subsides, and determination replaces it.

I put my hand on her cheek, praising, "That's my girl."

The crowd goes silent, and a new chill runs down my spine.

I turn, keeping Zara close, adamant to do whatever it takes for us to walk out of here alive.

Valentina steps in front of us and points at me. "The alliances your father worked tirelessly to put in place are now in jeopardy. The balance is off. Now, we must start again. His vision will not work without balance."

Zara's body stiffens.

I rub my thumb over her waist, tightening the rest of my grip. Valentina's words don't make sense to me, but I keep my gaze pinned to hers. I declare, "I don't know the full details of what my father wanted. But if the balance is off, we will start again, and I will ensure it comes to fruition."

Her lips form a taut line. Her glare intensifies.

My blood electrifies, racing through my veins. I don't understand what my father was trying to build or why I thought it was necessary to take part in it, but now, there's no way out. I enter The Underworld, or I'm not leaving this arena.

Neither is Zara.

What was she doing here?

I shake off the questions for another time. This isn't the time or place.

Valentina slowly puts her arm in the air. She asserts, "Then you've declared your fate, Sean O'Malley Jr."

Zara's hand grips the front of my thigh.

My bones turn to ice.

Valentina swirls her fingers in the air in circles.

Ten skull-masked men come on stage. They line up in front of the other couples.

Terror erupts on the men's and women's faces. A few men protectively tug their chosen bride to them.

The crowd stomps, lifting their wooden torches into the air, and the moon shines brighter.

Valentina throws her arms out and roars, "Cleanse The Underworld!"

The masked men on stage pull out their guns and point them at the couples.

A few women cry out.

A man yells, "This is our destiny too!"

There are two rounds of shots, and all ten couples fall to the floor. Bullet holes pierce each of their foreheads, and blood pools around them.

Zara's knees buckle.

I wrap my arms around her and bury her head into my chest, attempting to shield her from the red oozing around us.

Valentina's fiery stare burns toward me. She points at us, ordering, "Take your place on the altar."

I glance behind me, and another stage rises, along with a small staircase. A tall, muscular man in a black robe and the same skull mask waits in the middle of the stage. He holds a lit torch, but unlike the ones in the crowd, it's gold.

On the right side of him are twenty masked men. Their tuxedos are accented with pink. Rose boutonnieres are attached to their jackets, and they have matching bow ties and cummerbunds.

On the left side of the man stand twenty women. They're all dressed in the same eye mask and dresses as the women in the crowd, but they hold pink rose bouquets. The one closest to the man holds two, one bigger than the rest.

"Oh my God," Zara gasps, then glances up at me, eyes wide.

My stomach clenches. I attempt one last effort to get out of this, addressing Valentina. "You expect my bride to say her vows surrounded by death?"

The man in the robe speaks. His Russian accent thick as he booms, "You will address me now."

I spin toward him, clutching Zara as close as possible, hating that our backs are to the crowd and Valentina. I ask, "Who are you?"

He answers, "I am Kirill, King of the Omnipotence. Until you sit at the table, you don't make demands. Your blood caused their blood. So you have a choice to make now."

"What's that?" I question.

He points to Zara. "You vow your life to The Underworld and your bride. Or..."

My breath shallows. I don't need to ask about the alternate option. It's clear Zara and I end up on the floor next to the other couples if we don't proceed.

He assesses Zara, asking, "Are you ready to step into the truth?"

She stays quiet, her eyebrows pinned together, unable to speak or tear her gaze off him.

He warns, "When the Omni asks you a question, you answer, or there are consequences, Ms. Marino. Now, I won't ask again. Are you ready to step into the truth?"

"Answer him," I hiss.

She glances at me quickly, then nods at him. Her voice cracks. "Y-yes."

He continues, "You're ready to vow your life to The Underworld and your husband?"

Her chest rises and falls faster. She licks her lips.

I squeeze her waist.

"Yes. I'm ready."

Approval lights Kirill's eyes. He orders, "Then come forward."

The crowd stomps and lifts their torches, humming until the entire arena buzzes.

My heart races, but I grab Zara's hand and lead us forward until we're standing in front of Kirill, with the others surrounding us.

He holds his hand in the air, and the stomping ceases. The humming lessens in volume. He informs us, "Your actions have entitled you to a Ceremony of Exposure. There will be three phases. Pledge. Performance. Personalization."

Zara asks, "What do they entail?"

Kirill asserts, "You will find out as you go through the phases."

Valentina's voice interjects, "Get the room ready."

The humming stops. A cleanup crew, similar to the one at the underground fight, appears. They grab arms and legs and move the corpses off the stage. Others mop up the blood, sloshing it around and spreading it so the entire floor is stained maroon.

A buzzing sound begins, growing louder and louder until the atmosphere is electric.

Kirill booms, "The Underworld accepts your bids for initiation. Step forward and commit to your lives to each other and your new brothers and sisters."

Zara turns her nervous expression to me, and I lean into her ear, murmuring, "We made a pact years ago, so it must have been meant to be, right?"

Her gaze drifts to my lips, and my dick hardens. She pins her blues on me, and even through the white lace veil, the flush crawling up her cheeks is noticeable.

"Tell him you choose him," Kirill orders.

She snaps her head toward him.

He insists, "Tell him."

She refocuses on me and lifts her chin, squaring her shoulders. In a confident tone, she declares, "I choose Sean."

My adrenaline spikes and my pulse speeds up. The air around us turns thicker, and I once again debate about not going through with this.

It was what my father wanted, I remind myself, trying to shut down my nerves. Marriage is forever in my family. Zara's too.

Shit. Her father's going to kill me when he finds out.

My mother's going to be equally upset I did this without her.

What does she know about all this?

Why is Zara here?

"Let's begin," Kirill states, forcing me to put aside my worries and questions.

The buzzing changes to *oms*, but it's quieter and more intimate. The darkness of the night is at its peak, and the glow around the arena flickers, competing with the moon.

"Take each other's hands," Kirill directs.

We obey.

Zara takes a shaky breath.

I glance down at her chest. Her cleavage bounces as it rises and falls faster, making the ache inside me grow. I rub my thumbs over Zara's knuckles, and she gives me a small, soft smile.

Kirill asserts, "The vows you take tonight are never-ending."

Except I don't do forever.

O'Malleys don't get divorced.

How long until Zara and I are both bored?

He continues, "They supersede any previous loyalties and survive all future obstacles. They don't die through death. And the only thing more potent than your covenant with each other is your one with The Underworld."

I jerk my head backward, unable to stop, before I realize what I'm doing.

That's fucked-up.

Zara's forehead creases.

"Ah. You thought your vows to each other would be the deepest?" Kirill taunts.

My mouth turns dry.

Zara's expression shows her growing anxiety.

I squeeze her hands tighter.

Kirill asserts, "The Underworld is first. Always. Your partnership is second. Understood?"

No way in hell.

Kirill barks, "Answer me!"

"Understood. Zara does too, right?" I lie.

She licks her lips and nods. "Yes."

He peers harder at us, as if he doesn't accept our answer, but finally turns his head to the man next to me and orders, "Rings."

The man reaches inside his jacket pocket and hands one ring to Zara and two to me.

She glances at the black metal band and smiles, nervously blurting out, "It looks nice. Hope you like it."

A fluttering sensation hits my stomach. I open my palm and stare at the ring I selected and its matching band.

Please like what I picked out.

I didn't care about what any woman would think when I selected the diamond, but that was before I knew Zara would wear it forever.

She tries to peek, but I make a fist, teasing, "No peeking."

She claims, "I wasn't."

"Don't be a brat. You were," I mutter, then think about how many times I've wanted to put her over my knee and smack her juicy ass.

She smirks.

I'm marrying Zara Marino.

Jesus, help me.

Kirill instructs, "Zara, repeat after me. I, Zara Marino, take you, Sean O'Malley Jr., to be my husband for eternity, in The Underworld and all societies."

She clears her throat. "I, Zara Marino, take you, Sean O'Malley Jr., to be my husband for eternity in The Underworld and all societies."

Kirill continues, "I'll obey my husband and devote my life to The Underworld."

She repeats it.

He orders, "You may give him your ring."

She beams, holding the ring, teasing, "It's better than Kinsley and Kian's pipe cleaners, isn't it?"

I grunt, asking, "What made you think of that?"

She shrugs and slides the metal over my finger.

My pulse pounds harder between my ears. I stare at the metal band, wondering if this is some delusion in my mind.

Am I really standing here marrying Zara?

Kirill asks, "Sean, do you need me to repeat the vows?"

I stand taller and shake my head. "No."

Zara bites her lip, and her long lashes flutter a few times.

The ache in my veins grows stronger and hotter. I glance down at the barely-there lace at the bottom of her dress. I inhale deeply, refocus on her blues, and state, "I, Sean O'Malley Jr., take you, Zara Marino, to be my wife for eternity in The Underworld and all societies."

I look at Kirill, waiting for the next part.

"You have to obey me, Sean," Zara whispers.

I arch my eyebrows at her. "No way. O'Malleys don't obey. My father wouldn't have written that into a man's vows."

She scoffs. "Don't be sexist."

I ask, "What's my next line, Kirill?"

He answers, "I'll persuade, provide, and protect my wife while devoting my life to The Underworld."

"Persuade?" Zara questions.

Kirill nods at me.

I repeat, "I'll persuade, provide, and protect my wife while devoting my life to The Underworld."

Anger flares in her eyes. She turns to Kirill. "Seriously?"

"Do not question your vows. Not now or ever. Understood?" he warns.

"Don't take that tone with my wife," I snap.

He glares at me, threatening, "Then keep your wife in line. Now and in the future."

"It's not the Middle Ages." Zara huffs, but I put my hand over her veil-covered her mouth.

She glares at me.

"Quiet," I beg.

She closes her eyes.

"Thank you," I offer, and remove my hand, but when she opens her eyes, she's still pissed.

Kirill points at me, cautioning, "Your vows are not just words. They are to guide you for eternity. When in doubt, there are only three solutions. Persuade. Provide. Protect. There is nothing else."

Persuade. Provide. Protect.

He doesn't take his stare off me.

I nod. "Understood."

He motions to my hand. "You may give her the rings."

My chest tightens. I slowly slide the band on, then the diamond ring.

She stares at it, and I can't tell what she's thinking.

Shit. Did I fuck it up?

"I hope it's your taste," I say quietly.

Kirill interjects. "By the authority granted to me from the high and mighty Omnipotence, I now declare you, in The Underworld and all societies, eternal for life, Mr. and Mrs. Sean O'Malley Jr."

The *oms* stop. The crowd pounds their feet, raising and lowering their torches.

Kirill roars, "You may kiss your bride!"

A tornado of anxiety rips through my gut. I take a deep breath and lift Zara's veil.

The blush reappears on her cheeks, making my cock harder. I circle my arm around her waist and tug her against me. Then I slide my hand through her hair, tilt her head back, and move my mouth to her ear.

She gasps.

I murmur, "It's you and me forever, my little brat."

She trembles against me.

I kiss her lobe and then her neck.

Her hot breath hits my cheek, and adrenaline soars within me.

The stomping of the crowd turns louder and faster, keeping in tune with my beating heart.

I tighten my fist in her hair and kiss her jaw until I can't resist anymore.

All the years of stopping myself from having her have come to an end. The world spins, and my body rings with the energy of the arena.

My lips touch hers briefly, and I pull back, studying her.

She's looked at me with lust in her eyes too many times. Tonight, it's magnified into a thousand flecks of what's now mine and what's still to come.

I tease her with my tongue, continuing to watch her, unable to tear my gaze from hers.

She flicks back, staring at me just as closely, and diving deeper into my mouth.

The dam breaks. Our lips connect in an explosion of fire and ice, taunting us to go to the place we've always flirted with but never dared crossing into.

Everything disappears. It's Zara, me, and the devil giving us the green light.

It finally hits me that the stomping has stopped. The crowd chants, "Performance! Performance! Performance!"

I pull away, catching my breath as much as she is, needing more.

When can we get out of here and be alone?

The darkness begins to fade as dawn tries to break through. The crowd quiets.

Valentina shouts, "Phase two starts now!"

I spin with Zara and freeze.

All twenty-three corpses of the failed initiates hang from flag poles lining the arena. A bed with a white silk sheet is positioned in the middle of the original stage, directly over the fresh bloodstains. Candles have been arranged in the shape of a heart around the bed, and pink rose petals lie scattered around them, contrasting with the deep maroon of the blood-soaked boards.

Zara inhales sharply.

I pin her to my body, turning to Kirill, demanding, "What is this?"

He replies in a smug, dark tone, "The performance phase. It's time to consummate your marriage."

My throat turns dry.

"Sean," Zara whispers, her voice shaking.

I stand taller. "That's not happening here."

"It is, or your bid for initiation is over. And no one goes through partial initiation and leaves," he warns.

Zara glances around the arena, gripping my hand.

I open my mouth.

He interjects, "Any more resistance to fulfill your initiation will be considered a forfeit."

Zara closes her eyes.

The crowd stomps again.

Kirill steps closer and adds, "You always have two choices. That's it. There's never a third."

My gut falls further.

Zara turns to me. "Sean?"

I put my hand on her cheek. "I'm sorry. This is the only choice."

She closes her eyes and nods.

I demand, "Take down the corpses."

Valentina steps forward, declaring, "Their blood is on your hands. They stay. Now, take your bride to the bed or concede to The Underworld."

Against all odds, the room grows louder, the energy turning more frenetic.

Zara trembles harder against me, and I grip her tighter.

Valentina challenges, "Are you tapping out, Sean?"

The air in my lungs thickens. My fist clenches at my side. The last thing I want is for Zara, who is now my wife, to be subjected to this. My role is to protect her, not throw her into the depths of this sadistic society. Yet I know the consequences of not doing what they want. I'm about to answer when Zara speaks up.

She lifts her chin, squares her shoulders, and declares, "Sean O'Malley doesn't tap out." She turns to me, swallows hard, and orders, "Let's go."

Zara

Chapter

SIXTEEN

Though her face is partially hidden by her diamond mask, I can see the shock in Valentina's eyes.

There's no other way. Enough people have died tonight, one of whom I killed.

My insides quiver harder at the thought.

I killed someone. An innocent man pleaded for his life, but I slashed his throat and then stabbed him in the heart.

What kind of animal am I?

Valentina recovers, her lips pursing as she studies me closer.

Sean digs his fingers into my waist, but I can't tear my gaze from hers.

There's something familiar about Valentina. I can't put my finger on it, and I'm sure I've never met her before, yet the look in her eyes is almost comforting. It makes no sense to me, yet I can't shake it.

I'm sure she's stunning without her mask. I think she might be in her late twenties, maybe early thirties, and her sharp features remind me of a model on the catwalk.

One who'd eat me alive if I crossed her.

For some strange reason, I respect that trait in her. It's another aspect that feels intimate.

Somehow, I muster every ounce of bravery and don't flinch under her perusal.

Her expression morphs into one of approval, and she asserts, "Then don't keep us waiting. There are three stages of initiation, and you've only gotten through one. When the sun rises, you'll either be part of The Underworld or..." She pauses, pursing her lips, glancing at Sean, then back at me. "Not."

My stomach dives. At this point, the only goal is to get out of here alive with Sean by my side.

Valentina turns to face the crowd and puts her arm in the air. The gathering of people goes silent, and she points behind her, roaring, "Let the Performance test begin!"

Torches raise in unison, and the audience chants breathlessly, "Oh...ah! Oh...ah! Oh...ah!" They pound their feet and repeat the phrase over and over.

A buzzing ache fills my veins as I stare at the white silk-covered bed positioned in the middle of the huge bloodstain, pink rose petals strewn about, and the soft glow of flickering candles surrounding it.

"Zara," Sean murmurs in my ear.

I begin to turn toward him, but the bodies hanging on the flag poles, and the thousands of people watching us, steal my bravery. My heart beats so fast, I think it might explode, and my breathing turns shallow.

Sean steps before me, throws his arm around me, and slides his other hand into my hair. He pushes my face against his chest and murmurs, "I don't want it to be like this, but we have no choice. Forgive me before we do this." He pulls back and locks his conflicted, remorseful greens on mine.

I put my hand over his chest. His heart's pounding, just as out of control as mine, and I nod, stating, "I do."

A small amount of relief fills his expression, but it's short-lived. With his arm around my waist, he leads me to the side of the bed and then palms my cheeks. He presses his lips to mine, slowly sliding his tongue into my mouth and lazily kissing me until I'm clenching the lapels of his jacket, aching for everything I've deemed too risky for our friendship to survive.

The galvanic chanting lowers to a hushed tone, surprising me and pulling at the core of my desire.

Sean releases me, his chest rising and falling heavily, and keeps his eyes pinned on mine. He unbuttons his jacket and slides it off, then removes his bow tie and drops it on the floor next to it.

The chanting turns to only the women moaning, "Oh." The men continue groaning, "Ah." The thumping of feet continues.

A need sparks to life inside me, so intense my knees wobble. I've never experienced anything like it before, nor did I know something so powerful could consume me.

Sean drops his dress shirt, still watching me.

My gaze drifts to his defined pecs, sculpted biceps, and the V of his torso. Then he unbuttons his pants and draws down his zipper, and butterflies fill me to the point I can barely breathe.

His slacks slide down his toned thighs, displaying his half-erect cock.

Time seems to stand still. My pulse skitters as the reverberations in the air penetrate every cell in my body.

Sean breaks my trance, stepping closer and spinning me to face the rest of the arena.

I gasp, staring at the huge crowd of masked members of this world I know nothing about but was determined to join.

Sean's lips hit the curve of my neck, sending a shock wave of tingles down my back and straight to the ache between my thighs. He slowly unlaces the back of my corset, kissing my shoulders, then murmuring in my ear, "You've always been so fucking beautiful, you know that?"

I inhale a deep breath and turn my head, glancing into his eyes.

He gives me a chaste kiss, then he pushes my barely-there dress down my body. He studies me as the night air hits the front of my exposed body, and his warm frame heats my backside.

My nipples harden. My legs shake, and I swallow hard, glancing at his lips.

He steps closer, locks his arm around my waist, and his cock pushes into my back. Then he grasps my chin, pressing his thumb to the pulse in my neck. He tilts my head, holding it so I can't move, forced to stare at the crowd.

Heat floods my veins. I inhale sharply, holding my breath, my pulse climbing higher and higher.

His hot breath tickles my ear. His tongue teases my lobe. He declares, "All these people want you, my little brat. But you're mine now, and this group of strangers is staring at my wife's perfect, curvy body. So when we get home, I'm spanking your flawless fucking ass for getting yourself into this mess."

Adrenaline-spiked pulsations attack me. My thighs shake, but he holds me against him with his forearm.

He tilts my chin so I'm refocused on him, and adds, "They can't have you, my pulse. You're my wife now. I'm the only one who gets you."

Every sensation feels overloaded. My lips tremble.

He called me his pulse.

I'm married to Sean O'Malley.

For life.

His eyes darken. As if he can read my thoughts, he adds, "For eternity."

I gape at him, unable to move or speak.

Then his mouth and tongue take over, adding more fuel to the fire, burning my existence to ashes.

He spins me so I'm facing him, deepening our kisses, one palm gripping my ass, his other hand fisting my hair. His possession over me taunts me into wanting more until my body's aching and my arousal slides down my thighs.

The erotic moans of the arena heighten. The air between us turns balmier.

Sean retreats, his chest heaving, lips parted. He releases me, steps back, and assesses me, his gaze slowly drifting from my face to my toes. Then it moves back up until his greens glow with a look I've caught glimpses of but never been allowed to fully receive.

He's a bad boy concoction of a monster and a prince, meditating on the fight over his next move.

The chanting quiets, the stomping getting faster and louder, and grunts flare around us in unison.

Sean's eyes turn wicked. He steps closer, the back of my knees hit the mattress, and I fall onto the bed. He leans over me, his large frame casting a shadow around us, his forearms bracketing my cheeks.

"Oh! Oh! Oh!" women seductively interject, matching the vitality of the grunts.

I writhe under Sean, lifting my chin so my breath merges with his.

He moves his arm and runs his thumb over my nipple.

An "Oh!" flies out of me, matching the audience's as if in a song.

He lowers his fingers to the heat between my thighs, teasing it lightly.

"Take me," the women desperately call out.

I jerk my head toward the audience. My bravery disappears, and panic takes its place.

Sean turns my head back to him. "It's you and me, Zara. Forget about them and focus on me."

I gape at him.

His expression softens. He quickly kisses me and repeats, "Me and you. It's always going to be me and you. That's all that matters."

My eyes well with tears. I blink hard, hating the onset of emotions but unable to stop them. A million thoughts about what I'm about to do with thousands of strangers watching, the eternal vow I just made after killing a man, and the worry my friendship with Sean will be ruined, attack me.

He swipes at the first tear that falls and then lowers his mouth to my ear, asserting, "The time to cry is later, my beautiful wife. Don't show them any weakness. Focus on me. It's you and me and everything we've both always wanted."

I sniffle, taking a deep breath and meeting his eye. I ask the question to which I already know the answer, but for some reason, I want reassurance on. "You've always wanted this?"

He gives me another chaste kiss and confidently answers, "You know how much I've lusted over you, my pulse."

My anxiety fades. I've never heard Sean call any of his girlfriends a pet name, but something about him calling me his pulse seems sweeter than anything else he could call me. And I realize I love it as much as I love him calling me his little brat.

Sean demands, "Now, tell me you've always wanted me devouring you, Zara. Taking you to the point of no return and consuming you until you're spinning out of control with me inside of you."

I don't hesitate. "I've always wanted you, Sean."

Approval fills his expression. "Good. So it's you and me. Embrace the rest of this situation."

I nod, taking a final sniffle. "You and me."

He dips to the curve of my neck and kisses it, then murmurs, "Show everyone what they can't have because it's mine."

I slip my hand into his hair, clinging to it, as I slide the heel of my stiletto over the silk sheets and then raise my knees toward the sky.

His erection pushes deeper into my pelvis.

I tug his hair until his face is in front of mine, finding my courage and ordering, "Give me what I want, Sean."

His green eyes flare. His lips curve before they meet mine, and the dam breaks. The years of abstaining from the mystery and fascination of what we'd be like if we gave in to our desires come to an end. His mouth possesses mine with a burst of enthusiasm twisted with greedy need.

I dig my heels into the mattress, lifting my pelvis, craving to feel our bodies join together.

He holds my hip to the bed and taunts, "You don't run this show, my little brat. I do."

I open my mouth, and the chanting changes again.

Oms fill the air once again, but they aren't in unison, and it seems to never come to an end. As soon as one starts, another one begins.

It's chaotic, and creates a soft buzz inside me, adding to the ache I can't escape.

I turn my head, staring at the flickering torches and masked audience. Heat infuses my cheeks.

Sean nibbles on my breast.

I gasp and refocus on him.

He retreats to my lips, mumbling, "I get what I want first, my little brat."

"Please," I beg, trying to thrust my hips so he slides inside me.

A devilish grin erupts on his lips. He pins my cheek to the silk sheets.

The flames of the candles dance around me, turning the crowd blurry.

Sean's voice is gravelly when he says, "This is the only time they'll ever see you this way. Show them how gorgeous you look when I give you everything you need. Haunt their dreams and desires for the rest of eternity, my little brat. We'll see these people for the rest of our lives. And I want them to get a taste of what they'll never have because it's mine."

My adrenaline spikes. No one's ever seen me in a compromising position before. No man has ever told me to let others watch so they can be jealous. Surprisingly, the thought doesn't turn me off. It fuels what I'm dying to finally experience.

He adds, "Imagine being the villainess in everyone's fantasies. You're sometimes within touching distance, yet they're never allowed to reach out and take what they crave. They'll thirst for you in ways no one can imagine."

I stare at the crowd, the blurriness fizzling, and the masked congregation intensifying their *oms*.

"Don't hold back, my pulse. Instill misery in your pleasure."

His words create a new desire to bloom inside me. A demented picture of pain and suffering braided with envious emotions turns my reservations into a challenge. I embrace everything this moment is and can represent.

He glides his thumb over my neck, taunting, "Don't look away from them, my pulse. Terrorize them now and for all eternity."

The *oms* grow louder.

"Now, be a good little brat and show me you're sexier at coming than I dreamed all these years." He drops his face to my chest and returns to sucking my breasts, then makes his way down my torso.

"Oh!" the women moan as the men grunt.

Sean's palms press against the back of my thighs, and his mouth hits my throbbing pussy.

I writhe and inhale sharply, almost turning my head away from the onlookers, but I stop myself.

Haunt their dreams.

I'm only Sean's.

His tongue swipes over my clit, and his thumb rotates over the outside of my entrance.

My breath catches. He flicks faster, and I moan. Heat burns through my body, and my arousal dampens the sheet beneath me.

The noises from the crowd get louder, and all eyes are focused on me, as if they can see inside my soul.

He teases me further, flicking, sucking, pushing inside me but keeping me on edge.

I grip the top of his head, tugging him into me and begging while looking at the crowd, "Please!"

He doesn't allow me to come. He torments me until my body can't take anymore, and my body does something it's never done before.

Adrenaline slams into me, over and over, until I almost black out. I squirt all over him, soaking his mouth and chin in my orgasm, screaming, "Sean!"

The men groan "Fuck" so loud, I wonder if I actually heard it or made it up.

The women moan, matching their volume.

Sean laps up every drop, his own groan vibrating against my pussy.

The euphoria never stops, and I can't see the crowd anymore. Everything's white with the blur of flickering flames burning brighter and sensual noises growing louder.

He sucks me harder, my hips writhing.

A final release hits me, and I whimper, the adrenaline rush slowing. My heart races faster than ever before. I wiggle and finally admit, "I can't take anymore."

Sean lunges up, caging his hard frame over mine. He turns my head back to face him and slides his lips over mine, consuming me with the taste of my pleasure on his tongue. Then he pushes his forehead against mine. With a ragged breath, he asserts, "Now you're ready for me. And it's only you and me, my sexy little pulse."

"Y-yes." I barely manage to get the word out.

He slides his cock into my throbbing pussy, diving in as deep as he can in one thrust.

"Sean!" I cry out, clutching my arms around him.

He responds with more kisses, thrusting in and out of me in slow motion, pushing my desire to the brink of madness. His greens study me intently, watching my every reaction.

"Thank God I didn't know this all these years," he mutters.

"Wh-what?" I ask, then moan, blinking fast as his pace increases.

He clenches his jaw, glides his thumb over my cheekbone, and his hot breath slams into mine.

"Oh...oh...oh!" flies out of me. A new wave of adrenaline, different yet just as delicious as before, floods every cell.

"That's my little brat. Taunt my cock some more," he grits.

"I-I... Oh fuck!" I cry out, closing my eyes. The whiteness drowns everything out. All I can do is vibrate against Sean's body while gripping him tighter.

The chants ring out around us, beating into the tremors Sean keeps erupting through me.

"Jesus Christ, Zara," he barks, pushing my thigh toward my chest and thrusting hard.

"Sean!"

"Little brat," he belts out, and his cock thickens, then fills me deep with his warm cum.

Another high explodes within me. I can barely hold onto him, too exhausted from the onslaught of everything I always wanted but never knew could be this way.

He collapses on top of me. His ragged breath tickles my ear. His chest presses into mine.

I slowly return to reality as night breaks into early dawn.

The chant turns into a low hum.

Sean lifts his head, assessing me.

I smile up at him.

His lips twitch and then he kisses me. It's soft and sweet, and when he pulls back, he keeps his stare on me, claiming, "Mine."

"Yours," I reply.

Satisfaction fills his expression. He kisses me until I once again lose myself in everything Sean O'Malley.

The sound of clapping tears us out of our moment. Sean turns his head, as do I.

The audience roars with approval. It grows so loud we cringe from the shrillness.

Valentina steps next to the bed. Her expression matches that of the crowd. She holds out two robes, one pink and one black. She announces, "Bravo. You passed Performance. But can you handle Personalization?"

My mouth turns dry, and goose bumps pop out over my skin.

Sean jumps up, grabs the pink robe, and drapes it over my shoulders.

I slide my arms through it.

He pulls me off the bed and ties the belt around my waist, then kisses me gently. He takes his robe and secures it on his body. Then he wraps his arm around my waist.

Valentina points at something behind us.

We glance in that direction, and my gut drops.

Sean tugs me tighter to him as we stare at Kirill.

He stands next to a fire, holding a metal stick with something on the end, but it's too far to clearly make out what it is. Three men stand next to him, holding different objects.

Kirill dips the stick into the fire, and my gut spins. He pulls it out after a few minutes, and the end glows as hot as the flames. He pins his gaze on us and states, "It's time to make your final vows."

Sean

Chapter
SEVENTEEN

"Don't worry, I'm the only one who has to do it," I murmur in Zara's ear.

She glances up in horror, her eyebrows pinned together.

"It's fine," I assure her, leading her toward Kirill.

I knew this day would come. I caught glimpses of the skull branded on all the men watching the underground fight. I assumed it was a rite of passage into The Underworld.

It doesn't surprise me that it's happening tonight. While I'm not looking forward to the pain, I want the branded skull on me. It's my father's design—his vision and a symbol that I'm part of his world, even if I'm still unsure of all it entails.

It's a short-term pain, I tell myself, doing my best to show no qualms or fear about getting branded.

It's going to hurt like a motherfucker.

Short-term, pussy.

We step in front of Kirill, and the other objects the men hold become clear. The one closest to him has a piece of wood, I assume to bite down on. The second holds a jar of salve and some plastic wrap. The third man has a gold censer for incense and a lighter.

I look closer at the censer and realize it's the same skull design as the brand.

That's badass.

Pride fills me. My father designed a piece of art that represents something important. From what I gather, it's a symbol of change and loyalty. Seeing it in gold as well as stamped on the hands of strangers, makes me feel like he lives on and didn't just die a horrible death.

However, it happened.

I will find out who killed him and the rest of the details, I tell myself, knowing it will be easier now that I'm entering The Underworld.

A tense, eerie silence takes over the arena.

Kirill points to the man with the censer, and he lights the incense. The smoke rises out of cutouts in the roses. He walks around us, breathing loudly as if he's a dragon.

Zara gives me a funny look, and I stare at her sternly, thinking, *Don't say a word, my little brat,* and hoping she heeds my warning. I can only imagine the smart-ass things she might say.

When the thick scent encircles us, the man sets the censer on the floor between Kirill, Zara, and me. The smoke continues to rise from it.

Kirill turns to Zara and asks, "Are you ready to fully commit to The Underworld?"

The color drains from her cheeks. She glances at the hot metal brand and then at me.

Goose bumps race across my skin. I push her slightly behind me, and interject, "The branded skull is only for men."

Amusement fills Kirill's expression. "Where did you get that idea?"

I clench my jaw, pushing Zara farther behind me.

Kirill looks over my shoulder, then calls for Valentina.

I turn, moving Zara to the side so we're not behind Kirill, not fully trusting him not to hold Zara down and burn her.

Valentina steps in front of us.

"Turn," Kirill orders her.

She obeys.

"Lift your hair," he demands.

She reaches for her long, dark curls, gathers them in her hands, and twists them above her neck.

I inhale sharply.

Zara gasps loudly.

I clutch my wife tighter as I stare at Valentina's neck. She has the same brand as the men, but the roses are red instead of pink.

"Women are just as much a part of The Underworld as men. The importance of their role sometimes outweighs ours. Did you think otherwise?" Kirill questions.

Valentina lowers her hair.

I step back with Zara so we can see everyone. I answer, "I didn't suggest they weren't important."

His eyes narrow. "Yet you assumed they weren't worthy of wearing the skull?"

My chest tightens.

"Answer me," Kirill demands.

I blurt out, "Not that they are unworthy. But they're women."

"And?"

"I don't want my wife to go through the pain of being branded," I admit.

Valentina turns to Zara. She puts her hand on her cheek and softens her tone. "Have I gotten the wrong impression? You are not brave enough to finish initiation?"

I tug Zara back, not trusting Valentina or any of these people not to hurt her. I insist, "Of course she's brave."

Valentina snaps her glare to me. "Then why do you deem her unworthy of wearing the skull?"

I stay quiet, unable to think of a good answer, and clutch my wife to my body.

Zara turns to me. "Sean."

I break out in a sweat as I meet her eyes.

"It's fine," she insists.

"Zara—"

She puts her fingers over my lips.

My insides quiver. I release a breath through my nose.

She smiles, and when she's confident I won't speak, she removes her hand and faces Valentina. She lifts her chin and squares her shoulders, declaring, "I'm ready."

My stomach flips so fast, I swallow bile.

Valentina beams, praising, "Good decision."

I bite my tongue, reminding myself there's no way out of this. It's still a live-or-die situation.

Zara can't handle this pain.

"I'll go first," she says.

"No. You're last," Kirill interjects.

I snarl, "So she can see how painful it is and freak out before you do it?"

A dark arrogance overtakes Kirill's expression.

Valentina asserts, "Women are stronger than men. We birth your children. We stand by you when you're weak, and rise through the terror, bringing you with us to get to the other side."

I grind my molars.

Zara smirks at me, amusement flashing in her eyes.

I leer at her and make a note to add another session where I spank the shit out of my brat's pale ass.

"Step forward now or step away, Sean O'Malley Jr.," Kirill warns.

I glance at Zara one more time.

She points to Kirill, ordering, "Go on."

I begrudgingly step in front of him, still unhappy. Very soon, these people are going to burn my wife's perfect skin, and I can't stop it unless I want us to die.

Why would my father let women do this? I question as I stand in front of Kirill.

Low hisses fill the air, and the stomping of feet erupts once more.

My heart beats harder.

The man picks up the skull censer and circles us in more smoke.

Kirill booms, "Do you, Sean O'Malley Jr., pledge your heart and soul, loyalty and honor, to The Underworld?"

I don't hesitate in my answer. "I do."

"And do you promise to put The Underworld first?" Kirill asks.

No. My wife is first, dickhead.

I answer, "I do."

"When you stand before the stains of injustice, do you vow to slam the laws of The Underworld against all those who break them?" Kirill questions.

I don't know what the laws of The Underworld are, but I reply, "I do."

He looks satisfied. He turns and dips the metal rod into the fire again.

Fuck, this is going to hurt.

Stop being a pussy!

One man holds the wood to my lips.

I bite down on it, staring at the blue flames. A cold sweat breaks out on my skin.

Zara steps up next to me and grabs my hand.

I glance at her.

She rises on her tiptoes, kisses me on the cheek, and shoots me a brave smile.

My blood pounds faster.

Kirill pulls the stick out of the fire. It glows with smoke curling around it.

Valentina positions herself next to a small table and orders, "Kneel. Then make a fist and put it on the table."

I obey, and the man who gave me the wood holds my forearm against the table.

Zara kneels next to me and puts her arm around my waist. She murmurs, "You got this, babe."

Babe?

It's strange that we crossed the line. We weren't supposed to, and now she's calling me babe.

She's my wife.

How the fuck did we get here?

I look straight ahead, gritting my teeth against the wood.

The man with the incense circles me. The hissing turns into a chant mixed with more hisses and gasps. It makes my heart pound so hard that I think I might have a heart attack.

Kirill steps in front of me and announces, "Sean O'Malley Jr., you have proven yourself to be worthy of the skull—the mark that represents our eternal commitment. It overrides all law and order as you know it. So by the power of the Omnipotence, and with the full trust of The Underworld, you now may exercise the birthright you've earned to keep."

The women in the crowd shriek, and the men roar.

It startles me. I flinch, but the other man holds down my forearm right as Kirill pushes the skull against my hand.

I bite on the wood, roaring as loud as the crowd, trying to move my hand as my skin singes. The smell of it mixes with the incense. I gaze at my hand, and all I want to do is throw up.

"Breathe, Sean," Zara orders in a stern voice.

I turn toward her.

She grabs my cheeks, demanding, "Breathe!"

I realize I'm not taking in any oxygen. So I inhale short breaths through my nose, continuing to bite the wood.

She nods, smiling. "Good. Keep breathing."

Something cold hits my hand, and it's an instant relief. I refocus on the burned spot. The second man applies more balm to my brand and then wraps it in plastic.

The man who gave me the wood says, "You can relax now. You look like you're going to break your teeth." He releases his grip on my forearm.

I spit the wood next to me.

"Good job," Zara praises.

I stare at her, feeling semi-crazy, wondering how she can be so calm when she's about to have this done to her neck. I turn to Kirill. "Brand me on my neck instead of Zara."

He jerks his head backward.

Valentina's amused laugh fills the air.

I growl, "What's so funny?"

"You can't take another member's mark," she claims.

"Why not? She's my wife," I remind her.

She shrugs. "So what? That doesn't negate her duty to The Underworld or eliminate her obligation to fulfill initiation. Or allow you to steal her earned right to wear the skull."

"It does if I'm taking it for her," I declare.

Kirill warns, "Keep talking like that, Sean. We'll brand you in your neck, and Zara will still get hers."

"Listen—"

"Shut up, Sean," Zara interjects.

I snap my head toward her.

Her eyes turn to slits. "Don't say another word."

I open my mouth, and she puts her hand over it, threatening, "Enough."

Your ass, my hand, little brat.

She rises. "I'm ready."

Valentina puts her arm around Zara's shoulder. "Come with me, darling."

"Now she's your darling?" I mutter.

Valentina turns and says, "Zara and I hold no harsh feelings toward the other, do we?"

"No," Zara replies, raising her chin and pinning me with a challenging stare.

Confusion fills me.

Valentina laughs. "It's okay. Lots of men don't understand the sister-hood. Come on, darling. It won't hurt too long." She leads Zara back toward the bed.

I rush after them, and the other men follow.

"Zara—"

"I need you to lie on top of me, Sean," she says.

I freeze.

"I'm serious. Put all your body weight on me and hold my head in place," she orders.

The arena fills with hissing.

The air thickens.

Zara smirks, unties her robe, pushes it so it falls to the floor, and puts her hand on her hip. She teases, "Are you lying on me naked or robed?"

My breath catches. I lower my gaze to her tits, my erection perking up again. I mutter, "Fucking brat."

She bats her eyelashes and points at me, demanding, "Take your robe off. It'll be better for me if you're naked."

I arch my eyebrows.

She purses her lips, spins, and struts over to the bed. She slowly gets on all fours, then crawls to the other side, lowering her face first so her ass is in the air. She looks over her shoulder at me, then slowly slides her lower body to the sheets. Then her lips form a pout. "Why aren't you naked?"

"Fucking brat," I say, louder this time. I drop my robe, approach the bed, then grab her foot and press down.

She gasps and lifts off the bed.

I lunge my body over hers, then murmur in her ear, "This mark is going to be nothing compared to what my hand does to your ass."

"Don't tease me," she sassily retorts.

My dick digs into her backside, throbbing. I grunt.

Her smirk grows.

Kirill, holding the hot brand, kneels before Zara so he can meet her eye, and asks, "Do you promise to uphold the vows your husband just made to The Underworld?"

Her voice cracks as she answers, "I-I do."

He touches the back of her neck. "The skull is sacred."

"I know," she interjects.

"So you pledge your life to The Underworld and will defend it against its enemies?"

"I will," Zara agrees.

He kisses her forehead and rises.

"Don't do that again," I warn.

Arrogance washes over his expression. "An innocent kiss from an Omni is a privilege. It's a gift of a beautiful future."

"I don't care. Don't ever kiss my wife again. Not you or anyone," I threaten.

He grunts but steps back. He nods to the man with the wood.

The man holds it in front of Zara.

She bites down on it.

I stroke her cheek, reminding her, "Make sure you breathe."

She offers me a calm look.

Why isn't she freaking out?

Valentina twists Zara's hair into a tight bun, ensuring no strays. She adds, "Piece of cake, darling."

The crowd doesn't make the same chant as when I got branded. They resume their erotic *ohs* and *ahs*.

My cock hardens further.

The man with the incense jumps on the bed, waving the censer over our bodies. When the air is thick with the scent, and I can barely breathe, Kirill steps forward. He nods at me.

I add more body weight to Zara and press my palms against her head so she can't move. I lean down, kiss the spot on her neck that'll soon be burned, and murmur in her ear, "Just breathe, my pulse."

As soon as I lean away, Kirill pushes the skull against her flesh.

I cringe, watching her skin singe.

She whimpers, her body trying to jerk up, but I weigh too much.

I order, "Get the balm on her now!"

But the man already has it scooped out of the jar and ready to apply. He reaches over and layers it on her.

Her body relaxes.

I pet her hair, careful not to touch the burnt area, as plastic gets wrapped around her entire neck.

When it's secure, I slowly get up, tug her off the bed, and pull her into my arms. I kiss the top of her head, praising, "You did great."

She glances up. A few tears stain her cheeks. She asserts, "It wasn't that bad."

"No?" I question, shocked.

She shakes her head.

I confess, "I thought it hurt like a motherfucker."

She giggles.

I give her a chaste kiss, then say, "You were really brave."

"Thanks." She smiles.

The crowd breaks out in loud applause.

I spin us to face them, then freeze.

Their masks are all off. The sun has risen, and the torches no longer burn.

Valentina holds out our robes to us.

We take them and put them on.

She removes her mask, beaming as bright as Zara.

"I knew you were gorgeous," Zara blurts.

The look Valentina gives her is as nice as the one you'd give a best friend. She claims, "We have good genes."

"We?" Zara questions.

Something passes over Valentina's expression. It quickly fades, and she smiles brighter. "Yes. Us Italian women."

"Oh! Right," Zara says.

Valentina embraces her, then me. She retreats and turns to the crowd.

The applause dies down.

She holds her arms above her, crying out, "I now pronounce to The Underworld, Mr. and Mrs. Sean O'Malley Jr.!"

The applause resumes, and an SUV drives into the arena. It stops next to the stage.

Kirill still wears his mask. He opens the door to the back seat, then motions inside, stating, "It's time to go. We'll give you some time to yourselves, but your orders will arrive soon."

"Orders?" I question.

Darkness fills his expression. "Yes. Every member of The Underworld has them. We all have a duty to fulfill your father's vision."

"And when do I find out the entirety of his vision?" I ask.

"Soon. Now, go enjoy each other," he answers in a nonnegotiable tone.

"Sean, let's go," Zara says, tugging my arm.

I look at her.

"Please," she begs.

I glance around the arena as the sun rises higher. The masks cover the audience's faces once more. They begin stomping and raising the torches into the air again.

"Sean. Please," Zara repeats in a soft tone.

I cave and grab her hand, leading her to the SUV, wondering what we just committed to, but knowing all will be revealed soon.

And now, I'm going home with a wife, but not just any wife.

Zara Marino is my bride. There will be consequences in the outside world for what we've done tonight. I don't fully know what they are yet, but my gut says it won't be long until we find out.

Zara

Chapter

EIGHTEEN

Neither Sean nor I speak during the ride in the SUV. It's only a short time before we arrive at a private airport.

The sun shines brighter, and the driver rolls down the divider window. He announces, "There's a pair of sunglasses in the side door for each of you."

I glance down to find a designer case. Sean picks his up.

The driver suggests, "You might want to put them on. It gets pretty bright around here once you don't have the protection of the tinted windows."

Sean and I don't argue. We put our glasses on, and the SUV stops beside a plane. There's a huge body of sparkling turquoise water on the other side of the runway.

Sean doesn't open the door. As soon as the driver gets out, he says, "Do you know where we're at?"

I shake my head. "No idea. You don't either?"

"No," he admits uneasily.

"Do we need to worry?"

He grabs my hand and kisses it. "No. At least, I don't think so."

Anxiety fills me.

The driver opens the door and motions toward the plane, adding, "Have a safe flight home."

"Thank you," Sean says. He gets out and reaches in for me.

I take his hand, and he leads me up the steps and inside the private plane.

The same flight attendant that brought me here beams, chirping, "Welcome back, Mr. and Mrs. O'Malley. I assume you had a fabulous evening?"

Sean furrows his eyebrows.

I bite on my smile and nod. "That's one way to describe it."

Her lips twitch, then she steps back and adds, "I heard you gave quite the performance."

My cheeks heat.

Sean snarls, "Don't say things to embarrass my wife."

The flight attendant's eyes widen. She holds her hands in the air. "I didn't know it would embarrass her. I heard she owned the moment."

Sean's eyes darken. He glares down at her.

"You're fine," I tell her, then add, "Let's go, Sean." I pull him toward the back of the plane.

He mutters, "She better watch her mouth."

"Sit down," I demand, pointing at the seat beside mine.

He huffs and plops down.

I add, "You told me to ensure it was a good performance. Why are you mad at her?"

"You're my wife," he snaps.

"And?" I say, my stomach flipping, realizing we're going back to reality and I'm now married.

He stares at me.

I lean close to his ear. "Did you not want me to do what you told me?"

He sighs and closes his eyes. "No, you were amazing, actually." He opens them and locks his gaze with mine.

My stomach flutters. "I was?"

He glances down at my body, then back up. Even though we're still in robes, he claims, "Yeah. And sexy as hell just like now."

I put my hand on his thigh, stroking close to his balls but not touching them. I whisper, "We could do it again just for practice."

He slides his hand around my throat and lifts my chin. His grip isn't tight, but it's possessive and forceful.

I gasp as my desire spikes.

He moves his face closer. His hot breath merges with mine, teasing my lips. He sternly declares, "No one will ever see you in that position again."

"I didn't mean it like that," I say.

"No?"

I scoff and roll my eyes. "No. I meant you and me. Home in my bed."

Relief and cockiness mingle across his features. "Okay, good. In that case, I'll take you up on that." He winks and sits back.

I release my breath and shift in my seat, wondering what our new normal will be now that we've crossed the point of no return. I try to lift the window shade, but it's locked shut. I mutter, "What is with these people and all the secrecy? I thought we were part of The Underworld now. Why is everything still hidden from us?"

"Who knows?" he says and leans his seat back. "But I'm tired. Aren't you?"

I yawn, affirming, "Yeah. I am."

He grabs my hand. "Okay, let's go to sleep. If memory serves me right, this place is far away from home."

I don't argue. It only takes a short time until we're asleep. When I wake up, he's still passed out and holding my hand.

The flight attendant stares at us.

I sit up straight. "Do you need something?"

She smiles. "I just want to let you know that the back closet has clothes for you. We're going to be landing in a half hour. You might want to change unless you want to wear the robes," she says with an amused expression.

I grin. "No, I think we'll change. Thanks."

"Sure. Did you want anything to drink or eat?"

I shake my head. "I'm okay."

She stares at me for another moment.

My heartbeat picks up. I ask, "Is there anything else?"

She hesitates, then asks, "Will you and your husband participate in the Triangle of Souls?"

Confusion fills me. I admit, "I don't know what that is, but it sounds intriguing."

She licks her lips, glances back at Sean, then informs, "The wife gets to choose the third eye."

I question, "As in the invisible eye of Hinduism?"

She licks her lips again. "Yes. So you can experience true enlightenment."

I don't know what she means by that, and I feel like I'm missing something.

She opens her mouth and then shuts it.

I confess, "I'm lost. Can you explain what you mean?"

She nervously glances at Sean, then kneels in the chair in front of me and leans her elbows on the back. She lowers her voice, declaring, "You get to pick who leads you and your husband to full enlightenment. I would love to be your chosen one."

My chosen one?

I blurt out, "You want to sleep with us?"

She furrows her eyebrows. "The Triangle of Souls will bring you closer. You'll both have full enlightenment after our ceremony together."

She wants to sleep with us.

"Is this mandatory for members?" I question.

"No. Of course not. It's a gift you give each other."

I hold in my laughter and try to keep a straight face. "Thank you for telling me. I don't know if we'll participate in that ceremony, but if we do, you'll be at the top of our list."

"Really?" she breathes.

I hold in my laughter. There's no way I'm sleeping with this woman or letting her touch my husband. But I want to get out of the conversation and don't want to insult her. So I answer, "Yes."

"Thank you!" she replies excitedly.

"Sure," I reply back.

She gets up and points at Sean. "Do you want to wake him up, or do you think I should?"

"You better let me handle that job."

She softly laughs. "Okay. By the way, I did mean it as a compliment back there."

A mix of pride and uncomfortableness fills me. "Thanks."

"You're absolutely fascinating," she gushes, then spins and disappears behind the curtain.

A strange feeling comes over me. I decide it might be best to not tell Sean about my conversation with her.

I stroke his head. "Babe, you need to wake up."

He stirs.

"Babe," I say a bit louder.

He blinks a few times and stares at me.

"Babe, you have to get up. We need to change. We're going to be landing in a half hour."

He doesn't say anything for a minute, as if trying to remember where he's at and everything that's happened, and then it hits him. He gives me a funny look. He blurts out, "We're married."

My heart races faster. "Yeah."

"You're going to get bored of me," he teases.

I reply, "Maybe you'll get bored of me first?"

He shrugs. "Guess we'll find out." He rises and goes to the back of the plane.

A new fear hits me.

What are we going to do when we're bored of each other?

Please let him get bored of me before I get bored of him.

I get up and meet him in the back of the plane.

There's a summer dress, bra, and sandals for me. There's a pair of khaki shorts, a polo shirt, and slip-on shoes for him.

It doesn't take long to get dressed, and we return to our seats.

The pilot announces, "We'll be landing soon. Please put your seat belts on."

We do as instructed, and before I know it, we're landing. An SUV is waiting,

and after we deplane, we get into the vehicle. I stare out the window, watching the passing buildings and the Chicago skyline, wondering what's next.

The driver pulls up to Sean's place.

I turn toward him. "I guess I'll see you later."

His eyes turn to slits. "What are you talking about?"

I point out, "The driver's dropping you off first."

"Zara, we're married."

"Right. Well, let's go to my place," I say.

The driver puts the divider window down, as if he's been listening to us. He interjects, "You'll both go up to Sean's."

"I'm tired. I want to go home and get some rest," I object.

He locks eyes with me in the rearview mirror, sternly asserting, "As I stated, you'll both go up to Sean's apartment."

Sean says, "Zara, let's go." He opens the door and gets out. He reaches in for me, and I don't fight him. I take his hand, and he leads me into his building, up in the elevator, and down the hall to his door.

When we enter his apartment, we freeze. The table next to the door has a lit candle, pink roses petals scattered all over the wood, and our blood marriage pact sits next to it.

Sean picks it up, reads it, and mutters, "I can't believe you kept this all these years."

"Thank God, or I would've had to marry that other guy," I declare.

"Is he the one you wanted from the binder?"

My chest tightens. I lie, "No, I didn't want any of them."

"Are you sure about that?"

"Are we going to fight about this?"

He sighs and puts the blood pact down. "No, there's no point. Come on." We step into the family room, where I freeze again.

There are boxes everywhere. I question, "Why do you have boxes all over?"

"How would I know?" He walks into the kitchen, grabs a knife off the counter, returns, and rips a box open. He pulls out one of my sweaters. "I think this is all your stuff."

"What? How the hell would they get all my property here?"

He meets my eye. "How do they do anything, Zara?"

It's a good question. One I don't know how to answer. But I love my place. I'm not moving into Sean's man cave.

I walk over to another box and hold my hand out. "Give me the knife."

He obeys.

I rip open a box, and my gut dives. More of my clothes are in it. I close the box and put the knife down. I spin, declaring, "I'm not moving out of my place."

"You are. We're married," he grumbles.

"So? What does that have to do with anything? My place is way better. I put a lot of time and energy into it, and it's beautiful."

He declares, "I'm not living under your father's thumb."

"Don't be silly."

"You know damn well it's not silly. Now that you're married to me, you're not having your father's surveillance on you 24/7. Besides, they're not very good, are they?"

I put my hand on my hip. "Oh, like your surveillance is any better. How did all these boxes get in here with nobody noticing?"

He crosses his arms. "The Omni want us to live here, or they wouldn't have packed up your stuff and brought it here. I'm not about to start disobeying them."

"This isn't fair. I spent a lot of time making my place nice," I whine.

"What's wrong with my place?"

I glance around the apartment. The couches are brown leather, there's a video game console, and there's barely anything on the tan walls.

I point around, claiming, "This is blah! No woman wants to live in this."

"This place is awesome," he declares.

"You can't be serious."

"It is, and we're staying," he says, brushing past me, pulling his shirt off and going to the bedroom.

"What are you doing?" I question, following him.

"I'm tired. I'm taking a shower and getting something to eat."

"Sean, this conversation's not over. I mean it. I don't want to live here."

He spins to face me, and I run into him. He slides his hands through my hair, yanks my head back, and leans over me.

I inhale sharply, holding my breath and squeezing my thighs.

He hisses, "You know what I do to little brats?"

I don't say anything. My butterflies go crazy.

He continues, "I think it's time I show my wife what happens when she provokes me."

"Please do! You think you're the only one in charge, and you aren't!" I hurl.

"That's it." He releases my hair, scoops me up, and tosses me over his shoulder.

"Let me down, Sean!"

He grunts as he carries me to the bed. He sits and maneuvers me so I'm lying across his knees and then he yanks my dress up.

"What are you doing?" I say, gripping the bedspread and squeezing my thighs tighter, but I don't fight him. My body pulses with a new ache.

He rubs his hand on my ass cheeks, and my breath turns ragged. He claims, "I'm teaching my wife who's in charge and reminding her of her vows to obey her husband."

"That's a shitty part of the vows," I blurt out.

He raises his hand and then smacks it on my ass cheek.

"Oh shit!" I cry out as a new type of excitement explodes in my core.

He slides his other hand between my thighs, sticking his fingers into my dampness and then rolling them around.

I moan. "Sean, what the—"

A loud smack rings out, and a sting flares across my ass.

"Little brats get my palm stained on their ass," he roars, and spanks me again.

I inhale sharply, my pussy throbbing.

He slaps me over and over until I'm so damp I'm sure the bed's stained.

I grip the comforter tighter, whimpering.

He questions, "Do you still have a problem with my place?"

"We aren't living here," I grit out.

He rolls his finger inside me and smacks me once again.

I cry out, "Oh God!"

"Fuck, you're wet, my little brat. Why are you so wet?" he taunts.

"I'm not," I blurt out.

"Don't lie to your husband!" He smacks my numb cheek, and another round of pulsations erupts, mixing with the sting.

And for some reason, I want his handprint on my ass cheek. I don't know why. It's just like the skull. There was no way I wouldn't get branded with it.

He flicks his finger inside me and smacks me again, and a rush of endorphins flows through me, pushing me over the edge.

"Oh fuck!" I yell out, my eyes rolling, my back arching.

"That's my little brat. Come for me again." His palm lands another sting on me, and the orgasm bursts into a more intense throbbing.

"Sean," I cry out.

He thrusts his fingers and smacks me twice more, and I'm so dizzy all I see is white. He does it over and over until my arousal covers his lap. Then he tugs me up so I'm on my knees. He puts his arm around my waist and pushes my head to the mattress. He barks, "You want to come some more, you little brat?"

"No. Yes. No!" I cry out, delirious with pleasure.

"Which one is it?" he says, pushing his dick just a little bit inside me.

"Yes!" I shout.

He enters me in one thrust, and I moan. He grits, "You want to be a brat? Then I'm going to have to tame you." He slowly thrusts inside me.

But I'm already on the O-Train. I'm seeing stars, and I'd be unable to hold my body up if it wasn't for his arm around my waist. The high is so intense, I'm almost nauseous.

He grunts. "Fuck. You wanted to know what it would be like after resisting me all these years, my little brat? Well, this is what it's like being mine."

I whimper, my body convulsing and unable to stop.

He adds, "All those men and women stared at you...wanting you...needing you...craving you. Well, so do I. Except I'm the only one who's going to get you. You're mine. You understand me? Mine," he growls and then pushes deeper, his erection swelling inside me.

I hit another high, and his guttural groan fills the air.

"Fucking little brat," he spouts, his warmth filling me. He continues to thrust through it until his release drips down my legs.

When it's over, he collapses on top of me, then slides his arm under me and rolls onto his back, pulling me with him.

Both of us try to catch our breath and slow our heartbeats.

I glance up at him and, in a soft voice, say, "Sean, I mean it. I want to live in my place. You know how much time and effort I put into decorating it."

He sighs. "Zara, I don't care where we live, but I'm not doing shit without talking to the Omni first."

I huff. "So they rule everything now?"

Something passes over his expression.

Fear hits me. "Sean, don't tell me that that's what you mean. Don't tell me they get to control every single move we make."

He sighs and shakes his head. "No, I don't think they control every move, but they moved your stuff here for a reason. So until we can speak with them and tell them what we want, you'll have to deal with my place."

I shimmy out of his grasp, sit up, and groan, staring around his bedroom.

He tugs me back into him. "Is my place that bad?"

I glance at the bare walls and admit, "No, but can I at least put my stuff on the wall? It's so boring."

He smiles. "Yeah, I don't give a shit. Do what you want."

"Really?"

"Yeah, I don't care. If that's going to make you happy, then do it."

"Yay," I say, clapping, then lean in to kiss him.

It's meant to be quick, but he rolls me onto my back and kisses me deeply until he's hard again.

His greens twinkle. He rolls over, pulls me on top of him so I'm situated over his cock, and states, "I think you need more of a punishment."

Sean

Chapter

NINETEEN

Zara and I barely left the bedroom, only untangling ourselves from each other to order food and grab it at the door. Now, she's sleeping peacefully in my arms, with her leg draped over me, exhausted.

I stare at the ceiling, wondering again how we got here. There isn't a bone in my body that's upset I'm married to Zara. It's just ironic.

We fought for so many years not to cross the line, and now we've jumped so far over it, there's no going back. And I always knew it would be good between us, but this is better than I anticipated.

I glance down at her again, unable to stop the grin forming on my face.

Her lips are slightly parted, her long lashes dark against her skin, and her cheeks are still slightly flushed.

I mutter, "Fuck, I'm in over my head," then freeze, reprimanding myself when I realize it came out of my mouth.

She doesn't stir.

I carefully move her leg off me. She whimpers but doesn't wake. Then I slide out from under her, get out of bed, and toss on a pair of sweatpants. I grab the tray of take-out food and go into the kitchen. I scrape our plates, toss the leftovers in the trash, and load the dishwasher.

The doorbell rings, and I freeze.

Who could be here?

I glance at the bedroom, then walk to the front door and open it.

Brax stands there in his workout clothes, and he looks pissed. He questions, "So what the fuck happened the other night, and where have you been?"

"I can't get into it, and you know it," I assert.

He scowls. "Really? We're going to play this game again?"

One of my neighbors across the hall opens her door and steps outside.

I motion for him to come in.

He steps inside, shuts the door, and booms, "I need some answers. You can't just leave me hanging like that."

I shush him. "Keep your voice down."

He stills, then his eyes turn to slits. He glances at the door leading into the main room. "Why? Who's here?"

My heart races. I don't know what to tell him. I'm not prepared for this.

He jerks his head backward. "You're not going to tell me who's in there? Why not?"

I sigh and scrub my face. "I guess you're going to find out at some point."

"Find out what?" he asks.

I cross my arms and lean against the wall. "Zara's sleeping in my room."

His look of shock isn't surprising. He explodes, "You fucked Zara?"

I step closer, warning, "Don't talk about her in that regard."

Confusion replaces the shock. "What else do you want me to call it?"

"It's more complicated than that," I say.

He studies me momentarily and then his eyes drop to my left hand. Horror fills his expression, then he meets my eye. "Why are you wearing a ring?"

I put my hand in my pocket. "Don't, Brax. I need a good workout. Let's go to the gym and then we can talk about this."

"No, Sean. Tell me right now what the fuck is going on. Stop playing games with me," he snarls.

My chest tightens. I take several deep breaths and finally admit, "Zara and I got married."

His eyes widen. He gapes at me, but then his lips twitch. "You're fucking around with me."

"I'm not."

His face falls. "You're serious? You got married?"

"Yeah."

"Why would you do that? You two haven't even dated before. Or have you been sneaking around behind all of our backs?" he asks.

I shake my head. "No. It just happened."

He scowls. "It just happened? You got called away to whatever secret place you went to and came home married, but it just happened?"

My stomach flips. "Yeah."

"How do you even get into that situation?" he asks, his voice raising.

"Quiet," I reprimand.

He glances at my hand in my pocket, scolding, "Bro, I don't know what you've gotten yourself into, but this is crazy. You need to come clean with me. Who are these people, and what do they want?"

I ignore his statement and announce, "I'm going to change. I'll be back in a minute, and we can go to the gym."

"Why is your hand wrapped up?" he demands.

I close my eyes. I don't want to lie to Brax. We've never done that. Since the moment we met, we've always been honest and had each other's backs, but I don't know what I'm allowed to tell him.

"Don't keep me in suspense," he hurls.

Everyone's going to see it soon enough, I tell myself. I unwrap the plastic and hold my hand in front of his face.

"Holy shit! That must have fucking hurt."

I chuckle, admitting, "You should have seen Zara. She took it like a man. I took it like a pussy."

He arches his eyebrows. "Zara has one on her hand as well?"

Shut up, I tell myself, but answer, "No, it's on the back of her neck."

"Ouch!" Brax cringes.

I nod. "Yeah, but she was..." The memory of me lying on top of her while she barely complained, compared to my reaction, fills me. I grin.

"Dude, you're already soft on her, aren't you?" he taunts, pulling me out of my memory.

"I'm going to get changed. I'll be back out in a minute. Stay quiet."

"Aye, aye, whipped boy," he teases.

I groan, then go into the bedroom. I step into the closet and grab a T-shirt. I tug it over my head and then pull on a pair of socks and shoes.

I exit the closet and glance over at Zara. She's still sleeping, so I quietly leave the bedroom and meet Brax at the front door.

He points at my hand. "That thing looks gross."

"Oh shit. Hold on." I go into the bathroom and open the jar of salve that was magically left on my counter along with a roll of plastic wrap. I layer salve over the skull, wrap it, then return to my closet.

I pick out a pair of weight-lifting gloves and pull one over my hand, wincing as it slides over the brand. But it's a necessity. The last thing I want is for any of my uncles to see it. I know they will eventually, but I don't want to deal with it today.

Brax and I leave the apartment and get into his car. He pulls out into traffic and then glances over at me. "Luca know you married his daughter?"

My gut dives. "Nope."

Brax whistles. "He's gonna kill you, bro."

I grunt, but Brax is right. I put the seat back and close my eyes, not wanting to field any more questions. I order, "Wake me up when we get there."

It doesn't take long before Brax states, "Time to face the music."

"Keep your mouth shut," I warn.

He scoffs. "I'm not a rat."

"No shit."

"Then don't insinuate I am," he threatens, and slides out of the car.

I get out, and we hoof it into the gym. As I expect, all my uncles are there.

Killian booms, "Sean, where have you been?"

"I had shit to do," I tell him.

"You snuck out of the party, then disappeared for a day," Declan accuses.

"As I said, I had shit to do." I brush past them and go to the bench press. I order, "Spot me, Brax."

He doesn't argue and comes over. We get lost in our workout, and I'm relieved when I don't hear any more questions about my whereabouts.

Killian holds up a pair of gloves. "Want to go for a round?"

"Yeah, sure," I reply, setting the free weights down and walking over to him. I tug my lifting glove off and wince, forgetting about the brand.

Killian eyes my hand. "Why is your hand wrapped in plastic and all bloody?"

I glance down. The wrap is bunched up, barely covering the skull. It's a bloody, nasty-looking wound.

Killian grabs my hand, wrinkles his nose, and belts out, "Jesus. That's disgusting. What the fuck did you..." His expression goes slack, and the color drains from his face. He pins me with an angry look, snarling, "What did you do, Sean?"

I pull my hand away. "None of your business."

He grabs my shirt and pulls me toward him. "I asked you what you did."

"Whoa, what the fuck is going on here?" Finn barks.

"Nothing," I insist.

"Sean did something stupid," Killian spouts.

Finn turns to me. "What did you do?"

"I didn't do anything. Leave it," I state, but I know I'm fighting a losing battle.

"We have to get going, or we'll be late," Brax interjects, trying to get me out of this mess.

Finn warns, "Stay out of this, Brax. I mean it."

Brax clenches his jaw and gives me his I'm-sorry-but-I-tried expression.

Killian seethes, "I'm only asking one more time. What the fuck have you done?"

There's no getting out of this, so I reply, "I put my father's mark on my hand. Why is it such a big deal?"

Killian and Finn exchange a worried glance.

Killian fumes, "Why would you do that to yourself?"

Anger fills me. "I just told you it was my dad's design, and he had it on his hand. There's no reason I can't have it on mine."

Killian closes his eyes and shakes his head, grinding his molars.

Finn adds, "You don't know what you've done, Sean."

"Well, why don't you fill me in?" I question, my heart beating faster. I add, "I'm tired of all these secrets. If there's a reason I shouldn't have done it, then man up and tell me."

Nolan joins us. "Your dad had that on his hand, but people stole it. Somebody... Well, one of the Rossis stole his design. A lot of them have that on their hands. So do the Baileys. You shouldn't have branded yourself and especially not in the same place."

I scoff. "How was I to know? You could have told me that when we talked about it."

The three of them exchange another glance.

"Stop looking at each other and give me answers!" I demand.

They stay silent.

"God damn it. All of you! I've had enough of this. If you know something about my father, and if this means something, I want to know."

Killian declares, "We just told you that the Rossis and Baileys wear it. Hell, we even saw a few Petrovs with it. All we know is they had to have stolen it from your father. But you shouldn't have branded it on your hand. Who knows what it represents to those fucking bastards."

Finn asserts, "You're going to have to cover that up. Turn it into something else."

"No way," I blurt out.

"You need to. It could give our enemies the wrong impression," Nolan insists.

"The wrong impression of what?"

Killian seethes, "That you're a disgusting scum ball Rossi, for one."

"Or Bailey," Nolan adds.

Finn snarls, "Or fucking Petrov."

I rise, standing taller. "I'm not covering up my father's skull. He created it. He wore it. I have the right to wear it too."

"Don't be stupid," Finn adds.

"They stole it, so it's on them, not me. And now I'm done with this conversation," I assert.

Killian orders, "You're done when we say you're done. You're not going anywhere."

"Fuck, I'm not," I shout and stomp out of the gym with Brax on my heels.

We get into his car. He mutters, "Well, that went over good."

Still pissed, I spout, "Shut up, Brax. I don't want to hear it."

He turns on the engine and pulls out of the parking lot. "Okay, but you're in over your head. We both are."

I turn toward him. "What do you mean 'we both are'?"

He presses his lips in a straight line, staring at the road in front of him.

My skin crawls. I ask, "What aren't you telling me?"

"Nothing," he answers.

I sit back and study him.

He doesn't flinch, just continues to drive.

My stomach flips. "I see. So this is how it's going to be, huh? We'll both be part of The Underworld but never tell the other what's going on?"

Guilt flashes across his face, but then his expression hardens. He glances at me. "You claim you're not in a position to talk. Well, neither am I."

I open my mouth, then shut it. I turn and stare out the window, wondering how we got so deep into this mess.

My phone buzzes.

I glance at it and groan.

> Dante: What have you done, Sean?

My cell buzzes again.

> Liam: Get over to my house now.

> Dante: We need to talk. Your mom and I are still in town. This isn't a request.

> Liam: You've made a bad mistake. We need to fix it.

Dante tries to call me. I send him to voicemail just as Liam calls. I send him there too.

Brax points out, "They're not going to give up."

I close my eyes and sit back, trying to think about how to get around this, knowing the shit show is just about to start.

Brax drops me off, asking, "Do you want me to come up?"

"No, not right now." I reach for the door but my phone buzzes again. I glance at it, and my stomach drops.

> Fiona: You married Zara?

A close-up of Zara and me kissing after our vows, with my hand on her cheek and wedding band on full display, fills the screen.

"Fuck," I mutter.

Another text arrives.

> Luca: You're a dead man walking, Sean.

"Fuck! Fuck! Fuck!" I grit through my teeth.

"What now?" Brax asks.

I show him my phone.

"Shit."

"Yeah. Shit is right."

Brax's tone turns serious. "I wouldn't want to be on Luca's bad side."

"Gee, thanks for your helpful comments."

"Sorry."

"Whatever. He was going to find out at some point," I say, starting to open the door, then pause. I turn back toward Brax, asserting, "We're eventually going to need to figure out how to let each other know what's going on. You know that, right?"

He nods. "Trust me, bro. I don't like this either."

I hold my fist out, and he bumps it. I exit the car, enter my building, ride up in the elevator, and go into my apartment.

Zara's still asleep. I open the blinds and slap my hands together, booming, "Time to get up."

She flutters her eyelids. "What's going on?"

"Time to get up," I repeat, and pull the blanket off her.

"Jesus! What's the emergency!" She sits up in bed and glances over at the clock. "Sean, it's seven o'clock on a Sunday morning."

I step in front of her and cross my arms, looking down. "Yep. And shit's hitting the fan."

Her eyes widen and her face pales. "Did we do something to upset the Omni?"

"No. It's worse."

"Worse?" she frets.

"Yep. Our secret nuptials aren't a secret anymore. Our parents are still in town and will probably be here soon."

"Oh shit!"

"Yeah, oh shit is right. So get up, my pulse."

"When are they coming?" she asks.

I shrug. "My guess is the next fifteen to twenty minutes."

She groans.

I add, "Oh, and my uncles saw my brand."

She glances at my hand and then grabs it, horrified. "Sean, this looks disgusting. You're going to get an infection."

"It's fine," I say.

"No, it's not." She jumps out of bed and pulls me into the bathroom.

I stare at her backside.

My wife is hot as fuck.

She bends over and rifles through my cabinet.

I step up to her, put my hand on her hip, and suggest, "You can stay in this position if you want."

She giggles, rising with a bottle of hydrogen peroxide, then reprimands, "We don't have time for that right now."

"Says who?"

"Me. Now, give me your hand."

"That's going to hurt," I admit.

She arches her eyebrows, stating, "I didn't think the big, bad Sean was going to be such a baby."

I scoff. "Let's see how you react if I pour this on your brand."

She doesn't say anything, but her lips twitch. She grabs my hand, holds it over the sink, and pours the liquid over it.

I wince.

She stifles her laugh.

My wound bubbles with foam.

Zara grabs a wad of toilet paper, pats it dry, then gently coats it with salve. She wraps it tight with fresh plastic. Then she grabs my hand and kisses my knuckles. "There you go. Much better."

A warmth fills my chest. I stare at her.

She nervously questions, "Why are you studying me like I did something wrong?"

I blurt out, "Your dad's going to kill me since I didn't ask his permission to marry you."

She nods. "Yep. And your mom will be upset that she wasn't there."

"For sure," I state.

"Well, I guess there's only one thing to do." She turns on the shower.

"What's that?" I question.

"Shower." She smirks and then steps inside. She starts to close the door but then pauses. She pops her head out. "Are you coming in or staying out there?"

I chuckle, and my dick turns hard.

Fuck it. We have a few minutes.

"Why not?" I say, and step inside, pushing her against the tile wall while she shrieks.

Zara

Chapter
TWENTY

We get out of the shower and dry off. My phone rings when I step into the bedroom.

"Welcome to my world," Sean mutters.

I glance at it and groan. A new text pops up.

Dad: My beautiful, figlia. Tell me this is photoshopped.

A screenshot of Sean and me kissing after our vows, his wedding band prominently displayed, pops up on the screen.

My gut drops. I can only imagine the disappointment and hurt my parents must feel about what Sean and I did behind their backs.

I leave my phone near the bed and return to the bathroom. I dig through Sean's cabinet and call out, "Do you have a hair dryer?"

"No. But are you looking for this?" He appears holding my hair tool with an arrogant expression.

"Thank you!" I rise on my tiptoes and peck him on the lips.

He pats my ass. "Get ready. I'm sure they'll be here soon."

I roll my eyes, but my stomach tightens. "Oh, the fun."

"Yep." He exits the bathroom.

I plug in my dryer and turn it on. I only get a few minutes before Fiona steps inside.

She glares at me with her green eyes glowing hot.

I wince and softly say, "Hey."

"Don't you dare 'hey' me! How could you lie to me like that?" she accuses.

I shake my head. "I didn't. It's not what you think."

"Not what I think?" She holds her phone out in front of me, showing me the same photo my father sent.

"Fiona, I didn't mean to—"

"You didn't mean to what? Screw around with my brother behind my back while lying to me multiple times? Get married in secret with neither of our families there?" she hurls. Tears fill her eyes. She blinks hard.

I put my hand on her shoulder. "Fiona—"

She jerks her shoulder backward. "Don't touch me right now, Zara."

Guilt eats me. "Look, it just—"

She tilts her head, looking at me in confusion.

"What?" I nervously question.

She points at me. "Why do you have plastic around your neck?"

Oh shit.

She glances at the mirror, and her expression morphs to one of horror. "Is that blood?"

I step away from the mirror. "Listen—"

"What is it?" she shrieks, trying to spin me around, but I step backward.

"Zara, what did you do to yourself?" she frets, her horror turning to worry.

Sean walks into the room. "I told you to stop barging into my apartment, or I would revoke your access. You know you're supposed to ring the bell and wait for me to answer."

Anger takes over. She spins and jabs him in the chest. "You don't get to say that to me right now."

"Don't come in my home and act like you own it," he says.

She fumes. "Don't you dare act like what you two have done is right."

"What have we done?" he asks.

"Sean, don't," I warn, but I've never been able to get involved or stop their sibling fights.

They stare at each other with challenging expressions. Fiona shakes her head. "You're disgusting."

"Why am I disgusting?"

"You married Zara."

"Oh, so Zara is disgusting?" he questions arrogantly, crossing his arms. Then he adds, "I beg to differ. In fact, I find Zara rather appetizing."

"You're disgusting," she seethes.

"Stop it," I scold.

Fiona glances at his hand and then grabs it.

He winces. "Ow!"

Her voice rises again. "What the fuck is this, Sean? Why do you have plastic and blood on you just like Zara?"

He pulls his hand away. "It's not your business."

"No?"

"No, it's not," he says, clenching his jaw and staring her down.

I try again, softening my tone. "Fiona, let's go in another room and sit down and talk."

She turns to me, rage erupting from her. "Don't you think that would have been good before you went off and married my brother? And lied to everyone over and over, including me?"

My insides quiver. I hate I lied to her, even though it wasn't a full-blown lie like this one. But there's always been something between Sean and me, and she knew it. No matter how much I tried to escape it and not let it happen, it finally has. So now we're going to have to work through this.

"Please, let's sit down and talk," I offer.

Sean scoffs, "Yeah, get out of our bathroom."

She spins back to face Sean. "You're really pushing it."

His cockiness grows. "What are you going to do about it, Fiona? What Zara and I have done, we've done. It's not your business."

"Not my business?"

He smirks. "Yep. It's not your business who's in my bed or my house."

"She's not just in your bed, Sean. She's your wife now. Do you even understand what that means?" Fiona cries out.

Sean shuts his mouth and stares at her.

She's right. What we've done has consequences. They are deeper than what Sean and I have barely processed.

Sean leaves the room just as the doorbell rings. He turns back, accusing, "Thanks for sending that picture to Zara's family, sis."

Surprise fills Fiona's expression. "I didn't send any pictures to Zara's family. I wouldn't be the messenger of pain for her parents."

"Really? You seem a little out of control right now. Are you sure you didn't send one little text?" he taunts.

"No, I did not," she insists. "So whoever sent it to me must have sent it to them. Who did send it to me, anyway?" she asks.

Sean doesn't say anything.

She focuses back on me with fresh hurt in her voice. "Well, who was there? Who got an invite since I didn't?"

"Fiona, please. Let's go talk about this calmly."

A loud bang fills the air. My father's voice booms, "Open this door now, Sean O'Malley!" It's followed by more banging.

"Sean, go open the door," I urge.

My father warns, "Get out here, you piece of shit, before I knock your door down."

"Sean!" I push on his chest.

He sighs, muttering, "Let the games begin."

"This isn't a game!" Fiona snaps.

He ignores her and hurries to the other room.

We follow.

Within seconds, Dad pushes through the foyer. His fist is full of Sean's shirt, and Sean's walking backward, even though I'm sure he could hurt Dad if they got physical. Maybe not when my father was in his prime, but he's not a spring chicken anymore.

I shout, "Dad, don't!"

"Don't?" he spits, glancing at me. "Don't kill the man who stole my daughter's innocence?"

I groan. "Dad, stop. You're being extreme."

"Being extreme? He took my beautiful *figlia* and married her behind my back. Didn't even ask me permission."

"Dad..."

"Luca, let him go," Mom orders, but she's not happy with me either. Her expression glows with hurt and anger. And I can't say I blame either of them.

The anger in Dad's eyes intensifies. He barks, "I'm not going to let him go, my *stellina*. I'll do to him what every father does to boys who can't be men and step up to the plate. How dare you not do the right thing before you asked my daughter to marry you!"

"Dad, stop," I say as Dante and Bridget come through the door.

"How could you do this, Sean?" Bridget blurts out, as hurt as my mom.

"Because he's a fucking idiot," Fiona answers.

"Who asked you?" Sean bites out.

Dad grips Sean's shirt tighter, lifting him to his toes, and I know Sean could fight back. I don't know why he isn't. I guess it's out of respect for my father, which I appreciate, but I also want Dad to let go of him.

So I rush over and push between them. I demand, "Dad, stop it."

He glances down at me, then slowly releases Sean. He blinks hard, and pain fills his voice. "My beautiful *figlia*. How could you have done this? Do your mother and I not deserve to be at your wedding? Am I so horrible I didn't deserve to give you away?" He turns and snarls at Sean, "Or give this bastard permission to even marry you?"

"Dad, please," I beg.

"Luca, calm down. No one needs to have a heart attack today," Mom frets.

He glances at her with the same disappointed expression. "This isn't right, Chanel."

Sadness flares in her eyes. She affirms, "No one is saying it is, especially not me."

Dante interjects with a hollow voice. "You got the skull branded on you as well, Zara?"

The hairs on my arms rise.

Dad pales, his eyes widening. In a devastated voice, he shakes his head and gasps, "Zara. No."

I glance at Sean, not knowing how to answer.

"Why do you have plastic around your neck?" Fiona questions again, then orders, "Take it off."

"No," I reply and step closer to Sean.

He puts his arm around my waist.

"What did you do to yourself?" Mom questions, then steps behind me, tugs at the plastic and cries out, "Oh my God, your beautiful skin!"

I wince from the shot of pain on my neck.

"Zara's fine," Sean insists, tugging me closer. "Everything's fine. Everyone needs to calm down."

"What did you get my daughter involved in?" Dad seethes, his eyes glowing hotter.

My heart races faster.

Sean claims, "We put my father's design on us. Not a big deal."

"Not a big deal?" Dante snarls.

Bridget grabs Sean's hand, weeping. "Why did you do this? I told you not to do this!"

"You never told me not to put it on me," Sean argues.

Her face turns red with rage.

Fiona asks, "And why are you talking about my dad?"

Sean ignores her question and asks some of his own. "Why doesn't everyone tell us why they're freaking out? If the mark isn't a big deal, why are you all making it one?"

"Agreed," I add, wondering what my father and Dante know about the skull.

Do they know about The Underworld?

It's just another one of my father's secrets.

The room is quiet.

No one says anything.

Fiona finally breaks the silence, saying, "Mom? I need answers."

Tears well in Bridget's eyes, and she shakes her head.

Dante tugs her into him, asserting, "Your brother and Zara have done something stupid. That's all."

"What does it have to do with Dad?" she questions.

Sean speaks up. "Fiona, you remember the skull on Dad's hand?"

She furrows her eyebrows. "Um, maybe. I don't know. I..." Shame fills her expression, and she looks down.

Sean quietly finishes for her. "There's not a lot you remember anymore?"

Her eyes flow with tears. She swipes at them and then guiltily looks at Sean.

He gives her a compassionate look, offering, "I know."

She sniffles. "Why does it matter?"

Sean holds his hand up. "Dad had this skull branded on him. I got one, and so did Zara, but hers is on the back of her neck."

Mom snaps, "You've burned yourself? What would possess you to do that?"

More guilt eats at me. I hate not being able to answer them. But I also don't like how they seem to know something about whatever Sean's dad was up to.

In a stern voice, Bridget repeats, "I told you not to do it."

"No, you didn't. I never said I would put it on my hand," Sean claims.

"You know damn well what I meant," Bridget adds.

Dante warns, "Stop playing games with your mother, Sean."

Sean's face hardens. He tugs me closer. "What's done is done. Zara and I are married. We branded my father's mark on us as a tribute to him. That's it. It's a private moment between Zara and me, and it's not a big deal. Unless there's something else all of you aren't telling us?"

Fiona, Sean, and I stare at our parents.

My pulse skyrockets.

The longer they take to reply, the more I'm convinced they know something.

"You've made a bad mistake," Dante states.

Sean arrogantly replies, "Yeah? Why is that? You know something about my father you want to tell me?"

Dante gives Sean his challenging stare, then adds, "If your mother didn't want you to have that on you, then you should have respected her wishes."

Sean spouts, "Easy for you to say. Your dad didn't die when you were a kid. He's still alive and in his nineties."

Dante clenches his jaw.

My father accuses, "What did you pull my daughter into?"

"He hasn't pulled me into anything, Dad. We chose this. Together."

"You chose to destroy your body? To get married without your mother and me present and exchange vows with a man who didn't have the balls to ask for my permission?" he seethes.

"Okay, maybe we didn't do it the right way. But Sean's right, it's done," I insist.

Dad snarls, "So that's it? We're all expected to act like this is normal? And you two..." He points at us. "You broke your mothers' hearts. Now we're supposed to look the other way?"

I sigh.

Sean grips me tighter to him. He answers, "Unfortunately, that's how it's going to have to be, unless you want to have nothing to do with us again."

I gasp. "Sean, don't say that."

"You think you can take my daughter out of my life now?" Dad growls.

"No. But you're acting like this is an unforgivable event. As if Zara and I marrying each other is the worst thing that could have happened. I mean, there are a lot worse guys out there than me, Luca."

My father booms, "Don't you dare talk to me about whether you're worthy of my daughter's hand!"

"Dad! Sean! Please," I scold.

Fiona interjects, "Why did Sean put that skull on you, Zara? What's the real reason? He was my father too. I want to know."

"Fiona, it's nothing. It was a mark on your dad's hand. He designed it and was obsessed with it. It's just a gothic drawing," Bridget insists.

Fiona spins to face her mother. "If it's nothing, then why did you tell Sean not to put it on him?"

Anger flares in Bridget's eyes. She points at us. "Look how nasty their skin is now. Do you think I want my son branded? And Zara! Your beautiful neck. How did you even handle that kind of pain?"

Sean proudly states, "She took it like a champ! Way better than I did."

I glance at him, and my lips twitch. I blurt out, "You were a bit of a baby."

He winks at me.

Bridget roars, "You two think this is funny?"

My face falls. "No, but..." I glance back at Sean. "Well, he was way more of a wimp than me." I bite on my smile.

"This is not funny!" Dad shouts, his face purple.

I jump.

Sean squeezes my waist. "No, it's not funny. But here's what's going to happen. Zara and I are now married. You can choose to respect it or not. That's your choice. We hope you'll be happy for us. We've been friends for a long time."

"You chose the wrong daughter to do this with," Dad seethes.

"Luca, you know there's no one who will take better care of Zara than me. No man can protect her better from our enemies. And you can't deny that."

"Spoken from a man—no, a boy—who forced her to get mutilated!" Dad spouts.

Sean grunts. "I'm not a boy, and you know it."

"I'm not mutilated!" I protest.

"You intentionally burned your body! And for what?" Mom cries out, tears streaming down her cheeks.

"And he didn't force me. I wanted it," I add, guilt piling higher inside me.

Sean takes a deep breath and says, "I'm Zara's husband now. There's no more surveillance on her except what I deem necessary. From this point forward, she's my wife and my responsibility to take care of."

"Like hell, it is," Dad booms.

"Sean," Dante quietly warns.

"You don't dictate what goes on with my daughter's security," Dad fumes.

Sean puffs his chest out. "I do. I'm her husband, whether you like it or not."

"She's *my* daughter," Dad snarls.

Determination laces Sean's voice. "That's right, and that's why we want you to be part of our lives. But she's my wife, and I will protect her from now on. Any questions?"

Luca takes two steps, but Dante steps between him and Sean, warning, "Luca, cool it."

"Don't you tell me to cool it when it's my daughter," Dad barks.

"Things are too heated right now. We'll work through this at another time," Dante asserts.

"Mom, I want to know whatever you're not telling me about this skull and Dad. I deserve to know," Fiona insists.

Bridget sighs, shaking her head. "There's nothing to tell. I'm telling you the same thing I told Sean. It was just an image he obsessed over and then burned on his body."

"Are you lying again?" Fiona accuses.

Bridget's face falls, filling with fresh pain.

Dante points his finger between Sean and Fiona. "You two need to stop bringing up old ghosts. You know why your mother had to lie to you all those years, and she hasn't lied to you since. She doesn't deserve your disrespect."

"Then tell us the truth," Fiona pushes.

"I am telling the truth," Bridget cries out.

Mom interjects, "I think Dante's right. Things are too heated right now. We all need to cool down, take some time, and process all this. Luca, let's go."

Dad looks at her, not moving.

She softens her tone and puts her hand on his bicep. "Please, Luca, let's go."

He finally caves, giving Sean another angry look and me a sad one, full of disappointment. He mumbles, "My beautiful *figlia*," shaking his head, and they leave.

My heart aches. As mad as I was at him and my mother, I wouldn't ever want to hurt or disappoint them on purpose. Now they're in pain, and I caused it.

Dante asserts, "Bridget, time to go."

She glances between Fiona and Sean, tears still falling. "Everything I did was for you two. I wish you'd believe me."

Sean sighs. "We do believe you, Mom. We've always believed you after things came to light."

"Things that we still have questions about," Fiona adds.

Pain, fear, and horror wash over Bridget's expression.

I don't understand it. I only know what Fiona and Sean have told me, but it's not much. Bridget claims she had to hide them. She wasn't allowed to go back to Chicago and was only allowed to be in New York at her father's. If she had come back to Chicago or seen the O'Malleys after Sean Sr. died, then they would've been killed. She insists she did everything she could to keep them safe.

The O'Malleys forgave her when they found out she was threatened, and they also convinced Sean and Fiona to do the same.

However, Sean and Fiona have always wanted more details about who the people threatening her were and what happened to their father. She's never provided them with that information, nor has anyone else. So I can understand their frustration.

"Bridget, let's go. Come on," Dante orders as kisses her forehead, then he gives Sean another angry look. He glances at my neck, then shakes his head. He leads Bridget out of the house.

Fiona doesn't move.

I step next to her. "Fiona."

She whirls to face me. "What does my dad have to do with this?"

I shake my head and shrug my shoulders, lying once again. "It was just his drawing Sean remembered and suggested we put on us."

She stares at me, as if she can see right through me. "You know what's crazy, Zara?"

The hairs on my arms rise. "What's that?"

"I've trusted you my entire life. I never thought you were a liar, but now I clearly see I was wrong." She glances over at Sean. "And you?" A tear falls down her cheek. She scoffs. "You two deserve each other. Congratulations."

"Fiona!" Sean and I say at the same time.

She leaves the apartment, and I stand frozen, wondering how our actions could hurt so many people.

Sean

The Next Day

Chapter
TWENTY-ONE

Tingles tease me, and I groan. "Just like that, my pulse."

Zara smirks, slowing her rotation down. "What about this?"

"I said not to stop." I slap her bottom, but it's not very hard.

She tousles my hair, her pussy circling my cock at the same tormented speed, and then swipes her tongue against my lips.

I grab the back of her head and force her to keep kissing me until she's whimpering and quivering around my erection.

I grab her hip, mumbling, "You little brat."

She giggles.

I move her faster over me, thrusting deeper into her.

"Sean," she breathes, her eyelids fluttering.

I smack her ass harder, and she moans, her body convulsing over mine.

"You like that," I taunt, then smack her again as I thrust up.

"Fuck!" she cries out, her eyes rolling.

"This is what happens when you're a naughty little brat. I have to remind you who's boss," I grit through my teeth, pushing my pelvis as high as I can, our sweat merging.

"S-Sean!" she stutters, her voice hoarse, face bright red.

I slam her down one more time onto my cock, and a loud moan fills the air. Her entire body collapses over me, shaking intense tremors.

I hold her close, moving her hips faster, closing my eyes, blurting out, "Sexy little brat."

"Sean," she barely gets out, pushing her face into my chest.

And everything is fucking perfect.

She's perfect.

I still can't believe Zara's my wife, but she is, and I've not spent a moment wasting it.

The adrenaline builds in my cells, expanding them to the point they can't hold any more.

I smack her again as my throbbing erection slides deeper into her dampness.

She moans, her eyelids fluttering.

"That's it," I praise, swelling inside her until she's vibrating harder against me and whimpering.

Zings tease my nerves. Bolts of endorphins run down my spine, and my balls tighten.

The doorbell rings.

Her eyes fly open.

"They can go away," I state, raising and lowering her hips.

The doorbell rings again, and a loud pounding sound fills the air.

I shout, "Fucking go away!"

Her eyes widen.

I urge, "Come on, my pulse. You got a little bit more in you." I thrust harder and slap her ass cheek.

"Sean, I... Oh fuck!" Her eyes roll again, and her body convulses harder than ever. Her arousal soaks my pelvis.

I praise, "You fucking naughty little brat!"

A constant stream of rings comes from the doorbell, along with hard pounding.

"Go away!" I shout again, then my balls shrivel. A whoosh of adrenaline bursts out of my cells. I grunt, pumping hard and thrusting through it until I've drained everything I have into her.

Her convulsions slow.

We try to catch our breath as the doorbell and pounding continue.

"Jesus fucking Christ. Go away!" I yell out again.

Still flushed, Zara looks up and winces. "Maybe we should get that?"

"Fuck them." I push my lips against hers.

She giggles against my mouth.

The ringing and pounding doesn't stop.

I tear my mouth off hers, spouting, "Jesus Christ."

She rolls off me and rises.

"Where are you going?" I ask.

She grabs her robe and puts it on. "I'm going to go see who's at the door."

"Like fuck you are," I say, jumping up.

She arches her eyebrows. "Why not?"

"You just fucking squirted all over me," I point out. "My wife's not going to the door smelling like she just got fucked."

She smirks. "Really? Want to bet?"

"Don't test me," I warn.

She begins strutting toward the door.

I step behind her and spin her against the wall.

She gasps.

"You keep your naked, sexy ass, smelling like pussy juice, in this room."

Her lips twitch. "You do realize you have my scent all over you now?"

I grin. "You can squirt some more on me later. Don't you dare leave this room."

She giggles. "Yes, dear hubby. But go before whoever it is breaks the front door down."

I groan, annoyed at whoever is outside. I grab a towel, wrap it around my waist, then rush to the front door.

"Jesus Christ. Stop fucking doing that," I bark, then jerk the door open and freeze.

Byrne arches his eyebrows, taunting, "Is something wrong with your doorbell?"

"No, there's nothing wrong with my doorbell. Is there something wrong with your finger?"

"You weren't answering."

"I was busy," I state.

He chuckles, glancing at my towel. "I can see that."

"What is so important?"

"Aren't you going to let me in?"

I grumble, "Fine, whatever." I step back.

He enters the foyer, shuts the door, and wiggles a book before me, stating, "I brought this for you and your bride."

My gut dives. I don't like surprises from The Underworld. Maybe someday I will, but right now, I still don't trust anyone. So I cautiously ask, "And what would that be?"

"It's the laws that your father wrote."

My chest tightens, and my heart races faster. I gape at it.

He wiggles it again, as if it's a carrot, asking, "Well, don't you want to see what laws he created that govern us?"

I glance at him, admitting, "I don't know. Do I? I feel like this is a trick."

He squints. "There's no trick, son."

"No? Are you sure about that?" I question.

"Aye, why would I trick you?"

"Why wouldn't you trick me?"

Hurt fills his expression. "Is that what you think of me?"

I don't say anything.

He crosses his arms. "Have I not had your back the entire time?"

"Have you?" I ask, still suspicious.

Anger flares, replacing the hurt. He points up at me. "I have. And your dad would be disappointed that you question my loyalty when we were so close."

I blurt out, "You say you were close."

"We were," he insists in a stern tone.

I study him closer, asking, "How come my mom doesn't know about you?"

His eyes widen. "You asked your mom about me?"

I shake my head. "No."

"Good. She doesn't know about me, and we need to keep it that way."

"Why is that?"

"Because you shouldn't involve your mom in things she shouldn't be involved in," he states.

"So there's nothing in here that my mom knew about? My dad never said a freaking word to her about any of this?" I question, finding it hard to believe, and grab the book.

He hesitates.

Chills run down my spine. "Ah. So there is something my father talked to her about?"

He shrugs. "I don't know what goes on in a marriage."

I scoff. "Really? For some reason, I think you probably know what happens in mine."

He wrinkles his forehead. "No, I don't, son."

I stay quiet, giving him a challenging look.

He speaks first, announcing, "These are the rules. You and Zara need to memorize them. Your father wrote them. Every law has a reason behind it, and there'll be times when those rules will come into play. It's only then you'll understand why they're there."

"More riddles," I snap.

"Did I do something to you, lad?" he questions.

I just look at him.

He adds, "You seem pissed off at me today."

I think about his question, then I think back on all my interactions with him. I don't have a reason to be upset with Byrne. So, I apologize. "I'm sorry. You just caught me at a bad time."

"Really?" He glances at my towel and back up, grinning. He offers, "Sorry about that. And, lad, enjoy your honeymoon stage while it lasts."

"While it lasts?" I question.

He shrugs. "Sure. Everybody fucks like rabbits at the start, but then life happens, and you slow down."

I puff out my chest, declaring, "My dick's not slowing down."

Amusement fills his greens. He chuckles. "I hope you're the one man who can uphold that statement, son. If you have any questions, let me know." He turns and walks out the door.

I glance at the book. It's black, with the skull and flowers design embossed in gold.

I open it up, thumb through the pages, then close the door.

Zara comes out with a towel around her head and her silk robe on, questioning, "Who was it?"

"Byrne."

She tilts her head. "Who's Byrne?"

My gut dives. I realize I've never talked to her about Byrne. She must not know who he is.

She sighs. "Sean, don't tell me you'll keep things from me. We were both inducted into The Underworld. We don't need secrets between us anymore."

I hesitate.

Her voice turns stern. "Sean, we're married. Out of all the people in the world, you and I cannot have secrets from each other."

She's right, I decide. "Byrne's a man in The Underworld. He claims he was my father's best friend, but my mother doesn't know him."

Zara gapes, then questions, "You asked her?"

I shake my head. "No, but he says she doesn't know, and I shouldn't ask her."

Zara asks, "How do you know he's telling the truth?"

I admit, "I don't."

She bites on her lip, then points at the book. "What is that?"

I sit down at the table and pull a chair out.

She takes a seat next to me.

"He says it's the laws of The Underworld my father created."

Zara rubs her hands together and beams. "Ooh, this ought to be good!"

I chuckle. "You're crazy."

"Why am I crazy?"

"I don't know. Some things make my gut turn, and you spin it around into fun."

"Well, it's better we know than not know, isn't it?" She arches her eyebrows.

"I don't know. Is it?"

"I think so," she replies, and opens the cover. In a dramatic tone, she reads, "Welcome to The Underworld. The main goal is to get a seat at the table. Every level presents a challenge, but only the bravest and most deserving can earn a seat where they belong."

I take a deep breath.

She glances at me and wiggles her eyebrows, teasing, "Are you the most deserving and bravest?"

"No doubt," I answer, then quickly kiss her.

She continues reading. "There will always be 666 members who have a seat at the table."

I jerk my head backward. "666?"

"Yep."

"Isn't that number a sign of the devil?"

"Yes and no. In Revelations it's the mark of the beast, which had seven heads and ten horns, coming out of the sea. It's said to rule over all nations and tongues."

An uneasiness shifts in my stomach.

She adds, "It's a symbolic worldwide political system."

"Didn't know you were so informed on the history of symbols," I tease.

She laughs, then says, "It's also an angel number, representing a spiritual encouragement to refocus. We often focus on trivial things, obsessing over them to the point we lose sight of what's really important. So they say when you see 666, it's an angel nudging you to reassess the situation."

I stare at her.

She questions, "What?"

"How do you know all this?"

She shrugs. "It's interesting to me. But it kind of makes sense why your dad would choose it."

I arch my eyebrows.

She adds, "He brings both ideologies into play."

Confused, I ask, "How's that?"

"Well, if he really wanted to bring enemy families together, then he would need a new political system to rule over the families as one. And maybe he thought bad things were happening because families had lost sight of what's important and focused on trivial things. I don't know. Just makes sense to me," she states.

I ponder her statement then praise, "You're really smart."

She bats her eyes, beaming at me.

I point at the book. "What else does it say?"

She continues, "Memorize these laws. They are the rules that will guide you. They may not make sense initially, but every one is put forth to protect you and your loved ones. Each ensures your survival. Abiding by them will create peace throughout The Underworld and eventually outside it. Signed, Sean O'Malley, Founder."

I touch my father's signature, and the hairs on my arms rise, thinking about him holding this book and writing in it. I look away when emotions catch in my throat.

Zara puts her hand on my thigh. "Sean, are you okay?"

I take a deep breath and nod, admitting, "Yes, but this is hard sometimes. For so long, I buried so much of my father. I wanted to be him and remember him, but I also didn't want to, if that makes any sense."

Compassion fills her expression. She replies, "It does. Do you want to do this at a different time?"

I shake my head. "No. Keep reading."

She returns to the book, flipping the page, announcing, "There will always be 666 members who have a seat at the table. Revelation 13, with regard to 666: The mathematical results of "taking God's name in vain" and "changing times and laws" requires there are to be 666 members at the table at all times unless an unstoppable imbalance occurs. Should it happen, it must be filled on the seventh moon."

Confused, I admit, "That sounds like a lot of gibberish to me. Mathematical results with a name, times, and laws? Makes my brain hurt."

She bites on her smile and shrugs. "I know. But that's what it symbolizes and what your dad wrote."

I rub my hand over my face then ask, "Okay, what about the seventh moon? Why does that matter?"

Zara doesn't answer right away, but then snaps her fingers. "Seven is another number like 666."

"It is?"

"Yes. In Genesis 1, seven represents a full and complete world. That would make sense."

I mutter, "Or bad luck."

"Or good luck," she offers.

Silence falls between us for a few moments.

Zara's lips twitch. "Was your dad into witchcraft?"

"Not that I'm aware of," I reply, but the uncomfortable feeling returns.

"Okay, well, the seventh moon it is." She flips the page and continues to read all the rules.

Most are about loyalty and trusting your fellow brothers and sisters. Then we get to an amendment. The original rule states both husbands and wives must have a seat at the table. My father added, "unless grandfathered in," and wrote "amendment #1" next to it.

My gut churns. I glance at Zara, feeling uneasier.

She softens her voice. "Do you think your mom didn't know anything, or do you think she's lying?"

My chest tightens. I admit, "I want to believe her. Maybe she didn't know, or maybe she didn't want any part of this."

Tension fills the air.

"Why would my dad grandfather himself in if he thought this society was the answer to a peaceful world for his children? Wouldn't he want my mother by his side?"

Zara says nothing, her expression full of compassion.

"She has to know," I decide.

"Sean, you don't know for sure," she warns.

I leap up from the table. "I'm going to New York."

"Now?" Zara questions.

"Yep." I go into the bedroom and toss on some clothes.

"Sean, you're acting irrationally."

"Why am I acting irrationally? I need to talk to my mom."

"Sean, I don't think your mom knew anything. It seems to be painful for her too, bringing up your dad all the time and making her relive his death. It couldn't have been an easy time for her, knowing her husband had been murdered and having two young children to care for on her own."

My heart beats faster, and my gut dives. "Yeah, I know it was horrible for her, but I still need to talk to her."

"But what if she knows nothing and then you talk to her about stuff you shouldn't? The Omni will know!"

"I'll figure out how to talk to her about it without revealing anything," I claim.

"That's not possible."

"It is," I declare. I kiss Zara on the forehead and brush past her.

"Sean, you can't just fly off."

"I can and I will," I state as I leave the apartment.

I text my driver on the elevator ride to the lobby. Within minutes, I'm out of the building, in the SUV, and heading toward the private airport. I text my flight crew to get ready, and when we stop on the tarmac, I quickly get on the plane.

It takes a couple of hours to get to New York. When I get there, I go directly to the Marino compound.

I still have gate access, so I get to the front entrance and walk inside. I run into Dante's father, Angelo.

His face lights up when he sees me, and he grins. "Sean, what are you doing here?"

He's in his nineties, and still mentally sharper than anyone I know. He's also very mobile, thanks to this strict exercise program and diet his daughter, Arianna, insists on.

I hug him, replying, "It's good to see you, Angelo."

He hugs me back and then cups my cheeks. "I don't get to see you very often. I remember when you were little, and now look at you. You're all grown. A true man."

"Thank you. Is my mom here?"

He releases me. "I think she's in the sitting room."

I nod. "Thanks. I'll find you later, okay?"

"Sure." He pats me on the arms.

I brush past him, heading down the hallway. I enter the sitting room.

Mom's at her desk, working on her computer. She looks up. "Sean, what are you doing here?"

"I need to talk to you." I shut the door.

She rises. Her face turns pale. "What's wrong? Did something happen to Fiona?"

I hold my hands out. "No, Fiona's fine."

She releases an anxious breath. Even though we're adults, and Dante always assures her of our safety, she still worries about us.

I grab her hand and pull her over to the couch.

She sits, and I follow.

She softens her tone. "Sean, I know things were bad when we were in Chicago. I've been trying to think about how to get things back on track so there's no hard feelings between our family and the Marinos. I don't want that for you and Zara."

My heart swells. I admit, "I know we did it the wrong way. And I'm sorry for that."

She blinks hard. "Why did you do it like that? You know we love Zara. We would've been ecstatic for you had you done it correctly."

My stomach churns. "It just happened. You know how people in love are stupid and make bad decisions sometimes."

She pins her eyebrows together. "Well, when did you two start dating? And why did you keep it a secret?"

I take the easy out. "You know how Fiona is."

Mom nods. "Yeah, I do."

"Mom, I need you to focus, okay?"

"On what?"

"I need you to tell me what you know about Dad and the skull."

She sternly asserts, "Sean, I've told you all I know. Why do you keep insisting I know more? I don't. And if I did, I would tell you. But even Dante says you shouldn't have put that symbol on you."

"Dante doesn't know anything," I spout.

"Stop it. Dante's been a second father to you. You love him as one."

Guilt eats me. She's right. I sigh. "I know, but people don't make a big deal about nothing. So what's the real story?"

"I've told you all I know," she insists, hurt filling her expression and voice.

"You haven't," I accuse.

She starts to cry. She shakes her head with disappointment, grief, and anger in her expression.

"Mom, I'm sorry. I'm not trying to upset you."

She sniffles and looks toward the window. "Thinking about your father and how he died is painful. And I never liked that skull."

"Why?"

She turns toward me. "All it did was... It was painful for him when he got it, and it got infected, and it was disgusting. Then he went and tattooed it. It just seemed like self-mutilation to me. I've never understood it, Sean. And now you've gone and done it too, but you also put it on the back of Zara's neck. How could you allow that?"

More remorse fills me. But I know I had nothing to do with that decision. What I wanted didn't happen. It was out of my control. So I add, "I didn't force Zara to do anything."

"You're her husband. You're supposed to protect her."

"I tried," I say, and immediately regret it.

She studies me closer. "You tried what, Sean?"

"Just to get her not do it, but she wanted to because I did," I quickly lie.

Mom shakes her head in disappointment.

It rips at my heart. Yet I beg, "I need to know what you knew."

"I'm so tired of you accusing me of knowing something more. I've been honest with you," she insists and gets up. She puts her hand on her hip, and points at me. "You've never known how to let things lie, Sean. And you need to because I know nothing. I'm so sick and tired of being accused of things. I take full blame for what I did when you were a kid—full blame. But this? This isn't on me." More tears fall from her eyes, and it just makes me feel horrible.

I rise, deciding she doesn't know anything. Disappointed, I hug her, adding, "I'm sorry. I'll drop it."

She retreats and studies me.

"I will," I lie.

"Sometimes, I wish you weren't so much like your father."

"Meaning?"

She takes a few deep breaths, then states, "You're just as stubborn. And it tended to get him in trouble. So be smarter than him, Sean. Don't dig into things that have nothing to do with you, only to hurt those you love."

I ponder her statement.

She adds, "But he also did everything to protect your sister, you, and me. So lean into that, and ensure you protect your wife at all costs. Do better than you've recently done."

More guilt hits me. I cave. I vow not to bring my mom into this anymore. She doesn't know anything, and for some reason, my father didn't want her to.

Zara

Chapter

TWENTY-TWO

It's late at night. I have yet to hear from Sean, so I text him.

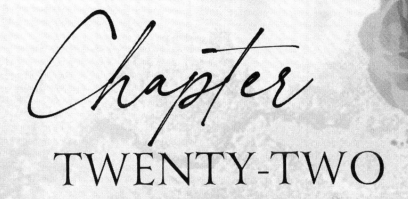

> Me: When will you be home?

> Sean: When I get there.

> Me: Seriously?

There's no response.

> Me: Thanks for being a dick, dear hubby.

I wait for a response, but the radio silence continues. I toss my phone in my purse, then go into the closet and grab a light scarf. I carefully put it around my neck so the plastic isn't showing.

I text my driver and then leave Sean's—our?—apartment. He pulls up to the curb just as I step outside. I get in before he can get out to open my door, and direct him to take me to Fiona's.

It's only a few blocks away. Since I have security clearance to her apartment, it doesn't take long before I'm standing at her door. I ring the bell twice.

She finally answers, glaring at me. "What do you want, Zara?"

I brush past her. "We need to talk."

"Why? So you can lie to me again?" she accuses.

I sigh. "Fiona, things are complicated. I didn't mean to lie to you. I'm sorry."

"Sure you are." She crosses her arms. "Is there anything else?"

"Don't be like that."

She studies me for a minute, then says, "Fine. But tell me what the skulls are really about."

My stomach churns.

She adds, "I saw how upset our parents were, so there's more to the story. And if my father was involved, I want to know. So tell me."

I decide to stop lying to her, mostly. I close my eyes, admitting, "Fiona, I want to tell you everything. I do. But I can't."

"Get out, Zara."

I open my eyes. "Please listen to me—"

"No, *you* listen to *me*. I'm tired of the lies. I'm tired of the secrecy. Just get out. Now!" She points at the door.

"Please. You're my best friend."

"Well, you have a funny way of showing that," she says. "Now, leave."

I decide it's best to let her cool off some more. "Fine, but I hope we can talk soon."

"Don't hold your breath," she warns.

I sigh and leave. I get in the elevator, but instead of stopping on the ground floor, it stops on floor three. The doors open.

Valentina beams at me from the other side. "Surprise!"

Confused, I question, "What are you doing here?"

She grins. "I'd like to tell you that. But you know how things are. Come on." She motions for me to get out of the elevator.

I obey.

She leads me down the hall to another part of the building. There's a service elevator. She pulls out a key card and scans it.

The elevator doors open.

We step inside, and she pushes the R button. The elevator ascends and then opens on the roof.

A helicopter is parked on the pad, its blades turning.

She yells, "I hope you like flying."

"Seriously?" I shout back.

She laughs and pulls me over to the helicopter.

The wind blows my hair everywhere. We climb inside, and the pilot helps us get situated. He hands us headsets, and I put mine on. Then he moves back to the front, prepares for takeoff, and lifts the chopper off the roof.

We're only in the air a few minutes before he lands at a private airport. We get off the helicopter and onto a private plane.

Within minutes, we're back in the air.

I question, "Where are we going?"

Valentina sighs. "Zara. I never know. You'll get used to it."

"I will?"

"Yeah. You'll get used to many things you never thought you would."

"Really?"

"Promise."

"Like what?"

She stares at me, then declares, "You'll learn to embrace the unknown because it always leads you forward."

I arch my eyebrows. "Why doesn't anyone ever give me a straight answer?"

She laughs, then says, "We have some time, so we should talk about something else...something important."

My pulse increases. "Am I in trouble?"

Her lips twitch. "No, not at all."

I relax, but then a new fear hits me. "Is Sean in trouble?"

"No." She pats me on the thigh. "Take a breather. Everything's fine."

I release an anxious exhale.

She studies me closer, and the familiarity sinks in again.

I blurt out, "Why do I feel like I know you, even though I know I've never seen you before the other night?"

She looks nervous at my question.

"Please tell me. And give me a straightforward answer."

"That's actually what I wanted to talk to you about."

"It is?"

"Yes." She opens her purse and pulls out a photo. I take it, and the hairs on my arms rise.

It's the photo of the woman, the baby girl, and my father. I gape at it, then snap my head toward her. "Why are you giving this to me again? Surely, you know I've already seen this."

"Yes, but you want answers, right?"

I nod.

She hesitates, then announces, "My mother is your father's sister."

My pulse increases. I state, "My dad only had brothers. The last one passed away last year."

She shakes her head. "No, that's not true. And your father and my mother were close."

"So we're cousins?"

She smiles. "Yes."

I suspiciously ask, "Why don't I know about your mother and you?"

She takes a deep breath, then reveals, "My mother fell in love with Marcello Abruzzo."

My eyes widen. I hurl, "The Abruzzos are horrible people! My father told me they don't respect women. They even traffic them!"

Her expression hardens. She swallows hard and nods, affirming, "That's correct, but not all of them are bad."

I cautiously admit, "I don't know if I can believe that statement."

Hurt fills her eyes. She claims, "It's true. And my father wasn't anything like the bad ones!"

I freeze as goose bumps raise along my skin.

She stares at me, then lowers her voice, insisting, "He wasn't like the other Abruzzos."

My insides quiver. The war between the Marinos and the Abruzzos has caused an incalculable amount of bloodshed. It's why it didn't make sense when my father was in those photos, looking happy with them. But there has to be more to the story, and maybe I should give Valentina the benefit of the doubt.

She adds, "I know this is hard to accept."

"It is, but my father looked like he was friends with them," I acknowledge, still confused.

"Yes, he looked like he was, but he wasn't," she claims.

"I don't understand."

She puts the puzzle pieces together for me, declaring, "That baby is me. I knew your father well as a little girl. But he didn't trust my father. He tried to get my mother to leave him, but she never would. My father was a good man."

"Then why did my dad want her to leave him?" I question.

"He was an Abruzzo. And your father refused to believe any of them could be good," she says, pain lacing her tone, then she tears up, adding, "My mother and I loved your father. But we also loved my father. He loved us. And your father was living a lie."

I defensively snap, "Meaning?"

"He was a spy sent to the Abruzzo clan so the Marinos could get intel on them."

"My father isn't a traitor," I seethe.

"He was in the Abruzzo's eyes," she states.

My stomach quivers. I stare at her, wanting to defend my father but needing to process what she's told me. The more I think about it, the more questions build within me.

She adds, "I never knew the truth until I joined The Underworld. I only knew your father was in my life and then suddenly he wasn't. None of them were for very long, though."

I furrow my brow. "What do you mean?"

She takes a deep breath. "As I stated, my father wasn't the typical Abruzzo. He knew your father was a traitor to the Abruzzo family, but instead of turning him in, he took my mother and me to Italy. We disappeared into the rural countryside. He made my mother promise never to contact your father again. In return, he only had interactions in The Underworld. He never got involved in Abruzzo business again unless the Omni ordered him to do so."

I gape at her, taking all of it in.

She stays quiet for a moment, watching me for my reaction, then says, "My father joined The Underworld because he believed in Sean O'Malley Sr.'s vision. He wanted peace between the families. He wanted me to not be scared to be an Abruzzo *or* Marino."

"Is that why Sean's father started The Underworld?"

"Yes. Hasn't your hubby told you everything he knows?" she questions.

An uneasiness fills me. "No," I admit, wondering why.

"I'm sure he would have eventually," she adds.

I shrug off the nagging feeling in my gut, then suggest, "Maybe we can talk to my father. Get him and your mom together again—"

"She's dead. So is my father," Valentina interjects.

I inhale sharply.

She swallows hard. "It's okay. They died together in a plane crash."

My heart hurts for her. I grab her arm. "Valentina, I'm so sorry."

She forces a smile. "It is what it is. But my father had a seat at the table. So did my mother."

"They were Omnis?" I question.

"Yes, and I'm getting closer to earning my spot, just like you are." She beams with pride.

Surprised, I admit, "I thought you were already at the table."

Her lips twitch. "Thanks for the compliment, but not yet."

"You're welcome."

I stare at the locked window shade and ask, "So you really don't know where we're going?"

"No. I only know about the situation and my orders."

I tilt my head. "What will happen when we get there?"

She laughs. "I can't tell you until we're there, but nice try."

I smirk. "Point for trying."

"Yeah, point for sure. And I'm sorry. I would tell you if I could," she claims and then stares at me for a moment. She finally adds, "It's really good meeting you and coming clean."

I smile and grab her hand. "Yeah, it is. I'm an only child, so it's nice to know about family."

"It is," she softly agrees.

A calm beat of silence falls between us.

Then something occurs to me. I ask, "The back of the photo said Aurora and Finzia. Who are they?"

"Aurora is my mother. My real name is Finzia Valentina Abruzzo. My parents started calling me Valentina when we moved to Italy. It's important no one knows I'm Finzia except for the Omni. Well, and now you," she explains.

I smile. "It's a pretty name."

She smiles back. "Thanks. You'll keep my secret, right?"

"Of course."

We talk for the next few hours about many things, but mostly about what our childhoods were like. When we finally land, we're led off the plane and down a hallway similar to the one I walked down before my initiation.

There's no spa setting when the door at the end of the hallway opens. It's a dark room. The only light is cast by several candles.

Two similar-looking women stand in a circle of flickering flames. Black rose petals surround them. They wear long, white satin gowns with spaghetti straps, and they're barefoot.

On one side of them is a small rectangular pool. The other side of the room has seven naked, fit, well-endowed men.

Butterflies erupt in my gut, and I glance nervously at Valentina.

"Don't worry, they're not for you," she murmurs.

What this is, and what am I about to be privy to?

Valentina takes my hand and leads me toward the two women. Once we reach them, she announces, "This is Maria Abruzzo, and this is Amalia Marino. They look a lot alike, don't they?"

"They sure do."

Valentina states, "Their blood is mixed. They're half-sisters, sharing the same mother."

"Wow. You look like twins," I blurt out, but they don't answer.

They both have olive skin, dark hair and eyes, a pointed nose, and thinnish lips.

Amalia is maybe an inch taller.

Valentina continues, "Zara, you get to pick which woman gets initiated into The Underworld."

My heart races. I glance at her, remembering what happened last time someone didn't get initiated.

She adds, "First, they'll pick which initiation they want. Then you'll decide who is worthy of completing initiation."

I shake my head. "I don't know how to choose."

Valentina nods. "Sure you do."

"Why can't we initiate both of them?" I ask, hoping there's some miracle.

Valentina's eyes turn to slits. She seethes, "One woman's a traitor. She's disclosed things about The Underworld to others that she shouldn't have. The other women has not. She has kept our secrets close to her heart. She's eligible to be initiated. So you must choose."

I gape at her.

"You can do it," she encourages.

"I don't know which of these women is a traitor," I scoff.

Valentina puts her fingers over my lips. Without room for negotiation, she asserts, "You will use your gut, and just know."

My anxiety escalates.

She refocuses on the women. "Now, before Zara picks, you two must decide which initiation you want. And it's up to you. Whatever you choose is what we will do if you survive."

I put my hand on my stomach. Bile rises, and I swallow it down.

Please don't make me kill anyone again.

Please don't make me kill anyone again.

Please don't make me kill anyone again.

I say this over and over in my head, but the dread in me grows.

Valentina points to the pool.

A man wearing a white robe and a skull mask kneels next to the water. He chants something low and incoherent.

She states, "You can choose the Ceremony of Water and Flames, which will baptize you into The Underworld. Or..." She points to the seven men.

They all stroke their erections, lewd expressions plastered on the faces.

Valentina continues, "Or you may choose the Binding of Flesh Ceremony. If chosen, these seven men will pound The Underworld into you."

I gape at Valentina.

"Don't look at me. Watch them," she instructs.

I refocus on the women.

Maria scans each of the men with a smirk on her face. "I choose Binding of Flesh all day and all night long. You can keep your Water and Flames."

Shock fills me at her response.

Valentina smiles in approval. "Excellent choice, although nothing is wrong with Water and Flames." She turns to Amalia. "And you? What would you choose? And there's no right or wrong."

Amalia looks at the men with just as much interest as Maria. She states, "Binding of Flesh. There's no other choice."

Valentina's tone grows stern. "But there is a choice. It's *your* choice. You're not being forced to do anything."

Amalia snaps, "There is no choice between water or men. I will always choose men and the force they can bring into my body. I look forward to my initiation." She lifts her chin, her eyes drifting over the seven suitors, then pins a challenging stare on Valentina.

"Well said, sister," Maria praises, then licks her lips, glancing at the men.

More shock fills me.

Valentina turns toward me. She announces, "It's time to choose, Zara.

Who is the traitor? Who is worthy to wear the skull and vie for a table seat, even though they may never get there?"

A flash of nausea passes through me. I look at Valentina. "I don't know. I can't decide. Please, do it for me."

"No." She lifts her chin and squares her shoulders. "*You* must do it. This comes from the Omni, not me. You must learn to rely on your gut and trust in it."

"Valentina—"

She puts her finger on my lips. "No more objections. Now, choose."

A claw scrapes in my gut. I step before Maria, studying her for what feels like forever. She never flinches, pinning her arrogant gaze on my anxiety-riddled one.

I move in front of Amalia, spending just as much time studying her. She gives me the same expression, but something passes in her eyes at some point, and I realize it's guilt.

Valentina asks, "Who will it be?"

I don't hesitate. I point at Amalia. "It's her. She's the guilty one."

"I am not!" she protests.

Valentina's face erupts in satisfaction and pride. "Good job. You are correct."

"I am?" I say with relief.

"Yes." She raises her arm and snaps her finger in the air.

A man appears with a Glock. He hands it to her.

Fear fills me.

Please, please, please! No!

She holds it out. "Now, kill her."

"Why me?" I question.

She gives me a sympathetic look. "Zara, I don't make the rules. This comes from the Omni."

Amalia takes several steps back, crying out, "I'm innocent! She's wrong!"

Valentina scoffs. "I know exactly what you've done, and Zara's one hundred percent correct." She turns back to me. "Now, shoot her."

Without thinking further, I point the Glock, pull the trigger, and shoot Amalia right in the heart.

She drops to the floor. Her blood stains her white dress, pooling all around her.

I stare at her in shock, feeling numb, wondering how I could do something so horrible once again.

Valentina spins me toward the men. She murmurs in my ear, "She was a traitor. You did well. Now, let's move on and enjoy the ceremony. This is one you'll remember, trust me."

I gape at her, my stomach flipping.

She leads Maria over to stand in front of the men.

A wall behind them opens. The largest bed I've ever seen, along with sex furniture, chains, handcuffs, and other tools, fills the area.

Maria slowly blows air out of her mouth.

Valentina asks, "Do you wish to switch to the Ceremony of Water and Flames?"

Maria scoffs. "Don't say such vile things."

Valentina's lips curve. She motions to two of the men.

They step forward and take Maria's hands. They lead her to the bed, with the others following.

Valentina states, "Follow me."

I obey, and she moves toward the others. As soon as we step past the wall, it slides shut behind us.

A reclining movie theater chair rises from the floor.

Valentina beams, pointing at it, ordering, "Sit down, dear cousin. The night's just beginning."

I do as she says, and she walks toward the door.

I call out, "Wait! Where are you going?"

She smirks. "This isn't my reward, it's yours. Enjoy." She disappears behind the door, leaving me bewildered and unable to look away from what's about to happen in front of me.

Sean

Chapter
TWENTY-THREE

"Zara," I call out as I enter the apartment.

She hasn't returned my text messages, and it's irritating me. I know she's upset. I shouldn't have texted her what I did earlier, but now she's just being immature.

"Zara," I call out again, but it's dead silent. My heart races faster. I dial her number, and it rings several times.

Her voice chirps, "You've reached Zara Marino. Please leave me a message, and I'll get back to you as soon as possible. Thanks!" A beep follows the message.

"Zara, call me," I say, then hang up. Then I pull up my texts.

> Me: Zara, message me back. Sorry I was a dick. Let me know you're okay.

I wait with my heart slamming against my chest. Nothing comes across my phone.

I text my sister.

> Me: I know you're pissed at me, but have you seen Zara?

A minute goes by, then I get a response.

> **Fiona:** She was here hours ago. We got into a fight, and she left. Why?

> **Me:** She's not home.

> **Fiona:** Maybe she left you. It would serve you right.

> **Me:** If you hear from her, let me know.

I call her driver. "Where's Zara?"

Calogero answers, "Sean, what can I do for you?"

"Where's my wife?"

"Your wife?" he asks.

"Where's Zara?" I say, forgetting that not everybody knows but surprised Luca hasn't updated him.

He replies, "I dropped her off at Fiona's. She hasn't come out yet."

"You dropped her off hours ago," I bark, fear overtaking me.

"Is something wrong?" he questions.

"Yeah. Find my fucking wife," I yell and then hang up. I pace the apartment.

Where the fuck is she?

I call Fiona.

"Sean, leave me alone," she says instead of a greeting.

"This isn't funny. Where's Zara?"

She lowers her voice. "Sean, I told you she left hours ago."

"Her driver is still waiting downstairs. She hasn't left the building, so where is she?"

My sister frets, "I don't know. She was here and left. Maybe we should call Luca."

"No, do not call her father. I'll handle this."

"But you don't even know where she's at," Fiona points out.

"I'll figure it out. She couldn't have gone far if she hasn't left the building." I hang up and fling open my front door, then freeze.

Byrne asks, "Want to figure out where your wife's at?"

"Where is she?" I ask in alarm.

"I'll take you to her."

"If anyone laid a hand on her—"

He holds his hands up. "Whoa, whoa, whoa. The Underworld doesn't hurt its members. You should know this. Or did you not read the rules?" He arches his eyebrows.

My panic starts to recede, but it doesn't completely go away. I snarl, "I mean it, Byrne, if anybody touched her..."

"Nobody's touching your wife. Now, come on." He takes several steps down the hall.

I follow.

We get in the elevator, and he hits the rooftop button.

I question, "Why are we going to the roof?"

"There's a helicopter up there."

"Seriously?"

"Aye," he replies.

Within minutes, we're flying over Chicago and then landing at a private airport. We board a plane, and once again, the window shades are locked so I can't see out.

I ask him, "When will all the secrecy go away?"

"When you have your seat at the table," he replies.

"But you know what's happening since you have your seat, right?"

"Aye, son, I know. But I don't have a seat at the table," he declares.

Shock fills me. I gape at him.

He asks, "Why do you look so surprised?"

"You claim you were my father's best friend. Why don't you have a seat at the table?"

"I don't want one."

I jerk my head backward.

He chuckles, then states, "Not everybody decides to take their seat."

"Why wouldn't you take your seat?" I press.

"Not all of us are cut out for it. I like my role. It's better this way. For me at least. But you..." He points at me. "You are meant to take your seat."

I stare at him.

He sits back and takes his tattered beret off. He runs his hands through his messy, orange hair, then says, "If you don't mind, I'm a bit tired. I'm going to take a quick snooze."

"Yeah, no problem," I murmur.

He puts his seat back and closes his eyes. He's soon snoring.

I stare in front of me, tapping my thigh, wondering what Zara is involved in, and vowing that if anyone has touched her, I'll kill them.

We finally land and get off the plane. It's a similar hallway to the one from initiation night.

We get to a door, and Byrne stops me from turning the knob. "Hold on a minute, son."

I glance at him, arching my eyebrows.

He pulls out a pocket knife and says, "You might want this."

Anxiety flares within me. "Why? What are they doing to my wife?"

He shakes his head. "Nothing. But take this. Your father gave it to me. It's time you have it."

Emotions choke my throat. I stare at the knife, putting my fingers over the Celtic knots, and then look closer. *O'Malley* is engraved on it.

Byrne says, "It's yours now."

"Thank you."

"Now, before you go in there, you need to know something."

"What's that?" I ask.

"There's a ceremony going on."

"If my wife—"

"Enough!" he barks, his cheeks flaring maroon.

I shut my mouth.

"The ceremony is not for your wife. She's merely watching it. If you go in there, you cannot get involved in the ceremony. Do you understand?"

I nod. "Yes, of course."

"Okay, now you may move freely about and do what you want, but do not interrupt the Ceremony of the Binding of Flesh."

"Binding of flesh?"

"Yes. You'll soon understand."

"Are they burning everybody?" I question.

He chuckles. "Not quite, but it's probably going to be pretty hot in there." He winks.

Confusion fills me. All I know is I want to get inside and make sure my wife is safe.

He pats me on the shoulder. "All right, lad, have a good evening. Anytime you're ready to leave, just come right back through this door. The plane will take you home."

"Okay, thank you." I open the door and step through it.

Byrne shuts it quickly. It takes me a minute to realize what I'm seeing.

Erotic sounds fill the air. Men grunt, and a woman cries out incoherent sounds.

The hairs on my neck rise.

Jesus, it's an orgy.

No, it's a gang bang.

One, two, three, four, five, six...fucking hell, there's seven of them.

The woman looks exhausted, yet not in a bad way. Her flushed face burns bright. The bed's soaked, and she's currently cuffed to a headboard with her ass in the air.

Two men push inside her. One's underneath her, and the other is behind her. A third stands next to her, holding her head to the side and thrusting his cock in her mouth.

Four other men stand beside them, rubbing themselves and waiting their turn.

I panic, looking around until I see Zara.

She's sitting in a movie theater chair, leaning forward and intently watching the scene. Her face is slightly flushed, and her chest is rising and falling in short bursts.

I rush over to her and kneel beside the chair, putting my hand on hers.

She slowly tears her gaze off them, and her eyes widen when she sees it's me. She murmurs, "Sean, what are you doing here?"

"What are *you* doing here?" I question.

"Shh."

The woman begins screaming, and Zara and I snap our heads toward the scene.

The man behind the woman is tugging her hair, her head tilted so far back, she's staring at the ceiling. He's ramming his cock into her ass. Another man's continuing to thrust inside her pussy. The third man sprays his cum on her cheek.

My first instinct is that they're hurting her, but then I realize they're not.

She cries out, "More! I need more!"

Two men approach, one on each side of her, and start tugging her nipples.

She shrieks, "Yes! Yes! Oh God!"

I glance over at my wife and lean toward her ear. "Is this turning you on?"

She holds her breath and then turns toward me, and I see the arousal in her eyes.

I keep my voice level but fear what she'll reply, asking, "Is that what you want? A bunch of men doing that to you?"

She whispers, "No, but I like watching it. Is that weird?"

A wave of relief hits me. I stroke her hair, tucking it behind her ear, and answer, "No."

She turns. "Is it strange I'm turned on?"

"Oh God, fuck me harder!" the woman cries out.

My lips twitch. "No."

Zara doesn't flinch, ordering, "Then fuck me now, Sean."

My dick hardens. "Here?"

She nods. "Yes, here."

"You're serious?" I murmur.

Her lips twitch, and she nods.

I rise, shed my clothes, and motion for her to stand.

She obeys.

I slowly tug her shirt off over her head, unbutton her jeans, and slide them to the floor. I push her back onto the seat and then slowly pull the denim off her legs.

She holds her breath in anticipation.

I run my hands from her ankles, over her shins, and up the insides of her thighs, then softly stroke her slit.

She closes her eyes and whimpers.

I move my mouth to her leg, kissing her until I get to her pussy.

The grunts from the men turn louder.

The woman cries out, "Two! I need two of you in my ass!"

Jesus fucking Christ.

Zara's eyes fly open. I slide my hand up her torso, playing with her breasts, and then suck on her clit.

"Oh," she moans.

I flick my tongue across her, then circle it, lazily lapping up her arousal and inhaling her scent, wondering why I waited all these years to take what was always due to be mine.

She slides her hand over my head, playing with my hair, and I increase the speed of my tongue lashing against her.

"Oh God," she quietly murmurs.

The woman screams, "Yes! Oh, fuck yes!"

I suck on Zara's clit until it swells, then shove two fingers inside her, and she moans loudly.

I mumble against her pussy, "So wet without me here, my little brat."

"I've been naughty," she whispers.

My cock hardens further. I take my time licking and sucking, flicking her at a torturous speed, enjoying every moment. Before I know it, even though I'm going slow, she's coming, gripping my hair, shaking against me.

"Oh my God, Sean! Oh my God!" she cries out.

I chuckle, then suck her harder.

She arches her back, and I lunge up, pushing her thighs to her chest, and enter her.

She moans.

I thrust in and out of her until she's convulsing against me, and I'm about to come.

But then a man steps next to us, his dick practically in my face.

I jump back. "What the fuck are you doing?"

He acts like nothing's wrong. "I came to join in. I've been thinking about your wife since your initiation," he declares, as if it's a compliment I'll appreciate.

I take my fist, pull it back, and hit him so hard in the nose, I break it. Blood spurts everywhere.

"Sean," Zara cries out.

I bark, "Put your clothes on."

She doesn't argue, grabbing her clothes off the floor.

Another man approaches, asking, "What's going on?"

I pick my jeans up off the floor and take the pocket knife out, whipping it open. I warn, "If anyone touches my wife, you're not leaving here alive. Is it understood?"

The scene on stage doesn't stop, the fucking continuing, the woman screaming and moaning her pleasure.

The second man puts his hands in the air. "Noted."

The one with the bloody nose rises, holding his face. "What the fuck did you do that for?"

I point my knife at him with the blade an inch from his chest. "If you ever touch my wife again or come near her, I'll fucking kill you."

"Easy, man. I was just in the moment," he claims.

"'In the moment'? You're supposed to be part of that ceremony, right?"

He looks back. "Yeah."

"You know what? Fuck you," I say, and slice my knife down his arm.

"What the fuck, man?" he shrieks, backing up.

I step closer, holding the knife out, and threaten, "Don't you ever even think about my wife again. Zara, let's go." I spin and grab her arm, leading her toward the door. I open it, move her through, then shut it.

I lock the knob and then spin her against the wall, fretting, "Are you all right?"

She nods. "Yeah. But, Sean, I don't think you should have done that."

"I didn't mess up the ceremony. They did," I claim.

Her expression turns more worrisome. "Sean."

"No one's touching you, Zara. No one's coming near you, and especially not with their dick near your face. They better not even think about it. Do you understand me?"

She nods.

I add, "Unless that's what you wanted?"

"Of course that's not what I wanted. I told you I wanted you, not any of them."

Relief hits me. "Good." I step back and grab my shirt from her, ordering, "Put your shirt on. Thanks for bringing my clothes." I kiss her on the lips.

She returns my affection.

I retreat, tug my shirt over my head, then slide into my jeans.

I lead her out and back onto the plane. We don't speak until we're in the air and I've calmed a bit. My heart finally stops racing, and I pull her into me. I kiss her head, adding, "I'm sorry if I scared you."

She looks up at me with tears in her eyes. She blurts out, "I killed somebody else."

My insides quiver. "What are you talking about?"

She starts to sob.

I tug her closer. "My pulse, what's wrong? Tell me what happened."

She wails, babbling, "I killed her. I had to choose who was the traitor, and I killed her. And Valentina is my cousin, but I killed the Marino

335

lady without thinking twice. Sean, I'm a horrible person!" She sobs, her tears drenching my shirt.

"Shh. No, you're not. Why were you with Valentina?"

"She just showed up."

"What do you mean she's your cousin?"

Zara pushes away, sniffling. "My dad had a sister. It was her mom, and she married an Abruzzo, but... Well, supposedly he wasn't a bad one, and my dad wouldn't believe it. He joined The Underworld. He believed in your dad's vision. He wanted peace."

I stay silent.

Her face falls further. "Sean, haven't you told me everything you know about The Underworld?"

I shrug. "We haven't had a lot of time to talk about things. But why haven't you told me what you know?"

She hesitates, then winces. "I don't know."

"Well, now that we're married, I think we don't have to worry about the secrecy."

"No more secrets, Sean," she states.

"Okay." I tug her back into me. "I'm sorry. Really."

"Why is it so easy for me to kill people?" she questions.

I lean down to look into her eyes, cupping her cheeks and brushing her tears with my thumbs. "It's in our blood. It just is. It doesn't make you a bad person."

"How can it not make me a bad person? I took two people's lives," she claims.

"You said Valentina said the woman was a traitor, correct? And you saw it in her?"

Zara bites her lip, and more tears fall. She nods.

"Okay then. She was a traitor. Traitors deserve to die, so don't worry about this any further."

She starts to sob again, and I hold her, wishing there was something better I could say to make her pain go away. But I'm unsure how, and I'm realizing that I need to get better.

I'm her husband. I need to protect her from this stuff.

If anyone's going to be killing anyone, it should be me, not her.

Zara

A Month Later

Chapter
TWENTY-FOUR

"Knock, knock," Amy's voice calls out.

I glance up from the briefing I've been working on and smile at her. "Hey, what's up?"

She steps inside my office with a box wrapped in brown shipping paper. She sets it on my desk.

The top has *Zara O'Malley* and *Private* handwritten on it.

My butterflies flutter. It's the first time I've seen my first name paired with O'Malley after it.

Am I changing it?

Yes.

No. I already changed it from Moulin to Marino when my father came into my life.

That doesn't have anything to do with taking my husband's name.

Amy interrupts my thoughts, relaying, "A courier delivered this. He said he was instructed to ensure you're the one opening it." She lowers her voice, wincing. "He's waiting outside your door. He's very persuasive."

I lean to the side, glancing around her body, and see a young man with a nose ring. He nods at me.

"Hey there," I say.

"You can't open it in front of anyone else," he blurts out.

I question, "Who's this from?"

"You'll know when you open it. Take care, Mrs. O'Malley."

Mrs. O'Malley.

He turns and exits my sight.

Amy stands on the other side of desk, her gaze pinned to the package. She whispers, "What do you think it is?"

I remind her, "It says it's private."

She nods.

"I'm the only one who's supposed to see it," I add.

"Oh! Yeah! Right! Okay!" She turns and walks toward the door.

"Thanks, Amy. Can you shut the door on the way out?" I say.

She looks over her shoulder, and disappointment flares in her expression and voice. "Sure."

She pouts and then mutters, "I never get to know any of the fun stuff." She steps out of my office and shuts the door.

I look at the box, staring at the writing, with my heart racing.

What did they send me now?

I can't be sure it's from the Omni.

Clients send me all kinds of crazy things, but they aren't always something I want to have in my possession. So I don't like surprises at my office.

I take a few deep breaths, reach into my desk, pull out a letter opener, and use it to slit the tape holding the box closed. I slide the inside box out and open the lid.

I remove a wad of red tissue paper, and find a small hard drive at the bottom of the box.

"What is this?" I mumble, deciding it must be regarding one of my clients.

My mind races through my current caseload, wondering who this could pertain to. I almost plug it into my computer, then stop myself.

I set the drive down and open my larger desk drawer. There's a laptop inside. I use it when I don't know what's on an external drive. Call it paranoia, but Sean lectured Fiona and me too many times on how to protect our technology from viruses.

I pull out the laptop. I turn it on and wait for it to load. Then, I slide the drive into the computer and double-click on the file.

A video pops up. The image it's paused on says "Happy viewing" over a black background.

A shiver racks my body. I take a deep breath, press play, and my gut immediately takes a nosedive.

My father, at a younger age, appears on the screen. There's no sound, but it looks like he's threatening a man, and they're arguing back and forth. Then my father takes out a knife and stabs the man several times.

In horror, I put my hand over my mouth, and the name Yury Ivanov flashes on the screen.

My gut churns faster.

Another man appears. My father shoots him in the head. The screen then shows the name Danny O'Connor.

Bile rises in my throat. I swallow hard, pushing it down, unable to tear my gaze off the screen.

Another man is killed by my father, and Arthur O'Malley's name appears.

A fourth man, called Kosmo Marino, also loses his life before the video ends.

I sit back in my chair, my gaze glued to the laptop, unable to calm my insides. Then I hit play, rewatching it, my head spinning with questions, just as horrified as the first time I saw it.

How could he kill anyone with those last names?

I killed my own blood, I remind myself.

I squeeze my eyes shut, trying to forget how I killed a Marino, as well as the man who wanted me to choose him at the initiation ceremony.

Something in me makes me watch the video again. Over and over, I watch my father kill men who aren't enemies.

I don't understand it, and I need answers. So I pick up my phone and go into my text messages.

> Me: Are you still in town?

It doesn't take long before my father replies.

> Dad: Yes.

> Me: I need to talk to you. Can I come over?

> Dad: Of course.

> Me: I'm leaving work now.

> Dad: I'll see you soon, my beautiful figlia.

I take a deep breath, toss my phone into my purse, then pull the drive out of the computer. I zip it in the inside compartment of my bag for safekeeping, then shut down the computer.

I last spoke with my parents in person when we saw each other in Sean's apartment. We've barely texted, and when we do, it always ends in an argument.

Now, there's no time to think about our strained relationship. The images of what I've done, especially to a woman who was my blood relative, won't go away. It mixes with the horror of what my father's done. The guilt eats at me, mixing with the unanswered question.

Why did he do it?

I leave my office and tell Amy, "I have to go. I'm not sure if I'll be back today."

She arches her eyebrows in question. "Where are you going?"

I'd groan inside, but I love Amy. She always wants to know everyone's business.

"Out," I reply, brushing past her and quickly stepping into the elevator. I text my driver.

The elevator stops on several floors. By the time I leave the building, Calogero is waiting. He opens the door to the back seat. "Ms. Marino."

"Calogero, I need to go to my father's house."

"Yes, ma'am." I slide into the back seat, and he shuts the door.

He walks around the car, gets in, then merges into traffic.

My parents' penthouse isn't far, but there's a traffic jam. When I finally get there, my stomach churns again.

Calogero parks, comes around to open the door, and pins me with a look of concern. "Ms. Marino, are you okay?"

I take a deep breath and step out of the car. "Yes."

"Are you sure? You look pale," he states.

"I'm fine. I'll text you when I'm ready to leave," I say.

He follows me into the building.

"Calogero, you don't need to walk me up to my parents' penthouse."

He chuckles. "You know I do."

I sigh and then remind myself to talk to Sean. It's been a month since we married, and he told my father he wasn't in charge of my security anymore. It may be time for him to make good on that so I don't have Calogero following my every move. Surely, Sean won't be this ridiculous.

We get in the elevator. Calogero punches the code for my parents' penthouse.

We quickly ascend, and the elevator doors open on the top floor.

My father's waiting for me. "My beautiful *figlia*," he says, pulling me into him.

I hug him back. It's been strange not having the usual relationship with my parents that I'm used to. As much as I've wanted to try and make things right between us all, I can't seem to do it. I've found it easier to ignore them while they're here.

"Is Mom here?" I ask.

"She just got back from her yoga class. She's in the shower," he states.

My chest tightens, and I meet his eyes with mine. "Good. I don't want her to hear us talking."

His eyes turn to slits. "What's going on, Zara?"

"We need to go somewhere private," I state.

Dad doesn't say anything as he leads me into his office and closes us inside. He points to the couch. "Sit down."

I obey.

He takes a seat and turns toward me. He grabs my hands. "Tell me what's going on."

I open my mouth, but I'm unsure where to start, so I snap it shut.

"My *figlia*, what's wrong? I'm your father. Tell me," he urges.

I blurt out, "Why did you kill them?"

The color drains from his face. "Kill who?"

My mouth turns dry. "The Ivanov man, for one."

His gaze hardens. "Don't speak such things."

"I saw it," I say, feeling emotional, tears welling in my eyes.

He studies me closer, holding his breath.

I add, "I don't know who I am anymore. I don't know who you are. And I don't know why you would kill an Ivanov."

His eyes blaze bright. He lowers his voice, trying to keep it steady. "I don't know what you saw, but you've never seen me kill a man."

My voice shakes. "You killed Yury Ivanov, Danny O'Connor, Arthur O'Malley, and Kosmo Marino."

His eyes widen.

"Don't lie to me, Dad. I saw it," I say, then swallow the lump in my throat.

"That's impossible," he mutters.

I shake my head. "It's not. I have a video of it."

He stares at me, momentarily speechless, then demands, "I want to see this video."

I shake my head. "No."

He seethes, "What do you mean, no?"

"It doesn't matter. The only thing on it is you killing those men."

"Who would send you such a thing?" he questions.

"Just tell me why you killed them," I beg.

He looks away and takes his hand off mine. He puts it on his thigh, and it trembles. I stare at it, and he slowly closes it into a fist.

"Dad?"

He jerks his head toward mine. "Who is doing this?"

"Doing what?"

"Sending you photos and videos about my past! Things you should not know and which are not your concern."

I soften my tone, putting my hand back on his. "I can't unsee what I've seen, Dad. Tell me why you killed them."

He snarls, "They were enemies."

"Ivanov? O'Malley? O'Connor? Your own flesh and blood, a Marino? How are they an enemy?" I cry out. And then the heavy remorse over the people I killed floods me again.

Bile tries to rise up my throat, and I put my hand on my stomach, swallowing it down.

"You look sick. Do you need the bathroom?" Dad questions.

I close my eyes for a minute, breathing through the nausea, then shake my head, claiming, "I want to know everything. And I know about Aurora and Finzia."

My father's face fills with shock.

A chill races across my skin.

He doesn't say anything for a few moments, then he asks, "How would you know about her? Who's revealing things to you that need to stay buried?"

I cry out, "Why does Finzia need to stay buried? There's nothing wrong with her."

He warns, "You don't know who she is."

"No, you don't know who she is!" I insist.

He puts his finger in the air. "Listen to me closely, my *figlia*. You are to stay away from her."

My voice raises. "I'm not staying away from her. She's my family. *Our* family."

"What's going on in here?" Mom interjects.

I glance at the door.

Her hair is wet, and she's in her pink robe. Her gaze darts between my father and me.

Dad blurts out, "Someone is poisoning Zara's mind."

"My mind is not poisoned."

"You don't unbury the dead. Is this your husband's doing? I'll kill him!" he snarls.

"No! Sean has nothing to do with this!" I declare.

"Then who is it?" he demands.

"I don't know."

"Don't lie to me!"

My eyes fill with tears. "I'm not! And Finzia is your flesh and blood. Do you even know your sister's dead?"

"Zara!" Mom gasps, putting her hand over her mouth.

The color drains from Dad's cheeks. He opens his mouth and slowly shakes his head. "What are you talking about?"

"You didn't know, did you?" I push.

"Zara, how did you get that information?" Mom asks.

Surprised, I ask her, "You know about Finzia and Aurora?"

"I told you I don't keep secrets from your mother. Of course she knows about them," he says.

"Then we should welcome her into our family. She doesn't have anybody anymore. Her parents are dead."

Pain flashes across my father's expression, but then he snarls, "Good. Another Abruzzo off this planet."

My insides quiver. "You're not being fair. He wasn't one of them."

"He was."

"Why are you any better when you've killed our family friends?" I challenge.

"Zara!" Mom reprimands, her voice shaking.

Dad's eyes blaze. "You don't know anything! I suggest you stay out of my business."

"Then explain it to me," I demand.

His face turns red. He fumes, "They were enemies. Traitors."

"Like you were?" I accuse.

His head jerks backward, a mixture of disbelief and betrayal on his face.

"Zara!" Mom scolds again, rushing to Dad's side and putting her hand on his shoulder.

He glances at her.

"Just tell me the truth. I'm not a child anymore."

My parents stare at each other.

"Let's just be honest for once and for all," I plead.

Mom shakes her head. She quietly tells my father, "This is getting out of control, Luca. Maybe the truth is best."

"She's my beautiful *figlia*," he says sadly.

She runs her hand through his hair. "Yes, but somehow she's learning bits and pieces. She should hear it from you rather than someone else."

He studies me.

My pulse races faster.

He finally says. "Finzia. She must be the one poisoning you."

"No, she's not!"

Dad grits through his teeth, "Her father was a disgusting Abruzzo. He stole my sister's life."

"How did he do that? You didn't even know she was dead until now!" I fume.

Another flare of pain erupts on his sharp features before the anger returns. He snarls, "He impregnated her. He made her fall in love with him. He made her part of that family—a family where she couldn't even be honest about the blood running through her veins!"

A tear falls down my cheek. I shake my head, asserting, "Not everybody's the enemy."

"You don't know who the enemies are," he snaps.

"But you always do?" I question.

He points at me. "You were not part of my past or that world. And I don't want you to have anything to do with it! Whoever's trying to pull you into it, I need to know."

I rise and lift my chin. "No one's pulling me into anything."

He turns toward Mom. "It has to be Sean."

Rage fills me. I explode, "That's not true! Sean does nothing but protect me, and for you to think anything different... Well, you should be ashamed of yourself."

"Zara, do not speak to your father that way," Mom scolds.

I turn to her. "You're just as bad as him. You cover up his secrets. You allow him to play the role of a traitor and then kill those who do exactly what he did."

"Zara!" Mom spouts.

Dad growls, "You don't know what traitors do."

"But what do *we* do?" I ask.

"We?" he asks, pinning his dark gaze to mine.

I freeze.

"My beautiful *figlia*, what have you done?" His voice is tinged with more than a little fear.

My chest tightens. I shake my head, lying, "Nothing."

There's something in Dad's eyes.

He knows I've killed people.

"Zara." He reaches for my hand, but I pull it back.

"I have to go." I stand and rush toward the door.

He follows me, Mom right behind him, demanding, "Zara, I want to know what you meant."

I spin to face them. "I meant that you and I have difficulty forgiving people or looking past things. I'm learning that we're wrong. And you're wrong about Finzia, Dad."

"I'm not," he insists.

"You are. But you know what's worse?"

He arches a brow.

"She misses you."

He flinches, then his expression goes stony.

A tear falls down my cheek, and I add, "She remembers you."

He clenches his jaw and looks away, blinking hard.

I continue, "She's all alone."

Dad doesn't say anything and won't look at me.

I wipe my face, declaring, "I have to go." I press the elevator button.

"Zara—"

"I can't stay, Mom," I interrupt, stepping into the elevator.

I forget to text Calogero, and I step out of the building.

He pulls up, and I slide into the back seat before he can get out of the SUV. He frets, "Ms. Marino, you're supposed to text me."

"I forgot. Please take me home."

He sighs, then drives toward my place, lecturing me on safety.

I look out the window and groan. "Not my place. Sean's."

"Yes, ma'am." He turns around and takes me to the apartment. He walks me up, and I don't argue, too exhausted to fight another losing battle.

When I get inside, I open a bottle of wine. I'm tired, mentally burned out, and emotionally torn. I hate how I don't have the same relationship with my parents anymore.

It hurts me that Dad can't even consider Valentina a good person just because of her father's last name.

I pour my wine, then take it to the couch. I curl up, take a sip, and put it on the table. I slide down, gripping the pillow.

At some point, I fall asleep.

"Hey, my pulse." Sean's tone is soft.

I blink hard.

It's dark, and the lights from the city shine through the windows.

"Hey," I reply.

His fingers stroke my cheek. "It's bedtime."

I sit up. "What time is it?"

"It's late. Come on." He scoops me into his arms, picking me up off the couch.

I bury my head in his neck, inhaling his scent.

"Are you all right?" he asks, walking into the bedroom. He pulls the covers back and sets me down.

"I don't know," I admit.

Concern fills his expression. "What's going on?" He sits next to me and unbuttons my blouse.

I sniffle. "I don't want to get into it. Not now, please."

He studies me for a minute. "Okay."

He helps me undress, then orders, "Scoot down."

I slide under the sheets.

He takes his clothes off and gets in next to me. He pulls me to him, spooning me and kissing the back of my neck.

I soon fall asleep, but I'm haunted all night by dreams of both my father and I killing people.

Every time I scream in my sleep, Sean's there, trying to find out what's wrong. But I can't talk about it. I'm too ashamed and confused.

He doesn't push, comforting me until I fall back asleep, then he holds me tighter the next time I wake up screaming.

When morning comes, we've barely gotten any sleep. Sean still wants answers, but I give him nothing, not wanting to talk about my sins or my father's.

Sean

Two Months Later

Chapter
TWENTY-FIVE

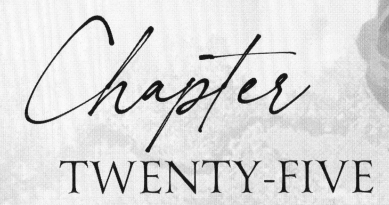

"Can you go to work a little bit late this morning?" I ask Zara.

She puts her lipstick down. "I suppose. What's going on?"

Excitement and a bit of anxiety fill me. I lean closer and declare, "I can't tell you."

Her lips twitch. She tilts her head and squints. "What are you up to, Sean O'Malley?"

I chuckle. "You'll see. Hurry up and finish getting ready."

She glances at her reflection in the mirror, shakes out her curls, then chirps, "I'm ready."

I pat her ass. "Good. I'll drop you off at work later." I grab her hand and lead her into the other room.

She giggles. "Where are we going?"

"It's a surprise, Mrs. O'Malley." I wiggle my eyebrows.

"The suspense is killing me," she admits, and grabs her purse off the table.

I guide her out of the apartment, through the building, and into the SUV.

As soon as we get inside, she questions, "Tell me again where we're going?"

I wiggle my finger in front of her. "Uh-uh-uh. I'm not spilling."

She huffs. "Aw. Just give me a little hint?"

I chuckle and add, "I think you'll like it."

She pouts. "That's not giving me a hint."

"Sorry. That's all you're getting," I declare, then kiss her hand.

My driver goes several blocks and pulls up to a building that's bustling with activity. There's a coffee shop, several boutiques, and a restaurant on the ground level.

She teases, "Aw, you're taking me to my favorite coffee shop and then on a shopping spree? That's sweet of you!"

"Nope!" I shake my head, grinning, and exit the car. I reach inside for her and help her out, taunting, "Guess again, my little brat."

She gushes, "Don't get me all hot and bothered before work."

I grunt, the space near my zipper getting tighter. I lead her past the coffee shop and into the residential lobby.

She asks, "What are we doing here?"

I nod at security. Casey motions for us to pass him, greeting, "Good morning, Mr. O'Malley."

"Morning, Casey."

"Is this Mrs. O'Malley?"

"It is," I reply, puffing my chest out. The pride I have that Zara's my wife grows daily.

Casey offers, "Nice to meet you, Mrs. O'Malley."

"You too," she replies, giving me a questioning look.

I push the button for the elevator, then lean closer to her. "When are you taking care of officially changing your name?"

Surprised, she arches her eyebrows.

I've never said anything to her about it. I've been waiting for her to do it, but now I'm growing impatient. It's time for her to take her rightful name—*my* name.

The elevator dings, and the doors open. People step out.

I lead her inside, press my hand on the pad, and the doors shut. I add, "You didn't think I would let you keep your maiden name, did you?"

She scoffs. "Allow me?"

"Yeah."

"You don't have the authority to give me permission," she claims.

"Like hell, I don't."

"Like hell, you do," she argues.

The elevator stops, and the doors open.

I usher her into a brightly lit, beautifully accessorized foyer. Expensive artwork with bright colors hangs on the walls. An intricately carved gold pot contains a light pink cherry blossom tree.

She points at it, asking, "How do they keep that alive in here?"

"The ceiling has indoor grow lights, and they make sure its soil has proper drainage," I tell her.

"Seriously?" She gapes, glancing up.

"Yep. But why don't you want to change your name?" I push, opening the door to the main area.

357

She steps through and stops just inside the doorway.

My anxiety spikes. I step up next to her and ask, "What's wrong?"

"That view of Lake Michigan is insane!" she gushes, then hurries across the perfectly decorated family room. She stands in front of the window, watching the waves crash against the shore.

I breathe a sigh of relief. "Yeah, it's pretty badass. What do you think about how the space is laid out?"

She turns and strolls over to the chef's kitchen, running her hand over the quartz countertop, stating, "These are gorgeous! I love how the blue resembles waves against the bright white." She steps between the oversized island and the back counter, taking it all in, then adds, "The view of the city is cool too!"

I nod, then grab her hand, tugging her toward the hallway. "Let's look at the rest of it."

"Whose place is this?" she asks.

"You'll see."

She lowers her voice, stating, "It's so early in the morning for visitors. Do they even know we're here?"

I chuckle, shaking my head. "Don't worry about it. What do you think of the bedrooms?" I open a door.

She steps inside the suite and raves, "It's beautiful!"

"Agreed. There are three other similar ones. And what about the offices?" I lead her to another room.

She glances at the modern white desk with silver legs, a designer couch, and more expensive artwork. "I want to work here."

I mentally high-five myself. Then I move her across the hall. A brown desk and a matching leather couch fill the space.

She tilts her head and blurts out, "If we lived here, this would be your office. I'd take the other one."

My lips twitch. I ask, "What about the gym?"

"Where is it?"

I step into the hall and point to another door.

She passes me and praises, "This is pretty kickass!"

Free weights, cardio and strength machines, an area with a hanging bag to kick are all situated on a wooden floor. Mirrors cover two walls.

I pull her out of the gym. "Come on. I want to show you the rest of it." I take her to the other side of the apartment and open another door.

The primary suite is just as stunning as the rest of the house, with a similar view of Lake Michigan as the main area.

"This place is incredible. But who lives here? Enough of the suspense," she says.

I puff out my chest, then step in front of a closet door. I open it and motion for her to go inside.

She gapes, glancing around. She mutters, "This is insane."

I've added some designer clothes and shoes, but the items don't fill the space. There's still plenty of room for our stuff, which is secretly getting packed as we speak.

I order, "Open the top drawer."

She arches her eyebrows. "I'm allowed to be nosy?"

I chuckle. "Yeah. Open it."

She bites on her lip as she obeys.

"Go ahead. Pull it out," I direct.

She holds up the black lingerie, smirking. "Well, this is interesting."

"Yeah, it's going to look amazing on you," I declare.

Her cheeks flush, and my cock hardens. She carefully asks, "Sean, did you buy this place?"

Pride fills me. "Yep. I sure did!"

Her eyes light with excitement, yet she hesitates before asking, "For us?"

I grunt. "Why else would I have bought it?"

She claps and jumps up and down. "Yay! Seriously? You bought this for us?"

Happiness floods me. Dmitri and Anna Ivanov's daughter, Mariya, helped me. "Yes. I had Mariya decorate it. Anna said she was ready to start taking on her own projects. Mariya said it was your style."

She tosses her arms around me, babbling, "Oh my gosh, it is. She nailed it! Thank you so much. Seriously? This is ours?"

I slide my hand onto her ass. "Sure is."

"Really?" she asks, tearing up.

"Yep." I put my hands on her cheeks and kiss her until we're both out of breath. I retreat and say, "Come on. There's something I need to do."

"What's that?"

Without answering, I pull her back into the kitchen. Then I announce, "There's something that sealed the deal for me."

"What was that?" she questions.

I move her to the side of the island, facing away from me, then reach around her and unbutton her blazer.

She turns her head and smiles, suggesting, "Don't leave me in suspense."

I tug her blazer off and toss it several feet away. Then I put my hands on her thighs, bunching her skirt to her waist.

She shifts, pushing her ass into my pelvis.

I put my face next to hers and nod at the window, instructing, "Look at the building directly across from us."

She pins her gaze on it.

"A floor below the penthouse," I tell her.

She refocuses her gaze and gasps.

Two men stand near the window with a woman sandwiched between them; they're all naked.

I announce, "That woman has two or more men over every morning at the same time. Always by the window."

"Shut up," she breathes, unable to take her eyes off the threesome.

I slide my fingers over the thin material of her thong.

She bites on her lip, her eyes full of fire.

One of the men sits on a lounger. The woman straddles him, and the second man leans over and kisses her neck.

"Holy shit," she murmurs.

I pump my fingers inside her, kissing her neck.

The same expression she wore at the Binding of Flesh appears on her face. She whispers, "Sean."

My lips brush her ear. I murmur, "I remember how you like to watch."

Her cheeks turn red.

I swipe my tongue over her lobe and splay my hand on her spine, pushing her onto the cold quartz. I release my pants and the sound of my belt hitting the floor ricochets in the air.

She inhales sharply, glancing back at me.

"Don't watch me. Watch them, my little brat," I insist. I take my foot and slide her feet farther apart.

She glances back at the throuple. Both men are inside the woman now.

"That's so hot," Zara blurts.

With one thrust, I push inside her.

"Oh my God," she cries out, and her insides pulse around me.

I don't hold back, thrusting into her at the same pace the men thrust into the woman. I bark, "Tell me how you like it, my little brat."

"Harder," she breathes.

The woman closes her eyes, her mouth in an O, her body convulsing.

I keep my palm on Zara's spine and grip her shoulder with my other hand. My cock slides in and out of her, creating a never-ending supply of tingles down my spine.

"Sean. Oh my God!" she chokes out.

The woman's face turns redder. The men pound into her harder, the one behind her tugging her hair so her face is pointed at the ceiling.

Adrenaline floods my cells.

"Sean, I'm going to—"

I slap her ass, and she shrieks, her pussy pulsating around my cock.

I slide my hand in her hair, tugging it so her chin's on the quartz. I pound into her harder, snarling, "You like what you see over there?"

"Yes. Oh my God, yes," she admits.

I ask the question that's kept me up at night; the one I haven't had the balls to ask. "Is that what you want, Zara? Me and another guy?"

She doesn't hesitate, stating, "No, only you. I just like to watch."

"You sure?" I question.

"Yes!"

Relief hits me. I say into her ear, "That's good, my pulse. No one gets you but me."

"Yes! Only you! Oh God! Oh fuck, Sean," she cries out, her body convulsing harder between me and the cool quartz.

I shout, "That's it, my little brat. You squeeze your tight pussy on my cock and come all over me!"

"Yes. Fuck me harder!" she screams in delirium, her stare still on the threesome.

"You like it when I talk dirty, don't you, my little wife?"

"Yes! Sean! Oh God," she breathes, gripping the edge of the countertop.

A tidal wave of adrenaline assaults me. I blurt out, "Jesus fucking Christ. You know how much I fucking love you, you fucking little brat?" I grunt, then release inside her, thrusting through it.

"Yes! I love it too," she claims, trembling so hard she's barely breathing.

I fist her hair tighter. "I don't mean sex, Zara. I fucking love you! Always have," I bellow, my erection swelling to the maximum point of pleasure.

She whimpers, her knees buckling, as I collapse over her, breathing hard, kissing the back of her neck.

I told her I love her.

She didn't say it back.

She blinks hard, then unglues her eyes off the scene across the way, turning her head to look at me.

I slowly slide out of her, grab a towel, and clean her up. Then I move her panties back over and tug her skirt down. I pull her backward, spin her to face me, and reach underneath her armpits. I hoist her up on the counter.

Breathing hard, she meets my eyes.

Oh shit. She's freaked out now.

I plant my hands on either side of her and lean closer. Vulnerability floods my chest. My voice is hoarse. "I meant it, Zara. I love you. I always have."

Happiness fills her expression. She cups my cheeks and blinks hard. "I love you too."

Surprise fills me. "You do?"

She smiles. "Yes. Of course I do."

My lips twitch. "Is it because I bought this penthouse for you?"

She laughs, teasing, "No. But since a happy wife makes a happy life, it was an excellent move on your part." She winks.

I chuckle and kiss her again, holding her tighter to me.

She slides her arms around me, one hand running through my hair, kissing me back with as much affection as I give her.

I retreat. "I probably need to get you to work now, don't I?"

She pouts. "You mean I have to leave this place?"

I shrug. "Sorry. You can come back tonight. I'll have all of our stuff moved in by then."

"You will?" she asks, beaming.

"Of course, my little brat."

She claps and then tosses her arms back around me. "Thanks. You're the best husband ever."

"There. That's what I've been waiting for," I admit.

She laughs, then her face turns serious. She tears up. "Thank you, though. This place..." She glances around. "It's amazing. Really. It's more than I ever could have wished for."

Pride fills me again. I kiss her on the lips, then reply, "Good. When you get home tonight, I have several more rooms I'm going to take advantage of you in."

She giggles. "Deal."

Zara

One Month Later

Chapter
TWENTY-SIX

The doorbell rings, and I retreat from Sean's kiss. "Are you expecting anyone?"

"No." He pulls me back to him and slides his tongue inside my mouth again. He palms my ass, squeezing my cheeks.

My core throbs, aching for him, burning for every crazy thing he's been murmuring he wants to do with me all night.

The doorbell rings again, and a loud banging echoes through the apartment.

I slide my hands on his dewy chest and push away from him. "Since you're wearing nothing, I'll get rid of whoever it is."

He grins. "I had a towel on, but you tugged it off me, remember?"

I glance at his freshly showered frame, then smirk. "Girl's gotta do what a girl's gotta do."

He chuckles.

The ringing turns to a nonstop barrage of dings.

I groan, stepping out of the bedroom. I rush to the door and whip it open, blurting out, "What are you doing here?"

Brax grins. "Taking Sean out for his bachelor party."

I arch my eyebrows. "Bachelor party?"

Fiona pushes past him. "Yep. And you're having your bachelorette party."

"Um, what are you talking about?" I question. I've barely spoken to Fiona. We've met for coffee a few times, but things are still a little strained between us.

She answers, "We're getting closer to the holidays. We need to make sure everything's good between us, so let's have a fun night. Besides, I can't hate you forever. You're married to my brother now."

"You're serious. You're taking me out for a bachelorette party?"

"Yep," she chirps.

"But I'm already married," I point out.

She scoffs. "Yeah, we all know. You two got married behind our backs, but we still get to have some fun. Go get ready. Put on a hot little dress."

"What's going on?" Sean interjects, stepping into the foyer, his towel wrapped tight around his waist.

I glance up at him. "Um, they're here to take us out for our bachelorette and bachelor parties."

"Bachelorette party? What are you talking about? She's already married to me," he states.

"Jesus, you two really are married. Go get dressed. We're having fun tonight without them," Brax asserts, his expression filling with mischief.

Fiona rolls her eyes. "Please. We welcome a night out without you. Come on, Zara." She grabs my hand, pulling me through the penthouse and into the bedroom. She adds, "This place really is badass."

My heart soars at her praise. "Yeah. Sean did an amazing job, didn't he?"

"Yeah. I didn't think he had it in him. Much better scene than his old place," she states, and pulls me into the closet. She slides hangers of dresses across the pole, then tugs out a little black dress. "Wear this one."

"Okay."

She glances at my shoe rack and selects a pair of stilettos. "These. Come on, let's go do your hair and makeup."

I laugh. "You're serious about this?"

"Yeah. All the girls are waiting. Come on."

"The girls?"

"Our cousins. Duh. Now, hurry. We don't want to be late."

We step into the bathroom, and she pulls out the seat under the vanity.

I sit down.

She picks up my curling iron and turns it on.

I cautiously ask, "So you're not mad at me anymore?"

"I'm always going to be mad at you. You and my brother are idiots," she declares, then smirks.

I laugh.

"I mean, you still need to tell me things," she adds, pinning her gaze on my reflection.

Anxiety builds within me. "Fiona, you're not going to try to get into this all night, are you?"

She sighs. "No. I shouldn't have brought it up. Not tonight. Come on. Let's get ready."

Our discussion turns to lighter topics, feeling more like it used to be, and part of me is relieved. There are still issues between us, and I wish there weren't any, but it's nice to feel like we're normal again.

It takes a half hour for her to do my hair while I finish my makeup. Then I get dressed, slip into my stilettos, and Sean walks into the room.

He announces, "He's making me leave now."

"Don't act so upset about it," Brax scolds.

Sean tugs me into him and kisses me, warning, "Be good tonight."

"I don't think I'm the one who has to be reminded of that." I huff, suddenly feeling like maybe this isn't such a great idea. I know what Brax and Sean are capable of when they're loose on the town. So I glance at Brax, threatening, "You two better behave. Remember, he's already married."

"Yeah, yeah, yeah," Brax says, waving his hand.

"I'm serious."

"Don't worry. I'll be good," Sean declares.

"Come on, driver's downstairs," Fiona says, grabbing my bag and handing it to me.

I glance back at Sean. "Have a good night."

"Be good," he repeats.

I laugh. "Don't tell me to be good. *You* be good."

"I already told you I will."

"Uh-huh. Sure. I know how guys are at bachelor parties," I state.

"Stop worrying," he orders.

"Fine." I raise onto my tiptoes and kiss him.

We go our separate ways, and I'm soon in Fiona's SUV. We have a fifteen-minute drive until it pulls up to one of the newest clubs.

I gush, "Oh, I heard this place is awesome."

"Yeah. The Wave's getting huge reviews. Kinsley and Kylie have already been here, of course," she adds, her lips twitching.

"Of course they have. Where are they?"

"Everyone's inside," she answers.

We get out of the car and stroll toward the line. Fiona steers me to the front, cooing, "Hey, Jason."

The bouncer eyes us over. His biceps bulge in his tight T-shirt. His black pants hug him perfectly. He looks me over and asks, "Fiona, who's this sexy woman with you?"

She puts her arm around me. "This is my sister-in-law, Zara."

He cringes. "Ugh, married woman."

"Yep. Sorry, can't have her," she sing-songs.

I laugh.

He lifts the red rope. "Have a good night, ladies. Don't do anything I wouldn't do."

Fiona smirks at him. "Don't worry."

We step inside the club. The music is so loud I can feel it vibrating through my body. We scan the area, and she points. "Oh, there they are." She leads me over to a VIP section.

Shannon, Kinsley, Kylie, Mariya, and a dozen other Ivanoff and O'Malley women are there. Part of me is relieved she only brought the younger generation. Not that I don't love my aunts and my mom, but things are still strained between us.

Everyone rises, and I hug and kiss them on the cheeks. Kinsley hands me a glass of champagne.

Fiona raises her glass in a toast. "To my sister-in-law, but let's pretend you're not married tonight." Her eyes twinkle.

I groan. "Fiona."

She rolls her eyes, laughing. "I'm kidding. But come on, we're going to have fun. To Zara."

"To Zara," everyone replies, clinking glasses.

I take a sip, and the refreshing bubbles slide down my throat. We sit down and talk for a while and then Kylie rises. "I don't know about you ladies, but I'm ready to dance."

"Me too," Shannon agrees.

A good-looking, maybe thirty-something red-headed man reaches out and grabs her arm.

She spins. "What are you—" Her words cut off as she stills.

"Wanna dance?" he asks.

Her cheeks turn red. "Okay."

I wiggle my eyebrows and glance at Fiona.

She shakes her head, grinning.

Shannon's usually the first to get hit on. We tease her that it has something to do with her red hair, but she really is stunning. She has all the best features of the O'Malleys and Ivanovs, which, when mixed together, makes her worthy of cover model status. And as much as she gets hit on, she always seems surprised. But she easily swoons over her suitors and tends to get a bit caught up in men earlier than she should.

The ladies disperse, and we follow them to the dance floor. We spend hours moving to the beat, and it feels good. It's like Fiona and I are back to normal.

Several men try to dance with me, but I don't allow it. It feels weird to get hit on, especially by guys I'd normally be interested in, when I'm married to Sean. But no bone in my body wants anything to do with them.

Why aren't I bored yet?

When's Sean going to get bored of me?

I continue to dance, happy that things are so good between us. Yet I can't help wondering when it'll end. Which one of us will be the first to want it to end?

We can't do anything about it when it happens.

We're married for eternity.

A horrible feeling hits me.

Fiona tears me out of my thoughts, yelling, "I need to go to the bathroom."

"I'll go with you," I yell back, needing to take a breather.

We weave through the crush of bodies, then enter the women's restroom. We do our business and then meet at the counter.

Fiona opens her purse and takes out her lipstick.

I do the same.

She asks, "So, are you tired of my brother yet? You can admit it." She glides the red stain over her lips.

"No, not at all."

She arches her eyebrows and puts her fingers together. "Not even a little bit?"

I think about her question and then shake my head. "No. It's been great, actually."

She wrinkles her nose. "I don't know how that's possible with Sean."

I laugh. "That's because he's your brother."

"Well, I'm glad you two are happy."

"You are?" I question, surprised.

She nods. "Yeah, of course. If you're going to do something that dumb, you might as well be happy."

I hug her. "Thanks for tonight. And thanks for"—I study her a moment—"kind of forgiving me."

Her lips curve into a tight smile.

"Admit it, you're forgiving me," I push.

Her face falls. "I'm halfway there. But I still don't understand how you could have gotten married without me."

"Sorry," I offer, for what feels like the hundredth time.

She grabs my hand. "At least Sean didn't fuck up your ring. My brother surprisingly picked well."

"He did," I agree, feeling a swell of pride as I stare at the most beautiful diamond I've ever seen. And in the family I come from, I've seen a lot of amazing bling over the years.

Fiona puts her lipstick in her purse. "Come on, let's go." She moves toward the door and opens it. She steps outside and runs into a man.

"Oh, I'm sorry," he apologizes with a familiar Russian accent. He grabs her as she falls backward, and tugs her into him.

Goose bumps race along my skin. I tense up, unable to keep myself from gaping at him.

A faded quarter-inch-wide scar mars his face. It starts at his right temple, moves diagonally over his eyelid, through his nose and cheek, and down to the left side of his jaw. He looks like a total bad boy, and would be great-looking if it weren't for the scar. He's wearing a designer black sports coat, black V-neck T-shirt, and dark jeans.

"I'm sorry," he repeats, pinning his dark gaze to hers. "Did I hurt you?"

I know that voice.

My heart pounds harder, and the hairs on my arms rise.

Fiona shakes her head and breathlessly states, "No, not at all."

He doesn't release her, peering at her closer as he says, "If I had to run into a woman, I couldn't have picked a better one. You're beautiful."

"Thank you. You're not bad yourself," Fiona replies, her cheeks flushing.

What is going on here?

Fiona would never say anything like that to a stranger. She'd play it cool and make him work harder for a compliment. And she wouldn't give a scarred-up man another look. She'd move right past him and onto the prettiest *GQ*-cover-worthy guy in the room.

He asks, "Can I buy you a drink? To make up for it."

"Sure."

It suddenly hits me who he is, and panic fills me. He may have worn a mask the entire ceremony, but I know that Russian-accented voice, and his height and build are the same.

Kirill.

Why is he here?

My insides quiver. "Fiona," I say, grabbing her arm.

The man jerks his head toward me, and his eyes widen, as if he's noticing me for the first time.

We stare at each other. My insides shake harder.

"Um, do you two know each other or something?" Fiona questions.

I hesitate, then lie, "No."

"I'm getting the impression you do," Fiona insists, giving me a look.

Kirill states, "I've definitely never met your friend."

I catch myself. "Yeah, I've never seen him. Besides, I would remember somebody that has—" I stop, realizing I shouldn't be pointing out his scar, and my cheeks heat.

His expression hardens. "It's okay. You can say it. Somebody with a scar like mine."

Fiona gives me a dirty look and turns back toward him. She reaches up and runs her finger over his cheek. "I think it's kind of sexy."

He stares at her, his jaw clenched, eyes burning with something I didn't see the night of our initiation. I realize it's vulnerability, but it's short-lived, and his expression quickly hardens.

"Come on, Fiona, let's go," I command, linking my arm through hers and tugging her away.

"Zara, what are you doing?" she shrieks.

"It was nice meeting you," he calls out.

"What are you doing?" she repeats, turning her head to look at him.

Why did he look like he didn't know I was here?

He's following me. He has to be.

I tug her down the hall and turn the corner.

"Zara!" Fiona scolds.

"Why were you touching him?" I question, my pulse still racing.

She huffs. "He's sexy as sin. He's got the bad-boy vibe down better than any bad boy I've ever seen."

I wrinkle my nose, knowing it's Kirill. "Seriously? He's also forty-something."

"So? Daddy can come home with me," she says, winking.

"Ew. That's disgusting."

"Why is it disgusting? He's hot," she claims.

"No, he's not," I insist.

"Whatever." She looks back, but we're halfway through the club and there is a crowd of people between us and where we left Kirill. She whines, "Now I don't know where he went. Thanks a lot, Zara."

"It's fine. You're not missing out. Look at all the hot guys around here. Guys our age too," I add.

She groans. "Please, Zara, don't be so vanilla."

I scoff. "I am not vanilla."

"You're acting like it," she says.

"No, I'm not."

We head back into the VIP lounge and sit. I pick up the bottle of champagne, but it's empty. I glance around, but there's no server anywhere in sight.

"I can't believe you did that," Fiona reprimands.

I point to a guy on the dance floor who's Fiona's type. He's tall, dark-haired, and looks like he could be the president of the country club. I state, "That guy's been looking at you all night."

She groans. "Yeah, I know."

"Then why don't you go dance with him?"

She wrinkles her nose. "Please. He's just another previous frat boy. He's probably just like Marcus."

I lean closer. "You have to get back on the horse. I know you two broke up, but it's time." I point at the guy again. "He would be a good one."

"Yeah, I'm sure he's amazing, especially in the sack. No, thanks, though. I need something different. I'm done dating these guys that are good on paper. They're horribly boring in real life. I need some excitement, and that other guy..." She glances around, and disappointment fills her expression.

"Fiona—"

"He was hot, Zara. I bet he knows what to do. And now, who knows where he went? I'm never going to see him again," she gripes.

Relief hits me. Kirill needs to never look at Fiona again. I wave my hand at the dance floor. "This room is full of eligible suitors. Look around."

The server comes in with a bucket, a new bottle of champagne poking out from the top. She sets it down. "Cristal, from the gentleman. He said he sends his apologies."

Fiona excitedly glances around. "Where is he?"

The server points to the balcony across the way.

We glance up, and my stomach dives.

Kirill stares intently at Fiona. He briefly glances at me and then turns his gaze back to Fiona.

The server fills two glasses and hands one to each of us. Fiona tears her eyes off of Kirill, but only for a brief second. Then she holds her glass in the air and nods at him.

Kirill nods back, and I shiver.

She takes a sip and smiles.

He turns and walks away.

"Maybe he's coming down here," she gushes.

"Fiona, he doesn't look like somebody you should get involved with."

"Oh, please, who says anything about getting involved with him? I can have some fun tonight." Her face lights up.

I groan, ordering, "Pick another guy. Look at the huge selection."

"Stop saying that. I'm not interested," she insists, then takes another sip, searching the crowd for Kirill.

He never appears.

I spend the night with my gut in knots, waiting for him to show up.

Fiona waits as well, but as time passes, she grows more and more upset. After an hour, we finally return to the dance floor. I make her dance with other men. We have a good time, but I can tell she's still thinking about him.

My only hope is that she never sees him again.

Sean

Chapter
TWENTY-SEVEN

The SUV pulls up to a strip club. The pink neon sign blinks: LEGS.

I groan. "Seriously?"

Brax's mischievous grin lights up his face. "You didn't think we'd go somewhere lame, did you?"

My stomach flips. I've never enjoyed going to strip clubs. It's not that I won't go, but I'd rather have my own woman grinding on me than a stranger who does it for any man who'll wave a few bills at her. But Brax loves them. So we've had plenty of crazy nights out at clubs.

Now that I'm married, this isn't a great situation to put me in. I suggest, "Why don't we go somewhere else?"

He grunts. "No way. This is your bachelor party, not a dinner with your pregnant wife."

I jerk my head backward. "Zara's not pregnant."

"I'm just giving an example of things to come," he states.

My gut flips, and I scowl, staring at the sign.

Brax opens his door. "Let's go. Time's ticking. The boys are inside."

I begrudgingly slide out of the car.

We enter the seedy establishment, and the thick air hits me in the face. The stench that seems to be a staple in strip clubs flares in my nostrils.

The music pumps loudly, and Brax slaps cash on the counter for our cover charge. He pushes me through the door.

There are eight stages with barely-dressed women dancing around poles.

"Ah, there they are," Brax declares, pointing at dozens of my cousins and friends. Women surround them, all fighting for their money.

I mutter, "This is going to be a shit show."

"The best of the best," Brax boasts, giving me a look that makes me cringe inside. I used to love that expression. Now that I'm married, nothing good will happen if I'm involved in whatever is going through his head.

L.J., Mikhail, Kian, and Romeo all have women on their laps. We approach them, and they're grinning like idiots.

I taunt, "Don't come in your pants, lads."

L.J. glances over, replying, "About time you showed up."

A server beams at us. "Can I get you a drink?"

"Jameson," I state.

"Bring the bottle," Brax orders.

I sit beside him, and women start making a beeline for us. Blondes, brunettes, redheads, white, Black, Latino, Asian, and Middle Eastern strippers all circle us like vultures, fighting for our attention and money.

Brax slaps a big wad down on the table, making it worse.

I groan. "Jesus."

"Lighten up, Sean, it's your bachelor party," he replies.

The server brings over a bottle and fills two tumblers.

I pick one up.

Brax holds his out to me. "To married life."

I clink his glass and then drink half of mine, cringing as the liquid scorches down my throat and into my stomach.

More women appear, and the air thickens from their heavy perfumes.

Brax tries to buy me several lap dances.

I deny each one; I'm not interested. The only one I want on my lap is Zara. But I do make a note of several of the women's outfits that would look way hotter on my wife. So I need to get to the lingerie store.

Several hours pass. I'm polite to the women but always turn them down.

Brax entertains several of them, as do my cousins. A redhead grinds on him, and a blonde rubs his shoulders.

Suddenly, I hear Byrne's voice come from beside me. "Looks like you're passing the test, lad."

The hairs on my arms rise, and I glance up.

He slides into the seat next to me and holds his glass out, commenting, "Looks like your boys are celebrating something."

Brax nods. "Aye. Except Sean isn't having any fun."

"I'm already married," I remind him, glancing at my other cousins.

They barely notice Byrne. They're too entwined with the women on their laps.

I refocus on Byrne, questioning, "What tests are you talking about?"

He takes a big mouthful of whiskey and leans closer. "Loyalty to your wife."

I lock eyes with him, snapping, "I'm always loyal to her. And I'm always going to be."

He nods in approval. "That's right. So you pass the test."

I glance at Brax, accusing, "You set me up."

He holds his hands in the air, offering, "Sorry, mate. He made me."

"Brax, go get a private dance," Byrne orders.

"Now?" he questions.

"Yeah, now."

"Excuse me, ladies. I need to share the love," Brax says, helping them off him and then rising to his feet.

They whine.

He picks up some bills and curls his finger at two other women. They bounce over to him and disappear into a private room with some of my other cousins.

I turn toward Byrne.

He leans closer. "It's time to go, son."

"Where?"

"Out the back door so others don't know you're leaving. There's a door down the hall, past the bathroom. I'm going to go now. You wait five minutes."

My chest tightens, and my heart races faster. I state, "I don't like surprises."

Byrne shrugs. "Sorry. That's the way these things work." He winks, finishes his drink, and gets up. "Congrats on your nuptials. I hope you and the missus are happy."

"Thanks."

Byrne disappears.

L.J. glances over, asking, "Who is that?"

"Just some guy I've met a few times. No biggie. I need to go to the men's room," I tell him, but he doesn't care. He's too interested in the woman grinding her pussy next to his cock.

I pass the bathroom and find the exit door. I glance behind me, to make sure no one's looking, turn the handle, and sneak outside.

Byrne's waiting in a black Mustang. I slide into the passenger seat, and he pulls through the alley.

I question, "Where are we going?"

"To the airport."

I snort. "Of course we're going to the airport. Let me rephrase my question. Once we're on the plane, where are we going?"

"You'll see," he says, his lips twitching.

"Do you ever get used to this? The secrecy's annoying," I add.

He shrugs. "Doesn't bother me."

Annoyed, I sit back in the seat and shake my head.

He glances at me, ordering, "Calm down, son. Nothing bad's going to happen."

I fume, "You said that last time, and a man tried to swing his dick in my wife's face."

He nods. "Aye. But you took care of it, didn't you?"

I freeze. "You knew that would happen?"

"No. But you took care of it. You didn't interrupt the ceremony on stage, and you didn't kill him. Yet you put him in his place. That was the right thing to do. If you'd killed him, well, that would've had dire consequences." He refocuses on the road.

A chill runs through my bones. I admit, "I could have killed him. It was hard to hold myself back."

"But you exercised restraint," Byrne adds, pulling into the private airport and parking next to a plane.

I open my door, step onto the tarmac, and shut the door.

He rolls down the window and calls out, "Have a good time."

I turn back. "You're not coming?"

"Nope."

My gut flips faster. "Why?"

"Not my place. See you soon." He revs the engine and drives off.

I take a deep breath, then walk up the stairs and into the plane, wondering what's in store for me. I step inside the cabin and freeze.

Zara's lips twitch when she sees me.

I grin. "What are you doing here?"

"No idea. I'm sure you know just as much as I do, which is nothing," she chirps.

I chuckle and sit down. I lean over and kiss her.

She retreats, her eyes turning to slits. "Why do you smell like perfume?"

I groan. "Brax took me to the strip club."

Her cheeks redden. She sneers, "Well, that was nice of him."

I grunt. "Don't worry, I just fended women off all night."

She mumbles, "Sure you did."

I slide my hand through her hair and tug her head back.

She gasps.

I lean over her face. "Don't worry, my little brat. You're the only one whose pussy I want rubbing against my cock."

She bites her lip, trying to hold back her smile.

I kiss her forehead, her nose, then her lips. I flick my tongue against hers until that ache grows within me.

The pilot comes on the speaker. "Please put your seat belts on. We aren't going far, but it's a little rocky tonight."

I release her, grab her seat belt, secure it, then do the same for mine. I pick up her hand and kiss the back of it, asking, "So, where did you go?"

She answers, "To that new club called The Wave."

"And how many guys hit on you?"

She smirks. "A lot, but I'm not sure it beat out the naked women trying to grind all over you."

"But no one did," I state.

She stares at me. "You didn't have any lap dances?"

I confess, "No. I hate those places."

She scoffs. "Sure you do."

I pin her with my gaze, and with my most serious voice, I assert, "I do hate those places. Ask Brax."

She huffs. "Right. I'm sure Brax is going to tell me the truth," she says sarcastically. "It's bros before hoes with you two."

"I'm not lying, Zara. There's only one woman I want rubbing against me, and it's you."

She briefly studies me, and she must see the truth in my eyes because she smiles. "Well, that's good."

I kiss the back of her hand again. "Yeah. So what do you think this is all about?"

"My guess is as good as yours."

The plane takes off and rises into the air, but not very high. The turbulence hits, and the plane shakes hard. After only fifteen minutes, the pilot announces, "We'll be on the ground shortly." The landing gear lowers, and within minutes, we're back on the ground.

Zara mutters, "Wow, that was quick," then she takes a nervous breath.

I stroke my thumb over the back of her hand, declaring, "Everything will be fine."

She turns, smiles, and softly states, "I know. I'm glad you're with me, though."

"Me too," I admit, my heart beating harder.

When the plane has come to a complete stop, we unbuckle our seat belts and get up. I lead her off the plane and through a dark hall, similar to the ones we always seem to go down. When we get to the end of it, I put my hand on the knob and pause. I offer, "Should we run back to the plane?"

Her eyes widen. "I think we'd be in trouble if we did that."

"Do you think anyone ever has?" I question.

She laughs. "Probably not. But I don't think we should be the first ones."

"I suppose you're right. Are you ready, my pulse?"

She nods.

I kiss her hand again and then open the door.

A low drumming fills the air. Candles flicker all over the room. There's a massage table and a chair with a table attached to it.

Seven couples line up across from one another. Women stand next to the massage table in little black dresses and soft pink stilettos. Their hair is wrapped in messy buns and their backs face us. All their brands pop with the same pink roses and shading as my father's.

The men wear black suits and ties that match the women's shoes. They face the chair and hold their closed fist to their chest. Their brands are prominently displayed, also colored like my father's.

Valentina stands between the table and the chair. She beams at us.

The hairs on my arms rise. I tug Zara closer to me, still not trusting Valentina, even if she is my wife's cousin. Zara may not have any reservations about her, but I'm not letting my guard down.

The drumming stops.

Valentina chirps, "Welcome to the Ritual of Color and Shadows."

Zara puts her hand on my thigh, as if to steady herself.

I ask, "What does that mean?"

Valentina's expression brightens. She announces, "It means you've earned the right to move up a level, but we're not going to stretch out your phases. There are two seats at the table that other members desire to fill. The vacancies need to be filled on the seventh moon, which is right around the corner."

My mouth turns dry. I've read and re-read the rulebook too many times to count. There may be 666 seats, but it's rare that one becomes available, much less two.

Zara squeezes my hand tighter and pins her blues to my greens.

Valentina continues, "The Omni have decided you'll get your pink color and shadows tonight. It's rare for anyone to get granted the Ritual of Color and Shadows, but you have approval. It's normally one ritual at a time, so the Omni are especially happy with you and your choices."

Pride radiates from Zara.

Valentina points to the massage table. "Zara, lie on your stomach. Sean, sit in the chair and put your hand on the table."

Zara and I don't say anything, quietly taking our positions as instructed, but I grab her hand.

She smirks, stating, "Don't worry. You can squeeze my hand as hard as you need to, Sean."

I chuckle. "I think you're going to have to squeeze mine harder."

"We'll see about that," she challenges.

I laugh, excited that my brand will now match my father's, and ecstatic we're moving up a level. We're one step closer to our seats at the table, and I couldn't be prouder that my wife is at my side.

Zara

Chapter
TWENTY-EIGHT

"Turn me out, turn me in," I sing, sliding into my robe and jamming to my new favorite song. I tie the belt around my waist, pick up the laundry basket, and step out of the closet.

I keep singing as I stroll into the laundry room and then put the basket on the counter. I separate the white clothes from the colored ones and start a pile for the dry cleaner.

A new song comes on, and I sing along with it. I check each piece of clothing in the white pile to ensure nothing is in the pockets, then toss them into the washing machine. I pour soap on top and turn it on.

I don't know all of the song's lyrics, so I hum to the beat as I repeat the process with the colored pile, setting each item aside.

As usual, Sean's pockets have things in them. Cash, coins, and a few pieces of paper with notes in his scratched writing. I roll my eyes, smiling as I check a pair of shorts, then move on to the dry-cleaning pile.

I pick up a pair of his black trousers and reach inside a pocket. I pull out a tube of lipstick, and feel ill. My pulse hammers as my stomach flips faster. I grab the counter to steady myself, staring at the cheap pink plastic tube.

That's not mine.

When did he wear these pants?

Friday. He wore them when we went to the charity event.

He had to leave early, claiming Liam needed him for some work emergency.

My hand trembles, but I force myself to open the tube. I slowly turn the plastic, and a half-used, hot pink cream stick appears.

Whose lips has this touched?

He didn't have lip marks on him when he came home.

How do I know that for sure, though? He slid into bed around three a.m. and fucked me, telling me how sorry he was for having to ditch me at the event.

He'd showered before he got into bed.

Sean wouldn't cheat on me.

Then why is some woman's cheap lipstick in his pants?

The more I recall the night my husband wore the black dress pants, the sicker I feel.

But anger mixes with the hurt, spinning inside me until it takes over. I stare at the lipstick, gripping the edge of the counter until my knuckles turn white.

Sean's palm slides around my body, slipping under my robe. His toffee and bourbon vanilla scent flares around me while his fingers torment me, softly gliding over my slit. His hot breath tickles my neck, sending tingles down my spine. He pulls the towel off my head, slides his other hand into my wet hair, and tugs my head back. His lips brush against my lobe as he murmurs, "How was yoga?"

My heart pounds harder, my chest rising and falling faster with too many conflicting emotions.

He teases, "Want to show me any new moves?"

I close my eyes, breathing through my nose, determined not to cry and tap into my anger.

There has to be an explanation.

Yeah, he cheated on me.

He lowers his hand, slipping two fingers inside me, pumping slowly.

I inhale sharply, hating how he can still create a reaction within me when I feel like I should hate him.

He wouldn't touch another woman.

He's bored with me.

I squeeze my eyes tighter, trying to stop the warring thoughts and chaotic trembles in my stomach.

There has to be an explanation for this.

Every woman says that when their man cheats on them.

He wouldn't!

What if he did?

He kisses my neck, pushes his erection into my spine, and mumbles, "I can't get any work done. I've been thinking about what I want to do with you."

"Did you do it with her too?" I spout, my voice cracking and tears welling in my eyes.

He freezes.

I push him back and then spin to face him.

Confusion fills his expression. "What are you talking about?"

I hold the lipstick in front of his face, demanding, "Who is she?"

He glances at the lipstick and then scowls at me. "You've got to be kidding me."

"Don't lie to me, Sean!"

"You think I'd cheat on you?"

"It was in your pocket!" I shout, a tear falling.

He wipes it off my cheek with his thumb, then keeps his palm on my jaw. In a low voice, he states, "Zara, I would never cheat on you. You're my wife."

My lips tremble. I seethe, "It was in the pants you wore on the night you left me at the charity event—on my own."

"That doesn't prove I cheated on you. And you know Liam called me for an emergency situation," he claims.

I scoff. "Don't insult me, Sean! Who is she? At least give me the courtesy not to lie to me. We both know you get bored."

His eyes turn to slits. "*I* get bored? What about you?"

I huff. "Me? You're going to flip this on me?"

His voice raises. "Don't act like it's not true! Every day I wake up, wondering if it's the day you'll toss me aside for a newer model."

I jerk my head backward, gaping at him.

"Don't act like you don't get bored faster than I do," he adds.

I jab the lipstick into his chest. "Don't you dare turn this on me! I've been nothing but a loving wife to you! You're the one who left me on my own at a work event and came home with some cheap whore's lipstick in your pocket! That's on you, Sean! Not me!"

He glances at the tube and then meets my eyes, his greens flaring with flames. He declares, "I was working, Zara. I've never seen that lipstick before, so stop accusing me of something I would never do."

"Bullshit!"

He snatches the lipstick out of my hand. He tosses it in the trash, steps closer, and pins me to the washing machine.

I lean backward.

He cages me in, pressing his erection against my stomach. He moves his head until his lips are an inch from mine. "I'm not a cheater, my little brat."

The ache in my core turns fiery. It happens every time he calls me his brat and gives me that angsty look. I hate myself for it right now, so I scold myself, and snarl, "Then how did it get in your pocket? It's not mine."

"I don't know. But it doesn't prove anything."

"Don't gaslight me."

"Don't insult me further," he warns, his chest pushing against mine, his gaze darting to my mouth.

My pussy throbs. I challenge, "Or what, Sean?"

Tense silence builds between us while the air turns hotter.

His hand drops to my waist. He unties the belt of my robe and then pushes the satin off my shoulder, taunting, "I'll have to show my little brat what happens when she accuses me of things I would never do."

"It was in your pocket," I say, but it comes out weak, and I hate myself for it.

His lips caress my collarbone, and I whimper, closing my eyes. I push my hands against his chest, but there's no force behind them.

He slides his hands in my hair and tugs my head back again.

My nipples harden, and I squeeze my thighs together.

Hurt fills his expression, and he demands, "Be honest, Zara. You know I could never cheat on you, right?"

I want to believe him but don't want to be gullible either.

"Tell me," he snarls through gritted teeth.

I whisper, "It's not my lipstick."

"Fucking bad little brat of mine," he mumbles. Disappointment flares across his sharp features.

My heart hurts, but I won't cave. I add, "Tell me how it got there if it's not what I think?"

"I don't know. Someone had to have put it there. I've never seen it before now. But I definitely wouldn't be so stupid as to leave it in my pocket if I were that type of guy," he states.

His comment reignites my fury. "Glad to know I need to look for other clues!"

"You shouldn't be looking for clues! I'd never cheat on you! I love you!"

"Sure you do!" I hurl as the washer spins at a faster speed.

His scowl deepens. He warns, "Last chance. Tell me you believe me and that you're just emotional right now."

Maddening rage fills me. I snap, "Fuck you, my cheating husband."

He jerks his head backward. He studies my lips and then slowly meets my gaze.

My ache intensifies.

He maintains, "I haven't slept with anyone but you since before we got married."

"Prove it," I challenge.

His eyes widen, smoldering with a dark fire. "That's it!" In a quick move, he spins me and pushes me over the washer, fuming, "Let me remind you who I belong to, my little brat."

"You should think about that before you fuck someone else," I hurl.

He grabs the back of my robe and shoves it to the side, where it hangs from my arm. The cold metal hits my body, and his warm palm splays against my back.

"Sean—"

A loud smack ricochets through the air. A sting erupts against my ass cheek and gnaws at my aching core.

He barks, "Let me make it clear, my little brat."

Smack!

"Oh God!" I mumble, blinking hard, my hands flailing to grip some-thing, but there's nothing but the flat top of the machine. The vibra-tions of the washer's cycle fly through my nipples, sending more shock waves through my chest.

"I love you and only you. Always have and always will," he declares, spanking me again.

A spasm hits me, and my voice cracks. "F-fuck!"

"Tell me to stop, my little brat, and I will," he claims, but it's also a warning.

He knows I can't ever tell him to stop when he touches me. He's a magnet, and there's no way to pull away from him. The moment we crossed the line, it became undoable. He knows it, and I know it.

He lowers his face to the side of mine, murmuring in my ear, "Don't ever accuse me of doing the unforgivable again, my little brat. You're my pulse, and you know it. And if you ever do to me what you're accusing me of, I swear to God..." He pins his dark gaze on me.

I hold my breath, and the machine switches to the spin cycle.

He spanks me again.

I yelp, and a throbbing wave of endorphins washes through me.

He slides his hand up my spine and wraps his fist around my hair. He kisses my cheek and then glides into me.

"Sean!" I whisper-shout, already feeling dizzy from the sensory overload.

His thick cock thrusts to the beat of the washer, and he lifts my head higher, turning it toward his face. His lips graze mine, but he doesn't slide his tongue in my mouth. He kisses me and then studies me, repeating it several times.

I try to resist, but I can't. Within seconds, my tongue rolls against his, and everything explodes around me. Adrenaline pounds through me, and his erection pushes deeper.

"That's it, my little brat," he coos against my lips.

My pussy spasms around his cock. Dizziness slaps me over and over until I'm shaking as hard as the washer and seeing white.

"You're my wife, Zara! My wife! You're the only one who gets me," he barks, thrusting faster.

Incoherent sounds fly out of me. I try to focus, but my eyes keep rolling.

Endorphins flood me, intensifying the spasms.

"My little... Fuuuuck," he booms, his body swelling and pushing mine past the point of no return.

A bigger orgasm hits me, and I squirt all over him. It runs down my legs and puddles around my feet.

"Good little brat," he grits, thrusting through his high for what feels like an eternity.

My adrenaline slows, my focus returning like a slow-motion picture. Then it's just Sean's sweaty skin against mine, our ragged breaths, and the cold washer vibrating under us.

He slowly lifts his body off of me, pulls me to my feet, and spins me to face him. He keeps me pinned to the washer as he grips the back of my head. "I mean it, Zara. I don't know where that lipstick came from, but someone put it there. They had to have. I've never been with anyone but you since we took our vows. Nor will I ever again."

I stare at him, my hurt and anger returning, wanting so badly to believe him but not wanting to be that girl; the one who stays and then realizes years later she's given her life to a man who doesn't deserve her.

It's Sean. He does deserve me.

I can't leave anyway. We're bound for eternity.

A new sense of panic hits me.

He kisses me. "Glad we got that sorted." He steps back and reaches for his shorts on the floor.

The realization I'm trapped and Sean could cheat on me for the rest of my life, consumes me. My insides quiver with fear. I snarl, "You're going to have to do better than that for me to believe you." I brush past him, exiting the laundry room.

He follows me. "This is bullshit! Grow up, Zara!"

I spin on him, jabbing him in the chest. "Don't you tell me to grow up! I wasn't the one with the lipstick in my pocket!"

An unknown expression fills his features. It tears through me, but my anxiety doesn't cease. He snarls, "I don't know where the lipstick came from, but I didn't fuck anyone else."

"Prove it," I spout, then stomp into the bedroom and slam the door. I lock it, then slide into bed, unable to stop the tears from drenching my pillow.

Sean

Two Days Later

Chapter
TWENTY-NINE

"Where did you put them, Zara?" I call out.

"Same place I always do," she snaps back from inside the closet.

"They aren't there," I bark, opening another bathroom drawer.

Things have been tense between us the last two days. She can't seem to get past the lipstick she found in my pocket. The only explanation I can come up with is that someone from The Underworld had to have planted it there. But my wife isn't taking my word for it. And I can't say I blame her, even though she should know I would never cheat on her.

She adds, "Then you didn't put them back where they belong."

"Ugh," I grumble, flinging open the bathroom drawer where Zara keeps her excess facial products, then freeze.

Inside, I see a black leather bag with the skull design embossed on it in gold. *Zara Marino* is printed under the skull. Beneath that it says *Zara O'Malley.*

What the fuck?

When's she going to change her last name?

My pulse skyrockets, and my heart hammers with anger, hurt, and curiosity. I pick up the bag. It's heavy, and I pull at the laces, opening it.

Reaching inside, I find it's full of gold coins with the same skull and flowers engraved on them. I take one out and study it, knowing it isn't fake. These are real, and worth a lot of money.

Why does she have these?

And why is she hiding them from me?

The air in my lungs turns stale. If I've learned one thing, The Underworld doesn't give you things for free.

What did my wife do to earn these?

Flashbacks of the Binding of Flesh ceremony race through my mind. My stomach flips, and my heart pounds so hard it might explode. I squeeze a coin in my fist and glance at my reflection in the mirror. I attempt to calm myself down, but it's pointless. I stalk into the bedroom.

Zara steps out of the closet, looking as beautiful as always, in a purple pencil skirt and matching blazer, and designer cream blouse.

I hold the coin up in front of her. "Something you want to tell me?"

She glances at my hand and pins her eyebrows together. "What is that?"

"You tell me," I state.

Fire burns in her eyes as she seethes, "Don't you dare try to accuse me of something. So tell me whatever this charade of yours is, because I'm not into your games, Sean." She goes over to the bed, sits down, then slides her heels onto her feet.

I cross the room, dump the coins onto the bed, and toss the empty bag next to them. I point at her names, accusing, "You're going to tell me you have no idea where this came from?"

She gapes at all the coins and picks one up. "Is this real gold?"

"Don't play with me, Zara. I want to know how you got this!"

Her eyes turn to slits. "I've never seen these before in my life."

"It was in the same drawer as your facial products," I bellow.

She glances at the coins again and then shakes her head. She softens her voice, claiming, "Sean, I've never seen them before."

I cross my arms. "That seems convenient."

"What does that mean?"

"The bag has your names on it! Even though only O'Malley should be there!" I add.

She rolls her eyes, then shrugs. "So what? Someone obviously put it there. It's not the first time The Underworld has left stuff in our homes."

"Yeah, like the lipstick!"

The same hurt that's filled her expression the last two days reappears. Her lips tremble, and she fires back, "That's convenient for you."

I cross my arms, fresh anger exploding within me. "Seriously? You still can't fathom that someone would try to fuck with us?"

"Why would they?"

"Who knows? But you know damn well I wouldn't cheat on you!" I roar.

"Do I?"

I scowl.

MAGGIE COLE

She adds, "We're already past our expiration date."

"What the fuck does that mean?"

"It means that the only one who's been in a relationship longer than we've been married is me. And only once. So it only makes sense you're bored. Nice of you to leave me at an event all alone to go do whatever it is you did with whoever it is you're seeing on the side," she snarls.

"I've told you I was working! Ask Liam!"

"Sure you were."

"I was!"

She stands and plants her hand on her hip. "And what was so important that you had to leave me alone at nine at night?"

"You know I can't discuss O'Malley business."

She scoffs. "Again, that's convenient."

I step forward and cup her cheek with one hand, calmly saying, "Zara, ask Liam. He'll confirm, and you can stop these ridiculous thoughts."

Her voice shakes. "You had lipstick in your pocket!"

"And you have gold coins in your drawer that you claim you didn't have any knowledge of until a few minutes ago," I point out.

She just stares at me, blinking hard.

I soften my voice. "Zara, you know I wouldn't cheat on you."

"You get bored, Sean."

"So do you."

"I'm not the one with lipstick in my pocket," she states.

Frustration swells within me. I snap, "Then tell me what you did to get

408

these coins. If you're so convinced no one planted that lipstick in my pants, then tell me what you did to earn that bag full of gold."

"Don't you dare—"

"Tell me," I interrupt.

She brushes past me. "I need to go to work."

"I have a right to know what they made you do," I demand.

She spins toward me and jabs her finger in my chest, asserting, "You have no right to question me on anything."

"Oh really? But you have a right to question me."

"I'm not doing this, Sean." She exits the bedroom.

I'm right on her heels. "You don't get to just walk away."

"I'm going to work. I have a briefing this morning. It's more important than discussing whatever ridiculous accusation this is," she declares.

I scoff. "Really?"

"Yeah. Grow up, Sean."

"No, you grow up!"

She grabs her purse off the front table and opens the door to the foyer.

I follow her.

She hits the elevator button, and the door opens right away. She steps inside.

I put my hand on the door and demand, "Zara, when you get home, you're spilling whatever it is you did for them."

She scoffs. "There's nothing to discuss. I've never seen that bag before today."

I scowl deeper.

She pushes the button and smirks. "Let's make a deal. You tell me where the lipstick came from, and I'll tell you where the coins came from. Oh wait, that's never happening, is it?"

"So you did do something."

"No, I didn't, you asshole. Now, take your hand off the door. I can't be late for work!"

My veins burn with rage.

In a low voice, she warns, "Remove your hand, now."

I slowly obey, then point at her, and declare, "I want answers tonight."

She huffs. "You and me both."

The elevator door shuts.

I groan and pound the elevator door.

Why doesn't she believe me?

My history doesn't exactly make me look innocent.

I've never cheated on anyone.

Yeah, I just never made it clear if I was committed or not.

She's no saint either. She gets bored too.

Fuck this. I need to work out.

I pick up my shoes, lace them up, then grab my keys. I get in the elevator and press the button for the ground level.

The elevator descends and stops on the sixth floor. The doors open, and Byrne stands there, grinning.

"Jesus. What now?" I mutter.

He steps inside and hits the basement button. "Lad, we need to talk."

I don't argue, knowing there's no point. The elevator takes us to the bottom level, and he gets out.

I follow him through several hallways. The musty odor turns more pungent.

He leads me past the storage units and then opens a door. He takes a small flashlight out of his pocket and steers us through several rooms until we can't go any farther. He shuts the door, then reaches up and pulls a string.

A single lightbulb creates a soft glow in the tiny room.

"Why are we here?" I question, glancing at the concrete walls and two metal chairs.

He points at one of the chairs. "Sit down."

My chest tightens. I normally don't get anxious. But I won't let my guard down until I get a seat at the Omni table and know what's going on. "Is this like a torture chamber or something?"

He chuckles. "No. But they can't hear us here."

I arch my eyebrows. "Who?"

"The Omni, who do you think?" he states.

"Oh."

He points to the chair again. "Sit."

I obey.

He sits across from me and crosses his arms over his chest while leaning back and studying me.

"I need to get to the gym," I tell him.

"It's time you know what happened to your dad."

I break out in a cold sweat, and my chest tightens. I open my mouth, but nothing comes out.

He leans closer. He looks behind him and lowers his voice. "You want to know the truth, correct?"

I blurt out, "I thought you said nobody can hear us. Why are you looking behind you?"

He shrugs. "Habit. But they can't."

"Would they be upset if they found out you were talking to me about this?" I question.

"About this? No. Not now. You've reached the level required to know the basics. However, I'll say more to you than what I'm allowed. And I don't do dumb things and take chances I shouldn't."

Nerves flare in my stomach. I ask, "Why are you risking your safety?"

He looks behind him again, shifts in his seat, and removes his tattered beret. "You should know what I'm going to tell you before you decide whether you want to take your seat."

A sense of excitement charges the musty air. I take a deep breath, claiming, "I want to know everything."

Byrne's green eyes glow in the dim light. His face falls, and pain crosses his expression, along with anger. "Your father wanted a utopia. He created a vision where everybody could live peacefully. You, your sister, and all the generations to come in all the families."

"Yeah, I've heard that before," I say, still pissed off that Zara and I are fighting, and that she thinks I'd cheat on her.

Byrne stares at me intently, then he blurts out, "Your father was back-stabbed by his sisters' husbands."

"What? Boris would never do that to Nora!" I assert.

Byrne shakes his head. "No, not by Nora's husband. By the twins' husbands—Shamus and Niall."

My eyes widen. I always forget about my twin aunts. They don't come around the family much. They were never fun or seemed like a big part of it, but it's still a shock to hear that my uncles would be involved in my father's death.

Byrne continues, "The O'Malleys had big enemies just like all of our friends. The Rossis, Baileys, Abruzzos, Petrovs... Your family was always at war...always fighting with them. When you were born, your dad met with members of the enemy families. All the men who had influence enough to make change were there. He did it behind your uncle Darragh's back."

The hairs on my arms rise. My uncle Darragh was Liam's father. He loved me and my sister. Everyone feared but respected him. The thought of my father going behind his back is a shock to me.

Byrne goes on. "So your father, along with Shamus and Niall, met with Lorenzo and Anthony Rossi, Tadgh Bailey, Salvatore Abruzzo, and Daniil Petrov, who had just come from Russia but spoke fluent Italian. No one on the O'Malley side had met him. After your father's death, he infiltrated the Marinos as a spy. When they discovered he was a Petrov, they killed him. You were in high school or the start of college. I can't recall the exact time."

I close my eyes, my heart beating faster. I shake my head. "Why would he trust those guys? I've heard about all of them. They were horrible men."

"Aye. But your father had a vision, and they pretended to agree with it. They'd all lost people close to them. Your father's brothers always told him he was crazy, but they didn't know he had been creating The Underworld behind their backs. He wanted to prove to them it could be done."

My gut flips. I admit, "My uncles seem to know *something* exists."

Byrne doesn't answer right away, then says, "They are aware your father attempted to start something, but they don't know the extent of it. They've only seen their enemies wearing the skull brand. And they can't get their minds past all the bloodshed and revenge to see what can be possible."

"*Can be*? Don't you mean what is? The Underworld exists," I point out.

Byrne shifts in his chair. "The Underworld is eighty percent what your father wanted. There's less war on the streets. Less death."

I grunt.

He scowls. "What's the negativity for, son?"

"Seems to be lots of death. Whenever I'm doing anything with The Underworld, people die."

"Yeah, but it's necessary in order to weed out the bad people."

"Isn't that what my uncles have been doing?" I question.

"Yes and no. People in your enemies' families have lost members they shouldn't have. So has your side. People who didn't do the evilest things and shouldn't have been killed but were because of their last names."

I cross my arms. "So the guys who murdered my father pretended to agree with his vision and then stabbed him in the back. Why? Just to kill him for fun?"

Byrne grinds his molars, then fumes, "They wanted to take over leadership with the Omni."

A deep chill runs through my veins. "But they're dead. So they didn't do what they wanted, right?"

He takes a few deep breaths, his expression darkening. "The ones who physically murdered your father are dead, yes. But there's one more thing you need to know, especially if you're going to sit at the table."

"What's that?"

He looks behind him again and then tells me, "Salvatore Abruzzo orchestrated your father's murder. He was supposed to be there the night your father died, but he got tied up in Italy. He's the only one still alive, and he has a seat at the table."

I squeeze my fists tight against my sides, seething, "That motherfucker lived, and now he's running The Underworld?"

Byrne nods. "Yes. You shouldn't trust him or those in the Omni he's closest with. However, it'll be hard to tell who the enemies are and who are in line with your father's vision. They're not going to stand out like a sore thumb. But Salvatore and his cronies are running it the wrong way."

"What are they doing?"

"Like you said, there's too much death."

"You just told me the deaths were justified."

He nods. "In some cases, but not all. Like the night of your initiation; those people didn't deserve to die. They earned their spots, just as you and Zara did. The Omni should have created a different initiation ceremony for them, not killed them."

I snarl, "That's Valentina's fault."

"No, it's not. Her orders come from the top. She's in just as much danger as everyone else," Byrne declares.

"She seems like she's in control," I state.

"She's not. And she's your wife's cousin."

"So I hear."

"Valentina has a good heart. She wants what your father wanted. She believes in his vision and is your ally," he insists.

I grunt. "Is she?"

"Aye, she is. And she's worked longer and harder to get her seat at the table. You'll get yours before she does, and it's not fair, but that's how The Underworld works," Byrne states.

I clench my jaw, trying to wrap my head around what he's saying.

He points at me, adding, "Your father was adamant that his generation could be better so his children could be safer. He didn't want your futures as bloody as his. He wanted your sister to have as much power as you, and for women to stop being harmed by these men."

"Fiona isn't cut out for this," I blurt out.

Byrne grunts.

"She isn't," I maintain.

"Did you ever think Zara would be?" he asks.

I contemplate his question.

In a firm voice, he asserts, "Your sister will have a chance to sit at the table next to you. The Underworld needs her as much as it needs you and Zara. If that's what the three of you choose."

I release a thick breath of air. "Why do you say 'choose'? Nothing will stop me from taking my seat."

"I'll circle back to your question in a minute. I warned your father not to trust those men. I told him he had to go about things differently, but he didn't want to heed my warnings."

"So my father was a stupid man?" I snarl.

"No, not stupid, just too positive at times," Byrne says.

I grind my molars, looking at the wall and trying to shove down all the emotions building in my chest.

Byrne adds, "I begged him to find different men to trust, but Shamus and Niall were family. When he brought them into the fold, they vouched for the others."

416

"You knew my uncles were bad?"

Byrne shakes his head, regret evident in the motion. "No. But I knew the others were. I wish I had known..."

My pulse rate increases. I ask, "Are you an O'Malley too?"

Byrne's face falls. "No, lad. I'm an O'Leary."

"An..." The blood drains from my face down to my toes. I jump up and clench my fists at my sides.

He nods. "That's right. My blood comes from your aunt Alaina's clan. I was the O'Leary your father entrusted with his Underworld secrets."

I lean closer, scowling at him. "But you didn't take part in his murder?"

He shakes his head. "No, son. Your dad chose me himself. When Shamus and Niall brought in the others, I warned him, but he wouldn't listen."

I pace the tiny room, absorbing everything Byrne has said, then accuse, "You didn't stop his execution!"

Anger flares in his eyes. He barks, "You think I wouldn't have done everything in my power to stop them from murdering him had I known?"

My insides shake harder. I pace faster, trying to breathe.

"Listen to me, lad," Byrne orders.

I spin to face him and pin him with a leer.

He warns, "You have to be careful if you decide to take a seat. You can't trust all of them."

I meet his eye. "I'll kill Salvatore and all the others."

"You can't kill an Omni. The rest will kill you in return," Byrne warns.

"They need to be weeded out," I insist.

Byrne nods. "Aye. They do. But you can't just go on a killing spree. At least not in plain sight."

"They need to pay for their sins," I seethe.

Byrne nods with defeat in his expression.

"Why didn't you take your seat? If you were chosen by my father to represent the O'Leary's, why didn't you do it?"

His face hardens. He insists, "I can do more out here."

"Then why would I take a seat?"

"You can do more from inside."

"That's weak," I argue.

"No, it's the truth, and you will see it someday."

I try to process everything I've learned.

He adds, "You must be careful when you take your seat. And there will be one more ceremony you must complete to solidify your position."

"Doing what?"

He closes his eyes briefly, then meets my gaze, answering, "Something you and Zara aren't going to want to do. But once you're in front of the Omni, you either go forward with it, or they kill both of you. So if you want the seat, you move forward with no qualms about following through, no matter what it entails."

Silence builds around us as we both stare at each other. Then there's another answer I need. I ask, "What about my mother? Why did she really keep us away from the O'Malleys?"

His expression betrays his sadness and discomfort at having to discuss this topic.

"Tell me," I demand.

He hesitates, then says, "You have to agree to never speak to your mother about this. It would bring her great pain and fear if she knew that you were aware of what happened to your father."

I look at him in silence.

"Promise me," he orders.

"Okay. I promise."

"Your vow is as solid as your father's? I don't have to worry about your word?"

Insulted, I answer, "Of course it's as solid as my father's."

He releases an anxious breath. "Okay. Your mother witnessed your father's death. She was there the night it happened, and they threatened her, just like she told you.

"She did everything for you and your sister. And don't think for one moment that she doesn't carry the nightmare with her. She relives it over and over. So don't you dare go adding to her grief."

A cold chill runs down my spine as horror fills me. The thought of my mother watching my father die is unfathomable. I barely choke out, "Tell me you're lying."

Byrne's sadness is palpable. "I'm sorry, son, but I'm not."

"One more question. Why didn't my dad tell my mom about The Underworld?" I ask.

Byrne sighs. "Your father didn't want her to worry. Until he had everything perfect, he wasn't going to bring her into it. He made that decision to protect her. He loved her and you kids more than anything."

Emotions tighten my chest. All the puzzle pieces now fit together. I ponder everything he's told me.

My thoughts get interrupted when the alarm on his watch rings loudly.

I arch my eyebrows in question.

He announces, "The seventh moon is almost here. Lad, are you sure you want a seat at the table?"

More determined than ever, I lift my chin and reply, "Yes."

He rises and then pats me on the back. "Okay, son. Don't hesitate to do whatever it is they require of you for the last ceremony. Every seat at the table requires a sacrifice. If this is what you want, then the offering you and your wife agree to will be the price you pay."

A shiver racks me at his ominous words.

He opens the door. "Let's get you on the plane."

Zara

Chapter THIRTY

When I get to work, I'm still fuming about our fight. Someone from The Underworld put those coins in our bathroom. But it doesn't negate the fact that he had lipstick in his pocket.

They put it there too.

I sigh and close my eyes, leaning against the elevator wall. My heart tells me that Sean wouldn't cheat on me. He's not that type of person, but he does get bored.

So do I, and I haven't cheated on him, nor would I.

I take a deep breath and open my eyes. Everything between us is better than I ever imagined it could be. Yet I'm always worrying about the other shoe dropping like it always did in my other relationships. The fact Sean has the same issues as I do when dating someone doesn't make my anxiety any better.

He wouldn't cheat on me.

I need to figure out how to trust in us.

What if he did meet up with another woman?

The Underworld planted that lipstick.

Did they?

The elevator stops on the fifth floor, and the doors open. People get off, and the doors start to shut, but a woman's hand shoots out between the doors as they're sliding closed.

The metal reopens, and I freeze.

Sylvia grins at me and says, "Hey, darling. Miss me?"

"What are you doing here?"

"Let's go for a walk."

I don't argue and push past the man in front of me. I quietly follow her down the hall, and she unlocks a door. We step inside an empty office.

Cardboard covers the windows. It's a smaller office than the one I work in and appears to be under construction.

"What are we doing here?" I question.

"We need to talk," Sylvia informs me.

"About what?" I ask, and glance at my watch, adding, "I have a lot of work to do today."

"Your schedule's been cleared," she announces.

I arch my eyebrows. "What do you mean it's been cleared?"

"It's been taken care of. You're not expected in the office today."

"You can't interfere with my work. I have important cases I'm working on," I declare.

She holds her hand up. "Yes, I know, but it'll be fine. Trust me. Besides, I thought you wanted to know about your father's past."

I sit there in stunned silence.

She arches a brow. "Well? Do you still want to know?"

"Yes, of course I do."

"Okay. Then that's why I'm here. Have a seat." She motions to a metal chair.

I obey, and she sits down in one across from me.

"Seems like an odd space to put some metal chairs when it's under construction," I comment.

She smiles. "I wanted to be prepared."

"You get an A for effort," I mutter, then cross my arms and legs.

"You and Sean going through a lot?" she questions.

My heart aches, but I keep a straight face and meet her gaze, not saying anything.

She leans over and pats my knee. "Don't worry, dear. Everything will be okay. I have faith in you two."

My stomach flips. I bite on my lip and wait.

She gives me another soft expression and then sits back. "Your father knows about The Underworld."

My eyebrows raise in surprise. "He does?"

She nods. "Yes. He didn't know Sean's father was involved, though. He had heard about it from Marcello Abruzzo."

"His sister's husband; Valentina's father?"

She affirms, "Yes."

"She's told me about her parents. Her mom is my aunt, I guess?"

"Yes, I know she told you."

"Of course you do," I sarcastically reply.

She laughs. "Don't worry. The days of everyone knowing everything about you will soon be over."

"They will?"

She smiles. "Yes. If you decide to take your seat at the table, all the spying and intrusions into your house will come to an end."

Anger fills me. "You planted that lipstick in Sean's pants, didn't you? And those coins in my drawer?"

Her face falls, and she shakes her head. "I didn't plant anything."

"Didn't you?"

"No. I'm not saying it wasn't somebody else, but it wasn't me. I don't know anything about that," she insists.

"Would you tell me if you did?" I hurl, tired of The Underworld interfering in my life. Yet I so badly want to believe Sean wouldn't cheat on me, and that they planted it.

Her expression turns stern. "Yes, I would tell you. You're at the final stage."

"Of?" I question.

A look what might be pride lights up her face. "Of getting your seat at the table. If you still want it."

I take a deep breath and slowly release it.

"You do still want it, right?" she asks, peering at me closer.

"Yes, of course," I say without a doubt.

She lowers her voice. "Even if you have to endure one more final test?"

A chill runs down my spine. "Like what?"

"No one gets a seat at the table without a sacrifice. I don't know what the Omni will choose, but you and Sean must be prepared for the ceremony. If you don't follow through, you know the consequences," she warns.

"Death," I mutter, the chill in my bones deepening.

She swallows hard, pinning me with a fearful look. "Yes."

I lift my chin. "I'm taking my seat."

She studies me for a moment, then smiles. "Okay."

"Tell me more about my father."

She licks her lips and continues. "Your father didn't believe an Abruzzo could be good. And it's not his fault. The killing during that time was excessive. The wars were never-ending. And the Abruzzos were doing reprehensible things to women and children."

"I've heard stories," I admit.

"You don't know the half of it," she declares. "Your father witnessed much of it. He only became a spy for the Marino family and infiltrated the Abruzzos because of his sister."

My heart beats faster. "Valentina's mom?"

"Yes. She fell in love with Marcello. Neither of them knew who the other was when they met. It just happened. They were star-crossed lovers and never meant to be together. They hid for a while."

My heart hurts, thinking of Valentina's parents, in love but being scared to show the world.

Sylvia continues, "Your father and the rest of your family were opposed to their relationship. But your aunt's love for Marcello and his for her was too strong. They ran away together and got married, and that's when your father infiltrated the Abruzzos."

"Marcello's family was okay with them being married?" I question.

Sylvia's voice turns sharp. "No. Marcello knew he could never tell them what blood ran through Aurora's veins. When your father infiltrated the Abruzzos, he was accepted as her brother, and no one was the wiser."

I blurt out, "That's a big secret to keep."

Sylvia nods. "And a dangerous one."

My stomach flips.

"Your father did it to protect her, and he tried to get her to leave many times, but she wouldn't. And Marcello loved Aurora so much, he allowed your father to spy on his family."

I blink hard, feeling bad for everybody involved, especially Valentina.

Sylvia tilts her head, watching my reaction, then states, "Valentina was born, and your father loved her. I'm sure he still does. But he couldn't get past Marcello being an Abruzzo."

"The Abruzzos do horrible things," I assert.

"Yes, they do. But Marcello wasn't like them. He didn't agree with human trafficking or bloodshed. He told your father about The Underworld. He wanted to solidify a better future for Valentina. But your father didn't believe that the Abruzzos could change. He didn't understand that Marcello wasn't anything like his brothers or other family members."

I ask, "He continued to keep my father's secret?"

Sylvia uncrosses and recrosses her legs. "He did. He never told the Abruzzos. After Sean Sr.'s death, Marcello and Aurora ended up fleeing to Italy with Valentina. They disappeared. Your father could never find them, and then it was too late. Marcello's brother, Salvatore, killed them during an Underworld ritual and took Valentina to raise as his own. She was sixteen at the time."

My insides quiver, and my heart hurts. "She didn't tell me that happened."

Anger infuses Sylvia's tone when she says, "Salvatore sits at the table. He's one of the most powerful Omni. Valentina was old enough to realize she had to play the game, but she has never forgiven him. She had to accept him as her new father figure, or she would have been thrown into a brothel."

Horror fills me.

"Your father only sees Valentina as being under Salvatore's wing; that she is his protégé. He doesn't know Salvatore killed Marcello and Aurora. He only knows that his sister married the enemy. Now, thanks to you, he knows she's dead."

Guilt for being the bearer of pain for my father assaults me.

Sylvia continues, "Luca's intentions are pure. He only wants to protect you."

"But now he knows that Valentina's alive. We can tell him—"

"You cannot disclose The Underworld's business to any outsider," Sylvia snaps.

"But she doesn't deserve to be alone!" I protest.

Sylvia's expression softens. "That's true. But Valentina's not on her own. She now has you. And I can't blame your father for not changing his mind; however, he can't know about The Underworld. So as much as you want to be angry with him, you need to make peace. If you don't, it will eat at you and, at some point, influence your decisions at the table."

"How's that fair to Valentina?" I question.

"It's not. But Valentina's fine. Like I said, she now has you and Sean. Correct?" She arches her eyebrows.

I blink hard and nod. "Yeah."

She crosses her arms. "Okay, so now you know. But if you carry this anger for your father into your seat at the table, you'll make mistakes.

Others will get hurt. So you have to make peace with the situation. He did what he did to protect his sister and niece, but ultimately he sees it as his failure."

I argue, "It's not his fault they fell in love. But he could have given Marcello the benefit of the doubt."

Sylvia holds up her hand. "You can't play the what-if game, Zara. Things were different back then. As I said, the war between the families was at an all-time high. You don't have any idea what it was like, or what your father witnessed. The things the Abruzzos did were unforgivable, even if Marcello didn't participate."

I close my eyes, trying to think of how to get my father to accept Valentina again.

Sylvia warns, "You'll go crazy trying to figure out the impossible. Some things are meant to be left alone, and this is one of those. If you cannot move past this, you cannot take your seat at the table. Do you understand?"

"Why can't I take a seat at the table just because I want to bring my family together?" I spout.

"There's more to it. The Underworld is not for everyone to know about, and you know that," she cautions.

"But you said my father already knows about it."

She sighs. "He knows what the intent behind it was. He does not know the extent of it, though, and he's never to find out. He does not have the capacity, just like Sean's uncles, to get over the past. But you don't need to lose your father, or your mother, over this."

I glance at the covered windows, my insides quivering. I don't want to lose my parents, but I also want to be fair to Valentina. Thinking of her alone on holidays or for major life events makes me sad.

Once again, it's as if Sylvia can read my mind. She repeats, "She has you. It's more than she's had since her parents died. Trust me. She's going to need you at some point."

I meet Sylvia's gaze.

She questions, "Are you able to separate the two? I need to know. Otherwise, you cannot take your seat at the table."

I take a moment to ponder her question. Then I nod and answer, "Yes. I will separate the two."

"Good. And are you willing to make the sacrifice at the final ceremony? No matter what it entails?"

My mouth turns dry. "Do I have to kill someone again?"

She shrugs. "I don't know what the sacrifice will be, but you must be willing to follow through. Otherwise, don't walk into the ceremony, because you won't walk out."

I shudder, not wanting to die.

What will they make me do?

"Zara, you don't have to do this. You can maintain your current level," she offers.

I lift my chin and square my shoulders. "No. I will take my seat at the table."

She rises. "Then we must go. The seventh moon is coming. We have limited time."

Nerves fill me. "It's going to happen tonight?"

She nods. "Yes."

I follow her out of the office and onto the roof, where a helicopter awaits. We get in and lift off, zooming over the city.

A thousand thoughts plague me, but the worst thing is my anxiety. It looms over me, getting worse as more time passes.

There's only one important question right now: What will I have to sacrifice to get my seat with the Omni?

Sean

Chapter
THIRTY-ONE

"Get dressed, then go through that door," Byrne directs.

I glance at the black suit.

He warns, "Remember, don't step out there unless you're willing to make a sacrifice."

My gut drops. I hate not knowing what's in front of me, but there's no other option. Zara and I have come too far not to take our seats at the table.

Byrne pats me on the back and states, "Good luck, lad." He disappears through the door we entered.

I grab the suit off the hanger, put it on, then step in front of the mirror. I stare at my reflection, trying to calm my nerves, muttering, "Don't be a pussy." Then I turn, open the other door, and the sound of chanting hits my ears.

"Om," the men boom.

"Ahhhh," the women follow.

The room reminds me of two college classrooms put together. Two women, dressed in gold lingerie, lead me down an aisle to the center of the room. They disappear, and I gaze around.

Hundreds of men and women fill seats, circling a center stage. Every row is higher, so everyone can see. A huge table, surrounded by seven women and seven men, is the only thing on the stage. There's plenty of room around it, so I wonder what else might get brought out once the ceremony starts.

The women in the audience wear long, black satin spaghetti-strapped dresses. And the men wear suits like mine. Unlike at initiation, no one wears a mask, and every nationality seems to be represented.

Zara appears, wearing the same black dress as the other women. She's guided toward me from across the room by two men wearing nothing but gold thongs.

I clench my fists at my side.

Jesus fucking Christ.

Touch her beyond escorting her to me, and I'll kill you.

They stop when they reach me. She unloops her arms from theirs, and they disappear around the side of the stage.

I take a deep breath and slide my arm around her waist.

She points her blues at me, full of anxiety and excitement.

I squeeze her waist and pin her closer to me, still unsure what the Omni will require of us, not trusting anyone in this room other than her.

A tall man rises from his seat at the table, and the room goes silent. His face has a diagonal scar from his right temple to the left side of his jaw. A familiar Russian accent fills the air, declaring, "Your consistent effort to earn a spot at the table has not gone unnoticed. Tonight will be the final test to prove you are worthy of the sacred role."

It's Kirill.

How did he get that scar?

He turns toward a man, stating, "Salvatore Abruzzo, you have won the honor of choosing the ceremony. What have you decided?"

The air in my lungs escapes in a *whoosh*. I feel like I've been punched in the gut.

He orchestrated my father's death.

My fist curls at my side, and I scowl at my father's murderer.

Salvatore, a short Italian man, rises. He scans Zara with a lewd gaze.

Deafening silence fills the air.

I grit my teeth, tightening my grip around her waist. I hold myself back from killing him, remembering Byrne's warning.

Salvatore announces, "Tonight, on the seventh moon, we will invoke the Ceremony of the Sacrificial Lamb."

A gasp fills the air.

Kirill's head jerks backward.

"What is that?" I blurt out.

Salvatore's lips twist. He gives Zara another lewd once-over, then turns his attention to me and declares, "Your wife is the lamb."

"Excuse me?" I burst out.

"What does that mean?" Zara murmurs, then shoots me a freaked-out look.

Salvatore points at the men sitting around the table and explains, "The seven of us will have her, and you will sit and watch. Kirill and I will enter her and cum inside her when the moon is at its brightest."

"Like hell, you will!" I protest, pushing Zara behind me and glancing menacingly between him and Kirill.

But Kirill's expression doesn't match Salvatore's. He looks uncomfortable.

So I object again, "No way."

Kirill clenches his jaw.

Salvatore steps in front of me, looking up and pinning his haughty gaze on mine. "Your seat at the table depends on completing the chosen ceremony. I have selected the Sacrificial Lamb. Your wife is our lamb. The sacrifice is yours. You will sit and watch or not earn your spot."

"The spot you stole from my father," I seethe, pushing Zara farther behind me and clenching both fists.

Shock fills Salvatore's expression. He snarls, "What did you say?"

"You killed my father."

"I wasn't present when your father took his last breath."

"You're just as responsible!" I accuse.

His lips twitch. He taunts, "Your objection to our ceremony means your sacrifice must double."

The crowd gasps again.

"Salvatore," Kirill warns.

It doesn't stop him. He states, "Fourteen men will now have her instead of seven. And I'm still coming in your wife tonight." He winks.

Any discipline I have breaks. I lunge at him, reaching for his neck and pulling him to the floor.

His hands flail, trying to pry me off him, but he's too weak for me. His eyes widen and he makes choking noises.

A chaotic feeling overtakes me. It's the same as when I was in the underground fighting ring, fighting for my life. I pin my body over Salvatore's and squeeze my grip tighter. His cheeks turn purple.

"Sean!" Zara shouts, but I barely hear her.

Blood slowly seeps into the whites of his eyes, and his attempts to pry my hands off his throat weaken.

"Sean!" Zara cries out again.

It doesn't take long before I realize there's no more life in Salvatore. I slowly get off him and glance at Zara, trying to catch my breath.

She has her hand over her mouth, and fear fills her eyes.

I jump in front of her again, looking around the room.

Tension builds, creating more dread within me. The audience stares at us, emotionless and silent.

No one stopped me.

A man at the table rises and declares in a Greek accent, "Your seats at the table are revoked. You have broken a sacred rule."

"Which would be what? Don't kill those who kill your father?" I snarl.

"Sean," Zara mumbles, reaching for my hand.

I look around us to make sure no one is within reach of her.

The Greek man answers, "The Omni are untouchable. No member of The Underworld can kill them. You will be sacrificed after your wife is given to the fourteen men. She will watch you die, then follow you in death."

"Override token," Kirill booms, stepping next to us.

The crowd erupts with loud gasps, followed by more tense silence.

My heart thumps harder against my chest cavity.

Zara digs her nails into my thighs, her knees wobbling.

The Greek man's eyes narrow.

I blurt out, "What does that mean?"

Kirill announces, "It means you're safe and will fill your seat with an alternate ceremony."

I stare at him in confusion, unsure why he's helping us.

Another man at the table interjects, "The committee has to approve. This is an unprecedented, serious violation."

"Approve it," Kirill orders.

Another man rises. He's bald, with huge biceps and wide shoulders. "The only way I'll approve is if Sean uses his token. And, Kirill, both you and Sean will owe us a nonnegotiable," he says, in what might be a Ukrainian accent.

I seethe, "Fine. Take my token. But the nonnegotiable doesn't involve my wife or me having sex with anyone else. From this point forward, sex is off the table."

An older Black woman with dark hair lined with gray streaks rises from her chair. She hands Zara a tube of lipstick. It's the same tube that she found in my pants pocket. She orders in a French accent, "Put it on."

Anger flares in Zara's voice. She snarls, "You planted this in our home?"

"Told you I didn't touch anyone else," I say to her.

"Yeah, well, I don't know anything about those coins!" she declares.

The woman with the lipstick states, "Your gold coins are a payment for the death of Salvatore."

My breath catches in my lungs. I recover and fume, "You wanted me to kill him?"

Kirill barks accusingly, "You wanted me to use my override token."

The Ukrainian man replies, "What matters is where we are at right now. Do you accept the solution, or do you want death?"

"As long as there's no more sex involving my wife or me, you can take my token," I assert.

He narrows his gaze. "So no token and a nonnegotiable not involving sex. Done?"

"Yeah. I'm good," I declare.

"Kirill?" he asks.

Kirill hesitates, then agrees. "Fine."

Approval fills the man's features. He looks around the table, ordering, "Hand in the air to approve, hands on the table to object." He raises his hand.

The others all follow.

"Good." He steps in front of Zara and me. "Do you vow to uphold the laws of the Omni, preserve the initiatives of The Underworld, and maintain secrecy of our utopia?"

"I do," Zara affirms, gripping my hand.

"I do," I proclaim, squeezing hers back.

He smiles. "By the power of the Omni, I grant you a seat at the table." He turns toward Kirill. "When we deem it's time, you will marry our chosen one."

Kirill objects, "You can't arrange my marriage, Fedir. I'm King of the Omni. Only I can decide whom I marry."

"All kings need a queen. You're forty-five, and you're past due to take a wife. You also just agreed to a nonnegotiable, so stop objecting. You know the rules," Fedir warns.

Kirill grinds his molars.

Fedir turns toward me. "You will give your sister, Fiona, to Kirill."

"No fucking way," I blurt out.

Fedir scoffs, pointing out, "You changed the course of your fate and your sister's when you didn't choose the redhead."

I protest, "I'm not handing my sister to him."

Fedir reminds me, "You agreed to a nonnegotiable. A broken agreement within the Omni is punishable by death. Is that what you want for you and your wife?"

"I'll use my override token," Zara interjects.

Fedir chuckles.

A chill runs through my blood. I tug Zara into me. "What's so funny?"

Fedir points at us. "You two have a lot to learn. You cannot use an override token for someone who doesn't have a seat at the table. And you can never use it for your husband's debt. A debt of one spouse is also the debt of the other."

"That's stupid," Zara says.

"It's one of the rules his father made," Fedir says, glancing at me.

Damn you, Dad.

I declare, "My sister is not meant for an arranged marriage."

"You are wrong. Your sister was meant to sit at the table. Your father wanted it," he declares.

"Not like this," I insist.

Fedir asks, "So you object to her marrying a man who stood up for you and saved your life and your wife's?"

I open my mouth but quickly shut it.

"Is there another man here you wish your sister to marry?" he questions.

I gaze at Kirill, breathing through my nose, staring at his scar-riddled face.

There is no way Fiona will ever be attracted to him.

He can't marry her.

"Well? Do you object? I can kill you, Kirill, and Zara now if you wish to backtrack on your promise," Fedir announces.

My gut flips.

I don't even know this guy.

I'll figure this issue out later.

"Fine," I state, vowing there's no way I'll let my sister get near Kirill.

Fedir asks, "Kirill? Do you agree?"

He grumbles, "Fine."

"Great! When it's time for Coronation, you'll give your sister to Kirill," he says to me, then snaps his fingers in the air.

Two men in gold thongs carry two seats onto the stage and put them at the end of the table, next to Kirill's spot.

Fedir motions toward them. "Please. Have a seat. Take your rightful places at the table."

I lead Zara to the seat between Kirill and me, for some reason deeming it to be safer than the unknown woman next to me.

Fedir announces, "My honored Omni, please welcome to the table, the Grand Duke Sean O'Malley and our Grand Duchess Zara O'Malley!"

Zara

One Month Later

Chapter
THIRTY-TWO

The woman behind the front desk stops and calls out, "Mrs. O'Malley?"

I stop and turn toward her. "Yes, Sheila?"

"The mailman said you need to start emptying your box, or he'll have to take it to the post office. He won't deliver anything again until it's picked up," she relays.

I wince. "Sorry. I don't know why we keep forgetting."

She smiles. "No worries. He said you have until tomorrow. Do you want to use this box?" She grabs one from behind the desk and puts it on the counter.

"That would be great. Thank you," I say, and pick it up. I go over to the mail area and unlock the metal container.

It's stuffed to the max. I tug several envelopes out before I can pull more than one piece at a time. I drop everything in the box and take it to the penthouse.

Yawning, I set the box on the table, remove my heels, and sort through everything, separating bills from junk mail. I get to the last piece and freeze.

Social Security Administration is marked on the envelope.

I yawn again, wondering why I'm so tired lately, then open the envelope and stare at my new Social Security card.

Zara Luciana O'Malley.

I smile, put the card on the table, then toss all the junk in the trash can. I set the bills in the basket and then glance at the time.

"Shoot," I mutter and pick up my phone.

> Me: Are you almost home? They'll be here in under two hours.

> Sean: Don't worry, my pulse. I wouldn't leave you to deal with them on your own.

> Me: Good hubby.

> Sean: The food will be ready for pickup in thirty minutes, then I'll be there.

> Me: Extra good, hubby.

> Sean: Happy wife, happy life.

> Me: Don't ever forget it.

> Sean: I won't. Trust me.

> Me: 😌😌😌

I go into the bedroom, take off my work suit, and pull on an oversized sweater. I step into my jeans, but I can barely get them zipped.

My body is going rogue.

I better start counting some calories.

I yank off the jeans and slide a pair of black leggings on. They feel tighter but not as bad as the denim.

My stomach growls, and I scold, "Stop that!" then I step into the bathroom and pull up my sweater, staring at my stomach.

How did I gain weight and not notice?

It's just my belly, I tell myself in relief, then freeze.

My boobs look huge.

My gut flips as I try to recall the last time I got my period.

Panic hits me. I order a pregnancy test online, select the expedited delivery option, and it arrives within ten minutes. I take it to the bathroom, open the foil, and pull out the stick.

My heart races.

No time like the present.

I sit on the toilet, pee on the stick, and set it on the counter. For the entire two minutes, I stare at it with anxiety flaring and then exploding when a plus sign appears.

I pick it up and gape at it.

Holy shit.

I'm pregnant.

What is Sean going to think?

We haven't talked about kids. Everything was about The Underworld. Now that we have our seats, the new worry is how to get out of Sean's debt without Fiona having to marry Kirill. And since we don't know when the Omni will decide it's time, we know the clock is ticking.

Sean gets flustered whenever we discuss it. We always end up in bed, with Sean on a mission to outperform our last sex session.

I'm not complaining, but it's made him a tad mentally absent lately. I don't know how he's going to react.

I enter the kitchen, grab my Social Security card, and go to my office. I open the closet and pull out my crate of gift wrap, sorting through different bags until I find a small black box with a gold ribbon.

I stick the pregnancy test and Social Security card in it, then secure the ribbon.

Within minutes, Sean arrives with bags of Italian food. He sets them down, kisses me on the lips, then wiggles his eyebrows, asking, "Are you ready for parentgeddon?"

I groan. "Let's hope it's not that bad."

He kisses me on the forehead and states, "I think we'll be good." He takes a tray of lasagna out of the bag.

"My dad did promise to try and forgive you for ruining all his fatherly wedding dreams," I add, recalling the conversation where I made peace with my parents and told him I wouldn't dig into his past anymore. But I also stipulated he needed to get over his animosity toward Sean. Mom agreed.

Sean cringes. "Can't say I blame the guy. If I had a daughter, I'd kill the guy who married her and didn't ask me for her hand in marriage."

"Well, aren't you old school," I tease.

He shrugs. "She better marry someone I approve of, or he'll be six feet under."

My butterflies take off. I reach for the box and hold it out to him. "I got you something."

His lips twitch. "You did?"

"Yeah. Well, two things, actually."

"Why do you look nervous?"

"I'm not," I lie.

He looks excited yet cautious. He unties the bow, lifts the lid, and goes still.

I babble, "I only planned on showing you my name change, but then I couldn't fit into my jeans and realized I hadn't had my period. Since you can't keep your hands off me, and I kind of forgot to refill my birth control, well...well, now we're having a baby."

He slowly lifts his gaze to mine. "You forgot to refill your birth control?"

My gut dives. "Yeah. Sorry. There's just been a lot going on." I bite on my lip.

He stares at me.

I blurt out, "Are you mad at me?"

He tosses the box on the counter and slides his hand around to the back of my head. He fists my hair and tugs it back.

I gasp, squeezing my thighs together.

He slides his hand over my belly. "My baby's in here?"

"Of course it's your baby. Who else's baby would it be? Don't even start that with me because—"

He slips his tongue in my mouth and kisses me until I'm whimpering.

"Is it a boy or a girl?" he mumbles, smiling against my lips, his greens twinkling.

I laugh. "I don't know. I just peed on the stick!"

"When do we get to find out?"

"Maybe we should let it be a surprise," I suggest, even though I'm dying to know.

"No way!" Sean declares.

"So you aren't mad?"

He grunts. "Don't be a little brat." He leans into my ear and palms my ass, squeezing my cheek. "Don't think this means I'm not going to bend you over my knee later tonight and spank you."

The ache in my core burns hotter. I murmur, "Don't tease me before parentgeddon."

"I should—"

The doorbell rings.

I glance at the clock. "They're early."

"No, I asked them to come now. I need to talk to your dad about work stuff," he claims.

I pout. "No work talk."

"Don't worry. It won't take too long. You and the others can catch up. But don't you dare tell them about the baby until I'm here," he adds, walking toward the front door.

I grin, happy he's as excited as I am about the baby. I toss the box into a drawer and follow him into the other room.

He opens the door to Bridget, Dante, Mom, and Dad.

We all exchange hugs and kisses and then Sean disappears with my father.

"You aren't going with them?" I ask Dante.

"No need," he says, and opens a bottle of wine. He pours a glass and hands one to each of us ladies. He holds his up and says, "Salute."

"Salute," everyone replies.

I pretend to take a small sip and then put it down. We gather around the island and make small talk until Sean and my father reappear.

I smile at Sean. "Everything good?"

He beams. "Yep."

Relief hits me. "Should we eat?"

He grabs my hand and kneels.

"What are you doing?" I question.

Nerves, mixed with a bit of arrogance, fill his expression. It reignites my ache as he says, "Zara, I didn't ask you to marry me the right way. I didn't give you the wedding I should have, and I didn't ask your father for your hand. That's on me."

I bite on my smile, knowing the truth about how we were married and the circumstances we faced.

He kisses my hand and continues, "Since we got married, everything in my life is now complete. You're the piece in my life I didn't know I needed. So I want you to marry me again, in front of our families, like we should have done in the first place."

I blink hard, but a tear drips down my cheek.

He pulls a ring out of his pocket. The trilliant cut, curve-sided, pink amethyst is as big as my wedding diamond. It matches the color in our brands.

I gasp, putting my hand over my mouth, gaping at it. Besides my wedding ring, it's the most stunning gem I've ever seen.

He grabs my right hand and slides it over my middle finger. "What do you say, my pulse? Will you marry me once more?"

"Yes! Of course I will!" I reply.

He rises, tugging me into him and kissing me.

Our parents cheer.

He retreats. Mischief brightens his greens, and he teases, "I didn't get you another diamond since I knocked it out of the park the first time."

I laugh. "You sure did! And this is equally as beautiful! Thank you!" I kiss him again.

"Let's plan a wedding!" Mom sings.

"Don't forget your other news!" Dad exclaims.

I freeze and look at Sean.

He groans. "Luca!"

I point at him. "You told him, didn't you?"

Sean shrugs. "Had to give him something so he would give me his blessing."

"What are we missing?" Bridget asks.

Sean slides his arm around my waist, grinning. He looks at me. "Do you want to tell them?"

"Tell us what?" Mom questions.

"We're having a baby," Sean and I proclaim at the same time.

"A baby!" Mom and Bridget both squeal.

Dante pulls out the scotch. "This calls for something a bit stronger than wine, don't you think, Luca?"

"Agreed." Dad tugs me into him. "My beautiful *figlia*. I'm so happy for you."

"Thanks. You're not mad anymore?" I ask.

He takes a deep breath. "It's time to move forward. We have a baby to spoil!"

I laugh, feeling more love and joy than I ever thought possible. I glance at my husband, remembering the night he told me to choose him.

Without a doubt, it's the best decision I've ever made.

Sean

Three Months Later

Epilogue

Mom's eyes glisten. She straightens out my bow tie, steps back, and smiles. "There. Perfect now."

"Thanks, Mom."

She beams brighter, declaring, "I always thought you and Zara had something special."

"You did?" I question.

She nods. "Sure. You two were always attached at the hip as kids. Then, when you got older, that magnetic pull was always still there."

I arch my eyebrows. "You could see that?"

"Of course. I'm your mother. Besides, you two were never good at hiding your flirting."

I chuckle, then pull her in for a hug. "I'm sorry I didn't do it right the first time."

She hugs me back. "I forgive you." She retreats and warns, "But don't pull a stunt like that ever again."

I chuckle again. "I won't."

Her face lights up more. "Good. Now that you're going to be a father, you have to remember your little guy will watch your every move."

More happiness fills me, mixed with a tiny bit of nerves. I can't wait to meet my son. Yet I won't lie and say I worry I won't be as good of a father as my dad or Dante. Dante stepped into a paternal role when I was in high school, and he kept the bar high. So I have a lot to aim for with my kid.

There's a knock on the door, and Dante booms, "They're ready for you."

My belly fills with butterflies, and I tell myself to calm down. I'm already married. Yet today feels even more important than our first marriage ceremony.

While we chose each other, neither of us would have considered ourselves ready for marriage. Today, the threat of death doesn't loom over us. No one is forcing us to say our vows. It's Zara and me recommitting to each other in front of everyone who matters to us.

Mom asks, "Are you ready?"

I puff my chest out. "I am."

The three of us leave the room and walk down the hall. Dante opens the door, and we step out onto the roof.

It's a new building complex the Ivanovs just finished developing. The stunning view showcases the best features of Chicago. Lake Michigan is on one side, and the bustling city is on the other.

When Zara and I were looking for a venue, Maksim told us to meet him here at sunset. One look at Zara gaping around, and I knew he was right. This was the perfect spot.

The Ivanovs graciously delayed the opening of the building for another few weeks, and transformed the rooftop into an even more spectacular setting.

In a few minutes, the sun will set, creating a vibrant glow around the city. Bright stars will twinkle over Lake Michigan. Outdoor lights already illuminate the perimeter. The best DJ in Chicago will play the list of songs Zara and I spent hours creating. Appetizers and dinner from Adrian Ivanov's newest restaurant will be served. Wine and booze will flow all night, and I'll dance with the only woman I've ever loved.

I take my place next to Brax, and he says, "If you need to run, my getaway car is waiting downstairs."

I elbow him.

He chuckles. "Kidding."

The music starts, and Fiona appears, wearing a black minidress and carrying a bouquet of soft pink roses. She walks down the aisle.

I wink at her and she smirks in return, which makes me chuckle again.

I have to figure out how to sway the Omni to make Kirill marry someone else.

Don't think about this today. The only woman I'm allowed to think about is Zara—no Underworld stuff.

My wife steps into the doorway, and I push the ill feeling away, trying to catch my breath.

Like always, my pulse is beautiful, sexy, and glowing. Her baby bump is showing, which only makes me adore her more.

Some men look for other women when their wives get pregnant, but not me. If anything, Zara and I have both been even more insatiable during her pregnancy, and the vision of her in her white satin wedding dress isn't helping the fire in my veins.

Luca offers her his elbow, and she loops her arm through his. They walk toward me, and I've never seen the old man look so proud. His grin is contagious, and I'm relieved we're back on good terms. I know I stole the moment he was owed, so I'm happy to give it back to him.

Zara pins her blues on me, and every feeling I have for her spins inside me like a tornado. I have to blink a few times, feeling overwhelmed that she's mine, now and for eternity.

They stop in front of me, and Luca lifts her veil. He hugs her and kisses her cheek, whispers something in her ear, then releases her. He steps closer to me and orders, "Keep doing what you're doing, son. My beautiful *figlia* is happy and loves you."

"I will," I promise.

He adds, "Remember, I'm the first to hold my grandson."

I chuckle. "You'll have to fight for that honor, Luca."

He chuckles and pats me on the back, then steps away.

Fiona takes Zara's bouquet, and I reach for her hand. I lean into her ear and murmur, "You look beautiful, my little brat."

Her lips twitch, and heat flares in her eyes.

The space in my pants evaporates. I take a deep breath and step back, holding her hands and caressing them with my thumbs.

The priest clears his throat.

We turn toward him.

He starts, "Dearly beloved, we are gathered here to witness and celebrate the union between this man and this woman in the presence of God."

I glance at Zara, and she bites on her lip.

Our parents insisted we get married in the Catholic church. Zara and I aren't super religious, but we agreed to a Catholic ceremony as long as it wasn't inside the actual church building. Zara said she didn't feel comfortable since she was already pregnant, and I was happy to have it elsewhere.

Earlier this morning, like every O'Malley before me, my uncles made me go to confession. I grumbled about not knowing what to say.

Killian handed me a copy of the Ten Commandments and told me to use it as a guide. He added that the priest can't reveal anything I tell him, and to wear something lightweight, like my T-shirt and shorts.

Declan claimed that was inappropriate and told me to put on pants and a button-down shirt.

Killian said, "Fuck off. No need to make the lad sweat to death in that box."

They went on and on, and I finally put on the dress clothes. When I stepped out of the confessional, Killian had a glass of water and a towel for me, but I didn't need to use it. He couldn't understand why I wasn't sweating.

After I said my piece in the confessional, I went to Liam's with all the guys, had a few shots, and hung out most of the day. I kept wondering what Zara was doing. I would have called her, but Fiona took her phone and said I had to stay away. She insisted that one man in our family would keep to tradition and not be in contact with the bride before the wedding.

Since we let everyone down the first time, I took one for the team and dealt with it.

But I've missed my wife all day. And now, the ache in me is growing, and I'm going to need to find a dark corner for us somewhere when our vows are over.

The priest says, "The couple decided to write their own vows. Sean, are you ready to share yours with Zara?"

Brax hands me the rings.

My heart races faster. I look at Zara, swallowing down the emotions pummeling me. I take a deep breath and vow, "I, Sean O'Malley Jr., take you, Zara Luciana Marino O'Malley, to be my wife for eternity. I'll obey, provide, and protect you always. My devotion is only for you, and I'll never get bored."

Zara's eyes widen in surprise and happiness, and she grins.

We had many heated debates about me saying I'd obey her. They usually ended up with me spanking her until she came, and I always told her there's no way I'm adding that phrase to my vows.

Seeing the happiness on her face proves it was worth it to swallow my pride. I slide her wedding ring and band on her finger.

The priest asks, "Zara, are you ready?"

Brax hands her my ring.

She beams at me, lifting her chin and squeezing my hands. She vows, "I, Zara Luciana Marino O'Malley, take you, Sean O'Malley Jr., to be my husband for eternity. I will persuade and protect you. I will be fully devoted to only you and never get bored."

I chuckle.

She slides my ring onto my finger.

The priest booms, "By the power vested in me, I now pronounce you Mr. and Mrs. Sean O'Malley Jr."

The crowd cheers.

The priest adds, "You may kiss your bride."

I tug Zara into me.

She inhales sharply, and the heat in her blues burns hotter.

I kiss her with every ounce of love I have for her, knowing that everything I've ever needed is in front of me.

We never knew why we both got bored with other people. Now I know why.

We were bored because we knew the other existed. We had small glimpses of what we needed, which only made us crave more. So, Zara was always meant to be mine. I was always meant to be hers. A blood pact might have saved us, but we made that promise because even in our drunken stupor, we couldn't fight the inevitable.

Our fate is together. Here or The Underworld. It doesn't matter where.

It's Zara and me for eternity.

* * *

A note from the author

Thank you so much for reading Bride by Initiation.
I was so excited to write the next generation Mafia Wars Series and I couldn't think of any better characters then Sean Jr. and Zara to start The Underworld. If you're wondering about their parents' books, *TOXIC,* is Bridget and Dante's story. *FLAWED*, is Luca and Chanel's!

Now don't worry! I've got one more super spicy scene for you with Zara and Sean! to download. So grab your icy cold drink and go to https://dl.bookfunnel.com/n6wb5oy9d8 to read for free!

Up next in The Underworld is *BRIDE BY CORONATION*. Think about this story as the *Princess Bride* collides with *Beauty and the Beast*.

Will Fiona figure out what Sean and Zara have been keeping a secret? How will she handle finding out her brother promised her to Kirill?

Will Kirill be able to rule as King of The Omni when Fiona becomes his Queen? And what's the scar across his face all about anyway?

Download Bride by Coronation at your favorite retailer or to grab audios, paperbacks, and ebooks at deep discounts visit Maggie's bookstore at www.maggiecolebookstore.com

And if you missed the family chart, go back to the beginning of the book. There's a great visual mapping out the Mafia Wars & Underworld families and each book.

BRIDE BY INITIATION-BONUS SPICY SCENE

You can find the bonus scene at:
https://dl.bookfunnel.com/n6wb5oy9d8

If you have any issues downloading this, please contact
pa4maggie@gmail.com.

* * *

Bride by Coronation is up next and available
June 1, 2025.

You can find it at your favorite retailer or head over to my bookstore
and check out discounted ebooks, audio, and paperbacks!
https://maggiecolebookstore.com/collections/paperback-bundles

BRIDE BY CORONATION

THE UNDERWORLD-BOOK TWO

THE
Underworld

BRIDE
by coronation

June 1, 2025
(cover coming soon)

MAGGIE COLE

My brother arranged for me to marry a stranger, one marked with a diagonal scar across his face and a tattoo necklace on his hand.

Neither disgusts me. They also aren't what scares me.

Kirill Petrov's a sworn enemy of our family and King of the Underworld. A towering man with darkness in his gaze, an unspoken promise of what he'll do to me, and something so deep in his expression it hurts my heart.

Yet the blaze of his allure only grows hotter, singing, until I can't resist him any longer... until I'm his Queen wearing his necklace night after night, staring at the beast inside his soul.

If I could, I'd kill that beast until the world saw my husband as the man I see—the man I love.

Except I give him my heart before I learn the full truth. And once you see the unforgettable, how can you go back? How can you forgive your husband for sins that aren't his, yet he's tied to? Especially when the people you love got hurt in the most vile of ways?

* * *

Bride by Coronation is available June 1, 2025.

You can find it at your favorite retailer or head over to my bookstore and check out discounted ebooks, audio, and paperbacks! https://maggiecolebookstore.com/collections/paperback-bundles

BRIDE BY CORONATION

CHAPTER ONE - THIS IS AN UNEDITED VERSION, SO PLEASE EXCUSE ANY ERRORS.

iona O'Malley

*B*itter cold slams into me the moment I step outside the Pilates studio. Wind whistles louder, and a blanket of thick, wet snow covers buildings, streets, and cars. Oversized flakes fall, making it nearly impossible to see what's ahead of me.

I reach my bare hand into my pocket, feel my credit card sleeve, and nothing else.

Great. I forgot my phone.

"Idiot," I mutter, shivering, digging my hands into my pockets deeper, and cursing myself for not anticipating the weather. My alarm didn't ring, and I ran out of my apartment in my sneakers, leggings, and a thinner winter jacket just in time to catch the last advanced class of the day.

The moment I stepped outside, I knew I needed more clothes. But it wasn't snowing, so I ran the entire eight blocks, happy to burn off the wine I drank at the dinner party I went to last night.

Now, I'm regretting putting my workout over my attire. My hot cheeks and sweaty skin only accelerate the chill creeping into my bones. I push myself against the harsh gusts, trying to walk faster, but every step is a fight. And the rising sun only serves to mock me, adding no warmth anywhere.

It takes me three times as long as it normally does to travel a few blocks. Nostalgia fills me from when I was a little girl and taxi cabs lined the streets. Now, you only get a ride if you order one, and since I don't have my phone, I'm out of luck.

Michigan Avenue appears, and I almost cross it, but at the last second turn. My brother, Sean, and his wife, Zara, who's also my best friend, live on the next corner. I decide I'll visit them and my new twin niece and nephew. I'll call my driver when I'm ready to go home.

Four doors and I'm there, I tell myself, picking up the pace, then the strongest blast so far barrels into me. I duck slightly, but it knocks me back two feet.

"Forget this," I mutter, yanking open the coffee shop door. I lunge inside, relieved to escape the torturous wind, and take a spot at the back of the line.

The rich, warm aroma of roasted coffee, nuts, caramel, and pastries fills the air. Hints of chocolate, cinnamon, and vanilla dance around it, comforting me. Indie music, grinding, hissing, whistling espresso machines, and whirring blenders fight for attention.

I study the menu, decide what I want, and step forward when the line moves, staring at the back of a well-built, broad-shouldered, tall man wearing a black wool pea coat and matching cashmere scarf. His dark, thick-wavy, medium-length hair is four, maybe six inches long in some parts. It's clean and styled but reeks of messy and the opposite of the country club men I usually date.

Wonder if he likes women tugging on it?

The bell over the door rings, and a violent burst of cold air hits my back. I lose my balance and step forward, knocking into the man.

"Crap! I'm so sor—" My mouth turns dry and air catches in my lungs. I gape at him, unable to believe it, feeling the same ache I haven't been able to escape whenever I allow myself to think about the stranger.

Surprise fills his sharp features, and a large dimple pops out under his scar. It's a quarter-inch faded white line with just a hint of red. It starts at his right skull, moves diagonally over his eyelid, through his nose and cheek, and down to his left jaw. His short-trimmed beard fits his face perfectly.

I wonder how long he's had the scar. I assume he's in his mid-forties, between ten to fifteen years older than me. It looks aged. In the last year, I've devised a dozen scenarios about how he got it.

My butterflies explode inside me, and the cold chill gets beaten by the heat flooding my veins. I've only seen this stranger once. It was over a year ago. I ran into him at a club when I was out with Zara. He sent a bottle of the most expensive champagne to my table, then disappeared.

His lips twitch. His dark eyes light up, and his deep, Russian accent hums in my ears, "I think you have an obsession with barreling into me."

I beam, "Or maybe you have an obsession with being in my way, so I'm forced to bang you?"

He arches his eyebrows in amusement.

My cheeks heat. I quickly add, "I mean, bang into you."

"Next," a whiny barista calls out.

He turns, steps in front of the counter but off to the side, then pins his heated stare on me. "What do you want, Fiona?"

"You know my name?" I blurt out, my pulse skyrocketing so fast I get dizzy.

He opens his mouth, then shuts it.

I bite on my lip.

"Can I help you?" the barista interjects in an annoyed tone.

The man claims, "Your friend said your name outside the bathroom."

"Oh, I forgot," I admit, recalling Zara interrupting my hot moment with Mr. Bad Boy.

"Sorry, but there's a line forming," the barista snaps.

The man narrows his gaze, scolding, "You're being rude."

The probably high-school boy, wearing a name tag that says Theo, shrinks. He cringes. In a nicer manner, he offers, "Sorry. How can I assist you?"

"Fiona?" The man asks, motioning for me to step next to him.

I obey and order, "Long macchiato, one pump caramel, one pump mocha, add whip." I turn to the man. "What's your name?"

Amusement flares over him. He states, "Kirill."

"And what would you like, sir?" Theo pushes.

Kirill doesn't take his stare off me. He answers, "Large coffee. Fiona, have you tried the Oatmeal Raisin cookies here?"

I shake my head. "No."

He turns toward Theo, "Add on two cookies."

"Name?"

"Bob."

I stifle a laugh. "Bob?"

470

"No one can spell or pronounce my name."

I add, "You definitely don't look like a Bob."

"Eighteen forty-five," Theo announces.

Kirill taps his card, displaying a tattoo of a hand necklace. Tiny pink hearts on top of crossed bones hang off a black chain. It runs over the sides of his thumb and pointer finger.

My knees weaken, and I grab the counter to steady myself. "You have a hand necklace?"

He freezes, then studies me, and the ache in my core turns into an inferno.

Theo interrupts, "Sorry. I'll agree your tattoo is rather fascinating, and I don't mean to be rude, but would you please step down to the end so other customers can order?"

Kirill shoots him more lethal daggers, then steps back. He motions toward the pick-up counter, his hand necklace on full display. "After you."

With wobbly legs, a racing heart, and zings flying through me, I force myself to get to the end of the counter.

A young girl with bright green hair, four nose rings, and three eyebrow hoops slaps two cookies, wrapped in paper sleeves, on the quartz. "Your drinks will be up in a moment."

"Thank you," I reply.

Kirill steps closer, unbuttons his peacoat, and the same delicious scent he wore the night we met in the club slinks around us.

I hold in my groan. The number of times I tried to find that smell at cologne counters is uncountable. I inhale deeply, basking in the leather, rosewater, saffron, jasmine, and other notes I can't identify.

"You aren't dressed very appropriately," Kirill states in disapproval, his eyes drifting over my body.

I squeeze my thighs together, babbling, "I was late for Pilates. When I got outside, it wasn't snowing, so I ran, thinking I'd sweat last night's wine out of me. I was at a dinner party. I didn't get drunk or anything. I just had a few more glasses than normal. Anyway, when I left class, the weather turned, and I forgot my phone." I stare at him, my heart thudding so hard that I'm sure he can hear it.

Tiny wrinkles crinkle around his dark eyes. He teases, "It's a good thing you didn't turn into an icicle. I'd have to defrost you in front of everyone."

My breath catches in my lungs. The throbbing in my core accelerates. I add, "I detoured to my brother and sister-in-law's place since the snow was beating me up too badly."

Something passes in Kirill's expression, but I don't understand what it means.

"Bob," the girl calls out.

I bite on my smile.

Kirill winks, picks up our drinks, and holds mine out.

I reach for it and freeze, gaping, while goosebumps cover my skin.

What is he doing with that on his hand?

The same skull adorned with roses that my deceased father designed and then branded on his hand is on Kirill. It sits on the same spot, near his thumb and index finger. It's also the same mark my brother branded on his hand, and Zara got on the back of her neck. I've asked them to explain what it means, but they only say they did it when they married as a tribute to my father. I don't buy it, nor does my mother or stepfather, Dante.

Kirill puts my drink in his other hand, then picks up his.

My voice shakes, "Why do you have my father's skull on you?"

Guilt flicks on him, then turns to a hardened expression. "It's nothing."

"Like hell it is!" I object.

"Take your drink, Fiona," he orders in a low tone.

I grab it, my hand trembling.

He snatches the bags of cookies and slides his arm around me so I'm forced to walk with him.

After several steps, I push away. "Tell me how you got my father's mark!"

"It's just a design I found. I don't know how it could be your father's," he claims.

I seethe, "Liar! My brother and sister-in-law have one, too!"

His eyes turn darker. He clenches his jaw, then sets his drink and the cookies on the table. He pulls out a chair. "Sit down."

"Tell me. Now," I insist through gritted teeth.

He steps closer, slides his arm around my waist, and tugs me into him.

A surge of electricity surges throughout every cell of my body. I gasp, my body molding against his looming frame.

His lips graze my lobe as he murmurs in my ear, "I said sit, Fiona."

I glance at his darkening features, illuminated by the faded scar, unsure what to do.

"Sit," he quietly repeats.

I cave, sitting and holding the macchiato with both hands too tight.

The lid pops off, and my hot drink slides over my hands.

"Ouch," I cry out.

"Shit!" Kirill sits, grabs napkins off the table, and secures my hands in his. He dabs the liquid until it disappears onto the paper and assesses my hand. With relief in his voice, he states, "I don't think you're going to blister or scar."

"How'd you get your scar?" I blurt out, then my chest tightens.

His head jerks backward, and pain crosses his expression. It's a small move, but enough to notice. He recovers, puts on his poker face, but grinds his molars.

I almost apologize, but I don't. He's wearing my father's skull. I want answers, and he hasn't given them to me yet. So it's time he starts talking.

He picks up his coffee, takes a large mouthful, and then sets it down, refocusing on me.

I fight the ache in my core with the fear over who he is and what he might be involved in. Since he doesn't answer me, I question, "Did you know my father?"

He continues not to speak and takes another sip of coffee, studying me.

Tension builds between us, creating an intense anger inside me, pushing me to the point I might explode.

I'm tired of asking for the truth about my father and getting nowhere. No one lets me in on anything. Not my mother, Dante, Sean, or even Zara. It's not her father, and she's more privy to information about my dad than I am.

I fume, "I want answers."

"It's not the right time," he declares.

Shock fills me. I accuse, "Not the right time? You have my father's mark on you, and you have the audacity to tell me it's not the right time!"

"Keep your voice down," he reprimands.

"No. Don't you dare tell me what to do!" I cry out.

Disapproval appears, and he pins it on me, breathing through his nose.

"Tell me," I demand.

He doesn't move for a moment, then unwinds his scarf from his neck. He leans forward, loops it behind my head, and secures the soft cashmere around me. He grabs the material in his hand and tugs me closer.

The ache resurfaces, numbing out the anger.

Kirill's hot breath teases my lips. He warns, "When I say it's not the right time, I mean it. It was nice having you run into me again. Don't forget to try the cookie. Have a good day, Fiona." He releases me and rises.

I stare at him.

He picks up the cookie, slides it in my jacket pocket, and then shoves the other in his coat. He turns and walks away, exiting the building.

I jump up, race toward the door, and face the bitter cold head first. The outline of his body is hard to see, but I jog as best as I can on the slippery pavement and catch up to him. I grab his arm, screaming, "You don't get to do that!"

He spins, wraps his arm around me, and moves me around the corner. He pins me against the wall, caging his body around mine. His fingers close around my throat, and he uses his wrist to lift my head.

Millions of sensations burst into flames, singing me so I can't even feel the cold air.

"Listen to me closely, little bird. It's not the time," he warns.

I take bated breaths, staring at his lips, craving for him to kiss me and squeeze tighter while anger and frustration swirl among my needs.

Surprise fills his expression. His erection pushes into my stomach. Seduction replaces the rage in his leer. He mutters, "Ah. I was wrong about you." His fingers tighten, loosen, then tighten repeatedly as he watches me.

My knees buckle, and I whimper, not flinching.

He presses closer, mesmerized by my reaction, and his face hardens. He releases me.

I take deep, shallow breaths, keeping my glare pinned on him.

He asserts, "A queen obeys her king. Don't forget it, Fiona."

I furrow my brow.

He steps back, ordering, "Make sure you dress appropriately from now on. I wouldn't want you to get frostbite and ruin your beautiful skin."

I gape at him.

"Until next time," he adds, then backs away, disappearing within seconds in the snow.

It takes several moments for me to recover. I don't understand how he could be so seductive when I want answers he won't give me.

I finally push off the wall, hurry past the coffee shop, and step into Sean and Zara's building. I nod at security and get into the elevator. I punch in my code and quickly get to the penthouse.

The doors open, displaying the magnificent cherry blossom tree in their foyer. I brush past it and open the door, stepping directly into the living area. The stunning view of Lake Michigan is barely visible, with ice frosting the penthouse windows in every direction you look. Flames flicker in the oversized fireplace, creating a soft glow. Soft music plays on the surround sound.

Zara and Sean are on the floor with River and Willow. One of the babies giggles from Sean's tickles.

"Don't worry! Daddy's coming for you next!" Zara coos.

"Sean, I just ran into a man with dad's skull on his hand in the same spot you put yours!" I announce.

They turn their heads. Zara's eyes widen. Alarm fills my brother's face. He demands, "Who?"

I rush over to them, sit on the couch, and cross my arms. I'd normally pick up a baby, but I'm too upset. "Tell me what the skull's about, and don't give me your song and dance."

"Fiona, who did you run into?" Sean demands, picking up Willow and holding her close.

Zara rises, leans down, grabs River, and states, "Nap time. Give daddy a kiss." She holds the baby in front of my brother.

Sean kisses him, then Willow, and hands her to Zara.

Zara shoots me an apologetic look.

I fume, "You're not innocent in this conversation either!"

She takes a deep breath, then replies, "I'll be back after I get the babies down." She exits the room.

Sean gets off the floor and sits next to me. "I need to know who you talked to and what they said."

I grab his hand with our father's mark. "A man who had this. He told me he couldn't tell me what it's about because it wasn't the time," I spout, making quotation marks with my fingers.

Sean's jaw twitches. "Who was it?"

"A man," I repeat.

His greens glow hotter. "Who, Fiona? Stop playing games and tell me who."

"Don't you dare accuse me of playing games! You and Zara need to stop hiding and spill whatever you know about Dad's skeleton," I insist.

Sean scrubs his hands over his face, then releases a stressful breath. "What did he look like?"

"Why? Are you going to tell me who he is if I tell you?" I ask.

He opens his mouth and then shuts it. He taps his fingers on his thigh, staring out the windows.

"Seriously?" I spout.

Zara steps back into the room and interjects, "Sean."

They lock eyes.

"What is going on?" I fume.

"Keep your voice down. The babies need to take their nap," my brother reprimands.

"Then you better start talking because—" My pulse pounds between my ears.

"What is it?" Zara asks.

I point at her. "You knew who he was, didn't you."

"Who?" she pins her eyebrows together.

"The man in the club with the scar," I reveal.

The color in her face drains, and she turns a fearful gaze on Sean.

Shocked, my brother asks, "You met Kirill?"

"Yes. Who is he, and why does he have Dad's skeleton?" I push.

Sean stares at the ceiling momentarily, grinding his molars, then answers, "I know you don't want to hear this, but he's right. This isn't the time, and any further information will only harm you."

"Meaning what?" I ask.

"You have to trust me," Sean insists.

I rise. "I'm supposed to trust you?"

He nods. "Yes."

I turn toward Zara. "I need to know."

She winces. "I'm sorry. Sean's right. We need to keep you safe."

I explode, "Keep me safe?"

"Yes," they say in unison.

Full of frustration and rage, I shake my head at them and spit out, "Thanks for nothing." I move toward the door.

"Fiona!" Zara calls, grabbing my arm.

"Don't!" I warn, shaking out of her hold.

Guilt is all over her expression. She holds her hands in the air. "Okay. But we love you. Please trust us."

I scoff, "You two deserve each other." I step into the foyer, slam the door, and vow that whatever they're hiding from me, I'll stop at nothing to find out, even if it's dangerous.

* * *

Bride by Coronation is available June 1, 2025.

You can find it at your favorite retailer or head over to my bookstore and check out discounted ebooks, audio, and paperbacks!
https://maggiecolebookstore.com/collections/paperback-bundles

READY TO BINGE THE ORIGINAL MAFIA WARS SERIES? GET TO KNOW THE IVANOVS AND O'MALLEYS!

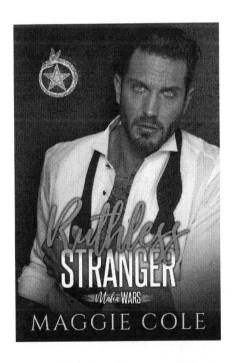

He's a Ruthless Stranger. One I can't see, only feel, thanks to my friends who make a deal with him on my behalf.

No names. No personal details. No face to etch into my mind.

Just him, me, and an expensive silk tie.

What happens in Vegas is supposed to stay in Vegas.

He warns me he's full of danger.

I never see that side of him. All I experience is his Russian accent, delicious scent, and touch that lights me on fire.

One incredible night turns into two. Then we go our separate ways.

But fate doesn't keep us apart. When I run into my stranger back in Chicago, I know it's him, even if I've never seen his icy blue eyes before.

Our craving is hotter than Vegas. But he never lied.

He's a ruthless man...

* * *

Ruthless Stranger is available on Kindle Unlimited on Amazon!
OR
You can find it at your favorite retailer or head over to my bookstore
and check out discounted ebooks, audio, and paperbacks!
https://maggiecolebookstore.com/collections/paperback-bundles

MORE BY MAGGIE COLE

Grab e-books, paperbacks, special editions, and audio at discounted prices!
Visit https://maggiecolebookstore.com/

The Underworld

Bride by Initiation (Sean Jr. and Zara)

Bride by Coronation (Fiona and Kirill) - June 1, 2025

Bride by Ritual - TBD

Mafia Wars - The Ivanovs & O'Malleys

Ruthless Stranger (Maksim's Story) - Book One

Broken Fighter (Boris's Story) - Book Two

Cruel Enforcer (Sergey's Story) - Book Three

Vicious Protector (Adrian's Story) - Book Four

Savage Tracker (Obrecht's Story) - Book Five

Unchosen Ruler (Liam's Story) - Book Six

Perfect Sinner (Nolan's Story) - Book Seven

Brutal Defender (Killian's Story) - Book Eight

Deviant Hacker (Declan's Story) - Book Nine

Relentless Hunter (Finn's Story) - Book Ten

*** If you're looking for Dmitri and Anna's love story, the book that created the Ivanov and O'Malley families, then grab book six of It's complicated: Secret Mafia Billionaire - Book Six

Mafia Wars New York - The Marinos

Toxic (Dante's Story) - Book One

Immoral (Gianni's Story) - Book Two

Crazed (Massimo's Story) - Book Three

Carnal (Tristano's Story) - Book Four

Flawed (Luca's Story) - Book Five

Mafia Wars Ireland - The O'Connors

Illicit King (Brody)-Book One

Illicit Captor (Aidan)-Book Two

Illicit Heir (Devin)-Book Three

Illicit Monster (Tynan)-Book Four

Club Indulgence Duet (A Dark Billionaire Romance)

The Auction (Book One)

The Vow (Book Two)

Wilted Kingdom Duet- (A Dark Bully Romance)

Seeds of Malice-Book One

Thorns of Malice-Book Two

It's Complicated Series (Chicago Billionaires)

My Boss the Billionaire- Book One

Forgotten by the Billionaire - Book Two

My Friend the Billionaire - Book Three

Forbidden Billionaire - Book Four

The Groomsman Billionaire - Book Five

Secret Mafia Billionaire - Book Six

Behind Closed Doors (Former Military Now International Rescue)

Depths of Destruction - Book One

Marks of Rebellion - Book Two

Haze of Obedience - Book Three

Cavern of Silence - Book Four

Stains of Desire - Book Five

Risks of Temptation - Book Six

Brooks Family Saga

Kiss of Redemption- Book One

Sins of Justice - Book Two

Acts of Manipulation - Book Three

Web of Betrayal - Book Four

Masks of Devotion - Book Five

Roots of Vengeance - Book Six

ALL IN BILLIONAIRES

The Rule - Book One

The Secret - Book Two

The Crime - Book Three

The Lie - Book Four

The Trap - Book Five

The Gamble - Book Six

The Cartwright Family - Holiday Billionaire Novels

Holiday Hoax - A Fake Marriage Billionaire Romance

Holiday Hire - A Billionaire Single Dad Nanny Romance

Holiday Rider - Coming November 1, 2025

STAND ALONE NOVELLA

JUDGE ME NOT - A Billionaire Single Mom Christmas Novella

ABOUT THE AUTHOR

Amazon Bestselling Author

Maggie Cole is committed to bringing her readers alphalicious book boyfriends and fiercely strong heroines.

She's been called the literary master of steamy romance. Her books are full of raw emotion, suspense, and will always keep you wanting more. She is a masterful storyteller of contemporary romance and loves writing about broken people who rise above the ashes. Her books can often be found hanging out in the top 100, even years after publication.

Maggie lives in Florida with her son. She loves tennis, yoga, paddle-boarding, boating, other water activities, and everything naughty.

Her current series were written in the order below:

- All In (Stand Alone Billionaire Novels with Entwined Characters)
- It's Complicated (Stand Alone Billionaire Novels with Entwined Characters)
- Brooks Family Saga- A Dark Family Saga – Read In Order (Each book has different couples)
- Behind Closed Doors-A Dark Military Protector Romance – Read in Order (Each book has different couples))
- Mafia Wars (Stand Alone Novels with Interconnecting Plot and Entwined Characters)
- Mafia Wars New York (Stand Alone Novels with Interconnecting Plot and Entwined Characters)
- Mafia Wars Ireland (Stand Alone Novels with Interconnecting Plot and Entwined Characters)
- The Underworld (Next Generation Mafia Wars Secret Society with Stand Alone Novels with Interconnecting Characters)
- Club Indulgence Duet A Dark Billionaire Duet – Read in Order (Same Couple)
- Wilted Kingdom Duet-A Dark Bully Billionaire Duet
- Interconnecting Plot and Entwined Characters)
- The Cartwright Family - Holiday Billionaire

Maggie Cole's Newsletter
Sign up here!

Maggie Cole's Website
authormaggiecole.com

Get your copies of Maggie Cole
signed paperbacks!
maggiecolebookstore.com

Pickup your Maggie Cole Merch!

Click here!

**Hang Out with Maggie in Her
Romance Addicts Reader Group**
Maggie Cole's Romance Addicts

Follow for Giveaways
Facebook Maggie Cole

Instagram
@maggiecoleauthor

TikTok
https://www.tiktok.com/@maggiecole.author

Complete Works on Amazon
Follow Maggie's Amazon Author Page

Book Trailers
Follow Maggie on YouTube

Feedback or suggestions?
Email: authormaggiecole@gmail.com

Made in the USA
Middletown, DE
06 March 2025

72348987R00291